The Diplomat's Wife

By the same author

The Dreambreakers

THE DIPLOMAT'S WIFE

Louise Pennington

CENTURY
LONDON SYDNEY AUCKLAND JOHANNESBURG

This is a work of fiction. All the characters and events portrayed in this book are fictional and any resemblance to real people or incidents is purely coincidental.

Copyright © Louise Pennington 1990

All rights reserved

The right of Louise Pennington to be identified as the author of this work has been asserted by her in accordance with the Copyright, Designs and Patents Act 1988.

First published in Great Britain in 1990 by
Random Century Group
20 Vauxhall Bridge Road, London SW1V 2SA

Century Hutchinson South Africa (Pty) Ltd
PO Box 337, Bergvlei 2012, South Africa

Random Century Australia Pty Ltd
20 Alfred Street, Milsons Point, Sydney, NSW 2061
Australia

Random Century New Zealand Ltd
PO Box 40–086, Glenfield, Auckland 10
New Zealand

British Library Cataloguing in Publication Data
Pennington, Louise
  The diplomat's wife.
  I. Title
  823'.914 [F]

ISBN 0-7126-3622-6

Typeset by Deltatype Ltd, Ellesmere Port

Printed in Great Britain by
Richard Clay (The Chaucer Press) Limited,
Bungay, Suffolk

*For Gina, my sister,
with love and grateful thanks . . .*

I have discovered the art of deceiving diplomats. I speak the truth, and they never believe me.
Di Cavour

It is better for a woman to marry a man who loves her than a man she loves.
Arab Proverb

I

It had been over five years. Hadn't it? Once she would have known even to the day, but a great deal of water had passed beneath that bridge of time, so much water that she wondered if the Karl she now saw standing across the vast glittering room from her was the same man who had made such raw, feverish love to her – and promises, many promises – in the exquisite gossamer of Blake's Hotel. Gossamer, because it had been a fragile thing, their coupling. Elizabeth's memory somersaulted inevitably backwards to the party, to London, to a walk along the Embankment at dawn, a magnificent pale purple dawn. It had seemed to her then in her naïvety that she had been waiting for someone like him all her life, because it had never been like that for her before, not that breathless need, that intense desire to reach out and touch. Her skin had been alive to him. And he had said, '– make me dizzy with a kiss . . .' They had only had that week, but those seven long, long days had had a timeless quality about them as if they could not end. But then he had flown away, back to the States and his other world, leaving behind the promises. Then had come the waiting: for the telephone calls, the letters, day after weary day, and even when the cold water of reality had begun to saturate her silly dreams she had still hoped. But Karl had never phoned, not once. And in that other time, a world away now, she had thought she had lost a part of herself. And now he stood only yards away and she felt the air catch and hold in her throat as he lifted his gaze from the glass held in his hand and his eyes strayed to the pale cameo of her face.

'Would you get me a refill please, John?' Elizabeth swallowed hard and turned swiftly and with practised ease to her husband.

'Already?' he asked gently and she saw familiar humour touch his mouth.

'Just a little extra to help me with all the witty small talk I shall be making on your behalf this evening,' she said too dryly.

'Okay, okay . . .' he replied quickly, and wondered at the sudden edge to her voice. He looked away from her and to a young girl carrying a laden tray of drinks and felt the guilty touch of his wife's hand on his arm.

'Sorry, I didn't mean to snap.' It had been too easy to see a shadow flee across John's big, open face. She could hurt him so easily, even now, after four years of marriage. And at that moment the guilt was twofold because she was looking back and reopening the past. Her eyes slid away from the safety of her husband's side to the other man who was only an arm's length away. She was amazed at the way her blood had begun to race, at the little breathlessness which made her mouth go dry even as her fingers curled around the comforting glass John handed to her. Elizabeth closed her eyes for a fleeting second. She had pressed the memory of Karl down, away from her life, a long time ago, because he had failed her. She supposed she had fallen for the easiest trick in the book. And she also supposed that she should despise men like that. 'Takers', Kate would have said, but Kate was several thousand miles away; she and Harry posted to the grey, polluted chaos of Manila. She missed Kate.

'Elizabeth –' She was propelled out of her thoughts by John's voice. 'Bruno and Maria Studer – from the Swiss delegation.'

Elizabeth looked into the older woman's thin, uninviting face; brown eyes magnified by the thick pools of her spectacles.

'They've only just arrived in Vienna.'

'. . . and living in a hotel . . .' Maria Studer's mouth pulled into a tight, unforgiving line. 'We were virtually given no warning, no time to get even a little organized.' Her skeletal hand reached out and pierced an olive with a cocktail stick. 'We had practically been promised another year in Paris and then they surprised us with this circus!' Mme Studer pierced another olive with angry relish. 'My husband is too old for conferences . . .'

'I'm sorry,' Elizabeth offered gently. 'But Vienna is a comfortable place, if a little expensive.'

Mme Studer raised her eyes skywards and her mouth began to open in disgust, but before she could speak her husband was plucking at her sleeve and guiding her to another introduction, a man waiting at her side.

Karl Nielsen took the thin proffered hand and dutifully squeezed the cold limp fingers before straightening and switching his attention immediately to the other woman who stood waiting just behind. It *was* Elizabeth. There was a beautiful flush to her face as she looked back at him, as her forehead creased into a soft frown, and he wondered how she was, how she had been, and if she had ever thought of him. It seemed a long time ago, London and her, and those long-short days which were beginning to unfold in his mind with sudden and unexpected ease. He remembered that he had planned to call her, or that he would write, but there had been other things in his life then – obstacles – his job, Gabrielle, and that constant painful itch due to lack of funds; that most of all. London had come to seem disproportionately far away for romantic interludes and he had deliberately pushed Elizabeth out of his mind because it had seemed to him then that there had been no other choice.

His eyes travelled over her in one practised second. She had not changed very much, not really, but there was a sureness about her that had not been present in the girl he had met five years before. As his gaze lingered on her face he was caught and held by the moistness of her pink painted lips and the soft flare of her nostrils as she looked back at him. And there was still that thick mass of toffee-coloured hair, but now it was pinned, tamed, so skilfully. Perfectly diplomatic. He found himself wondering briefly what it would look like now if it were unclipped and allowed to fall free around her lovely face. Corny, perhaps, but he couldn't help himself.

Before, in that other time, Elizabeth had always worn her hair loose, long and just a little wild. And when they had lain together she had let it trickle tantalizingly along his skin and he had reached up and buried his fist in its heaviness, locking and twisting his fingers as he pulled her back down to him. Karl wanted to smile then, at himself, surprised at the vividness of the memory, surprised that he could remember so much.

He felt his eyes searching her face with unexpected eagerness, but there was a shadow behind her unblinking stare as he took her hand, and a cool, taut smile as he lifted her warm fingers, Viennese style, to touch his mouth. She had not forgotten him, and she had not forgiven him. He smiled a little at this new-found knowledge. London had been an oasis, a beautiful stop-over on his way back to the States and Washington. And he *had* meant all he had said to her then despite what she might think, but there had been no *time*, no way to make allowances for Elizabeth's presence in his life.

He had always managed to live above his means with astonishing ease – beautiful things, women, 'the Washington fast-lane' had all taken their toll, and five years ago his bank balance had read less than zilch – until Paris had happened and his meeting with Claude at that international trade fair. Then, finally, things had begun to turn around. Karl's eyes dimmed as he remembered his initial hesitation, but it had been a momentary thing, just as Claude had known it was. The slim, effeminate Frenchman had read the need in his face with uncanny skill, had known how easy it would be to persuade him. It had been the best deal he had ever made. Karl swallowed slowly and pressed down that deep, low chord of doubt which sounded somewhere in the back of his brain. Beautiful things had always fascinated him; he was greedy for them. And sometimes the greed was too much to resist and he allowed himself to be seduced. Deliciously, willingly. Because he wanted to, because he was exhilarated by the risk of having it all, no matter what the cost. His thoughts returned to Elizabeth and the cold, taut smile. She would never understand, he supposed, women rarely did.

'Karl Nielsen, from the US delegation – my wife, Elizabeth.'

Karl glanced at her husband and was surprised. But naturally she would have married, naturally someone like Elizabeth would have a husband somewhere, somehow.

'Yes . . . we have met.' He smiled as he saw barely concealed curiosity in John Thornton's eyes.

'Oh?' John said and looked expectantly at his wife.

'It was in London, John,' she responded lightly, 'some years ago.' Blood soared into her face. He would know; John would only need to look at her.

'Yes, I remember it very well,' Karl continued easily, 'a plane was delayed due to appalling weather conditions – we were stuck at the airport for hours. Heathrow, wasn't it?'

She nodded stupidly at his lie, as the dim beauty of that room at Blake's took shape and fled away. There had been no real need to lie. Now they were like conspirators and John stood beyond them, on the edge, like an unwitting fool.

'There's Caroline, the British cultural attaché's wife . . .' She smiled stiffly. '. . . I wonder, would you excuse me?' She moved away not waiting for a response, angry and somehow humiliated, and crossed the room towards her friend, cursing under her breath. She knew she was overreacting, it was all past and his lie merely a smooth way to cover over what had happened between them. After all, she was married now, safe, with a child. And as a picture of Christopher slid into her mind she was instantly soothed. Safe. But it was still an irony that Karl should be here, of all the places in the world he could have been posted. She felt a mocking blade of guilt pierce her as she neared the other side of the room, because she had known all the time – it had been so easy to discover where he was because his name had glared at her from the list of delegates – and not really so surprising to find him at the same conference as her husband because their careers were curiously almost parallel. And in any event the world of diplomacy was a small one, wasn't it? Conference diplomacy even smaller. A tight, humourless smile grazed her mouth. Perhaps she had willed him here through all those unrelenting days and nights of longing, perhaps there was justice, after all. But she sighed inwardly, touched by sadness. Five years ago she had never thought of conferences, of diplomacy, of Vienna – other worlds – she had been too busy being in love with him.

'What do you want?' Sam's voice was flat and expressionless.

'I just wanted to speak to you – what's wrong with that?'

'Because I'm busy, Natalie, really busy – I should be on my way to an important reception,' he said with exaggerated patience.

'I want to see my baby,' she said sulkily.

'I'm bringing her over at Easter, you know that. The conference will recess then.'

'That's too long to wait, Sam.'

'I didn't want it this way, Natalie.' He had never even dreamed that it would end up this way. He felt the old spectre of depression beginning to wake, like a nasty, grinning spook.

'I've booked my flight.'

The silence was heavy then and he couldn't even hear the faint sound of her breathing. For a moment he wondered how he would feel if she had just died, suddenly, at the end of the telephone in the process of begging him for permission to visit their child. It would look good in the papers.

'Don't do this, Natalie.'

'I love you, Sam,'

He sighed wearily, the performance never varied.

'It's over. How many times do I have to tell you?'

'I made a mistake,' she persisted and then quickly corrected herself. 'Okay – a lot of mistakes. But I've changed, Sam.' There was silence again. 'People *can* change . . .'

He didn't believe that and she knew he didn't believe that.

'Sam – *please* . . .'

'I can't stop you coming here, Natalie.' Unfortunately.

'You could at least try and be nice about it.'

'I was nice before, remember? And look where it got me.'

It was her turn to sigh.

'We could at least try – for JoJo's sake.'

Sam gritted his teeth. Don't call her JoJo, Natalie, it tastes bad in my mouth. 'I wondered when you'd bring her into this.'

'She's my daughter as much as yours, Sam.'

'You should have said that a long time ago.'

'How many times do I have to say it – I'm sorry, I'm sorry, I'm sorry.'

'Let's just leave it, Natalie.'

'I don't want to leave it.'

He imagined her face – golden brown, almost perfect, frowning softly. 'Maybe we could take JoJo out together?'

'And play happy families?' He sighed heavily, angrily. 'Give it up, Natalie. Give it up, for Christ's sake.'

'What about JoJo? Don't you care what our split might do to her?'

'You'll push me too far . . .'

'How far, Sam? How goddamn far?! It's about time you started thinking about someone else besides yourself.'

Now that was rich – coming from his almost ex-wife. Sometimes he thought he actually *hated* her, really *hated her*. Like wanting to reach out, through the phone, and put both hands on her neck and squeeze, and squeeze, and squeeze. He closed his eyes. But some well-meaning 'friend' had told him that hating was too passionate, too 'feeling', too close to that over-used word, love. And that scared Sam. Maybe indifference just took time.

'Natalie – *don't*, okay? Just *don't*.'

'Don't *what*, Sam?!'

Golden face would be ugly now with anger. He had seen it before and wanted to forget.

'Don't give me any more bullshit. It wasn't too difficult to get custody of Joanna and you know all the reasons why. Do you want me to spell it out?'

There was a pause then and a vivid picture of her formed in his mind – frowning, mouth tight, cheeks shot red with silent fury.

'I have changed, Sam, really I have.' But her voice was gentle now, too soft. Natalie's bedroom voice.

'You never have known when to quit, have you, Natalie? But I have.' He caught a sharp, tired breath. 'It's too late. Okay? Too damn late.'

'Then why don't you stop wasting your precious time and go to your bloody reception, you heartless bastard!!!'

The phone was put down with a crash and Sam winced. He stood quite still for a moment staring down at the mute receiver, wondering how it had all come to this. He shook his head gently, glad that he had taken the call in his bedroom rather than in the hallway because then Clara would have heard every word. Clara, the nanny with the laughing face: a Filipino whose English was surprisingly good, who had four children somewhere, never had a letter, never complained, never looked unhappy. He wondered how she did it. Joanna loved her and that was everything, but it didn't seem right that she should love a comparative stranger more than her own mother. He supposed sadly that it was much better than no one at all.

Absently he pushed the stray lock of black hair back from his forehead and smiled bitterly. Natalie change? She had said that before the break-up and she still went on saying it, almost as if she really believed it. A tiny doubt began to seep insidiously into his brain. Could she be trying . . . ? Natalie? Once she had seemed soft, sweet; once he would have believed every word she said because he had wanted to and because he needed all those carefully hoarded dreams he had woven to exist, *to be*. Not now. Because she had taken them all and stuck pins in each one so that there was nothing left except souring memories. Sam swallowed, shut his thoughts off abruptly and shrugged; she was probably just missing a few home comforts and she knew that he had always been a soft touch. At least until Joanna. He walked slowly into his child's bedroom. Like a fairy grotto. Sam almost liked this time of day the best when she was totally still, all her features soft, sleeping, perfect. He still marvelled at the fact that she had come incredibly from him; from one tiny, minuscule cell. But there had been Natalie too. And Natalie, despite everything, was beautiful. Wasn't that why he had fallen in love with her in the first place? He smiled dryly; fallen in lust would be a better way of putting it.

He had met her at the UN in New York and had literally been bowled over by her from the first, and she had done everything she could to snare him. Maybe she had guessed in some obscure, clever, feminine way how easy it would be to wrap him around her sexy little finger. She had guessed right. Sam sighed with exasperation and leaned down to kiss Joanna's small clenched fist before leaving the room.

'Never let anyone tell you, kiddo,' he murmured softly, 'that there's anything trivial about fornication.'

He had not listened to his friends' barely veiled criticisms of Natalie, not the talk, the slithering whispers of wild parties, wild boyfriends and silver cruets filled with coke and other tasty little numbers. After all, beautiful women attracted gossip like that, at least that was how he had convinced himself. But somehow he had never been able to look his mother in the eye and talk about 'how close' he had come to this, his latest, girlfriend. And ultimately his mother had been right about his wife, though she had never directly opposed him when he had decided to marry Natalie. 'She glitters a lot, Sam,' was all she had said. And he had not really understood at the time. Much later, after Mom had died and Joanna had had the accident, he understood.

'What are you wearing?'

Felix stared stonily at her from the bottom of the marble steps.

'It's new – I wanted to look just a little different tonight . . .'

'Why?'

Genevieve clutched at the loose folds of her dress, a sick feeling gathering in her stomach.

'The opening reception – there'll be so many new people there,' she replied lamely, beaten down by his gaze.

'My dear Genevieve,' his dry voice snapped at her, 'it's not a fashion show, and why should you imagine that anyone will be interested in what *you* will be wearing?' Felix pulled at the cuffs of his shirt sleeves in irritation. 'You merely appear as if you are trying to recapture your lost youth.' He sighed dramatically. 'Please go and change.' Felix turned away from her dismissively and began reaching for his overcoat. 'You have just under five minutes if we are not to be outrageously late.'

Genevieve stood mutely in the painful silence which followed, her eyes coming to settle on her husband's partly bowed head, the word 'but' hovering, frightened, behind her lips. She had taken such care with her appearance this evening. Such care. She had thought that he would be *pleased*, pleased that she'd made the effort. Genevieve swallowed the lump in her throat and walked back the way she had come. But she never seemed to please Felix, somehow she was always found wanting. She moved unseeing past the living room and on up into the wide frescoed gallery which preceded her dressing room. For a long, unhappy moment she stared at herself in the full-length mirror which confronted her as she stood in the doorway. It was only a black taffeta dress, a little more fitting than usual and an inch or so shorter, but only a black dress. Genevieve realized quite suddenly that she had looked forward to wearing it, that it had given her a little more confidence than usual. Confidence. She closed her eyes and felt tears begin to burn behind her lids.

'Mama – I thought you had left?'

Genevieve blinked quickly and turned with a silly, bright smile fixed on her face; her daughter was standing in the frame of the doorway. She looks like me, she thought with a trace of sadness, but prettier, much prettier than I.

'I have to change, darling.'

Sophia stared at her mother, a puzzled frown creasing the smooth, white forehead.

'But you look so nice . . . even Gunther noticed.'

'Your father doesn't like it,' she said gently and then added quickly, 'You know he's usually right about these things.'

Sophia watched her mother's face and was reassured by the quick, easy smile. The dress slipped down, making a pool of black ink on the thick white rug.

'It made you look younger somehow,' she said finally.

'Well . . .' Genevieve replied awkwardly as her cheeks reddened '. . . I don't really need to look young any more, do I?'

'Oh, Mama!' Sophia shook her head in exasperation and smiled as if her mother had made a joke.

'I'll wear the blue check,' Genevieve said, almost to herself, and moved to the long fitted wardrobe. 'Thank heavens it's only just been cleaned.'

Sophia stepped outside the door as her mother lifted the dress from its plump silk hanger.

'Papa's calling.'

Genevieve closed her eyes briefly in panic. 'Tell him I'm just coming.'

As her daughter disappeared from sight she caught a glimpse of her reflection in the mirror and automatically began smoothing down her straight brown hair. It had been cut too short and there was a pale shadow circling her neck which the sun had never seen. The black dress had had a high fastening, the blue check hung limply at the shoulders, its small peter-pan collar falling short of her white forty-four-year-old neck. Everything would look rushed now, everything would look dull. She was sure she had looked better in the black, more assured, but perhaps Felix knew best.

Genevieve sighed heavily and glanced once more at herself, seeing a set of fragile features sitting in a white face, large dark eyes fringed with black lashes glistening ominously. Once they had been her best feature, but at that moment they seemed to protrude unkindly, rising out from her face, anxious and afraid. She smiled sadly and turned away. And Genevieve was a beautiful name, she thought wistfully, but she was over forty and plain, always plain. A long time ago Felix had called her 'pretty-plain', but that had been before they were married. Her husband's voice broke abruptly into her reverie and the sickness in the pit of her stomach seemed to tighten like a knot.

'Don't shout, Felix – please don't shout,' she said softly to the empty room.

Sophia watched her mother run to the top of the stairs, her handbag flying clumsily behind her. Her father was angry, but he was often angry these days. She drew a guilty breath. But Papa was, after all, very busy, and over the past few weeks with the lead-up to the conference he had seemed to be more at work than at home, so naturally he would be overtired, irritable, and naturally he would expect that the household should run smoothly in his absence, her mother to play her role perfectly at his side and she and her brother to fulfil the dreams he had for them.

She shivered slightly as she watched her father from the window guiding the car out of the drive. Their world had always revolved around Father, it seemed to make life very simple, very straightforward, and she had never questioned it. Sophia could never imagine leaving home, going to university, having a boyfriend without the consent of her father. They were a very traditional family, she supposed, her friends had told her as much, but she didn't mind; there were no conflicts inside the walls of her home, no unexplored territories, no unknowns.

Sophia moved across the room and ran her slim fingers along a row of books. Everything was in its place, everyone in their place. Her eyes slipped to the large sketch-pad lying by the side of her chair where she had left it: and there was her sketching. She had a small hope that her father might consent to allow her to attend an art school, her mother had said that she would speak to him 'at the right moment'. Sophia flicked slowly through the pages, pleased with the flowing lines etched in charcoal. Sometimes she thought she could sit for ever, sketching, losing herself in each line, each careful stroke. There were several of her mother, that taut, nervous smile on her pretty face; only one of her brother Gunther and at least a dozen of her father's severely handsome face. No smile, she thought curiously. She suddenly realized that her father rarely smiled. Her hand reached up and pulled the cover down over the black and white pages, and her eyes slid back to the window. It was beginning to snow.

'I thought we could go to the castle at the weekend.' It was a statement not a suggestion.

Genevieve sighed inwardly.

'Oskar's driving down from Munich,' Felix continued, 'I've also invited a couple from the British delegation, the American ambassador to the conference and the German bilateral ambassador and his wife.'

'We will need someone for the American ambassador, and Oskar, won't we?' Her mind automatically began to turn over female possibilities in their circle. Oskar was not an easy man to please, in fact she never knew whether her small efforts to please him succeeded or not. Genevieve wondered why he had never remarried after the death of his wife nearly twenty years ago; after all, he was rich, intelligent, cultured, charming . . . She frowned. Oskar *was* charming, but there was little warmth in that charm, she realized. Sometimes she thought that Oskar was simply bored beneath those heavy-lidded eyes.

'I have already arranged for Simone to entertain the American.' He paused, face staring straight ahead. 'Why not let Sophia come along and play escort to Oskar – it would do her good.'

Genevieve blinked as her husband's words cut sharply into her thoughts.

'But isn't she a little young for such a dinner . . . and she has her art on Saturdays . . .' Sophia would hate cancelling her lesson.

'Sophia is almost eighteen, Genevieve – not a child – and her art lesson can wait.'

'But she so looks forward . . .' Her voice began to wither and die as Felix's gloved hands tightened around the steering wheel.

'She will attend the dinner, Genevieve.' Then he sighed dramatically. 'You pamper her too much.'

Do I? she thought guiltily.

'I try not to, Felix,' she replied. 'Indeed, I have thought that it would be good for her to get away from the protection of the family and fend for herself.'

'What do you mean?'

'I think we might consider sending her to a good art school – she has talent, Felix.' But it was useless. All the time she had known it would be useless, and she didn't know why.

'There would be little point,' he said in a voice that discouraged any further discourse. 'She is only likely to meet someone we would not approve of.' He sighed again. 'I'm surprised at you, Genevieve . . . isn't it you who always looks so wary at some of the unappetizing arty types we see in certain cafés, and wasn't it you who told Sophia not to go to the flea market at the Nashmarkt on weekends because of the "unsavoury young men" who run some of the stalls?' He laughed then, but it was not a kind laugh. 'The Nashmarkt is full of "arty types" . . .'

'That's not what I meant, Felix,' she said quietly.

'It is not a good idea,' he said. 'Sophia has led a sheltered existence, too sheltered perhaps.' He paused for a moment and Genevieve found herself looking at him. 'She would find it very difficult to adapt to such a life – God only knows what would happen.'

'But she's a good girl.'

'I'm not disputing that,' he said tersely. 'But she is young for her years, too naïve . . . surely you can see that we should look for a more secure, traditional future for her than permitting her to undertake the hazardous existence of an art student.'

She sat uncomfortably, painfully, in the silence that followed.

'But she will be so disappointed . . .' she said finally, miserably.

'I have had many disappointments in my life.'

Genevieve looked nervously down at her hands as if he had admonished her. What disappointments? Was she a disappointment? Sophia? Was it her fault? Her eyes lifted guiltily and she caught a sad glimpse of herself in the glass of the car window as they drove beneath the boughs of black, leafless trees. She had hoped for this one thing for Sophia and she had failed her. Perhaps if she had phrased it a different way, asked him at a different time? But in her heart she knew that the answer would have been just the same. Her eyes darted once more to his hands as they rested on the steering wheel. So sure. Felix was sure of everything. Genevieve realized with a touch of shame that she envied him.

Specks of snow began to hit the windscreen of the car and she thought of Schloss Bletz, of old memories, old sadnesses. There were too many disquieting echoes there – her father, her mother, the past. But Felix adored it, in his own understated way, she knew that. It was he who had got her father out of debt, he who had rescued the family name, he who had ultimately married her. She wasn't fool enough to think that Felix had married her for love, that would have been too much to ask, but her title meant a great deal to him and she was glad of that. It was her father who had finally agreed to 'pass on' the title to his future son-in-law – for the proper price, of course. She sighed inwardly. It had worked out well. And hadn't she been in love with him? Her eyes were drawn inevitably back to her husband. He was still good-looking, handsome; tall, slim, muscular. Genevieve tried to recall the excitement she had felt when they had become engaged at last, when he had kissed her for the first time and she thought that she would faint. But she had been so young then, so foolish, full of dreams.

She smiled wistfully and glanced again at her husband's profile, as stiff as if it was carved in stone. And immediately she saw a vision of Sophia, her sketches, her disappointment. Genevieve closed her eyes and turned back to the window. It was one of the things they shared, a love of art. It had been such a joy to discover when Sophia had still been very young that she loved to draw; then as she had grown there had been art galleries, exhibitions, trips to Florence and Venice. She swallowed slowly; it had been her own dream as well as Sophia's that her daughter might attend a good art school. A private, secret dream, ruined now, of course. Felix was probably right, but in the half-shadows of the car her hands clutched each other, twisting and turning, white knuckles and fingers digging into the soft flesh of her palms. Could she do nothing right? Felix obviously thought not, and Gunther sided with his father, albeit silently, but she could see the veil of contempt behind his eyes. Gunther had always been his father's son. But Sophia was hers, they were friends. She looked down at her hands and watched them uncurl, forcing the fingers to stretch outwards over her skirt, making herself relax. Perhaps she could tackle Felix again – later, tomorrow. But she was so clumsy, so awkward, full of cowardice.

Genevieve shifted her gaze back to the black face of the window, suddenly feeling very tired. There was still the reception to be got through and then the arrangements for the weekend to be put in hand. With guilty hope she wondered if the snow would last and settle, filling and choking the narrow roads leading up to the castle. It had happened so often in the past. Once, many years ago, they had been cut off for days. She had been a child then and had woven pretty dreams around the dazzling whiteness which had transformed Schloss Bletz into something beautiful. She smiled softly in remembrance. But, after all, she was a countess, with a rich handsome husband, beautiful, healthy children and even a fairy-tale castle to complete the picture. People would laugh at her if they thought she could possibly be unhappy. But she wasn't, was she? Not with so much, not with so many gifts. It was ridiculous.

Kristina stared at herself in the mirror of the bathroom cabinet. There were dark circles under her eyes and her skin had a white, tired look about it. Slowly she massaged some moisturizer into her cheeks, her forehead and the lines that were beginning to make thin bands around her neck. She didn't suppose the sleek, glossy ointment could keep its extravagant claims, but it was better than nothing at all. Perhaps if she managed to get to bed before midnight a few times a week she would see an improvement, but she closed her eyes at the thought. Even as she did so she heard the slow, faltering steps of her mother as they made their way to the bottom of the stairwell, and her stick, tip-tapping, tip-tapping. Sometimes Kristina thought it would drive her mad.

'Will you be late tonight . . .?'

Silence.

'Kristina – can you hear me?'

For a moment she was tempted not to reply, to keep up the pretence that she couldn't hear her mother's dry, rasping, nagging voice rake what peace of mind she was trying to muster.

'No – I won't be late.'

'It was almost three in the morning last night – I heard you come in.'

'I know, Mother, I can tell the time.'

'Will you be seeing him again?' The voice was louder now and Kristina knew that her mother wuld be leaning forwards on her stick so that she could hear more clearly her daughter's reply.

'At the weekend.' It was a lie. Manolo had stopped seeing her over three weeks ago. They had slept together a few times and then there were simply no more phone calls. Kristina drew a sharp breath; he was leaving Vienna anyway, going back to Spain and a home posting and, naturally, his wife. The same old story. If she told her mother the truth there would be a lecture, a long lecture, about standards and morals and 'what did she think she was doing with her life?' – and worse still: 'too old, too old', like a worn-out horse that had outlived its usefulness.

Perhaps if dear Mother in her infinite wisdom had not forced her into an early marriage things might have worked out differently. She had been nineteen and Frederico a middle-aged, over-cultured member of a minor Italian aristocratic family. She had been beautiful and Frederico had been rich. A perfect match. 'A good marriage is essential,' her mother had said, meaning, of course, that it was measured by the property a potential husband, or wife, possessed. Frederico had been charming and distinguished in a very formal, stiff sort of way. Dull. She wondered why it was that rich men were so often dull, or unattractive, or solitary, or over-wary as if the world was teeming with people lying in wait ready to relieve them of their money. His home, a large red-roofed country house overlooking a sea of grape vines, was also dull, even simple – a bachelor home, where there was neither charm nor gaiety, little love or warmth. And as the months and years had passed she had wondered if Frederico knew the meaning of *affection*, let alone love. He had lived his life and she had lived hers. Occasionally he had visited her apartment and they had made love in a mechanical, accepted kind of a way, but otherwise they hardly touched. They never kissed each other. But at least Frederico had not been unkind and on occasion had even put aside his habitual frugality and been surprisingly generous. Her eyes slowly closed, tight, as memory took her and those days dry as dust seeped like sand into her consciousness.

Kristina blinked and stared blankly back at her reflection in the glass and began rolling mouthwash around her tongue before spitting it angrily into the basin. She had tried with Frederico, tried very hard. But it was as if he had already decided that he was old – at forty-six! – that it was too late to change. And she had been too young and headstrong to be shut away from a world which seemed to grow farther away each day. God, the loneliness! Perhaps if she had loved him a little to begin with . . .

They had divorced eventually and Frederico's round sallow face had shown neither pleasure nor displeasure, and because his family had made sure that she had signed a marriage contract before their wedding she found herself left with virtually nothing after seven years of marriage. Her mother had raged impotently that she would take him to court, but she had known that it was useless and in any case didn't want the scandal, and finally she had turned the full force of her anger and frustration on Kristina because she 'hadn't tried hard enough'.

Ultimately she had returned home, to Vienna, because there had been nowhere else to go and for a short, brave period she had thought of running away, but finally lacked the courage. She had taken a secretarial course and brushed up on her languages, something she was good at, and then for the first time had found herself a job. She had been twenty-seven, over ten years ago. Kristina stood back from the mirror and surveyed herself critically. Suppressing a sigh, she blended some more rouge on the still good bones of her face, then there was mascara, a touch of eyeliner and some lipstick called Rot Dame which always made her smile and made her lips just a little too red.

'Your car's here . . .'

'I'm coming, Mother.' Coming, coming, coming.

How many times had she asked herself why she was still there, still enduring the taut, dying relationship with the only real person she had in the world. Wasn't the true reason lack of money? To live well in Vienna one had to be *seen* to live well – like living in the right area, being seen at the right restaurants or walking down the Kärntner Strasse in one's mink, with one's little dog. Kristina smiled wryly; she might not have the last two, but she certainly lived in the right area. Her mother owned a beautiful apartment on two floors in the First District, overlooking the Stadtpark. And she certainly got taken to the right restaurants – not always with the right person, or for the right reasons, but she supposed she was keeping part of the pact she had made with herself.

'Kristina – your car!'

She winced as her mother's voice tore into her thoughts. Sometimes she wondered if living in the First District was worth the sacrifice of living with her mother. Sometimes she thought she was desperate . . .

The car drew up outside the Hofburg and her eyes were drawn to the lights flickering brilliantly through the windows. She had no invitation to the opening reception of the conference; she was not on the 'diplomatic list' as a freelance interpreter. It made her feel second best; outside the magic circle. Sighing heavily, she climbed out of the car and told the driver to wait.

Kristina ran into the building waving her pass like a flag and to her office on the first floor. Lying in a drawer were two tickets for the opera which she had forgotten in her rush to leave the building that afternoon. Whatever sacrifices she would make for Fritz that evening she would at least have a night of *Tosca* to dream about when her head eventually hit her own pillow. And it had taken over an hour to get them, the queue being particularly long that morning, and she had almost been late for one of the first meetings. Her ankle turned on the marble floor as she closed the door with a slam behind her. She cringed briefly in agony and realized with relief that no real damage had been done, yet felt the sudden and inexplicable sting of tears. But the tears were quickly replaced by angry impatience at her own weakness. Kristina took a deep slow breath and began walking carefully back the way she had come. An open door leading to the office of the British delegation stood ajar and she frowned, but then recognized the young woman who was waiting impatiently by one of the telex machines.

'Working late?'

The young woman turned, startled, her cheeks flushed. Pretty.

'I'm doing someone a favour – I said I'd pick this up for the bilateral ambassador as it's not really connected with the conference proper.' She started to smile. 'You may not have realized it, but I'm with the embassy, not the delegation.'

'Well, everything's been rather chaotic over the past two weeks,' Kristina responded, and smiled back. Laura, wasn't it?

'But I think by next week there should be some semblance of order and I'll be back in my office.'

'I hope you're right,' Kristina replied and then added quickly, 'I'm afraid I must go – don't stay too late.'

'I can't . . . I have other things to do too . . .'

Which meant the opening reception, or a man, of course. Kristina returned a mechanical smile and pulled the door closed. Laura was a successful woman in a man's world; she was also very attractive, which was unusual for a female diplomat – perhaps because there were so few, she thought absently. Well, at least Laura had something worth holding on to even if she stayed single, which was doubtful. She caught a breath, depression beginning to loom threateningly as she made her way down the thick stone steps. She tried to switch her thoughts to the opera, to Fritz, to the conference year which seemed to stretch out before her and which she had persuaded herself would be full of opportunity. New hope, new men. Because, after all, that was what she wanted – a man. There was no pretending in her any more. She was, and never would be, the career type. But it would be her own man now, not someone else's, not someone who would walk into her life one day and out the next. Using her. She had had plenty of those, and always in that foolish part of her heart she had tried to convince herself that they would finally really want *her*, not her hot, asking flesh alone. And she *was* hot, she knew that too. She would cling to each one as if there had never been anyone else, her voice rising higher and higher as if it was the last time, as if she would never make love again.

She went out into the darkness and the cold air hit her face like a slap, and her eyes began to water as she walked towards the car. Sometimes she thought she was dying inside.

Sam stood hesitantly on the threshold of the Hofburg ballroom, his eyes scanning the ever thickening crowd for his ambassador. Fortunately the head of his delegation was a tall man, well over six feet, and Sam spotted him with ease.

'Ambassador Gurney...?'

'Sam, good to see you.' He gestured outwards at the gathering masses. 'Quite a party the mayor has laid on for us.' His eyes passed searchingly over the younger man's upturned face. Somehow Sam was managing, but he really did have his hands full – literally left holding the baby. Maybe he looked a little tired and maybe the separation had given him a few white hairs, but it was better than that God-awful grey plateau he had just climbed down from.

The ambassador had met Sam's wife once, in New York, and just as he had been led to believe she was, indeed, quite something; languid and lush, too sensual, like an over-ripe fruit. And when Natalie Majors smiled she had a way of sliding her tongue along the edges of her teeth, as though she was relishing something censored or forbidden. Not the sort of woman to marry, not if you wanted to live happy. Ms Majors was the sort of woman you kept in a penthouse flat, with a mink coat in the closet and a credit card for Bloomingdale's. Sam had never even seen her coming. And when she had finished playing her games and her husband had had enough, she had left him with a baby, a baby she had never really wanted in the first place by all accounts. Sam had taken it all on and somehow he seemed to manage, yet they weren't the most appropriate of circumstances for a very bright US diplomat. But times change. Thirty years ago it would never have happened, but then thirty years ago the world was a very different place. He smiled back at Sam and wondered if he knew that Natalie had been having an affair with one of the big boys in the White House before latching on to him. She had been ditched because Donahue's wife found out, and lucky because it hadn't gotten into the papers. It hadn't been very lucky for Sam.

Dan Gurney's eyes moved briefly to another member of his delegation, Karl Nielsen. Karl was a different man altogether – cool, calm, and unmarried. Dan smiled to himself because instinctively he knew that his counsellor would never allow himself to be hooked by any woman. Karl was too clever for that, too damned calculating. And he looked good on it, almost too good, because looking good was easy when you had only yourself to think about.

'Sure is – *quite* a party,' Sam agreed and slowly turned away from the close scrutiny of his ambassador, pressing down the beginnings of irritation. Everyone was expecting him to have a breakdown, or turn to drink, or something, but it wasn't going to happen. Natalie had done her worst and he had faced it and got through it. With every day that passed he was beginning to feel a little better about himself. But what he didn't need was her coming back and poisoning his peace. Not now. Sam sighed inwardly and let his eyes travel over those nearest him.

Several couples could be overheard making the usual small talk, and not far away a tight knot of eastern Europeans looked on self-consciously, their suits dark; wifeless with pallid faces. Despite all the changes which were taking place he still pitied them a little; it was hard toeing a rather blurred party line, hard to go back to empty, faceless apartments with no woman to take the sharp edges away. Most Eastern Bloc wives were doomed to stay at home. Maybe the party didn't yet trust their comrades as much as they wanted the West to think. He swallowed slowly, realizing that he was wifeless too, but at least that was his own choice. Natalie's open arms reminded him of a minefield, likely to blow up in his face at any moment.

'How's Joanna?'

'Fine, sir.'

'If you have any problems, just let me know . . .' Daniel Gurney looked away from Sam, a frown creasing his forehead. '. . . Right now I think we'd better play the game . . .' He smiled. 'I'll see you later.'

Sam took the gentle hint and moved away from his ambassador, glad to escape the probing, if kindly, eyes.

But Dan Gurney was not thinking of his first secretary at that moment, he was letting himself, foolishly, be taken back to all the hurting again. It amazed him how easy it was to imagine that she was standing there beside him as she always had done and sometimes, sometimes, he could even forget that Judy was dead, but that was happening less and less now and he was glad because he didn't like the reawakening of that heart-wrenching pain when he realized that she wasn't there at all. His eyes scanned the room, the people, the dim faces. How she would have loved all of this – that finally humanity had discovered it was becoming an endangered species and decided to do something about it. Once she had said to him in that quiet, deadly way of hers, 'Don't you *care* that we're all beginning to choke on our own garbage?' He hadn't taken her seriously, but then no one in the right places had taken anyone seriously when it came to dying wildlife, polluted air, shrinking rain forests. Environmentalists had almost been put in the same boat as revolutionaries or crazies, and no one had ever heard of the word ozone. Until now, because now it was a political issue at last and the average politician had had to go green, or perish. And somehow, between now and the autumn, the hundred and twenty-four countries attending the conference had to take a much bigger step beyond the Hague Declaration and actually create a new global body charged with enforcing environmental protection. Dan smiled softly; Judy had got him in the end. In her dying she had handed him her concern for all the things he had taken for granted throughout his life. But it couldn't replace her. And maybe that was the cost.

Sam looked around for a drink. His lips were dry and deep down somewhere he felt the quiet thunder of a headache beginning to stir. Natalie was that quiet thunder. He wondered vaguely whether there were people who really were *bad* for you, who could actually make you feel physically ill; or relationships that were simply doomed from the start, like a terminal illness. His mind slipped back to his ambassador. Dan had been married over thirty years until his wife's death two years ago and Sam was sure that he had hardly looked at another woman before or since. A marriage made in heaven, he thought wryly, and then felt a little ashamed because he was only envious. And he was fortunate serving under Dan Gurney, who had a brilliant reputation and a sense of humour to go with it, not like his last taskmaster who wet his pants if he had to make a decision.

'Mr Cohen?'

Sam turned and found himself looking into a face he did not immediately recognize.

'Countess Dhoryány . . .' she offered.

He felt a blush creep up from his neck.

'We met over dinner . . .'

'I'm so sorry . . .' he said quickly, 'it was the Austrian ambassador's, wasn't it?'

Genevieve smiled.

'That's right,' she said, 'it's never easy fitting the right name to the right face at times, especially under these circumstances,' and then added swiftly, nervously, 'my husband is always telling me that I have a mind like a sieve.'

'I'm sure you don't,' Sam said kindly.

'None of us is perfect, Mr Cohen,' she responded, still smiling.

'Your husband is deputy in the Austrian delegation, I understand.'

'Yes.'

'I imagine that must keep you pretty busy.'

'I suppose it does, but that's all part of my role, isn't it? In any event, our two children are almost grown up, which makes things much easier – not like some of the young wives here.'

'Actually, I have a two-year-old daughter myself.'

'And your wife is with you tonight?'

'My wife is in New York.'

'I see, but she and your daughter will be joining you soon?'

'I'm afraid my wife will be staying in the States, we're separated, but my daughter is here with me.' He sighed silently, noting the cheeks of the Countess as they began to glow pink.

'Oh . . . I see . . .' But she didn't really see at all. Genevieve cringed inwardly. She had let her tongue run away with her and now she had placed them both in an embarrassing situation.

'It suits us both fine,' he said with an effort.

'I do apologize, Mr Cohen . . .' she stammered '. . . I didn't mean to pry.'

'Sam – please.' His mouth tilted easily into a smile. 'And there's really no need to apologize.'

'Sam . . .' she repeated feebly. But his name sounded awkward on her tongue and all the time her mind was whirling with the knowledge that he was managing alone with his two-year-old daughter. She thought of his wife in New York, totally free, and seemingly unperturbed. Genevieve felt slightly stunned. She could never contemplate leaving her family and certainly not Sophia. Guilt crept automatically into her head as she realized the shape of her unwitting thoughts. She could never leave Felix, of course, either. Never, that would be impossible. He was like the sun, the moon and the stars, and the children and she revolved inevitably around him.

'I think we shall have a busy evening ahead of us,' Sam said, gently changing the subject.

'Yes, I think we shall.' She looked nervously back at him. 'Actually, I'd better make my way back to my husband – we're expecting the German ambassador at any moment.'

'Good luck,' Sam responded humourously as she turned away and was surprised when she called back at him.

'You know – if ever you need a hand with your little one, I shall be only too glad to help.'

He nodded his thanks and watched her as she wove cautiously through the groups of people. Like a trembling bird. But he shifted his gaze from her uneasy figure, upwards, to the magnificent painted ceilings and the dazzling chandeliers which hung at intervals above them.

The Hofburg had quite a history if he remembered correctly. On making his triumphal entry into the old Habsburg city, Hitler had given his first speech from one of its balconies to the seething masses who had welcomed him – there had even been jubilant church bells for the Catholic Führer as his motorcade had passed through the streets of

Vienna. Sam blinked; maybe he had even walked across this same floor with a similar glittering crowd, except someone like Sam wouldn't have been allowed within shooting distance of the place.

His heart grew dark as he thought of his mother. She had lived in Berlin and then moved with her family to relatives in Vienna just before the Anschluss of 1938. The frying pan into the fire. She had dyed her hair blonde in an effort at fooling the Nazis and amazingly it had actually worked for quite a while, but ultimately she and her family were betrayed and finally Ruth Kraus was detained in Mauthausen concentration camp from the spring of 1944 until her release by the Allies in 1945. But her first husband and four-year-old daughter had not been so lucky. She had never seen them again. They had never broken the law, she had told him, they had always been good citizens, but in the end it never made any difference, they were always *Juden*. They never forgot that. Somewhere in the Third District of Vienna there was an apartment which belonged to his mother's family, but it was pointless trying to reclaim it. They had tried that once.

For a brief, wretched moment Sam was shaken by memory as he recalled her face as she had told him the whole story when he had been too young to know or really understand – except her desolate, frightening crying which had almost broken him. She had wept great racking, ugly sobs as if his very asking had opened the floodgates of time. He had never asked again.

Sam's eyes darted to the distant figure of the woman he had been speaking with. But it was difficult to keep hating, to keep the dreadful memories alive, particularly with someone as innocent and so obviously naïve as Countess Dhoryány. And she was a victim of sorts; he remembered her husband quite clearly: a tall, cold bastard. Now *he* was a different ballgame altogether.

It was beginning to freeze and Laura pulled her coat more closely around her as she walked through the massive stone archways of the Hofburg and out towards the Ringstrasse. There was a wind and it bit into her skin. Suddenly she felt tired – and homesick, which surprised her somehow. At the weekend she had driven tourist-like to the Schönbrunn Palace and walked through the shadows of the perfectly symmetrical building into the grounds beyond. Her feet had taken her past the carefully carved gardens and on up to the Gloriette, which gave her a blue, panoramic view of the city. She stood there a long time as the afternoon waned, until the perfect blue had become laced with fine strands of purples and golds as dusk drew in. Her hands had been stiff with cold. On the way home she had stopped at a café and drunk two cups of coffee topped with plumes of whipped cream, amongst all the old ladies, the couples and the smoke, and had thought of home. Eventually she had turned her eyes to the window and the opera house across the street. A long time ago someone somewhere had called Vienna the City of Dreams, but at that moment its baroque beauty was grey, devoid of all dreams, and the streets almost empty. Like a museum. Her lips had moved into a ghost of a smile. Andrew would have laughed, said she was being emotional, over-imaginative. Laura shivered as a sudden gust of wind tore at her clothes.

She missed him, more than she had thought possible. Yet it had ultimately been her decision to take the Vienna posting and postpone their marriage; it had been difficult to refuse the appointment, particularly as it meant that she would become second secretary, the youngest to do so in her year, *and* it would also involve political reporting, something she was beginning to relish after her stint in the West European department of the Foreign Office. But Andrew had been so calm, so damn cool about it all. It infuriated her that *she* had had to be the one to choose, as if somehow she had been railroaded into it. Not Andrew, never Andrew. How sweet of dear old Fate to allow her to fall in love with a fellow diplomat who was also a bit of a chauvinist. She drew a sharp breath. Even he could not completely contain his surprise when she had, after all, accepted the posting. He had not thought that she could do it – not choose a career instead of him. In his own inimitable way Andrew had forced her into it, but neither of them would admit it. Now she would test herself and him. At least, thank God, his time in London had been extended for another six months and he had not been sent to the back end of nowhere for a three-year stint, which would make meeting him virtually impossible. Laura laughed silently. Somehow she couldn't see Andrew allowing himself to be sent to the back end of *anywhere*, it didn't fit into the glittering career he had mapped out for himself. She had once jokingly mentioned a posting in Lagos and he had almost turned pale. Oh, no, not Andrew. Not the stupefying heat, the flies, the chaos, the boredom.

Laura sighed in a slow, weary fashion. And now, she supposed, she was doing something stupid. Perhaps if Andrew had returned her telephone call, or even been home when she had called again, she might not have accepted the dinner invitation, but now it was too late to turn back. The Imperial Hotel loomed up, floodlit and pompous, and she swallowed slowly as her feet automatically took her into the spacious, marbled foyer.

Meeting Ralf had been a chance encounter; he had simply backed into her car in the car park at Schönbrunn and then after the usual exchanges, offered dinner as some compensation. She had refused, but he had called her at her office on Monday and she had finally let him persuade her. It had been his voice that had done the persuading – slow, foreign, languid – and the echo of Andrew's telephone ringing, ringing, ringing. She pushed a curtain of her dark, thick hair angrily back over her shoulder and deliberately switched her mind back to the West German's call. Ralf had been quietly persistent, quietly tempting. He had the sort of voice, she realized, that could paint pictures of pleasure with infinite ease, and ultimately she had consented to his invitation because his silky words had seduced her. And she had thought she was beyond that sort of obvious seduction. Because, of course, that was what it was. Even as she turned right and into the small piano bar she felt a guilty flush seep into her cheeks as if she had already committed the sin of sleeping with the man who was so patiently waiting for her, as if his voice had said and done it all.

She saw him then, a broad man, powerful, saw his wide mouth slide into a slow smile. She should not have come, she knew that. This man, this situation, was like wading incautiously into dangerous waters. But Andrew had left her little choice. Laura looked back at the man called Ralf and squeezed out a smile. Suddenly home seemed very far away, suddenly and with searing clarity she realized that she did not want to be in Vienna. City of Dreams. Sadness caught in her throat and Andrew's face drifted effortlessly into her mind as she felt the warm moistness of this man's – the stranger's – lips linger on her hand. Damn you, Andrew, Damn you.

Elizabeth slid past a group of unfamiliar faces. Her eyes darted back to John who was still standing on the other side of the now crowded ballroom. She felt she could breathe again, felt colour slowly returning to her face and wondered again how memory could play tricks with such ease. Over five years and yet it could all have happened yesterday. It was as if her heart had stood still, as if it had stayed open and vulnerable, just waiting for him. For Karl. She moved into the banqueting room beyond and to the vast table which filled the centre of the room. The white linen tablecloth set with silver was covered with delicately prepared food and she found her gaze passing uninterestedly over the myriad plates of smoked salmon, the bowls of sugar-coated fruit, baby ducklings in green aspic, tiny little pastries and exquisitely filled chocolates, but she paused and her eyes settled with quiet admiration on the centrepiece, a life-size effigy of an eagle moulded in ice, its claws embedded in a small sea of caviar. It was, no doubt, the Habsburg eagle and she smiled a little dryly before taking her place behind a fringe of people who had gathered at the edge of the buffet and waited with unusual patience; she was empty, but not hungry. The waiting was an escape from the small talk, and from John.

Guilt crept stealthily into her face as she thought of her husband. She had met him a year later, a year after Karl; somehow she had always thought of it that way. She knew it wasn't fair, not the way things had happened, not the comparison. John deserved more than that. He had sat across from her at a dinner party and she had known from the way he had looked at her that they would see each other again.

Left to herself she would have done nothing about it because she had wanted someone to resurrect the passion she had felt for Karl, and John was not the man to do it, she had known that from the first. John's love was of a safer, gentler kind. But he had pursued her and she had been flattered.

He was twelve years older, a successful diplomat from a very wealthy family. His great-grandfather, an English–American, had literally struck gold in the hell days of the Yukon, lost an arm through frostbite and gangrene, and then returned, homesick and tired and old. But William Thornton, or Old Bill, as John loved to call him, had not been too old or too tired to marry, and he had sired three sons to prove it, dividing his ever-growing and carefully invested fortune between them. The Thorntons became richer and more respectable with each generation.

Elizabeth supposed that John had been curious about her lack of interest in his wealth and connections. That was unusual. It was also true. She had also showed little enthusiasm in their relationship for several weeks, but John had persevered and she had grown used to him – to his kindnesses, his generosity, even his love. He had loved her from the first and it was difficult to ignore someone so sincere as her husband, so good. Because John was good and it always made her feel guilty. As if he knew . . . But even John had his limits and one night he had simply said to her that he knew she was not really interested in him – that he was wasting his time. Elizabeth blinked for a moment as memory prompted her, as a picture of his familiar face slipped into her consciousness.

He had terminated their relationship on the spot – kind, good, predictable John. She had been speechless with disbelief as he had closed the door of his car and driven away. For a few long moments she had stood on the pavement as a breeze, like a whisper, had played with her hair and carried the scent of him away. She had waited two days, two long, excruciating days in which she had battled with pride, selfishness, foolishness and ultimately something called love. In the end she had telephoned him and it had been like trying to reach out and touch him across an ever-widening chasm. She remembered her heart jumping in panic because suddenly she had realized that John Thornton mattered to her very much indeed. They were married six weeks later, two weeks before John's posting to Madrid.

Her hand tightened around the white napkin in her fingers. She wished she had never seen Karl, had never met him because she and John *were* happy, despite the creeping spectre of memories. But she couldn't change what had happened, could not undo what had been done and said. And Elizabeth knew in the deepest part of her heart that she didn't want to.

'Hello, Elizabeth . . .!'

Elizabeth turned, knowing she was caught. The round, slightly bulbous brown eyes of Madeleine Lindahl swept over her with obvious and barely concealed interest.

'Madeleine – how was Sweden?'

'Cold, dark, dull . . . it is better anticipating a year in this merry-go-round than stay at home.' She sighed. 'But then, of course, Sweden is not my home.'

Elizabeth gave a dry smile in response. Madeleine was originally French, had spent her childhood in England and after 'exploding on to the London social scene', married Olaf – 'because he was so much sweeter' than the other men she had met. Madeleine rarely had a good word to say about anything or anyone. She was always intimidatingly smart and incredibly thin. Like a razor. Tireless wife, tireless hostess, tireless charity fundraiser. A *Vogue* classic. Her husband was charming and long-suffering and John liked him for his almost unswerving sympathy for the West despite his country's neutral stance. They had met in Madrid during the course of military and human rights talks held the previous year.

'How is John – and Christopher?'

'Both very well. And Olaf?'

'The same – my dear husband never changes, but we all have our crosses to bear.'

'Oh, Madeleine – that's not fair,' Elizabeth replied, shaking her head.

'I know, I know . . .' the older woman responded a little sheepishly and then added quickly, 'I *adore* your dress by the way – Victor Edelstein if I'm not mistaken – must have cost a small fortune . . .'

Elizabeth swallowed and felt blood soar into her face. Madeleine was right, but she hated the familiar accuracy of her guesses. The dress *was* an extravagance, but John had insisted and she had been unable to resist the exquisite creation in red ruched silk. She had quashed her guilt by sending a donation to one of her favourite charities.

But Madeleine seemed impervious to Elizabeth's discomfort and rattled on with the speed and monotony of an express train. 'Have you met the Austrian deputy and his wife?' Now she was switching to the subject which mattered to her most. Gossip.

'No, but we're having dinner with them at the weekend.'

'Titled . . . at least his wife is . . . I understand *his* is not quite, shall we say, "authentic" . . .'

'Oh . . .' Elizabeth replied wearily.

'I had coffee with Clare Carter yesterday . . .'

'How is Clare?' She made an effort because she liked Clare although they had only met once or twice. And Clare needed sympathy from any quarter with their recent move barely completed, three children under seven and a heating system which had decided it would only heat half of their huge, grim apartment. When Elizabeth had seen her last she was still surrounded by a slowly shrinking mountain of cardboard boxes.

'Depressing,' Madeleine replied. 'It seems there is some talk that Oliver may not get Brussels, after all – it could be back to London for them after the conference.'

'But I thought it had all been confirmed?'

'Apparently not.'

'Poor Clare.' A home posting which would mean a massive drop in pay; finding a place to live in London at an exorbitant rent, new schools for the children. Clare had been hoping and praying they would not be sent home.

'Well, Elizabeth – what one loses on the swings one gains on the roundabouts, as they say – and after all, London is a great deal better than Khartoum, or El Salvador, or Ho Chi-minh City.'

'Very amusing, Madeleine, but we both know it's not quite as simple as that.'

'They knew a home posting was likely . . .'

'Then why was Brussels ever mentioned? In any event, there are months ahead in which everything could change again. I would have thought it too soon to even talk of a next posting.' It took an effort for Elizabeth not to let her irritation show.

'But we are all at the mercies of our respective foreign ministries, Elizabeth.'

Madeleine was being at her patronizing worst.

'I am aware of that.' Elizabeth's voice came too sharp.

'You seem, if I may say so, a little distracted this evening.'

Elizabeth sighed impatiently. 'Do I?'

'I've obviously caught you at a bad moment . . .'

Madeleine's eyes had begun to glitter, a bad sign. They had never liked each other, merely sharing a mutual interest in the small, exclusive world in which they had to exist. It had always seemed to Elizabeth that they had circled one another warily – she reluctantly enduring the older woman's trivial jealousies and patronizing gossip, and Madeleine capitalizing on the younger woman's lesser experience and innate reserve.

'Perhaps you have . . .' Finally, she had allowed herself to be provoked. Another time she might have reconsidered the reply she made then, but she didn't care. Behind Madeleine a man stood and Elizabeth knew he was waiting for her, knew that he saw the boredom and barely concealed impatience in her face and the darkness in her eyes which told their own story as she gazed back at him.

'Hello, Karl.' His name on her tongue. How many times had she dreamt this, lived this moment?

She thought then how much a voice could say when words said so very little, wondered at that instant heat burning her face.

'Elizabeth.'

She felt Madeleine's eyes, knew that even she would have sensed something not quite right. It didn't seem to matter. Not then. But Karl moved past the other woman, giving her a brief cursory nod.

'Perhaps you would excuse us.'

Under any other circumstances Elizabeth would have smiled at the expression, which made Madeleine seem briefly comic. But then Karl's hand was cupping her elbow and Madeleine disappeared from view as he guided her away from the table, sliding a glass of white wine into her soft, open hand.

'If you really are hungry, I will get you something.'

She looked back at him. 'No – no, thank you.' So formal.

A silence fell between them, a powerful silence which seemed to breathe many different meanings as the vast room retreated and the sea of faces dimmed.

He studied her for a long moment and then allowed his mouth to take over as he smiled.

'How are you?'

'Well,' she replied and was amazed at how steady her voice was, how light the word sounded. 'But we did not meet at Heathrow – at least that is not how I remember it.'

'I apologize.' He paused. 'I didn't wish to embarrass your husband.'

'John is not so easily embarrassed,' she said with a trace of sarcasm. 'And naturally he is aware that I have a past – as we all have.'

He watched her carefully, slowly, as if deciding what he would say next.

'You know I didn't forget.'

She hated the part of her which seemed to rise in eagerness at his words. For a split second their gazes locked; it was like going backwards, like pulling aside a flap in time at that point when her heart had come open.

'It's a long time ago, Karl.'

'I left it unfinished. I know that.'

She gave him no answer as memory stung her, recalling with sudden and surprising intensity that feeling of disbelief when he had not called and how she had waited – sure, certain that she had not been mistaken and that he *had* loved her.

'But it doesn't matter now, Karl. Does it?' She smiled with an effort. 'We've both moved on and our lives have changed.' She thought she saw a shadow of confusion settle on his handsome face, but then the moment was gone and he was returning her smile and she felt the breath catch in her throat because it seemed to her then that he could see inside her.

'Perhaps we could have lunch . . . for old time's sake.'

'I don't think so.'

His eyes shifted slowly to the drink held in her hand and he saw the untouched wine shudder and break into tiny yellow ripples against the side of the glass.

'It would not be so much – just lunch, Elizabeth.'

Only he had ever been able to say 'Elizabeth' and make it sound rich, sensual, potent.

'I don't think so, Karl,' she said again and wondered at the calm in her voice. But her eyes were drawn reluctantly to his lips; remembering.

'Think about it,' he said slowly. 'I'll call you.'

'Please don't.'

She lowered her eyes and then looked away, across the endless faces, searching for John.

'I must go.' She placed her glass on the empty table beside him.

He said nothing as she walked away. She had said no, but he would have been surprised if she had said anything else. Karl swallowed the tightness in his throat. Elizabeth moved him and he did not want to be moved. He lifted the glass of wine she had left so carefully behind and let the smooth liquid slide slowly into his belly. She was angry and her anger excited him, just as it had done once before, and suddenly he was unable to stop his thoughts sweeping backwards to that last time and was amazed at the clarity of the image which took shape in his mind. Elizabeth beneath him, Elizabeth smiling: warm, melting, sweet beyond belief. His tongue slid slowly, carefully around the rim of his mouth. Elizabeth. He wondered how he had forgotten so easily. Karl let his gaze drift away, to the other side of the glittering ballroom where she would be standing, dutifully, next to her husband. He would call her because he couldn't help himself. Because he wanted her now, wanted Elizabeth's lovely, hot, open mouth.

2

The day seemed carved from crystal, sharp and starkly beautiful. Snow blanketed the close hills and thin sunlight polished them so that Genevieve half imagined that they might be made of glass. She blinked and turned her gaze to the windows of Schloss Bletz glittering in their casements and to the massive shape of the castle itself, its dour beauty reaching out to the small lake which lay black and compliant at its feet. It was not much past dawn, but she had been unable to lie open-eyed in her bed any longer so she had dressed warmly and wandered out into the frozen grounds. The fitful light made her eyes feel leaden, but pinpricks of snow stabbed at her upturned face and stung her skin into life. A wind was beginning to bite and she wondered if their guests would arrive safely before more snow fell. She lifted her gaze to the bruised sky and thought she saw a brightness, a lessening in the thick grey clouds. It had not been so bad, this visit, it had not conjured up the same grim heaviness, the same feeling of servitude she had so often felt in the past. And Sophia loved it. Both of the children did. But there was more than love here for Felix. Genevieve supposed it was 'all' to her husband; a symbol of everything he had ever wanted in life. Although, of course, he would never say so.

She turned away from the white, paralysed gardens and on to the stone-flagged path which ran parallel to the lake. For a moment she leaned against a broken fragment of wall and stared downwards into the thick, black water. Her brother had died here. He had only done as she was doing – looked into the face of the lake – and the wall had simply crumbled at his touch, like sand, and Heinrich had crumbled with it. As if he had offended some deity, some ancient, long-forgotten god of this little, arrogant piece of water. She had been twelve then, Heinrich two years younger. Even now, even after all the years that had passed, she could still hear the sound of his body as it broke against the spit of rocks, the sodden, jerking splash as it came to rest in a ring of water. A wind clawed at her hair and her mind was dragged inevitably backwards, as the grief came creeping, rising. Always like this. Her lovely, fragile mother had faded then, wilted and slowly died in the room above the water. Her father had remained, as always, at a distance, but when she had dared to look at him through her child's eyes his aloofness had become something awesome suddenly; scathing, and there had been a sick, unhealthy feeling

– big, like a fist – tightening in her belly as he had walked away from her. Her fault.

Genevieve closed her eyes as they began to burn. Slowly she lifted her head back and let the tiny specks of snow fall on her face so that they melted and trickled in disarray down her face. But she did not speak of Heinrich now and Felix never asked any indelicate questions which might bring the past tumbling into the present. It had only happened once and her husband had vowed he would never ask again. She was so emotional, and he hated that. Genevieve looked back into the water and tried to press all the old desolate memories down. Because she could not walk away, or go back to Schloss Bletz and Sophia, and talk and smile and be Genevieve whilst this sadness was upon her.

'Good God . . .'

Elizabeth looked up, jarred out of her thoughts. John was still hidden behind his morning newspaper and she was relieved to note that he could not have seen the shadow of boredom which had passed unmistakably across her face.

'What is it?'

'Do you remember Peter Brandt?' John put the paper to one side and looked back at her. 'Stuart's brother-in-law . . . we met him in the summer, over dinner?'

Elizabeth frowned as she searched her memory.

'He's a journalist . . . tall, blond . . .' John said softly. 'Or was . . .'

She remembered him then, remembered he had been wearing an awful purple tie as if he had borrowed it from someone for the occasion. He had been rather witty, rather sweet with his thin, too-long yellow hair.

'He's dead.'

She blinked rapidly as she caught her husband's fixed stare. 'How?'

'Murdered near the Tanzanian–Zambian border.' John looked away from her. 'Hacked to death.'

She swallowed. 'Are you sure it's him?'

Rather witty. Rather sweet.

'Not many journalists called Peter Brandt, late twenties, nephew of the Home Secretary . . .'

'John – how horrible.' She reached across the table as he passed the newspaper to her. If it hadn't been for the Gorbachov/China meeting, Peter's death would have made the main headline. Instead it was relegated to a space halfway down the page and a photograph of him laughing with a hat on. 'Home Secretary's nephew murdered'. Her eyes ran down the carefully worded columns and sub-headings. . .

'butchered'... 'ivory'... 'ruthless'... He had been murdered by ivory poachers some twenty miles from the border.

'Poor bloody fool.' John stood up and moved towards the window. His brief visit to Africa six years previously came back to him in all its intense, confused beauty. He had stayed at a lodge somewhere in the vast emptiness of the Serengeti and watched the sun rise brilliantly from the rim of the plains, he had slept and waited at a well-known watering hole with the mosquitoes, the flies, and the heat beating on his back through a canvas roof. There had been a kill at the water, a sudden madness of dust and kicking; a shriek. He thought unwillingly of Peter Brandt, alone, running beneath that cruelly exquisite sun.

'We'd better make a move, John.'

He turned back to his wife. She was trying to switch his mind away. Elizabeth was good at that. Did she know how easy she made it for him? There was no contest, no choice in the way he looked at her or the way he wanted her.

The road snaked away from the direction of the Danube and they began to climb. Elizabeth looked back and saw the black arc of the great river as it began to disappear from view. They had followed the almost straight road to Bratislava and the Czech border, but had finally veered to the left as they neared the border. The weather had held, but the snow lay thick and frozen across every field, along every bank, abutting every road as if it merely waited. There was a chance of more snow tonight and she thought of Christopher. He had accepted their going with only a trace of reluctance, but he would be happier at home with Grace, his nanny, with his toys and his books.

She smiled softly as a picture of him struggling over each page came vividly into her mind. Almost four and he could read. It had been her own proud surprise for John when she had helped their son through his first sentence. Motherhood had taken her unawares, but it had taken her all the same. Sometimes, sometimes when she looked into his flawless, soft, baby face she would find herself drawing a sharp, wondering breath, despite the familiar painful echoes and despite the wound which had never really healed.

'I hope we won't be snowed in...' She glanced at John. 'I promised Christopher we'd be back in time for dinner tomorrow.'

John did not immediately reply and when he did she realized that his thoughts were elsewhere.

'There'll be a hell of a stink...'

'You mean about Peter Brandt?'

'There'll have to be – I can't see the Home Secretary sitting lightly on this.'

'What can he do?'

'Add pressure,' he said quickly. 'Ostensibly there is an all-out ban on the ivory trade but there's still an illegal international network operating. Even now, after all the shouting and wringing of hands – and don't forget George Adamson's death for basically the same reason – the poachers are still obviously going about their business with virtual impunity . . . some with the help of their own government.' He sighed. 'For instance, the average game warden is not armed with an AK47 like the average poacher. The average game warden, my love, is lucky if he has a nice sharp spear to stick up the average poacher's backside.' He shook his head. 'Sorry . . .'

'Don't apologize, John, you don't lose your cool enough . . .'

'Oh.' He frowned. 'Why, do you think that would be good for me?'

'Perhaps.' She forced a smile. 'You're too controlled.'

'That sounds rather, shall we say, unpromising, if not dull . . .'

'No, I didn't mean that,' she said, floundering suddenly. 'Anyway, getting back to what you were saying . . .' she added quickly, trying to change the subject because it seemed she would hurt him somehow, in this present mood, 'do you think Peter Brandt was trying to prove the connection between poacher and government, get actual evidence of corruption in high places?'

'Possibly.' He sighed again. 'Maybe his murder will provide the impetus needed to get to these so-called high places, but I don't envy anyone the task; the trail must stretch at least halfway round the globe – Zaïre, Zambia, Tanzania, France, the Middle East, Singapore, Hong Kong, to name but a few.'

'Mr Poon . . .'

'Our man in Hong Kong, but he's slipped out of the picture in recent times, things got too hot.'

'Surely the bad publicity and the ban together will go a long way in bringing the trade to a halt?'

'That's what everyone's hoping. But don't forget the reserves – protected, but very poachable – and declining numbers and bans on imports play straight into the hands of the black marketeers, making tusks even more valuable, and the Middle East and Chinese markets, particularly, have little time for the sentimentalists of the elephant – if they want ivory, or black rhino horn, or whatever, they will have it.' He glanced at her with a frown on his face. 'And there is this everlasting problem of corruption which is rife from the top to the bottom in certain African countries, and naturally in such countries where poverty is the norm, a local man turned poacher will take the opportunity of earning the equivalent of three years' wages from one day's poaching, he would think himself a fool not to.' John shook his head. 'And Britain's decision to let Hong Kong sell its stockpile of tusks was no help at all. At least, thank God, that's over.'

Elizabeth turned back to the window and tried to conjure up the searing heat of an African plain, but the whiteness outside would not let her.

'Was Peter married?' she asked softly.

'He wasn't last year.' He looked back at her, immediately regretting his glib response and then brought her hand up quickly to his lips. 'Sorry, I've gone on too much – and it's not a nice subject.'

'Don't apologize – I'm not made of glass, John.'

He turned back to the road, a little reduced by the sudden edge in her voice.

'Are you worried about Chris?'

She sighed inwardly, guiltily. 'Not really,' she said and then added half in apology, 'I'm just a bit tired, that's all.' It was almost true, at least that she had been unable to sleep soundly, that her mind had turned over and over, bringing back the past in glorious stinging Technicolor so that it had not been John who made love to her as the grey dawn had crept stealthily into their room, but Karl – Karl's hands, Karl's mouth, Karl's body filling her with slow, deliberate pleasure.

It was not really the time of year to go sightseeing, Sam realized, but he needed a walk, and he needed to get to know the city a little. He bent open the book held in his hand with forceful resolution and began walking up the Weihburggasse towards the Franziskanerplatz, a small square housing a Franciscan church. He stood for a moment on the corner of the square and let his eyes wander upwards to the old roofs and then downwards and through an archway over a narrow cobbled path which ran away into a pretty sheltered courtyard. Old Vienna. For a few minutes he had sat in one of the dark, ornate pews of the church, empty but for a cowed old woman and a youth with long hair. There were flowers carefully arranged at the base of each gilded statue; hushed, shadowy corners of muted light and marble humbled beneath the richly ornamented walls and ceilings. His gaze had followed the sculptured walls upward to the centre and he had found himself looking into the face of a Jesus Christ. This Jesus had a sweet, handsome face without a line of pain, or suffering, or anguish, or even slight displeasure at the follies of the humans the face was compelled to look down upon. Sam caught a tired breath. He didn't belong here; he didn't really belong anywhere. Even his Jewishness had left him.

The wind tore at his coat as he pulled the heavy wooden door closed behind him and he shivered as he moved forward again, but the sound of someone's stereo made him stop and he began to smile. Scott Mackenzie. Somehow it seemed a small marvel to him then that he should be standing in Vienna in the middle of winter with the wind whistling around his ears and hearing the dulcet tones of 'San Francisco' calling to him. Because it did call to him. All that reckless, languid beauty which had made him breathless too long ago because it seemed that youth, arrogant youth, could finally change the world. Sam swallowed as a vivid, crazy picture of the Monterey Pop Festival soared sweetly into his head. The music bound them all – Hendrix, Joplin, The Mamas and The Papas, Otis Redding. The police had flowers around their necks. Everything – everyone – had seemed warm, benign. He had lost his virginity that long, hot summer of love when anything had seemed possible. But the dream, all the dreams, had withered and died, or so it seemed. His father had called it 'intense self-indulgence', his mother had smiled and said that she was jealous. Sam shook his head gently and made himself walk away. What a baby he had been then! But for a while it had worked, or so it seemed to him. People *had* cared.

His visions dimmed. Where had Natalie been then? In first grade. He shrugged, pushing the image of her face away. She would have loved it all, but she had been born too late. Instead, as if to make up for her loss, Natalie had had her party later when all the flowers and the music had died. She supped the legacy of the sixties like the elixir of life. He wondered if anyone had had any idea that when she had had access to sensitive national security documents, some of the country's top secrets, she had been on cocaine for at least two years. She had told him later, one long night after their marriage, after several and more flutes of champagne. The cover on the bed had been deep blue, he remembered, satin, and she had fallen, naked, across its slick, glossy surface. 'They never knew, Sammy . . . not the ones who counted anyway . . .' She had laughed then in that low throaty way. 'No one knew about good ol' Natalie . . .' Her roving gaze had finally come back to rest on his face and she had smiled then, a smile he had come to know well: the long brown legs had opened; slim, knowing fingers had run across her belly, down down to the dark fur at the apex of her thighs and Natalie had arched her back, squirming against the slippery satin. He had stood in the doorway, paralysed, sick with desire as her hands had moved again, slowly, surely upwards to caress her own breasts. Sam closed his eyes as if it would shut out the vision. Good ol' Natalie.

As he approached the Kärntner Strasse the grey cold drove him into a café and he sat at a Formica table staring out at the people as they walked gingerly along the icy street. The hot chocolate he had ordered made his fingers tingle as he lifted it to his mouth and let the sweet, sticky warmth slide down to thaw his insides. She was coming too soon, of course, he wasn't ready for her yet. Sam drew a breath and dropped his eyes to the safe round rim of his cup. Three weeks she had said and there had been nothing he could do or say that would persuade her to change her mind; she had even managed to find him at the Hofburg and drag him out of a meeting with the lie that it was urgent. The urgency had been the day and time of her flight. He felt a stab of anxiety as he thought of Joanna; because Natalie would be charming, Natalie would be impressively affectionate. Even to him; he knew that too. But she would be staying at a hotel, so at least her visits could be scheduled and he would make sure that they would be scheduled to suit him. Yet hovering in a bleak, sordid corner of his mind was the knowledge of his own weakness and suddenly he doubted his resolution, because he knew that, even now, after all that had happened she would find a way of anticipating him, and as the thought took shape and fled away it was replaced by odd, disturbing slices from the past as they slid furtively into his mind to taunt him. Natalie had seduced him, literally; she had driven him slowly, oh, so slowly to such a pitch of fevered want that he had cried out beneath the calculated ministrations of her skilful fingers and tongue. And even as he sat in the anonymity of that Viennese café he felt blood rush into his face at the memory, felt the raw, unwilling heat of desire tease his loins. That had been a long time ago. Another planet. But since their separation there had been no one else. And that was dangerous, wasn't it? Sam lifted his eyes to the window and pressed the thought down. He didn't want to think about that now, not just as he was discovering this newfound peace. And there were other women, weren't there? But even as he drained the last drops from his cup Natalie's face stole reluctantly into his head and he could only see her moist red mouth, lips parted, the slick pink tongue sliding across perfect white teeth.

'You may find this place a little formal, but the food is always good and the service excellent . . .'

Laura looked back at Ralf and tried to pull her lips into a semblance of a smile. He is used to women, she thought, almost matter of fact in his expertise. She couldn't imagine Andrew bothering to explain his choice of restaurant – they would just go there because it was near, or because he felt like a curry or a Chinese. A vivid picture of his face the night before she had left London took shape: a little sullen, the wide, thin mouth pulled up on one side, the clever eyes half hidden as he played with his coffee spoon. A dinner to say goodbye. The Bombay Brasserie . . . his choice . . . even then. Somehow Andrew had discovered the trick of always getting his own way with the least trouble and it had been one of the things that had made her decision to come to Vienna easier. She frowned softly, sure that it hadn't always been like that. In the early days he had tried to please and impress, but the pleasantness had become dutiful, the need to impress no longer existed. Familiarity breeding contempt, she supposed. Perhaps, then, it was as well she had left London and his veiled warnings behind her to stew for a while. Oh, she still missed him, she couldn't fool herself about that, but he hadn't exactly been overzealous with his phone calls since she'd arrived in Vienna and there had only been one letter. One letter. But, of course, he was free now to all intents and purposes, and she was the one who had given him his freedom on a silver platter. And Andrew, despite everything, was good-looking and charming when required. Why shouldn't he be too busy to write? Why shouldn't he be out there, at the parties, at the night-clubs? She had practically given him *carte blanche* to do so. But Andrew didn't like night-clubs.

She sighed softly, pushing the thought aside with an effort and switching her attention to the menu, letting her eyes run through the delicious descriptions of fish, shellfish, veal and cold and warm salads. Ralf had made it easy for her; after the lush dinner at the Imperial he had met her for lunch and then casually offered dinner again at the weekend. It had been difficult to refuse, and he wasn't pushing her – no pressure, no cheap passes or persuading her to go back to his flat 'for coffee'. It had taken her years to discover that a lot of men took acceptance of 'coffee' as a code-word for sex; sometimes she wondered whether she was soft in the head.

'You seem a little preoccupied, Laura.'

His voice snapped her out of her reverie, and he surprised her once again with his almost perfect English; except for that slight, unmistakable foreign lilt.

'I'm sorry . . . but it's been rather a hectic week . . . I've been dividing my time between the embassy and the conference and I think I'm only just beginning to come down to earth.' Not quite true but it didn't matter at that moment.

'Your ambassador will no doubt be glad to have you back with him – full-time.'

'Yes . . . yes, I suppose he will.' She found her eyes meeting his across the table.

'And you have three years in Vienna to look forward to . . .?'

She blinked. Three long years. 'Yes – that's right.'

'Your enthusiasm is overwhelming.'

'I'm sorry.'

'Don't be. After all, it's your privilege; it can't be easy moving to a new place, a new country every three years and leaving friends and loved ones behind.'

Laura looked back at him as his mouth tipped into a sympathetic smile. 'No, it's not.'

'And you have left one particular friend behind?'

For a moment she hesitated. 'Yes – does it show that much?'

'You have a very expressive face.'

She found herself blushing. It seemed, somehow, an intimate thing to say. 'We had, you might say, a fundamental disagreement.'

'Ah . . .'

'His career versus mine.'

'And you won?'

'I'm not sure now . . .' she said slowly and smiled with a trace of sadness.

'Forgive me, I didn't mean to pry.'

'Please don't apologize,' she said quickly. 'Anyway, it's hardly a suitable topic when you've been kind enough to invite me for dinner.'

'No kindness. You're very good company,' he lied. Apart from being nervous she had almost been morose, but he had suppressed his natural impatience with careful, practised ease. 'And Vienna can be lonely for a businessman who merely flits in and out.' That was a half truth. Ralf let his eyes travel over her face, the white neck, the opening of her blouse. But Laura *was* very attractive and he was sure that eventually he would find the object of the exercise very palatable. 'Now, why don't we eat . . .'

She watched him as he turned his attention back to the menu and then to the nearest waiter and wondered why she should feel just faintly, vaguely irritated. She had never seen herself in the role of 'good companion'; yet Ralf had gone out of his way to keep in touch with her. In fact he had persisted until she agreed to see him again – surely he had more in mind than merely friendship? Perhaps after the initial chase he was wondering whether she was worth the effort. In any event, she chided herself, did it really matter whether he made a pass at her or not, or was she getting neurotic? For a moment Laura hid her discomfiture behind the safe wall of the menu until she heard the sound of wine being poured into her glass.

'Corton-Charlemagne . . . a superb white wine . . . perfect with shellfish . . .'

Laura matched his stare as she lifted her glass. 'As well as knowing good wine, you speak French well too?'

'And Italian, and Spanish, and Hungarian.' He saw her eyebrows rise. 'I need them all – for my job.'

'It must be very interesting.'

'It is.' He swallowed some wine. 'Although many people seem to find computers a little boring.'

'I have to use one.'

'IBM?'

'How did you guess . . .?' she replied dryly. He was smiling and suddenly she realized she was beginning to enjoy herself.

'Easy . . . do you want to talk about it?'

'I don't think so.'

He laughed. Beautiful teeth. In a split second his knowledge and his laughter had somehow tipped the invisible scales in her head and she found her eyes appraising him in a new way. Ralf was very different from Andrew, but there was nothing wrong with that; dark to Andrew's fairness, broad compared with Andrew's perfectly tailored proportions.

'You're staring.'

'Sorry . . . I was miles away.'

'May I ask what were you thinking?'

'You remind me of someone.' She felt a faint blush of pink at the lie.

'And you remind me of someone.'

'Do I?'

Almost.

'The last time I was in Greece. She was dark like you . . . quite lovely.' He let his gaze slide to the window.

Laura drew a breath, waiting until her own voice broke their silence. 'Can I ask what happened?'

'She was too young – much too young,' he said quietly. 'Just sixteen, the daughter of an old friend.'

'You sound, at the very least, disappointed.' And it annoyed her, just a little.

'Disappointed? No . . . not really, not in the way you think.' He looked back at her. 'She was not much more than a child. I admired her purity, that is all, if that doesn't sound overly sentimental. The essence of beautiful old Greece.' Ralf smiled. But he had had her all the same, and she had had no idea, little Nina, as he had closed the door of the kitchen and forced her to the hard mud-packed floor. Except her eyes, those great round liquid eyes, had swelled and grown large with fear. Georgios had owed him and he had taken.

'Greek history is a hobby of mine.' He leaned across the table and poured more wine into her glass. 'Perhaps, after dinner, you might care to see the artefacts I've collected over the years.' He watched her face, amused, knowing what she was thinking. 'My apartment is only five minutes' walk from here.'

She knew that already, she had looked it up on her street map of Vienna. Laura smiled with a trace of uneasiness. So this was it, the pass. She shifted her gaze to his shoulders and to the powerful arms leaning so casually on the table. Perhaps she was wrong. It would sound puerile to refuse.

'Yes, I'd like that.'

'Good.'

But there had been no pass, no subtle or unsubtle attempt to move closer, to touch. Throughout the visit Ralf behaved impeccably. Even as they stood together in the deep spotlit alcove which housed most of his collection there was a carefully measured gap separating them and she was forced to concentrate on his voice and his words and on the exquisite exhibits he held up for her to see. She actually found herself involved, interested as he gave a brief, potted history of each piece.

'Take Pan,' he had said, 'who, according to Greek myth, was supposed to have been so ugly at birth – with horns, beard, tail, and goat-legs, that his mother ran away from him in fear . . .' He pushed the black stone figure into her hands and she felt distinctly repelled by the feral, sub-human face which looked back at her.

Ralf smiled. 'Pan stands for the devil, or upright man, of an ancient fertility cult . . . master of orgies,' he remarked softly, 'the only god who died.' He took the figurine back and returned it to its place on one of the illuminated shelves. 'But my favourite is this lady, of course.' And he lifted down a beautiful bronze and then stood behind her and made her run her hands over the full roundness of the Goddess of Desire, Aphrodite. 'So real, isn't she?'

And she had nodded in response as the blood soared into her cheeks because the closeness of him and his hands on her hands and his voice and his words aroused her suddenly with appalling ease.

But then he moved away from her, still smiling, and his role as museum guide came to an end and she wondered whether he was playing a game with her, teasing, because she had not imagined the way his fingers pressed, pressed against her own, had not imagined that hot breath on the curve of her cheek as he had extolled the obvious virtues of the Goddess of Desire. But then he had taken her back into the main room and the mood had snapped and she was forced to switch her admiration away, to his wonderful use of space and a room which seemed to run the whole length of the building, for ever. White on stark white, broken only by polished wooden pedestals and more Greek statutes, but these were large, unflawed, modern. The *pièce de résistance* was the magnificent terrace, paved in black and white marble, giving a panoramic view of the city. She found herself gasping softly at the sea of snow-covered roofs, the floodlit beauty of St Stephen's and the ordered loveliness of a fairy-tale Vienna.

'It's just – beautiful.'

'I thought you would appreciate it.'

He made coffee then, superb, rich Turkish coffee. Finally, he had said, quite simply, 'I think it's time to take you home.' She offered to take a cab, but he flatly refused.

'It's the Schellingasse, isn't it?'

She nodded in acquiescence and wondered why as they neared the door she should feel a nagging trace of disappointment. He had not put a foot wrong, at least nothing which could be construed as the pass she had been expecting, which was what she had wanted, wasn't it? Any feminist would have a field day with her, she thought wryly. Or perhaps it had simply been too long since she had played this game and she was way out of touch. But perhaps, after all, it was only good old-fashioned curiosity, because there was no getting away from the fact that Ralf *was* different. She slid past him, taking in again that faint musky scent of aftershave, the clean, soapy perfume of his skin. And there was something else, something which she could not grasp which stole stealthily, carefully away beneath the surface of her consciousness.

'I don't want you to leave me alone.'

Kristina stared at her mother, hating the moment. 'But I have to go . . .'

'I'm ill.'

'The doctor said that there is nothing really wrong.' Kristina swallowed slowly and forced her gaze to the portrait of the Emperor Franz Joseph I hanging above the huge fireplace, like an ancient monument. We should charge people to visit 'our home', this capsule of old Vienna, for the pleasure of breathing the last sour air of a bygone age.

'What do doctors know? – "Nothing really wrong",' she sneered. 'I have a *bad heart*.'

'He said that you were tired, that resting today and tomorrow would . . .'

'I *don't care* what he said.' She shook her head, the surprisingly luxurious curls unmoving.

Kristina almost wanted to smile; she had been using Kristina's hairspray again which meant that she had climbed the stairs to her daughter's quarters.

'Mother,' Kristina said gently, 'this is important to me – I *want* to go.'

The old woman looked up. 'Why, Kristina? Not *another* man, surely?' Her mother smiled then, but not with kindness.

'Actually, no . . .' she replied tautly, 'this is a special favour.' And it was the truth, for once.

'I don't believe you.'

'I don't care if you don't believe me.'

Her mother's head began to nod ominously. 'I don't care,' she repeated, '*I don't care*. Someone will carve that on your headstone, Kristina.'

'I have to go, Mother.'

'Don't leave me.'

It was her last plea, the last time her voice would sound gentle, merciful. The performance hardly ever varied. Kristina closed her eyes. She hated her then, hated the pleading most of all. Her coat lay discarded over a chair, and she moved across the room to put it on.

'And *LOOK* at you . . . just *LOOK* at you!' Her mother's words gushed cruelly at last, her fists thumping the wooden arms of the chair in thwarted rage.

Kristina tried to shut out the sound, concentrating on her coat – the buttons, the belt, the softness of the black velvet. Anything.

'Your skirt is too tight, your lips too red . . . they must *laugh* at you.' For just a moment she seemed to relent and her voice softened again. To the pleading. 'Don't you see, Kristina – you are *too old* for such things – too old.'

But the door closed with a soft slam and the old woman was left alone in the room, grey curls still, mouth trembling, ready to speak again.

The streets were frozen and as she walked gravel crunched beneath her feet. Kristina took deep, slow breaths of the cold air, fighting for control, fighting the tears in her eyes. And the despair. Her mother had an excellent way of *creating* it, as if she could conjure despair from the night air like an evil perfume. She glanced at her watch; she would be just acceptably late and by the time she reached the Mahlerstrasse her face might look frozen, but at least not despairing. Or maybe it would show, seeping out from beneath her make-up, deepening the small lines which had begun to take their place at the edges of her eyes. Kristina sighed heavily, watching the white fog from her mouth cloud and disappear into blackness.

'Kristina!'
'Sorry I'm late.'
'Nonsense . . . we have another few minutes before we have dinner.'

As Monika took her coat Kristina discreetly ran her eyes down the length of her friend's dress. Too much gold, she decided neutrally, and breathed a small sigh of relief. Perhaps her own skirt was a little tight, but she was practically under-dressed compared with Monika. Besides, she thought defensively, my bottom is one of my best, almost unchanging, assets . . . and I don't have many of those left.

'My thanks again for standing in at the last minute, Kristina, I was almost desperate.'
'Really, it's no trouble.'

If only, if only they all could have seen the nasty little cabaret her mother had performed and as she walked into the drawing room she realized with sudden searing insight that they probably would pity her.

The drinks were pleasant and after a few minutes Kristina began to relax and became aware that she knew only one other person in the room besides Monika and her husband, an Austrian, who was also one of the delegates at the conference. Kurt was solitary and apparently homosexual, one of the few she had met who made it rather obvious, with careful disdain, that he had little time to spare for the opposite sex. God forbid if Monika had decided to sit him next to her . . . And please God not the paunchy Greek who had made a clumsy pass at one of the conference attendants. She glanced around again and settled on an attractive Spaniard. Oh no, no more Spaniards. Before she could muse any further Monika was ushering them into the adjoining dining room.

She did get the paunchy Greek, but at least on her right side was seated a nice American. At first she had thought him young, thirtyish, but when he turned towards her and she was able to see his face fully for the first time she realized that he was probably more her own age.

'Sam Cohen – hi.'
'Hi . . .' She smiled back at him, the inevitable question sounding in her head. Married? And for a brief, burning moment she hated herself.

It was one of the most enjoyable evenings she had spent in a long, long time. Kristina even found herself being charming to the paunchy Greek. But it was Sam. She actually *liked* him; he made her laugh; he seemed a nice, uncomplicated man and she had thought that such men had ceased to exist. He had asked for her telephone number.

'But he's married, Kristina . . .' Monika said as she brought out her coat.

Kristina looked back at her, not allowing herself to speak. The other guests had left and they were alone, only the sound of Monika's husband, Herbert, could be heard as he poured himself a drink in the adjoining room.

'He didn't mention it,' she replied feebly.

'Do they ever?' Monika responded with a knowing, irritating smile. 'I know because one of Herbert's girls had to pull him out of one of his meetings to speak to his wife long-distance.' She began helping Kristina on with her coat. 'He has a little girl, too.'

'A little girl?'

'Oh, Kristina . . .' Monika said with exasperation. She had known her friend too long to pretend any longer; there had been too many times when she had had to wipe away the tears or pour a stiff drink. And there was the ever-present shadow of her gargoyle of a mother. Monika shivered slightly before continuing, 'Why do you think I put Christos next to you. . . ?' She saw Kristina's face fall. 'I know he's not perfect, but he's a man and free and with a good career – he told me he found you very attractive.'

Kristina silently buttoned her coat. The paunchy Greek who made passes at conference attendants; she was reduced to that.

'I must go, Monika, it's getting very late.' She cleared her throat.

Monika looked back at her. 'I'm sorry . . .'

'It was a lovely evening.'

She walked away knowing that her friend still watched her, unable to turn and wave and say goodbye and see the pity held in her eyes.

'You look wonderful.'

John let his eyes travel over the lovely curves of his wife sheathed in black velvet, the rigidly cut bodice emphasizing glorious shoulders and the creamy opulence of the breasts he loved so well. She seemed perfectly at home in the magnificent surroundings of the castle, as if she were mistress here instead of the fragile Austrian countess who had greeted them on their arrival. He caught his wife's gaze as it came to settle on his face and as she fastened the sapphire earrings he had given her for their first anniversary. He never forgot. But she was not totally his, Elizabeth never had been. He wondered whether he loved her too much.

'Thank you, John.' She grinned. 'You look rather distinguished yourself.'

She smiled back at him, a full smile, no hint of any effort. It was *just for him*. Quickly he shifted his stare because all at once he wanted her, and knew she would see it. His mouth went dry and he was swept by dizzying, crushing need.

Elizabeth paused in front of the mirror, seeing the unmistakable flush of desire in her husband's face reflected in the glass. She had also seen the helpless joy in his eyes as her lips parted, her face lighting up as he stood watching her, almost in awe. At that moment there was only John, as if the world had retreated and everything was very simple, suddenly. He could touch her soul sometimes, reaching inside to negate the temptation and wretched guilt which had begun to make her miserable. She was touched by shame and her hands came up to hold his face and gather him into her arms. They stood, wrapped in silence, for a long moment, his head cradled in the curve of her neck.

'Why can I reduce you so easily, John . . .?' she whispered. 'You shouldn't let me . . .'

He lifted his head up and stared into her face. 'Because you always have.' His smile was boyish then, slightly sad. 'And there's nothing I can do about it.'

She reached up and brushed his lips with her own, prising them gently apart with her tongue so that he would take her. Almost instantly she was rewarded by his strong hands gliding down her back, pressing her against him so that she would feel his growing hardness and the breath catching like a tight knot in her throat. He groaned softly and pressed his forehead against her own in frustration.

'We have time, John . . .'

He drew a breath. 'But your dress . . .'

'John, John,' she said in mild exasperation. 'It doesn't matter . . . pull it up . . . pull it up.' Her mouth closed over his again and then traced the curve of his jaw to his ear. 'I want you now, John, not later.'

Oh, and so did he. So did he.

He swallowed slowly, catching the material between his fingers, letting it ride up over her thighs and the lush roundness of her buttocks. John pushed her gently against the wall and lifted her so that his entry would be made easier. There was no self-control now, no questions as his need took over and she welcomed him ardently, her legs locking around him as the searing heat of their pleasure began to build and build and there was only her closed eyes and open mouth begging him. Elizabeth begging him, breathing his name.

Sophia looked out beyond the window to the thin grey thread of evening skyline which was now fading into blackness. Her eyes drifted to the massive fists of purple cloud which were drawing together, blotting out the stars one by one and, like a child, she wished on the last, the final pinprick of light.

'You're ready . . . good.'

It was her mother's voice. She had heard her quiet knock and timid step into the room, but had not turned. Sophia's eyes were drawn to her own long slim fingers and the carefully buffed and polished nails normally stained black with ink or smudged with charcoal.

'Please – Sophia.' It was a plea. 'For me.'

Sophia closed her eyes.

'A few hours, that is all.' Genevieve sighed softly. 'Your father wants this so much.'

'Why, Mama?' she asked finally.

'Sophia, Sophia.' Genevieve found her eyes travelling over her lovely daughter. She had combed the long chestnut hair herself, chosen the pale pink dress and the delicate chain around her neck. 'We have discussed this already; you are nearly eighteen and it is time to take your place with your father and me at some official dinners.'

'I missed my lesson.'

'I know, but only this once. And there is always next week.'

'Have you asked Father yet – about my studying art?' She turned slowly and Genevieve felt her eyes quaver and shift beneath her daughter's gaze. Not now, Sophia.

'No,' she replied quickly. 'Not yet.'

Sophia's eyes seemed to grow large suddenly, luminous, like a frightened puppy.

'Forgive me, Mama,' she said softly. 'I have been so rude, and I know it is not your fault.'

'There is nothing to forgive.' Genevieve circled her with her arms. 'Nothing at all.'

'It is just that everyone else will be so much older than I am. What shall I say? How will I pass the whole evening standing and talking – about *what*, Mama?'

'You are a charming young woman, Sophia, do not forget that,' Genevieve parried. 'Talk of your art, school, Austria. Remember most of our guests are from other parts of the world and know little about Vienna and Austria in real terms.' Then she smiled. 'And also remember to ask – and to listen, that is the secret. You will be surprised how much people enjoy talking about themselves!'

The faintest of smiles began tipping the edges of her daughter's mouth and Genevieve took a slow, barely audible sigh of relief; perhaps, after all, it would be all right. But then there was the art question and Felix's adamant refusal. She had lied to her daughter, but she had had little choice under the circumstances. Her mind swept backwards to the conversation with her husband in the close confines of the car; it had been the wrong time, she would ask him again. But even as she tried to convince herself, a flicker of fear came into her heart, driving any calmness out, letting the old familiar feeling of inadequacy seep in.

'Mama?'

Sophia's voice startled her as it broke in upon her uneasy thoughts.

'I was not concentrating, as usual.' Genevieve attempted a small laugh and looked into her daughter's softly frowning face. There was the dinner to be checked and the place settings. And Felix would be waiting. She swallowed and reached for Sophia's hand.

'Come, we shall be late.'

Dan Gurney sipped at his sherry, white and dry, just how he liked it. It was impressive, he realized – Schloss Bletz: the lake embraced by forest, the lonely grandeur of the land; like taking a step back in time. He only wished he could like Count Dhoryány, his host, but liking such a man was difficult and he would not begin to try, he had learned that lesson a long time ago. At least his stance for Austria in the conference was a relatively comfortable one because its record for conservation and care of the environment was so good, but it fought a losing battle on one side of the country – totally blocked in by the East and its runaway and escalating pollution.

'You seem deep in thought, Mr Ambassador.'

Dan turned abruptly and found himself looking into the face of his host.

'I was thinking of your somewhat problematical neighbours.'

Felix frowned.

'The East.'

'Ah.'

'We will have an interesting battle on our hands over the next few months.'

'I assume we will also be tackling our "problematical Western neighbours", Ambassador Gurney.'

'Daniel, please.' He couldn't imagine Count Dhoryány calling him Dan. Not at all.

'Daniel,' he repeated carefully and then continued. 'After all, the list is almost endless: toxic spills in the Rhine river and the North Sea, dying seals, lead emissions from cars, acid rain . . .' He paused. 'You are, of course, aware that the UK is probably the largest contributor of acid rain to both Sweden and Norway alone, and that the US deposits six million tonnes of acid on eastern Canada each year . . .'

'I am aware, Count Dhoryány.'

'Felix, please.'

'Felix. You have an impressive home,' Dan remarked, changing the subject.

'Thank you. It has been in my wife's family for over five hundred years,' he said and then added, 'before America had even been dreamed of.' The corners of his mouth turned upwards into a sardonic smile. 'The central keep dates from the early twelfth century, some outer walling and the east tower were added during the Middle Ages and the somewhat unusual addition of the baroque tower much later, of course.'

'Of course,' Dan replied with a trace of sarcasm.

'As you might imagine, as well as great age, Schloss Bletz also has a great history.' He gestured extravagantly towards the window and the terraced gardens as if he were about to make a speech. 'You are probably not aware that this part of Austria was invaded by the Turks in the first half of the sixteenth century . . . there is even a small collection of Turkish art and weaponry in the great hall.'

'Actually, Felix, I majored in European history.'

Felix's eyes examined him rather sharply.

'And I was waiting for the right moment to say . . .' Dan continued easily '. . . that you have a very fine example of rococo painting on the ceiling of the garden room – Maulpertsch, isn't it?'

'I am impressed, Daniel.' He smiled tightly. 'I'm afraid that we continentals tend to have a somewhat "traditional" view of the American.' He laughed, but Dan was reminded of a smirk.

'Well, we all have to live and learn, and change, Felix.'

The eyes looking back at him seemed to open wider, one arrogant eyebrow arching.

'The conference, for instance,' Dan continued, deciding to get down to business. 'Presumably the grouping of a hundred and twenty-four countries will give us all ample opportunity to take some fairly drastic action in the not too distant future.'

'Fortunately Austria has an excellent environmental record.'

'True.'

'And we are suffering at the hands of our neighbours, and not just our Eastern Bloc "friends".'

'That's also true, but somehow we are all going to have to take a wider view, Felix, not just of "our country", or even "our immediate neighbours", but a global view.'

'Rather idealistic . . . people, countries are little more than the health of their economies . . . and cleaning the environment will cost a great deal of money which most of our "friends" around the conference table will not be prepared to spend.'

'Right again, Felix – so we shall either have to persuade them, educate them, or buy them off.'

'With whose money, under what conditions?'

'That's what we're here to find out.'

'I wish I shared your obvious optimism, Daniel.'

Dan sighed inwardly, wondering why he had brought the subject up, here, now. He looked across the room, his gaze drifting to that of his host's wife; a pretty woman, fine featured, but too thin. For a moment he watched her move, nervously, like a puppet – eyes wide, with a wooden smile fixed on her face.

'The key word is *change*, Felix,' he continued wearily.

'As long as it does not cost too much money,' the Austrian persisted. 'It always comes down to money in the end.'

'And ignorance and stupidity.' Dan blinked and turned reluctantly to look into Felix's face and the man drew back a little.

'There are many difficult and complicated issues at stake, of course,' Felix said carefully.

'That's quite an understatement, Felix. At the moment we stand at the bottom of a long and almost impossible climb.' He thought of Judy. 'Good words of intent cost nothing, all we have to do now is fulfil them, which will undoubtedly prove expensive, controversial – and probably very unpopular in many cases.'

'Well, we must start somewhere.' The man was ridiculously passionate about it all, almost embarrassingly so.

Dan gave him a humourless smile. 'That's right, Felix, we must, because if we don't we may find ourselves going the way of the dinosaurs.'

'Your mother tells me that you paint . . .' Elizabeth said, looking into Sophia's shy, uncertain face.

'A little . . .' she said slowly, 'but I prefer sketching, although my teacher is pressing more and more watercolours on me.'

'Do you do portraits?'

'Oh, yes.' Her eyes seemed to grow larger with repressed excitement.

'I have a small son, would you sketch him for me?'

'But I have only done my family and a few friends.'

Elizabeth studied the girl's face, it was almost perfectly formed and there was a gentleness about it, like that of a faun or a doe. A madonna's face.

'May I see?'

The brown eyes looked downwards, but Sophia's pretty mouth was smiling with barely concealed pleasure.

'Please?' Elizabeth pressed a winning plea into her voice.

Sophia lifted her eyes from her hands and nodded in response. 'I was sketching this morning, in the garden room, my portfolio is still there.'

'The garden room . . . yes, your mother showed me.'

Elizabeth looked towards the double doors. 'The next room. Shall we look at them there?'

Sophia glanced across the drawing room before replying; her father was busy with the American and her mother with the German ambassador's wife. She nodded and they slipped out through the partly open door and into the flagstoned hallway. Elizabeth shivered.

'It's always cold, even in summer,' Sophia said in response.

'But you like it here very much, don't you?'

Sophia lowered her gaze again as if she had just been found out. 'It's so old, so big – like a grand and very old man.' She loved the castle, the feeling of solidity all around her, the thick dark wood and thicker walls; its age, its wisdom. There was curious comfort in knowing that it would still be here long after her parents were gone, and long after her own death. She looked up and Elizabeth let her eyes follow to the high vaulted ceiling which soared above them, a massive crystal chandelier hanging like an enormous jewel from its central arch.

'It is usually closed off during the winter because of the threat of snow, but when the weather is better we often come.' She looked back at Elizabeth, face radiant. 'It is my father's favourite place, too.'

'Oh, yes?'

Sophia nodded.

'And your mother?'

Sophia's face seemed to darken a little. 'Not so much, I think.' She wondered if she had said too much, but she liked this woman. 'My mother's brother died here.'

'Oh . . . I'm sorry.'

'It was a long time ago, Mother was a child.'

'What happened?'

'There was an accident.' She paused and her voice grew quiet as a picture of her mother's tense, anxious face formed in her head. 'He fell, badly, into the lake. Mama was with him when it happened; she was twelve, I think.'

'How terrible.'

'Yes. We never talk about it.' Sophia flushed guiltily and wondered again whether she had said too much.

'Let me see your sketches,' Elizabeth said.

Sophia nodded, smiling in relief, and then led her guest into the adjoining room.

For a few long seconds Elizabeth stood just inside the doorway and once more took in the glorious ceiling and the delicately painted panels bearing birds, fruit, scrolls and exotic nymphs which formed three of the main walls. The fourth was of a fairly recent design, the panels being of rich, stained glass and leading through ornately carved French doors out on to the wide, paved terrace. She inhaled deeply and wondered whether it was too sumptuous, too perfect. Her gaze slid back to the glass panels and the view of the lake which lay black and thick beneath the steep walls of pine.

'Beautiful – isn't it?' Sophia said quietly.

'Yes.'

Sophia's voice had grown small and Elizabeth found her eyes pulled back to the young girl's. The portfolio was lying on a low table against a wall and as Sophia pulled the black laces undone the sketches fell free, spilling outwards like confetti. Elizabeth bent down and began helping her to pick them up from the floor.

'But you're really very good!' she exclaimed and savoured the thick white paper between her fingers. 'This is your mother.' Genevieve's face had been caught and recorded in expertly knowing lines and shadows; her daughter had captured the nervousness, the unease almost too well, had somehow brought out from within deep tones of pain so that they seemed to lay open on the page, naked and exposed.

'Mother worries so much . . .' she said, as if in apology.

Elizabeth glanced at the young girl beside her as a moment's odd little silence fell between them.

'And this, of course, is your father.'

'Yes.' Sophia gave her a searching look. 'He is very handsome, isn't he?' she said proudly and then giggled softly. 'All my friends think so.'

'Yes, I . . . yes, he is.'

'And this is Gunther, my brother, but I have only done one or two of him because he is so boring!'

Elizabeth studied the pages in her hand and then shifted her gaze back to Sophia's face.

'You will sketch my son – please?'

Sophia smiled, obviously delighted at the implied compliment. 'If my parents agree.'

'Don't worry, I shall persuade them!'

Sophia began slipping the sketches back into the folder and then turned sharply as the door opened behind them.

'There you are.' Genevieve smiled tightly at Elizabeth as her eyes immediately took in the portfolio and her daughter's sketches. 'I wondered where you both were.'

'I'm so sorry...' Elizabeth said quickly, 'but I cajoled Sophia into showing me her work, and I must say she's very good indeed.'

Genevieve nodded and closed the door quietly. 'Yes, yes she is.'

It was now or never. 'I wonder if you would allow her to sketch my son?'

'Of course.'

'Mama is busy trying to persuade my father that I should attend an art school,' Sophia interjected.

Genevieve turned away as if she had noticed something in the garden.

'I hope he will not prove too difficult to convince...' Elizabeth offered. 'I am sure he realizes how talented his daughter is.'

'You see, Mama,' Sophia chuckled.

Elizabeth was drawn by Genevieve's stiff nod of the head, and her eyes travelled down the silk-clad arms to the small fists which were tightly clenched so that the knuckles showed white. She swallowed and looked exaggeratedly at her watch.

'I think my husband will be wondering where I am.'

Genevieve seemed to give a small start. 'Yes, of course.' She glanced quickly at Elizabeth and then turned to her daughter. 'Come, Sophia, we will be keeping everyone waiting.'

'God! Save me from dinners like that!'

'It wasn't *quite* that bad...'

'Oh yes, John, this one should be given a special prize.' Elizabeth sighed dramatically and kicked off her shoes. 'And besides, you didn't have to spend the whole time sitting between our host and Oskar von der ... whatever...'

'Von der Heyden.' He added, 'Of von der Heyden Chemicals fame.' He smiled in sympathy. 'Not much of a talker, I gather.'

'It was like getting blood out of a stone.'

'I liked the German ambassador.'

'Yes, his wife's nice too.' She frowned a little. 'Embarrassingly perfect English which shames my German. I shall have to make more of an effort.'

'You said that about French.'

'Thank you, John.'

'Just a joke.'

She shook her head and smiled. 'Sorry, I think I'm tired and it has been rather a long day.'

'At least the wine was wonderful.'

'Naturally we have our host to thank for that . . .' she said sarcastically and then lay across the bed and stared wearily at the ceiling. 'I would have enjoyed it more if we hadn't had to endure his ridiculous performance on wine tasting – swirling it around, holding it to the light, *breathing* it, rolling it over his tongue, and then that final pomposity when he tilted his head back and let it trickle down his throat.' She laughed in exasperation.

'Well, at least he kept you entertained.'

'Yes, when he remembered to lift his eyes out of my cleavage.'

'Felix?'

'Yes, Felix.'

'Doesn't seem the type.'

'Believe me, John.'

'Okay, okay, I believe you.' He held up his hands in mock fear.

'God, that poor woman.'

'They have a charming daughter.'

'Yes, very.' Elizabeth sat down in front of the mirror and unclipped her earrings. 'She wants to go to art school.'

'Is that a problem?' John moved into the bathroom.

'From her mother's reaction to an innocent question on my part – yes.'

'Maybe they have other plans for her.'

A tap squeaked and water began to pour into the basin. Elizabeth stared back at her face in the mirror.

'I think they have.'

'Sorry, I can't hear you.' John was cleaning his teeth.

'It doesn't matter . . .' But it did matter somehow and she didn't really know why. She moved over to the window and saw only utter blackness; no moon, no star, no shadow. She shivered a little as the shriek of a night owl broke the thick, heady quiet and she was suddenly touched by sadness, because there was about Schloss Bletz a feeling of greyness, heaviness, dreams lost and forgotten, or broken, or ended, or never begun.

Genevieve began brushing her hair. Fifty strokes. Fifty in the morning, fifty at night. She reached for a bottle of skin cleanser and began wiping her cheeks with neat pieces of cotton wool in swift upward strokes so that her face gradually took on an unnatural shiny look as if the neat balls of cotton wool had taken away her colour too, and the shadows, and the lines, so that the face that looked back at her was not Genevieve, but someone else, a stranger who only came at night. She removed the slick white cleanser with toner the colour of lemon juice and then reached finally for a jar of night cream, a gilded, highly ornamental jar which reminded her, curiously, of one of her dead mother's gold bracelets.

'A successful evening on the whole . . .' Felix's voice startled her as he emerged from his dressing room.

'Yes, Felix, it was.'

'Simone was drunk.'

'Only a little, Felix, I'm sure no one noticed.'

'The American ambassador did . . . her hand kept squeezing his arm . . . thank God it didn't disappear beneath the table . . .'

Genevieve closed her eyes.

'You will cross her off our list.'

She made no answer.

Felix stood looking at himself in front of the long dress mirror and then began to slip his jacket from his shoulders.

'I only hope she drank enough to put her out for the night; it would be intolerable if she started wandering about the corridors in a drunken stupor.'

'I'm sure she won't do that, Felix.' Genevieve's eyes widened in surprise.

'She is not always a rational woman, my dear.'

Felix opened the huge oak cabinet and carefully placed his jacket on one of the thick padded hangers, a barely discernible frown disturbing his face. Simone had made a scene in the ground floor cloakroom; she had literally thrown herself into his arms, pawing at his shirt, rubbing her face and thrusting her big, flabby breasts against him. He had been disgusted, what was she thinking of? Their brief affair had been over for several months and still she slobbered over him like a bitch on heat. She was old enough to know better, for God's sake. It had been a mistake from the very beginning. He shook his head and began sliding his black-clad feet out of the hand-made shoes and inserting wooden shoehorns into each of them. The woman was a sex-mad fool.

'Did you count the cutlery?'

'It was all there, Felix,' Genevieve replied tiredly.

'And my collection of silver miniatures?'

'Yes, Felix.'

He gave a brief snort of satisfaction.

'I shall never forget that weekend last summer when we played host to almost half the diplomatic community . . .'

Genevieve sighed, knowing what was coming next.

'Appalling . . . four of the dessert spoons were missing and two silver pheasants . . . the dwarf ones I picked up in Jacques Perrin in Paris . . . not to mention that crude little man from the Romanian embassy filling his pockets with my cigars.' Felix began removing his trousers. 'Appalling. That sort of thing never happened in my father's day.' He shook his head. 'The war changed *everything*.'

'I liked the British couple.'

He paused for a moment, one leg still covered by a baggy trouser leg.

'Yes.' His mind instantly inserted a vivid picture of Elizabeth Thornton and he smiled to himself. 'Thornton's a very wealthy man.'

'Really?' she replied uninterestedly.

'Yes. It might be worthwhile cultivating their friendship.'

Genevieve moved across the darkened room. There was only one lamp left burning and a shaft of light from the bathroom illuminated a rectangle of the polished wooden floor. It had been her parents' boudoir, a massive room with heavy drapes of burgundy velvet and old Persian rugs on the floor. A huge oak chest sat at the end of the bed, covered with carvings of cupids and garlands of flowers. Just like the bed itself, a period beauty she supposed, but it had been her parents' and finally her father's. She never felt happy in this room, in this bed. The covers had been turned back and she climbed into the cool embrace of cold white sheets.

'Oskar was on good form.'

'Was he?' She hadn't noticed. For her, Oskar was always the same.

Felix glanced sideways at his wife. 'He seems to have taken quite a liking to Sophia.'

'Has he?' Genevieve sighed inwardly, wanting sleep.

'Once she's gotten this art nonsense out of her system we should get them together more often.'

Genevieve swallowed, only half listening, not wanting to resurrect the art question now. Tomorrow, perhaps.

'Young girls often get foolish ideas in their heads,' Felix continued easily.

Her jaw tensed. 'It's not a foolish idea, Felix.' She looked up at him, finally drawn. 'And I don't think Sophia wants to get her art out of her system.'

'Well, she will have to try.'

Felix hung his perfectly creased trousers in the cabinet with an impatient sweep of his arm.

'Couldn't we let her pursue some study for just a year, Felix? We could send her to a local school so that she wouldn't have to leave home.'

'No, Genevieve.' He turned towards her, face stony. 'I think we have already discussed the matter and I said no.'

He walked into the bathroom.

'Felix . . .' she pleaded. 'Sophia has talent . . .'

She heard him sigh dramatically.

'How many artists have *real* talent, Genevieve, how many? And are *you* a competent judge, or even Frau Taucher?' His voice had taken the tone of a very patient father talking to a rather naïve and not very bright child. 'I hope you haven't been encouraging her?'

Suddenly he was standing in the shaft of light from the bathroom, naked legs slightly spread, his hands unbuttoning the crisp whiteness of his shirt with sharp little movements of thumbs and fingers.

She remained silent.

'Well – have you?'

'I know how much she wants this, Felix,' she said quietly.

'She is hardly old enough to know what is good for her.'

'*Please*, Felix.' She made a soft, despairing sound.

'Genevieve, I have already said "no" more than once.'

He disappeared into the bathroom again as if the conversation was at an end.

'Just a year . . .' Her eyes began to fill with tears.

'Do you have trouble hearing me?' His voice was raised now as if he wanted to be sure that she heard him, that there was no mistake.

'I promised her that I'd talk to you.'

'Well, you have kept your promise.'

'That's not enough,' she said thickly, feeling sick now as well as tired.

He came back into the room. 'I beg your pardon?'

'*Please*, Felix.'

He looked at her, at the small white face, the large irritating doe eyes, and felt a surge of unreasonable anger.

'I want her to marry Oskar.'

The words dropped like stones into the room and the silence that descended was weighted, palpable. He hadn't planned to tell her like this, but the futility of their conversation and her unusual obstinacy had pushed him beyond endurance.

Genevieve looked up at him, her eyes widening, the breath catching audibly in her throat.

'You can't mean it,' she whispered.

'For heaven's sake, Genevieve, don't look so stunned! Oskar is an extremely wealthy man – an excellent catch for any girl.' And if any man's daughter was going to marry Oskar, it would be his; von der Heyden was a byword for wealth in the right circles and besides, Oskar was lonely, he had said as much to him only last month and he could tell, from the way the man looked at Sophia, that he certainly admired her, at the very least, and with a little subtle persuasion it would surely not take too much to convince him that pretty, unspoilt Sophia would make an ideal match.

She stared at him in bewilderment, unable to comprehend immediately. 'You *do* mean it.'

'Of course.'

'But why? Why, Felix?'

'Why?!' His voice became chill and his mouth drew into a small, thin line. 'Don't be ridiculous.'

She shook her head, the blood draining from her face. Felix watched her for a moment and then realized that he was standing almost naked in front of her unseeing eyes; he reached for his robe and the rustling of the silk made Genevieve blink.

'He is too old, Felix – and Sophia looks upon him almost as an uncle.'

'Oskar is only a year older than I.'

'But you are Sophia's father.'

His eyes darkened with anger at the implied insult. 'What a remarkable observation, Genevieve.' He spun around on his heel, dismissing her, and walked back into the bathroom, closing the door behind him.

She inhaled deeply as if she were recovering from a blow to the stomach and her eyes lifted mechanically to the ceiling and the patterned beams, then downwards to the far wall and the enormous ceramic stove which sat fat and bloated in a black corner. In the bathroom Felix was finishing his toilet, she could hear his careful, precise movements, the creak of the polished wooden seat as he sat down, the muffled sound of the paper roller as he pulled off the selected number of pieces. There were always six. She heard him shift a little as if he were making himself more comfortable and then he muttered, moaning softly as he broke wind, and she closed her eyes. Genevieve sighed raggedly and caught the heavy coverlet tightly in her fingers. She tried to wipe the evening away, to sleep, but a tear too heavy to hold back was squeezing itself out from the corner of her eye.

There had been no more snow. Dan shifted impatiently from one foot to the other as he looked out on the frozen gardens from the breakfast room. He had had enough of Schloss Bletz, he wanted to get home. And home, in Vienna, was his light and airy apartment looking on to the magnificence of the Karlskirche. By now the smell of coffee would have permeated the kitchen and the hallway and he would be standing next to the stove cooking ham and eggs, the *Herald Tribune* neatly folded alongside his plate, waiting to be read.

'Daniel – I hope you slept well?' Felix strode towards him from across the long narrow room.

'Fine, thanks.' Not true. He had been cold and had found himself hunting for an extra blanket amongst the myriad cupboards in his room. Then Simone had come visiting. He had wondered later how she had found out where he was sleeping. A servant? Felix? Surely not.

Fortunately he had not responded to her frantic, drunken whispers through the door and eventually she had given up and he had stood shivering in the darkness until her uncertain footsteps had lessened and died away. He had toyed with the idea of letting her warm his bed, literally, but toying was all it was. He was getting too old for that sort of thing and drunken, lonely women were definitely not his style.

'I see you've breakfasted already.'

'Yes, I do apologize, but I'm always an early riser and I really do have to get back to Vienna and finish a report which has to be ready for tomorrow morning.'

'That's a pity. I had hoped to escort my guests on a walk in the grounds.'

'Actually, Felix, I took the opportunity before anyone was about this morning.'

'I'm surprised you didn't see my wife.'

Dan raised his eyebrows.

'She couldn't sleep . . . and now seems to have caught a slight chill.'

'I'm sorry.'

'Oh, it's nothing.'

'Will she be down for breakfast?'

'No, I'm afraid not – I've insisted she return to bed.'

'Perhaps you would give her my best wishes and thanks.'

'Of course.'

They looked at each other for an awkward moment.

'I'll just go and fetch my bags.'

'I'll organize that.'

'No, really.'

'I insist – after all, that's what I pay the servants for.'

'Thanks,' Dan said dryly and watched Felix's retreating back as he made his way out of the room. He turned to the silent gardens and was snapped once more out of his reverie as someone else came into the room.

'Good morning.'

'Good morning, John. Sleep well?'

'Like a log, actually.'

'I wish I could say the same.'

'Oh, dear . . .' John smiled in sympathy.

'I'm just about to leave.'

'So soon?'

'Well, apart from feeling slightly shattered, I do have some work to get on with once I get back.'

'Ah.' John began pouring himself some coffee. 'I take it this is for the plenary meeting?'

'Right.' Dan sighed softly. 'I've been waiting on an assessment from the World Bank on the effects of the projects for which they provide funds.'

'This is connected with the "debt for nature" idea?'

'Right again.' Dan shook his head gently. 'Naturally the commercial banks don't like it and naturally it will be difficult to implement.'

'I had noticed the rather lukewarm reception it has received so far.'

'Well, at least it's a start.'

John took a long, life-saving gulp of coffee.

'And there's still the wildlife issue.'

'That's a separate commission to be headed by the Swedes.'

'You heard about the murder of that British journalist in Tanzania?'

Dan nodded. 'Your Home Secretary's nephew.' He shook his head. 'Ivory. I thought we were beginning to knock that on the head.'

'That's like expecting the Japs to cease slaughtering the dwindling number of whales . . .'

'No doubt you've heard that they have a new "scientific" plan for harvesting whales.' Dan snorted with contempt. 'I think it was the late Sir Peter Scott who called this so-called plan "international hooliganism on the high seas".'

'And they keep denying it, of course.'

'Of course.'

Dan sighed heavily and thought of his office and the wide, long desk piled high with papers, reports and letters of protest from people all over the world.

'I've received ideas on working strategies and suggestions from groups as far apart as The Self-Employed Women's Association to an outfit called Earthscan.'

'So have I, and some of them aren't bad, except that they all want us to work miracles overnight.'

'With particular emphasis on the rain forest question and the global warming trend, no doubt . . .'

They looked at one another with a smile.

'It seems a long way from Madrid and talks on human rights.'

'Or the reduction of long-range missiles.'

'I think maybe it's an improvement,' John said quietly.

'I think you're right.'

Elizabeth walked into the room unobserved and stood for a moment watching the two men as they looked outwards beyond the window to the white hills.

'I hope we're not going to have more snow.'

They both turned abruptly as she spoke, shoes knocking on the polished wooden floor as she walked towards them.

Dan looked at her with pleasure and just a touch of envy. No drunken Simone, this. In her wake came Felix, and Dan drained his coffee cup and placed it back on the table.

'My bags are ready?'

'In the boot of your car,' Felix said and then focused his attention on Elizabeth.

'Good morning.' He gave a clipped nod of his head which was supposed to veil his eyes as they travelled down the length of her body. John longed to smile.

After Dan's departure Felix joined them for breakfast and was quickly followed by Sophia and a somewhat pale Oskar.

'Where is Mother, Papa?'

Felix brought his head slowly up from the boiled egg he was cracking with careful precision.

'She has a slight cold, Sophia, and will not be down for breakfast.'

'Shall I go and . . .'

'No, that will not be necessary,' he said quickly and with unnecessary force.

Sophia's eyes widened a little and then wavered beneath his uncompromising gaze. Elizabeth exchanged a brief but meaningful glance with her husband.

'Coffee, Sophia?'

For a moment the young girl did not reply, but then slowly switched her attention to Elizabeth.

'Thank you.'

They were all saved, even Oskar, by the entrance of Simone, one hand placed dramatically across her forehead.

'I am ill . . . so ill.'

Felix frowned. 'Perhaps a very large schwarzer might help,' he remarked dryly, pushing the coffee jug towards her.

She seemed not to hear him and remained standing in the doorway.

'May I get you something?' Sophia asked, rising from her chair.

Slowly Simone lowered the hand from her brow. 'What a good child you are.'

Sophia blushed.

'I think I am going to be sick.'

But Simone still stood there, unmoving, in the doorway, only her large breasts and the unhappy bulk of her stomach twitching a little beneath the tight confines of her dress. But suddenly she did move and Elizabeth was surprised at the speed with which she vanished from view. It all happened in a split second – her face draining of colour, her disappearance from the doorway, her hasty footsteps followed quickly by an abrupt halt as she vomited.

John closed his eyes and put the piece of bread and butter he had been holding back on his plate. He darted a glance at Elizabeth and then switched his glance back to his host. Felix was sitting paralysed in his chair, his lips pressed together, his face turned a murderous red as the retching went on and on and on.

Elizabeth slid into sleep on the way back to Vienna. She and John had released themselves from staying at Schloss Bletz any longer by pleading the reasonable excuse that more snow was likely. She awoke as they neared the outskirts of the city and only then did a brief flurry sprinkle freezing white specks across the windscreen of the car. Her eyelids lifted slowly open and she realized that it was the music coming from the cassette player which had triggered her into wakefulness.

'What's that?'

'What's what?'

'The music?'

'I don't know – one of Grace's, I think.' John's eyes slid sideways. 'Don't you like it?'

'Yes – I like it.' Elizabeth straightened her head to look out of the window. 'I just haven't heard it in a long time.' She wanted to smile, smile at the perversity of Fate. 'Hotel California' had been with her five years ago in another car, in another cassette player. She swallowed slowly as the sweet, searing memory of that long, long week with Karl rose like a sensuous, teasing ghost to haunt her. Even now.

John leaned forward and turned the sound up. 'Okay?'

She nodded in response, unable to look back at him and say 'no'. The husky lament of the guitars filled the car, the gentle exotic words spilling out in a torrent ' . . . and still those voices are calling from far away . . . mirrors on the ceiling, they drink champagne on ice . . .' She caught a breath and let herself be taken back, back; the music stroking her memory with skilful, furtive fingers ' . . . you can check out any time you like, but you can never leave . . .'

3

Karl had never liked his voice; Claude spoke in a quick, high staccato, occasionally touched by a nasal twang which irritated.

'I wanted this to be the last time, Claude.'

'Everyone always says that, my friend.' He laughed.

'The risks are beginning to outweigh the advantages.'

'Come, come Monsieur Nielsen . . . things are not *that* bad.' He sighed theatrically. 'Now, for me it is another story. And, after all, you have friends, and the friends are very good to you.'

'Let me think about it.'

There was silence for a moment.

'You may think about it, Monsieur Nielsen, but you will still come back to Claude with the right answer. I know you. I will call again in perhaps two days.'

Karl's eyes drifted to the white wall of his apartment, to the two narrow masks he had carefully placed in the centre. They were made of wood, incredibly beautiful, inky, black wood; faces with closed eyes, hollow cheeks and the wide, fleshy beauty of an African mouth. They were not the same, these mouths; a close observer would notice that the mouth of the woman was more lush, just open, the tongue lifted tantalizingly upwards. Karl swallowed. He had picked the masks up in Malawi during his sojourn in South Africa. He had gone there with only curiosity and had left with a deep, wild longing to go back. The masks were exquisite and, of course, he had paid too much for them, two thousand dollars each, but he had had to have them. He looked into the mouthpiece of the telephone and realized all at once that Claude had gone. It didn't matter. Karl lifted the brandy he had been drinking to his lips and sighed softly. It *was* the last time, at least as far as Claude was concerned. He held the liquid in his mouth for a moment and then drank it slowly, letting it sink warmly into his stomach. There would be something else, he supposed, but he would have to think about that later.

His eyes strayed back to the mask of the woman and her partly open mouth and immediately he thought of Elizabeth. She had been unable to refuse him finally and from the tone of her voice he had been able to tell that her husband had been in the room. He had left several messages, but she had never returned his call and he would have been disappointed in her if she had. Now it was all right, now she had directly agreed to meet him because she had been unable to say anything else. He had enjoyed her voice, smiling at her obvious discomfiture, and he had surprised himself with the sudden surge of excitement which had immediately produced an image of her flushed, oval face in his mind. It had been a long time since he had felt like this about a woman, this urgency. He was not an emotional man, not given to wild fantasies and longings like so many of the women he had bedded. Even when he had allowed himself to be faithful for a while and even when he had explained that he would never marry, they would still pursue, still cling, still love, until it almost suffocated him. That had been Gabrielle. But even she, in the end, had lost him. Karl drained the glass in his hand. He supposed Elizabeth would have been the same, but he had been unable to give her the chance to find out. Elizabeth was married and he wanted her. There was a sort of ironic beauty in that, a sort of delicious risk. He looked back at the mask on the wall, at the lovely, plump beckoning mouth and his lips tilted into a smile.

'I just wish it had more light . . .'

Elizabeth nodded in agreement as Clare showed her around the apartment. It was dark, it was dreary, it was cold.

'Was this all Oliver could find? There are some lovely houses at Grinzing – with enormous gardens.'

'He doesn't want a long drive to the embassy,' Clare replied a little defensively, adding quickly, 'And we are fairly close to the Stadtpark which almost makes up for the lack of a garden.'

Elizabeth followed Clare into the drawing room which still awaited the touch of an organized, caring hand to give it some semblance of order and sense of comfort. Clare had not had the time and Oliver was fast becoming a workaholic according to John, hence his wish to be within shouting distance of the embassy. Oliver had been overlooked for promotion once again and now the chance of a posting to Brussels after the conference seemed very slim; he was obviously blaming himself.

'It's so nice of you to come.'

'I was looking forward to it.'

'Cake?'

'Thank you.'

Clare sliced the fruit loaf carefully and began pouring steaming coffee into heavy china cups.

'How are the children?'

'Fine. It's just the usual school thing.' She sighed. 'We've managed to settle Jennifer into a local school, but we're still trying to find a suitable nursery for Phillip.'

Elizabeth watched Clare push her hair back from her face; she was clearly tired.

'Is the baby still not sleeping through the night?'

Clare responded with a dry, knowing smile. 'It's better, but not that much better.'

'God, you must be worn out.'

'I manage, Elizabeth, and Oliver's actually very good.' She shook her head. 'They say it gets better after the first year.' She began to laugh. 'I've always wondered who "they" were!'

'If I can help at all . . .'

'I find talking over a coffee helps enormously!' She laughed again. 'But, no . . .' Clare continued more seriously '. . . we manage.' She paused. 'Of course, more money would help. I had no idea Vienna was so expensive!'

'I was rather surprised myself.' But it hadn't really mattered, she thought guiltily. John was wealthy, wasn't he? And what would Clare Carter know of thousand-pound gowns, or a permanent membership at Champneys? Poor Clare was too busy juggling her limited resources and wondering whether she could look forward to a decent night's sleep. Elizabeth stared into her coffee cup for a moment and wondered whether she was spoilt, wondered whether she took it all for granted. She thought of John suddenly, and Christopher. She lifted her head up and smiled mechanically back at Clare. And she was meeting Karl.

'You won't believe this . . .' Clare's voice continued brightly, 'but my mother has offered to send us a food parcel every month!'

'Oh, Clare . . .'

'Yes, really.' She qualified it by adding, 'Well, at least clothes for the children and the odd luxury.'

'I don't think the great British public would believe you if you told them!'

'Sometimes I wonder myself.' She started to laugh again. 'But you have to have a sense of humour in this business, especially if you're "a wife". Maybe the powers that be will feel sorry for us one of these days and give us a raise.'

'I hear the Dutch have actually had a cut in pay . . .'

'God forbid!' Clare sighed and looked to the window. 'I wouldn't mind the inconveniences of a hardship post, but Oliver would hate it, says he'd die of boredom.' She turned back to Elizabeth, a gentle frown on her face. 'You know – he'd suffer the privations of London rather than the easy life of the Far East or Africa and much more money.'

'He doesn't really have a choice, Clare.'

'I know.' She picked up her coffee cup. 'Maybe it's just as well.' She smiled wistfully. 'I always wanted to have my own business, you know, I was doing a degree in economics when I met Oliver.'

'What happened?'

'His first posting – to Helsinki.'

'You gave up your degree?'

'I didn't have much choice really. After all, I loved Oliver and I knew that running my own business was hardly compatible with being a diplomatic wife.'

'Do you have any regrets?'

'Sometimes, Elizabeth.' Her eyes deliberately looked back. 'Don't you?'

'Sometimes.' Elizabeth gave her a small smile. 'I worked in publishing; I loved it for a while.' Inevitably she thought of Karl. Her gaze slipped to her coffee cup in the awkward silence that followed. She had had to leave Faith's finally, there had been little choice.

'I expect you will be going to the Opera Ball . . .?' Clare asked quietly, adroitly changing the subject.

'Yes, we are – an invitation from the Austrian Foreign Minister.'

'I must say, that is one experience I would like to share – but it's hideously expensive!'

'I'm afraid so.'

'And the trip to Prague and Budapest?'

'No, I can't make it. Will you?'

'The logistics are too difficult to contend with – and naturally the expense, although Oliver did say we would manage if I really wanted to go.'

'Madeleine Lindahl needs any responses by Friday.'

'I was hoping to give her mine today, she said she would be here.'

Elizabeth was surprised that Madeleine had even agreed to come. Clare was not her scene. Clare would be 'depressing, uninteresting, parochial'.

'She's probably simply late – Madeleine is not renowned for her time-keeping.' In fact, Madeleine made an art of being late, as if it was her right and hers alone to appear long after everyone else, to make an entrance.

'I must say I find her a little awesome!' Clare said, grinning. 'She's so tall, so elegant – and those amazing eyes, like black stones.' She sighed. 'I'm afraid I feel like crawling under a stone when she comes anywhere near.' Her hands fell into her lap and self-consciously she brushed some crumbs from her skirt. 'And as for you, Elizabeth – I just don't bother to think about it!'

'Oh, Clare . . .'

'No, really. I don't know how you always manage to look so good. I'm sure, even if I had the right bone structure, or whatever, I'd still look as if I'd just gotten out of bed!' She shook her head. 'I've no idea about these things and anyway, when I see myself in a mirror, I'm always reminded of a horse . . .'

'You do yourself an injustice.'

'No, I don't, Elizabeth.' Her face had grown serious. 'And you are too modest. John must think himself a lucky man.'

Elizabeth smiled with an effort; hating the praise because she did not deserve it, not when it was all so easy, not when she was about to risk it all because of a torch she had held for too long and which still smouldered hot and furtive in her heart.

The woman's dress had been torn from top to bottom and her innards exposed. Laura drew a breath. But they had left a string of pretty pearls around her neck.

'It is only a wax dummy, Laura.'

She turned to Ralf and forced a smile.

'It looks so realistic.'

'That, of course, is the idea.' He smiled back at her. 'Joseph II was a man with an eye on the future, an intelligent man. He wanted his military doctors to have the best means possible for studying anatomy, before they were let loose on his army.'

Laura shifted her gaze back to the mutilated waxwork figure in the glass case. Her eyes traced the line of the woman's long brown hair which had been allowed to hang loose and lovely over one arm, a macabre contrast to the bloodless inner organs which stared back at her.

'She could have been pretty.'

'Probably.' He leaned closer. 'After all, it is always somehow more shocking to see something lovely violated than something ugly.'

'Yes, I suppose so.'

'Basically, my sweet Laura, we are all merely the sum of the rather gruesome organs which hide within us.' He looked back at the woman in the glass. 'She could have been made just ordinary, plain, with straight unappetizing limbs. But, no, she is pretty, with long curving legs, succulent hips and a string of pearls draped around her neck.' His mouth tipped upwards on one side. 'She could be you, Laura.'

She blushed, secretly embarrassed that she should be so pleased at the compliment. Ralf was still a mystery. She knew he appreciated her, knew he noticed her, but that was as far as it seemed he wanted to go.

Instinctively she knew that he was not homosexual. And there was something about his hands; big, strong hands. He had a broad, almost Slavic face, a wide mouth and beautiful teeth which she saw only rarely. When Ralf smiled or laughed he was transformed, but he did not laugh often. It was nearly a month now since they had met and she was beginning to feel relaxed with him. He had shown her much of Vienna, had even procured magnificent and almost unobtainable tickets for the Opera Ball in three days' time. He was very different from Andrew, but Andrew had made her choose, Andrew had pushed her away, not trying really to understand. She sighed inwardly as Ralf took her arm.

'Come, we will leave the grim details of the Josefinum for the sparkling jewels of the lost empire.'

'The Hofburg?'

'The Schatzkammer, or Imperial Treasury, of the Hofburg.' He stopped and turned towards her. 'You have no wrap around your neck and it is below freezing today.' He removed the black cashmere scarf from his own neck and began winding it securely about the exposed skin of her neck. Laura glanced up at his face as his hands played near her throat. It was unnerving somehow to have him so close to her, facing her, his mouth only an inch away. She could see each dark eyelash, the fine lines which ran either side of his nose, feel his breath on her face. He lifted his eyes from the black cashmere scarf and looked back at her and for a split second their gazes locked. Laura caught a tight, inaudible breath, felt the blood pound through her veins. But he smiled suddenly and the gaze was gone and there was his voice stinging her into life.

'I think we should hurry, the Treasury closes in an hour.'

'Yes . . . of course.' She allowed him to take her arm again, felt the sure warmth of his arm moving down her back as he guided her down the marble steps. A lacerating wind tore at her hair as they came out of the building. And she thought of Andrew and London and was surprised and a little sad at the twist in her thoughts. She wondered where he was, what he was doing. And who he was with. But Ralf claimed her as they came to his car, his arm reaching possessively around her waist as he leaned past to open the door. His lips grazed her cheek and she was caught by the musky man-smell of him, by the power in his grip before the heat from the car wafted dizzyingly around her and Andrew was gone.

Sophia hugged her school books against her chest as she walked along the narrow cobbled street. The winter air froze her cheeks and her breath came in white bursts of fog. She had planned to have a *heisse schokolade* at a local café with some friends, but had declined at the last moment because she was not in the mood for café talk, for her girlfriends' chatter of boyfriends and new clothes. Her parents had argued the previous night, which was almost unparalleled; her mother had actually spoken back to her father. Sophia sighed heavily; it had been because of her and her desire to go to art school. And there had been something else, something to do with Oskar von der Heyden, but the door to the drawing room had ominously closed then as if they had known that she stood in the doorway of her bedroom, fist clenched against her mouth, heart racing; listening, listening.

She bowed her head a little as she turned into the unprotected expanse of the Parkring and waited at the kerb for a tram to pass and the lights to turn green. The wind tore at her hair and impatiently she pushed it back over her shoulder. The gesture made her look up and her eyes travelled absently over the passing cars. A blue Mercedes. Her father's. Automatically she lifted her hand up as if to wave, but he had not seen her. A soft frown wove itself across her forehead as she took note of the woman sitting next to him, a blonde woman she did not know, quite young.

The lights turned to red, but Sophia did not cross the Parkring, instead she stood at the edge of the pavement and watched her father's car as it turned right and then left, passed the Marriot Hotel and then slowed to a halt as her father parked. But in a moment he was getting out of the sleek blue car and walking quickly to the passenger's side. He opened the door and helped the woman get out and then glanced up and down the busy street, but he did not see his daughter standing watching him from the kerb of the Parkring.

Something inside Sophia rose in protest as his hand glided smoothly across the lush fur of the woman's coat and with reluctance her feet began to move, but not away from her father to catch the U-Bahn and the train safely home, but in his footsteps – right, into the Weihburggasse and across the street to the SAS Palais Hotel. For a long, long moment she hesitated, willing him to turn around and see her, willing him to say goodbye to this woman who was younger, much younger than she had thought.

The uniform-clad doormen tipped their caps at him as he guided the blonde woman through the gleaming glass doors of the hotel, her high heels taking quick, ridiculous steps on the deep red carpet, her face turning to Felix's, and smiling with rich, red lipstick; a pouty, intimate smile which was rewarded by his beautifully tailored arm coming up to drape itself across her plump shoulders and press her against him.

Sophia felt a little sick, felt dread and disbelief pulse through her like vague, gnawing pain. She moved across the street and walked past the curious doormen and into the hotel foyer. Her father had gone. She swallowed slowly and took a seat in a corner. A pretty waitress with fragile oriental looks took her order for coffee and placed it on the marble-topped table with a sympathetic smile. Sophia wondered if she knew, wondered if everyone in the world knew, except her. She took a sip of the strong, hot coffee and then pushed the steaming cup away. She did not want the coffee, did not want to sit here in this lovely room, full of strangers, waiting for her father.

It was not quite one and a half hours. Sophia looked at her watch. Not quite one and a half hours. They emerged from the lift laughing – the girl and her father; and there was one last quick embrace as the girl's hand slid slyly inside her father's jacket and Sophia closed her eyes. For a split second her thoughts swept backwards to the security and ease of the past, to countless times when she had observed her father at home, at his desk, with her mother. Tall, handsome, good? Father. Her eyes flicked open again and she lived the painful scenario once more as Felix moved to the hotel reception area, no doubt to pay his bill. In a brief moment of abstraction she wondered if he would pay for the room as if he had spent the night there, or otherwise would they charge him by the hour?

Even as the ludicrous thought passed through her head he was turning around, surveying the room; and he saw her. There was a rushing in her ears as their eyes met and she could hear her heart pounding as if she had just run a wild, mad race. His face seemed to drain of blood, but then the blue eyes were narrowing and she saw anger in the handsome face and suddenly she felt afraid. But he said nothing, did nothing. Felix acted as if his daughter was not sitting across the room from him, her eyes staring back round and swollen, desolation written clearly on her face. He turned back to the desk, paid his bill and escorted the girl in the fur coat out of the hotel lobby and into the icy street.

For a few minutes she waited, hands clenched in her lap, eyes lowered, gazing at the polished floor. There was an ache in her dry throat, a terrible sadness gathering inside as she let him walk away like a stranger. Now she wished with all her heart that she had never seen him today, that she had let him drive away from her and she had simply gone home, on the U-Bahn, like every other day. She longed for the safety of little things suddenly, longed for her mother. Genevieve's pretty waif-like face soared searingly into her head and she wanted to cry out because this was something she could never talk about with her mother; it was as if a crack had suddenly appeared in her life which would get bigger and irrevocably spread, shattering every illusion she had ever cherished, corroding all the things she had ever held dear.

Sophia stood up and opened her purse, watched her hand tremble as her fingers mechanically lifted out the number of schillings for her coffee. It had begun last night, she thought with numb bewilderment, everything had really begun last night – her parents' quarrel, her father's anger at her mother's insistence and then Genevieve's pleading voice until the door had ominously closed. Sophia swallowed slowly; she had awoken this morning with an anxious feeling trapped deep in her chest which had stayed with her, weighing her down, and then she had seen her father.

She willed her feet to move and found herself walking through the bright, plant-filled lobby, through the sleek glass doors and out into the Weihburggasse. Her eyes moved furtively up and down the long, narrow street. Of course, he had gone, of course he would not be sitting waiting for her in his blue Mercedes, the blonde girl by his side. Misery gripped her as the raw, wounding picture of a small white hand sliding skilfully inside her father's jacket poured rapier-sharp into her mind. Her eyes began to brim as her feet took her back to the Parkring and the first lap of her journey home. Sophia sighed wearily, biting back the tears. But it was not home, somehow, any more. In the space of a few short hours everything had changed and for all time. She lifted her head up and let the wind burn her face, her scarf snapping backwards, waving behind her like an unhappy flag. The sky was grey and heavy and low, and she thought she saw more fine specks of snow begin to fall. Sophia moved across the wide tree-lined road towards the train station and home. Home was where her father was and she drew a quick, despairing breath at the weight of grief held in her heart. As if he had died.

Elizabeth supposed that Do & Co would be known as chic to Vienna's beautiful people, and as she stood hesitantly in the doorway she caught a glimpse of Nicki Lauda giving an audience to a few admirers at a table in the centre of the room, but her eyes slid easily away and travelled across the scores of heads to a far corner where Karl was sitting, watching her. As she stared back at him her mind seemed to freeze up and time slowed, but she forced her legs to move, forced herself to weave her way through the tables and the people and the strange, faraway buzz of conversation which fell away the closer she came to him.

'You look wonderful.'

His voice – rich, American voice, full of old promises.

'Thank you.'

He had stood up to draw back her chair and as he moved past her she caught a sharp, inaudible breath because she could not believe the effect his closeness still had on her, could not believe that the years which had come and gone had changed nothing. Nothing.

'I'm glad you could make it.'

Her eyes lifted to his face. 'You were very persistent.'

'I know . . . I'm sorry.' He smiled. 'I couldn't help myself.'

Blood began to seep slowly, inexorably up her neck, into her face.

'I wanted to see you . . . with no strings . . . just us . . . just to talk.'

'You could talk to me on the telephone.'

There was a subtle change in his eyes. 'I said I wanted to *see* you.'

'I'm married, Karl.'

His dark eyebrows came together in a frown. 'I owe you an explanation.'

'You owe me nothing, Karl.' Oh, God, but he did. 'As I told you at the reception – it was a long time ago and our lives have changed.'

'I had commitments, there were things I had to sort out,' he continued as if she had not spoken.

'Don't, Karl.' She looked away from him.

'Listen to me . . .' His hand reached across the table and grasped her shaking fingers, but she pulled immediately away as if she had been stung. His eyes darted to her face and he saw in an instant the conflict and the old longing in Elizabeth's lovely face.

'There is no point in this conversation.' She tried to rise, but his hands pulled her back down to her seat. 'Please . . .' The pleading was her undoing, and his, because their eyes met and locked and she allowed his hands to slip back along her arms so that they could take the fingers which still shook.

'Will you pour me a glass of wine?'

'Of course.' His hands slowly withdrew and Elizabeth swallowed with relief. Her nerve was almost gone. There was a dim, vague thought somewhere in her head that she should get up and walk away, that this would be her last chance, but she did not move, instead her hand reached out to take the glass of wine which Karl passed to her.

'Why are you doing this?' Her voice was controlled now, almost normal.

He looked back at her and was surprised once more at the need which rose up inside him and he could not give her a true answer because he did not know himself.

'I want you.' Perhaps it was that simple.

She felt giddy for a moment and her heart seemed to jump in quick and sudden panic.

'I have a husband, Karl.' She winced a little at her choice of words, as if she was talking about a car, a house, an appendage. 'And I love him.' Even as she added the trite phrase Elizabeth wondered at herself, at the same question which kept rising inexorably into her thoughts that if she loved John, how could she think of Karl, see him like this, *be* here?

'Then why have you come?'

Because she wanted to, it was as simple as that, and for a brief second she hated him.

'Your face says everything, Elizabeth,' he said gently. 'It always did.'

'You could leave me alone – you could find someone else.'

'I can't.' He shook his head. 'And I don't know what you mean by "someone else".'

'This is madness.'

'Perhaps.'

She looked away from him, her gaze seeking the safety of everyday things.

'You *must* leave me alone, Karl.'

'I told you – I can't.'

He shifted his gaze from her anxious face to the soft hand which wove itself carefully around the stem of her glass, as if she would anchor herself there.

'And you will see me again, Elizabeth, because like me, you won't be able to help yourself.'

She made no answer.

'So sure of yourself . . .' she said, finally. 'You always were.'

'It's the way I am. Sometimes I have wondered whether it's a virtue or a vice.'

'You walked away.'

'I had little choice.'

She smiled.

'I thought about you.'

'But not enough.'

He sighed and then studied her sharply until her eyes wavered beneath his gaze.

'You will let me see you.'

'No, Karl.'

'You will.'

'Don't . . .'

'Elizabeth . . . Elizabeth,' he said softly.

She shook her head, but her eyes were inevitably drawn back to his face as memory took her, as all her good resolutions began to wither and die because, like he had said, she would not be able to help herself.

Kristina stared reluctantly at the two remaining salads on display, they looked a little wilted and sad, but she picked up the nearest turkey and ham with a sigh and walked back to her table in the dining room allocated to the Environmental Talks at the Hofburg. For a moment she looked at the salad and wondered why she suffered the deprivations of her diet for no good reason. 'Still hoping to catch a big fish,' her mother had said cruelly when she had noticed the piece of dry toast looking unhappily back at her daughter at breakfast. Kristina sighed again, even a small fish would be something, but a nice unmarried fish, please, she prayed silently.

'Hi.'

Startled, she looked up and found herself staring into the face of the American, Sam, she had met at Monika's dinner party.

'Hello,' she replied a little stiffly.

'May I join you?'

'Please do – the seat is not taken as far as I am aware.'

He was married, Monika had said so. She pressed down her disappointment because she had actually liked him and that really was a change, she thought with sudden amazement. How many men had she really liked? What a sad fool she was.

'The talks are really under way now,' Sam said conversationally as he sat down. 'And by the looks of things you girls are being kept pretty busy.'

'With a hundred and twenty-four countries present, interpreters are naturally a very useful commodity.'

His smile was a little forced as he looked back at her, confused by the edge of hostility in her voice.

'Do you have a favourite language which you prefer to speak?' he asked amiably.

'I like French, but also English.'

'I could tell,' he said quickly. 'At the dinner.'

Her eyes examined him sharply. 'Really – how?'

'You seemed so relaxed, so fluid.' He offered her a bread roll. 'I was impressed.'

Kristina sighed inwardly. She had heard all these lines before. With a quick shake of her head she refused the bread roll. Someone close by dropped their cutlery loudly on a table surface and the sound jagged on her nerves.

'I thought I might pay a visit to the English Theatre here.'

'Oh, really.'

Sam frowned at her studied coolness. Goddamnit. He was only trying to be pleasant. At the dinner she had been like a different person – warm, humorous. Nice. So nice he had wanted to ask her out, but now he was not so sure.

'I understand it's pretty good,' he said with an effort.

'I believe so.'

Silence fell between them. Sam looked self-consciously about the busy room, wishing he was anywhere else but here with this difficult woman.

'Have you ever been to the States?' he said at last.

'No.'

'You should try it some time.'

Kristina ceased studying her salad and looked up. Didn't he understand yet?

'Why?' she asked coldly, but the coldness was becoming too much of an effort, it did not suit her, she was just not made to be cold.

Sam looked back at her, startled by the shadow of contempt in her face, but he persevered, unable now to turn back.

'It's got just about everything – amazing people, amazing places, the best hamburgers in the world. The Empire State building.' Christ, he sounded inane and he felt the telltale tingling of a flush seep into his face.

She could see his embarrassment and suddenly felt ashamed. After all, he hadn't actually asked to see her again, but her instincts told her that was what he intended. She sighed softly and smiled despite herself.

'Maybe one day . . .' she said.

'I was born in Boston.'

'As in the Boston Tea Party?'

'Right.' Relief was beginning to filter through him. Maybe she was just having a bad day and he had come along at the wrong time. Inevitably he thought of Natalie and her moods; bloody, vengeful moods. Christ, she used to make my life hell, he thought in wonderment.

'I knew someone who went to the Harvard Business School – that's Boston, isn't it?' she offered. His name was Frank, Frank Spick. His name had always made her want to laugh. There was something comic about a name like Spick. Frank had had a big square head set on too narrow shoulders. With sudden clarity she recalled the one and only time they had made love. Frank had had a penis the size of a man's thumb and because he was so self-conscious their lovemaking had become a mockery, but he had tried so hard and she had lain there writhing in pretended ecstasy until he had finally climaxed. But he had known, she was sure of that. Poor Frank. He had never asked her out again, but she had liked him all the same and she knew it would never have occurred to him to think that the size of his penis had not mattered to her in the least.

Sam's voice broke into her thoughts. 'I did Law there.'

73

'And then Washington?'

'Right.'

'You enjoy your work?'

'Have up to now – these talks are really interesting.'

'Some of the delegates do not seem to take them terribly seriously.'

'They're the stupid ones.' He sighed heavily. 'Somehow pollution and a hole in the ozone layer don't sound as exciting as Star Wars and long range missiles, but in their way they're just as deadly.'

'Do you really think this convention might actually achieve something?' Kristina realized that she was interested, and the knowledge warmed her somehow. It had been a long time.

'It will have to,' Sam said seriously. 'I went back to school to learn about what's happening.' He shot a glance at her. 'It's frightening, Kristina.'

She nodded, liking the way he had used her name. 'But it's not too late?'

'No, it's not too late – yet,' he replied softly. 'And in a way this is the greatest challenge man has had to face, and what's so good about it is the fact that we can do it *together* – globally – if we really want.'

'You're an idealist.'

'I was once . . . I thought I'd lost it somewhere.'

'I don't think so.'

He smiled.

She swallowed. 'I've got to get back.'

Sam blinked as she abruptly stood up. 'I thought . . .' he stammered. 'The English Theatre . . .'

Her eyes travelled over his face. 'I'm very busy.'

'Perhaps one night next week.'

'No, I don't think so.'

He blushed. 'Lunch then?' It was his last shot.

She looked at the freckles sprinkled delicately across his nose. Gentle face. 'I . . .'

'Monday?' he gushed.

A sense of helplessness spread through her. 'Yes.' She drew a breath. 'All right.'

'I'll meet you here – twelve thirty?'

She nodded and took a step away from him.

'Monday, then,' he said finally.

'Monday,' she repeated parrot fashion.

Kristina walked away, her feet clicking on the marble floor. There was something about him, something unmistakably nice, but then her thoughts swept back to Manolo and Fritz and Frank Spick and an apt American word slipped unkindly into her head: 'sucker, sucker, sucker.'

*

Her mother was out. Sophia lingered in the kitchen, not wanting to go up the stairs and past the drawing room where she could hear her father reading the newspaper.

'Make me a coffee.'

Mechanically she reached for the coffee pot and poured her brother a cup of the black, steaming liquid.

'You've been crying.'

'No, I haven't,' she replied too quickly.

'You have.'

She turned away from him and ran a glass full of water.

'Why?'

'Leave me alone, Gunther.'

'Come on, Sophia – tell me.'

They were different, she and her brother, he was cold where she was warm, he was arrogant where she was soft. She suddenly realized that he was like their father.

'Go away.'

He came across the room and put his hand on her face, squeezing the cheeks together, making her mouth pout, hurting.

'You are a very, very silly girl.' He sighed theatrically. 'You should know by now that you don't say things like that to your big, clever, handsome older brother.'

Tears began to course down her cheeks.

'Don't be such a baby.' He released her and went back to his coffee. He studied her for a moment. She was a pretty girl, even very pretty, but fragile like glass, and it was her fragility that irritated him. He was aware that his mother irritated him also, always. She was *so weak*, so incredibly subservient that sometimes it sickened him, and Sophia was the same. He knew he was like his father and was glad. Life was easier and treated you better when you knew exactly how to get what you wanted, knew exactly how to manipulate people. He thought his father a master.

'Sophia, would you come to my study for a few minutes?'

Gunther turned, startled, at the sound of his father's voice. His sister walked past him without a murmur and followed their father up the stairs. Gunther's eyes narrowed and he waited until their footsteps had lessened and died away before making his way softly to the door of the study.

'Why were you in the SAS Hotel this afternoon?'

Sophia could not look at her father, it was like being with someone she did not know, and then with a surge of sadness she realized that she had never known him.

'Answer me.'

'I was waiting for you.' Her voice quavered and she knew that she wanted to cry, but he would not like that, so she kept her head down, lowered, afraid.

Felix stared back at his daughter, hating the awkwardness and the fact that Fate had dealt him some cards that he did not know how to play.

'What did you see?' He had to ask, he had to find out just how much she knew.

She did not answer. Her eyes were fixed on her knotted fingers, on the fingernails, on the small mole on the back of her right hand.

'What did you see, Sophia?'

'You were with that girl.'

She looked up suddenly and he was a little shaken by the ashen face, the shocked eyes. He looked away to the window and the safety of the garden.

'She is a friend.' He qualified his futile words. 'An old friend.' He had known Eva for three weeks, he had simply seen her ample proportions walking seductively along the Ring and had stopped the car and asked her if she'd like coffee. Naturally she had said yes after taking in the Mercedes, his clothes, his face. They had been to several hotels since and it had been his mistake to come to the centre of the city, the first time, because he hadn't been able to wait any longer, and it was quick and convenient – fitting her in between meetings. He had bought her some fabulously sordid underwear which had lain too long in the boot of his car. His mistake.

'Yes, Father.'

She sat staring, not seeing, suffocated by the silence in the wood-panelled room and the hot, dry air.

'I did not want you to misunderstand the situation.'

She made no answer.

'You haven't, have you, Sophia?'

Sophia's blank gaze came back to settle on her hands. It would pass, this dreadful moment, and perhaps later it would slide away into the recesses of her memory with the little white hand slipping slyly inside her father's jacket.

'Have you?'

'No, Father.'

'Good.'

He looked back at her and felt curiously naked as her eyes lifted from the twisting fingers in her lap to his white face. For a fleeting moment he was touched by shame.

'I expect you have some school work to do . . .'

Sophia nodded and stood up. Felix did not move from his place by the window until the door had closed softly behind her and then he shut his eyes tightly, his mouth falling sullenly open whilst he swore and cursed at the empty room.

'You really are a silly little bitch.'

Sophia caught a startled breath and turned to find her brother leaning against the door-frame of her bedroom.

'I want to do some sketching, Gunther.'

'You mean you want to cry, don't you?'

'What do you want?' she asked wearily.

'You have broken a cardinal rule.'

Her eyes grew round as if she knew what he would say next.

'Let me explain.' He smiled patiently, but it was not a kind smile. 'You don't follow your father when he's busy with his mistress.'

She winced.

'Most men of any standing have a mistress, Sophia – didn't you know?'

She shook her head uselessly.

'It's a fact of life.'

He didn't move, but remained leaning against the door-frame staring at her.

'I want to sketch, Gunther.'

'It's not the end of the world, Sophia.'

She shook her head once more and her hand reached to the door handle as if she would close the open door.

'It's an accepted practice . . .' He sighed. 'Men have always done it.'

She said nothing.

'For God's sake,' he sneered. 'All Father's friends have mistresses – or, at least, see a different woman besides their wife from time to time. You'll marry one day and your husband will have a mistress.'

'No.' She was surprised at the sound of her own voice.

'You really are ridiculous.'

'I want to sketch, Gunther.'

'Father took me to the Gurtel on my eighteenth birthday . . .' His mouth had pulled into a leer because he was remembering the big, black prostitute his father had allowed him to choose for himself; she had been standing near a seedy night-club wearing very little except a short white leather jacket and thigh-length boots. It had cost 500 schillings, excluding the not-so-cheap champagne they had had to drink in the night-club.

'I don't want to hear you.'

Gunther laughed. 'You should grow up, Sophia.'
She looked into his face. 'Why don't you like me?'
'Don't be stupid.'
'I think you are the one who is stupid, Gunther.'
His eyes glittered. 'Mother knows.'
She swallowed. 'No.'
'Of course.' He shook his head slowly, comically. 'She just pretends it's not happening.'
'No.'
'It's true, Sophia. Why don't you ask her?'
Gunther walked away.

It was beautiful, their sitting room, Elizabeth thought, and walked slowly towards the large, high windows which overlooked a small cobbled courtyard. Sometimes it was so quiet that she could imagine they were living in the country somewhere, not in the middle of a European city. The walls of the sitting room were a very pale pink, with the cornicing and carvings picked out in white, and in the corner was the traditional Viennese ceramic stove – huge, friendly, strangely elegant. She sat down and looked up at the painting of John's dead mother, Jennifer, over the fireplace. She had liked Jennifer, they had grown close in the short time they had known one another, but then she had died, finally, of the multiple sclerosis which had dogged her health for so many years. Jennifer had been a liberal thinker, she had even had a brief fling when 'John's father was driving me insane'. Elizabeth smiled at the portrait, remembering Jennifer's words, she had been a little shocked at the time. 'I had to, Elizabeth,' she had protested, 'in the early years of our marriage he was intolerable, like living with a spoilt schoolboy who still needed mothering; I kept asking myself, what about me? I don't think Edward really gave a damn until it was almost too late.' Elizabeth sighed. But John wasn't like Edward, John was a good husband and she loved him. But he had come after Karl and she and Karl were somehow 'unfinished' and there was nothing she could do about it.

'You look tired.'
Her husband stood on the threshold of the large, lovely room, loosening his tie.
'So do you.'
'And we have the Opera Ball this evening.'
'I'm afraid we do, but at least we have until the opening ceremony at ten p.m.'
'I shall have to grin and bear it, then.'

He kissed her on the top of her head and she looked up into his face, crushed suddenly by guilt. She couldn't do it to him, not such a betrayal. Somehow here, now, in the security and comfort of this beautiful room, it did not seem possible.

The Opera Ball – ball of balls. Elizabeth leaned out of their box and gazed with fascination at the sea of people, at the perfectly dressed men in perfect white tie, at the dazzling gowns accompanied by equally dazzling jewellery, swaying in time to the 'Blue Danube', the best known of Strauss waltzes. Eighty young couples had made their entrance into the 'adult world' during the opening ceremony, eighty virginal white dresses, their owners with glittering tiaras in their hair, floating beside eighty young men in tails, their hands moist with sweat in white, white gloves as they paraded their partners before the mass of people who watched and waited as the champagne began to flow and the Opera House became a dome of pleasure for one long night. It was pure decadence, she thought with amusement, and with champagne at over £200.00 a bottle it had to be – all this amazing extravagance just to see, and be seen. Across the magnificence of the ballroom she could see a TV team hunting for the many VIPs present. They would not have to look far – Kurt Waldheim stood to their left and Princess Caroline of Monaco to their right.

'It takes my breath away – just a little,' John said, coming beside her.

'I know what you mean, like taking a step back in time to the Court Opera Balls of old Imperial Vienna.'

'I'm afraid it's wishful thinking on the part of the Viennese,' he said softly. 'Old world dreams forced to blend with new wealth and power. There must be as many counts and countesses, barons and baronesses here as there are chandeliers.'

'That's the Duke of Braganza, isn't it?'

'Yes – pretender to the throne of Portugal, so I understand.'

Elizabeth grinned.

'If you would like to put your champagne down, we can join all these Euroroyals and Eurohopefuls.' He smiled and offered her his arm in a mocking, affectionate way. 'By the way – you look wonderful.'

'Thank you.'

She had bought the Catherine Walker dress six months previously and it had been hanging tantalizingly in her wardrobe waiting to be worn; a champagne silk sheath scattered with sequins. She pressed the thought down that she had been wearing champagne silk when she had met Karl; it was an unnecessary memory, a pinprick to unsettle her again. Echoes.

*

The waltzes seemed to go on and on until John took her arm and they began to make their way back to their box. Through a gap in the crowd Elizabeth saw Madeleine, almost too dazzling in a gown of vibrant bronze lamé, dancing with the French ambassador. Her face was flushed, her mouth pulled into a wide, toothy smile which made Elizabeth want to laugh. She shook her head gently and followed John up the silky marble steps, stopping as she saw him smile and give a small wave at a couple coming towards them, a pretty dark-haired young woman and a Marlon Brando look-alike.

'Laura Drummond – my wife, Elizabeth,' John said and then added, 'Laura works at the embassy proper, but she helped us out in the delegation office at the beginning of the talks.'

'Hello.' Elizabeth smiled and then looked towards the man standing next to her.

Laura blinked. 'Oh, I'm sorry – this is Ralf Müller.'

Ralf took Elizabeth's hand and brought it to his mouth with exactness and then John was shaking his hand and Elizabeth could see how closely her husband was scrutinizing the man; his curiosity was obvious and she was slightly puzzled. As they moved away from the couple and back to their box he was shaking his head good-humouredly.

'I'm sure I've seen him somewhere before.'

'I must say Herr Müller is rather good-looking . . . has an almost Slavic look about him.' She laughed. 'Reminds me of Marlon Brando.'

'I wish I knew who he reminded *me* of,' John said vaguely.

'It will come to you.'

He turned his head and stopped abruptly. 'There's Laurence – would you mind if I had a few words, I'll see you back at the box . . .'

She nodded as he walked away and towards his ambassador, who was standing with another member of the delegation. She sighed softly, used to the indistinct line between business and pleasure which diplomacy was never able to draw. People bustled past her as she moved against them. The atmosphere was intoxicating and she hummed to herself as she neared their box, smiling at a ravishing young couple who looked as if they had just stepped out of some baroque fantasy. But it *was* a fantasy, this arena of vanity, and it seemed so easy to slip sideways into the myth of Vienna, so easy to be seduced by the enchantment of the dream.

'Elizabeth.'

Her heart jumped and for a brief second her eyes closed at the sound of his voice.

'Elizabeth.'

She turned slowly, not wanting to, but unable to do anything else.

He stood in front of her, his face almost solemn, taking her breath away; beautiful in the perfect black and white of his evening dress.

'I didn't know you would be here . . .' Stupid thing to say.

'I'm a stand-in, a last-minute stand-in.'

He took her arm. 'Will you join me in a glass of champagne?'

'I was on my way back . . .'

'A few minutes won't stop the world turning, will it?'

She said nothing.

There was no one in the box to which he escorted her. There was a bank of pink and white carnations hanging along the lip of a carving and she fixed her gaze on them, the blood shooting through her veins. She heard a burst of raucous laughter coming from somewhere close and her eyes grew large as she looked back at him, as if they would be caught, as if she had already done something of which she should be ashamed.

'It's all right,' he said softly and his hand came up to caress her cheek.

She closed her eyes. There was a wild feeling trapped in her chest. He kissed her gently and she shuddered, knowing that it was too late now, knowing that she would regret the moment for the rest of her life, but it did not matter, not then. His hands stole along the bareness of her shoulders and her head went back helplessly. Their lips met again and her mouth parted immediately, her fingers sliding upwards into his hair to pull him closer, to make him want her, make him feel the staggering need which had taken control of her limbs, her mind, her heart. The raucous laughter sounded again from somewhere faraway. There would be regrets, a thousand of them, but she would have this, just this.

Laura climbed into the warmth of Ralf's car. She was shivering.

'It must be ten years since I've been to a ball, I'd forgotten how exhausting they can be.'

'It doesn't show.' His eyes slid sideways, flicking over her, undressing her in his mind.

'It must be very late,' Laura said carefully, suddenly excited by the obvious appreciation she could see in his eyes.

'Only just after two.' He looked at the car key held in his gloved fingers. 'Shall I take you home, or would you like coffee?'

For a moment she pretended to hesitate, but then nodded and was rewarded by a broad grin.

'I like it when you smile . . .' she offered a little shyly. 'You should do it more often.'

'But then I wouldn't seem so mysterious, would I?' he said and turned back to the windscreen and started the car.

And he *was* mysterious somehow, computer expert or not. She shifted her gaze to the window as the car began to move out of the cold grey tomb of the underground car park. The streets were clear of snow, but there was an icy stillness and the sky seemed black and brittle as if it could break. She snuggled down into her velvet cape and glanced at Ralf's powerful profile, then her eyes slid to his glove-clad hands resting lightly on the steering wheel. She swallowed, suddenly unsure of him again. Every time she felt secure, the sense of security would just as quickly dissolve into mist and she would be looking at a stranger. It was unnerving, as if there was something invisible which lay just out of reach; hiding. He darted a glance at her as if he had felt her eyes and smiled again and one hand came over to hers, lifted it and brought it quickly to his lips.

In weak moments she had found herself inevitably comparing him with Andrew, but there was no comparison because the differences were too great. Her thoughts came back to the letter she had received from him yesterday, a letter not saying very much, a noncommittal letter, no mention of his lack of phone calls or the fact that when she called he was hardly ever there. But what did she expect? She supposed it was really over between them and the thought made her sad, made her wonder at her decision to come to Vienna. Even her work had disappointed so far; the ambassador and his deputy were not good at distributing the workload and sometimes she actually found herself with little to do, or saddled with mundane protocol matters, and unless things changed radically once the Environmental talks were over, the day-to-day workload would become even less stimulating.

'The man who introduced himself this evening – John Thornton – what does he do exactly?'

She blinked as Ralf's voice broke into her thoughts. 'Deputy to the Talks.'

'They have a separate delegation office, I suppose?' he asked.

'That was the idea, but Laurence Dymoke, the ambassador to the conference, decided that the facilities in the new British Embassy were too good to resist, so now they're billeted with us.' She smiled wryly. 'Although I'm not sure if Sir Nigel Howard, my own ambassador, is too thrilled.'

'Two ambassadors under one roof . . .' he said. 'I hope they get along.'

'Well, they've both got rather large egos, so I think that most of the time they try to stay diplomatically apart.'

He laughed and she felt strangely relieved, wondering again at the capacity for the pendulum of her moods to swing. There was nothing *wrong* with Ralf, it was *her* and Vienna, and Andrew and her work which did not sit quite right and, at least, she had a career and now a man who made demands on her which was what she had wanted, wasn't it? The car was speeding past the Parliament building and Ralf's apartment was literally just around the corner. Her eyes caught the Goddess of Wisdom standing on top of the fountain, cloaked in frozen snow, and she wondered wistfully whether she had any of her own. They were slowing down and she glanced at Ralf's unmoving profile in the half light. She began unclenching her fists which had been hiding in the folds of her skirt. They were clammy with cold sweat.

She had been totally unprepared for his lovemaking, totally unprepared for the astonishing skill of his hands, his mouth, his tongue. Even before he had touched her, when he had slowly, ritually undressed himself, his eyes never leaving her face, she had known then that he had deliberately waited for this moment as if he had timed it perfectly down to the last waiting second. For a fleeting moment the breath had caught and held in her throat as she had looked back at him and seen for the first time his massive shoulders, the enormous breadth of his chest tapering down to a surprisingly narrow waist and widening again to tight buttocks and huge muscled thighs. He had tremendous physical strength, that was obvious; the biceps and chest muscles were beautiful, as if they had been carved, as if there was no blood or bone beneath, but only cold stone. She was reminded of Michelangelo's David, and a marbled Hercules she had seen once, somewhere. When he approached her she did not move and she knew somehow that that was what he wanted, that he would be in control. But then he was drowning her in his strength, obliterating any qualms, any indecision. She heard herself whimper as he came behind her, his hands sliding upwards, his breath hot on her neck, his stroking quickening, quickening. For a brief second she froze as he whispered close to her ear, using words that at any other time in any other place would have shocked and disgusted. He turned her slickly on her back, brought her legs over her head in one swift movement and took her roughly and so suddenly that she cried out. She looked into his face and the eyes that looked back at her were flat and expressionless, and she felt a tiny shrinking inside because she was afraid, but then his lips tipped slowly into a smile and he moved her again so that his open mouth could cover hers, let his hands glide softly down over her moist, hot back so that his fingers would find the secret place between her legs. She closed her eyes as the pleasure began to build, but then inexplicably he released her, changing his position, starting again, as if he would drive her mad. She became aware of his fingertips languidly massaging the base of her spine, his tongue trailing the curve of her breast, the thick shaft of his penis just touching the inside of her thigh. And all the time she was burning with desire, dazzled and made giddy by his careful hands. He lifted her abruptly and she gasped, catching his thrust as he brought her against him and she opened her mouth to scream as he moved finally, rhythmically inside her. There was ecstasy here, black ecstasy, and for long searing moments she fed upon it, but too quickly it was slipping away and she was left with a vague feeling of being out of control – that this was not love, or even affection, but a ritual, a practised, exquisite ritual which had very little to do with her.

John watched Elizabeth as she unclipped her hair and let it fall.
'What's the matter?'
'I'm fine – really.'
He remained standing, still looking at his wife, watching the thick honey-coloured hair.
'Why do you shut me out?'
She looked up, stung, a little shocked by his perception.
'I don't shut you out, John.'
But she did; Elizabeth always had.
'You do,' he said softly. 'Perhaps you don't realize it, but it's there all the same.'
She looked back at him from the mirror and swallowed deep in her throat.
'I'm just tired, that's all.'
'So am I.'
She continued combing her hair, taking shelter in the nightly ritual.
'Please, John, let's just get to bed . . .'
Wordlessly he pulled the bedclothes back and climbed into the coolness of the sheets. His head sank slowly into the heavy pillow, his eyes straying to the ceiling where a light still burned. It was inexplicable how the evening had changed, as if some god of misery had brought his great fist down halfway through a Strauss waltz so that nothing was quite the same again. He couldn't explain it, anyway, not the change in Elizabeth, her forced gaiety, the sudden brittle smile, that confused, sad look he had caught in her eye when she thought his gaze had been elsewhere. He drew a sharp, weary breath. But he *was* tired – they both were and tiredness had a way of playing tricks; tomorrow he would put tonight and the Opera Ball behind him. He turned over on his side and watched her as she moved across the room to the bathroom. He wondered why loving her should be such pain and yet such pleasure, wondered why he should love her too

much. Because he did, and sometimes the knowledge scared him, particularly when he imagined what his life would be like without her. But they had a good marriage, even very good; he shouldn't jump at shadows, shouldn't let the old fears come walking in because of a shaky evening. He was tired and the tiredness let his guard down, let the feeling of grey melancholy which was hovering just out of sight seep in around the edges.

4

It was a surprisingly enjoyable cocktail party. Elizabeth took a sip of the gin and tonic in her hand and let her eyes drift across the room to the host and hostess, an Australian–Irish couple, Greta and Dan Mulhall. Greta, a vivacious redhead, was representing Australia at the Talks, her husband Dan was a poet-writer. His last poem, 'Irish Darkness', had won critical acclaim both in his home country and abroad. Diplomacy worked for them, Elizabeth realized; Greta loved her work and Dan found it relatively easy to adjust to a new environment; his writing certainly didn't seem to suffer from the trauma of moving from one country to another at regular intervals. There were many diplomatic couples who paid a toll sooner or later for the constant pressures, and divorce was consequently high, and sometimes children rebelled or had schooling or personality problems. It was difficult for some little ones to adjust, and the adjusting often got harder as they grew older. Elizabeth thought of Christopher. John had suggested that boarding school in England might be an answer at some stage, but she had refused such an idea absolutely; Christopher would stay with them as long as possible. She frowned a little, convinced that parental love should be able to surmount almost anything. Despair touched her for a moment because she was risking all of that now, for all her fine words. She was a fraud, a hypocrite, not likeable for the insistent, helpless thoughts she had of Karl, not likeable for the love that she would share with him. In his bed. She assumed it would happen in *his* bed, in *his* apartment. Not a hotel. Please, Karl.

'Elizabeth . . .'

Her eyes were drawn quickly, nervously to Madeleine's face.

'I'm sorry, I seem to have startled you.'

The Frenchwoman's face was openly amused.

'Just a little, Madeleine, I was miles away.'

'That was more than obvious, Elizabeth.' Her mouth turned upwards into a dry, knowing smile. 'But I won't ask what you were thinking.'

'Nothing of interest, I can assure you.'

Madeleine looked back at her carefully and made no answer. Elizabeth felt herself blush.

'How was Hungary – and Prague?' she asked, in an effort at breaking the quick, awkward silence.

'Beautiful,' Madeleine replied. 'Everything – the hills, the villages, the wonderful buildings – clothed in snow. Budapest is glorious, the old royal palace, the history, the people . . . I adore it. Quite extraordinary.' She took a deep breath so that the nostrils of her long, thin nose came together. 'Let us hope *glasnost* continues and is not a hiccup in the darkness. I think I would weep if the great Russian bear brought its miserable foot down again on Budapest.'

'And Prague?'

'Still miserable.' Madeleine shook her head. 'Any change will take longer there, I fear . . . but Prague Square – beautiful, beautiful.' She turned the full force of her gaze on Elizabeth. 'You should have come . . .'

'How is Olaf?' Elizabeth asked, changing the subject.

'Boring me to death with his constant references to ozone, pollution, rain forests, etcetera, etcetera.' She drew a weary breath. 'You would think we were all living in an open sewer.'

'Perhaps we are.'

'Oh, not you as well, Elizabeth.'

'It's difficult not to be affected by what's happening.'

'What *is* happening?' She took a large sip of Perrier water. 'Mass hysteria.'

'I think you know better than that.' Elizabeth gave a sardonic smile. 'Or perhaps it has something to do with the fact that the green movement is weaker in France than almost any country in Europe . . .?'

'That has nothing to do with it.' She responded too sharply. 'The fool has even asked me to get rid of my fur coat, my mink – now how is that supposed to help the ozone layer, for God's sake?'

Elizabeth laughed. 'For one thing, I think it's called good public relations – after all, the Second Commission is on the wildlife issue.'

Madeleine sighed dramatically. 'It's all *so tedious*.' Her eyebrows came together in a frown. 'In any event, I have never cared for public opinion – so mediocre. All those "green" people in their plimsolls and crumpled dungarees.' She sighed again. 'Life used to be such fun, now one can't even breathe without having to think about it.' She took another sip of water. 'How is John, by the way? I thought he was looking just a little pale.'

'Really? But he's fine, Madeleine.'

'And you?'

'Well,' Elizabeth replied, a little puzzled. 'As you see.'

'I saw you in Do & Co,' Madeleine said. 'Last Wednesday, wasn't it? I was only passing and had hoped to get my usual table, but naturally I didn't dream of joining you – you both looked so, how shall I say, *cosy* . . .' Her tone was intimate and unpleasant. 'After all, Vienna's such a small world.'

Elizabeth looked back at her, hating the blood which was creeping into her face. Of course Madeleine had been leading up to this all the time.

'Yes, I think it was Wednesday,' she answered, deliberately vaguely, amazed at the calmness in her voice.

'Nice man. The American, I think?'

'That's right.'

'Karl, isn't it?' she probed.

'Karl Nielsen,' Elizabeth finished for her. There was no point in prevaricating.

'You seem to know each other very well.' Madeleine was almost smirking.

'Karl had a lengthy relationship with a good friend of mine.' It came easy, the lie, she thought with a touch of shame.

'Really?' Madeleine responded. 'When was that?'

Elizabeth swallowed hard. 'Why are you so interested, Madeleine?'

'Oh, you know me, curiosity is one of my attributes.'

'Some people might call it something else.'

'That's not a nice thing to say, Elizabeth, you disappoint me.' But Madeleine still smirked. 'So touchy – one might think you had something to hide.'

'Not the slightest little thing.'

The older woman's eyes examined her sharply for a moment and then her face relaxed and Elizabeth's sigh was almost audible.

'I think I shall fly to Milan next week,' Madeleine said abruptly, her gaze shifting covetously to Elizabeth's dress. 'I need some new clothes, something to brighten up these dull, diplomatic days.'

Elizabeth forced a smile. Go for God's sake, Madeleine, just go.

John swore inwardly. Morton was being pompous in the extreme and also self-righteous.

'We must turn good intentions into deeds – there has been enough talk.'

But John *did* agree with him, despite the pomposity and innuendoes; both knew the United Kingdom with its massive industry and population had far larger pollution control problems to deal with than its Scandinavian neighbours.

'Of course, that is why we're here, isn't it?'

'We have all agreed . . .' Morton's monotonous voice continued '. . . at least the developed nations, that we must take more stringent measures to limit output of CFCs, yet there is still considerable reluctance – cloaked by the word caution – by too many Western countries.'

John sighed. Morton was naturally including the UK in his little speech, but thank God, the Secretary of State for the Environment, with the Prime Minister's final blessing, had at last begun to put words into action and was no longer playing second fiddle to the Prince of Wales when it came to environmental issues.

'And if the developing countries are to be prevented from following the same path,' he added, 'it is only fair to compensate them – that is where the International Environmental Fund will play its role. As the Indian delegate mentioned at today's meeting, the developed states are responsible for ninety per cent of the present damage to the ozone layer.'

'It will cost some two hundred million to replace the present CFC plants in the Third World,' John interjected. 'How do we share the bill?'

Morton had the grace to blush.

'Norway will play its part,' he said defensively.

'There is also a further six billion needed to replace all use of CFC gases.'

'I know, John.'

'And remember that our Chinese "friends" are demanding the free transfer of technology and if that doesn't happen the use of CFCs in the West might end, but still be exported to the Third World.'

'Like DDT . . .'

John spun around and found himself looking into the face of Dan Gurney.

'Our old friend "the pesticide",' he said dryly.

'We were talking about our new friend, "the CFC".'

'CFC poisons the atmosphere – DDT poisons man direct.'

'I thought the use of DDT was prohibited.'

'Oh, sure, but the US, for instance, still manufactures over eighteen million kilos a year for export – and largely to the Third World.'

'Do you want me to quote you on that?' John responded with a grin.

'I don't think so . . .'

'You really do your homework, don't you, Dan?'

'Yup . . . the average Central American has eleven times as much DDT in his body as the average American citizen.'

John took a gulp of his gin and tonic.

'I think I'm getting a bit bug-eyed with all these statistics.'

'Aren't we all.'

They moved over to the window.

'Any news on that ivory murder?'

'You mean our Home Secretary's nephew?' John asked and then added, 'No, not at the moment, although I understand that no stone is being left unturned.'

'It's a vast, corrupt network, John, and from the inquiries I have made over the past few months it could even involve the cooperation of politicians and fellow diplomats.'

'That's not surprising considering that we can travel without customs and security checks.'

'Exactly.'

'You're really *very* involved, aren't you, Dan?'

'Is it so obvious?'

'I didn't realize you were becoming an expert.'

'I'm not – still just an amateur, but I have been asked to advise on the Wildlife Commission, so I think they can see that I'm keen,' he said in a mocking tone. 'Something I inherited from my wife.'

'Inherited?'

'She died two years ago.'

'I'm sorry.'

'I am too.'

Instinctively John's eyes scoured the room for Elizabeth.

'You have a lovely wife.'

John darted a wary glance at the American ambassador and then nodded slowly in response. 'Yes, I know.'

There was a note by the telephone. Sam read it quickly. Natalie, of course. He cringed inwardly and wondered why she was still able to destroy his peace with such ease. Any tentative happiness, any stealthy good humour evaporated instantly when she came back into his life and he began reaching for his antacid tablets. He let out a tired, exasperated breath and picked up the receiver. It would be about 3 p.m. in New York. Upstairs he could hear Clara putting Joanna to bed, could hear the soft, sweet tone of his daughter's voice as she asked yet another question.

'Why . . . why . . . why?' Sometimes he ran out of answers. Sometimes the fact that she had no mother to speak of pierced him because he couldn't pretend to give her it all. Natalie had been no mother and there was no pretending otherwise. Her baby was either booze or coke, whatever was easiest to reach.

'Who is it?'

The line was good, she could even be in the next room. He couldn't imagine that.

'Oh, Sam, hi!'

Like old friends.

'I got your message.'

'I didn't expect you to call back so soon.'

'Life is full of surprises.'

'Don't, Sam.' Her voice was soft then, almost gentle, almost convincing.

'What do you want, Natalie?'

'I just wanted to let you know my arrival date.'

For a split second he wished he smoked. 'You've already told me that, Natalie, or have you changed your mind?'

'By one day, Sam, just one day.'

'I don't want you here.'

'Don't be angry.'

'You know what I think.'

'It's only for three days.' Her voice was teetering on a whine. 'Give me a break.'

'Give *me* one and don't come.'

He could hear the sharp intake of her breath.

'How's JoJo?'

'Joanna's fine.'

'Can I speak to her?'

Pleading little girl's voice. In a small burst of fantasy he tried to picture her as a child, a little girl, but quickly failed.

'She's asleep.'

Almost.

'I need to see *you*, Sam.'

'I'm tired, Natalie.'

'Don't put the phone down, Sam, wait a minute.'

'I told you, I'm tired.'

'And I'm coming whether you like it or not – next Friday, the twentieth.'

'Thank you for the good news.'

'Try and be civilized about it, for JoJo's sake.'

He closed his eyes in disbelief.

'*Jesus-H-Christ!* When – just when – have YOU EVER done anything for JoJo's sake? Just tell me?'

'Okay, okay – calm down.'

They had said it all before, but suddenly there was rage and bitterness and humiliation joggling for release.

'Don't tell me to calm down – just get off the line and out of my goddamned life.'

'I'll see you next week, Sam.'

She put the phone down with a soft click and for a few long seconds he stood there holding the voiceless receiver mutely in his hand. Finally he walked slowly into his study and opened his drinks cabinet. He stared unseeingly at the array of bottles and then mechanically reached for a bottle of twelve-year-old Glenlivet. The drink soothed him a little, spreading calm through his veins so that the spectre of Natalie began to recede. It would only be three days. He cursed softly, gulping the drink down and pouring himself another. His eyes lifted to the ceiling of his study and the dozen or so model planes which hung at various angles and heights; they were sometimes a solace, his planes, a little escape for a while as he watched them or put together a new model. Generally they were World War II planes and he had quite a collection now from the early Spitfires, to Lancasters and even Messerschmidts. He smiled slowly because his study would never be big enough to hold them all. There was a house in New England, a beautiful big colonial mansion in white, built on an enormous cellar. He shook his head gently; he hadn't wanted to go back there in a long time.

He switched his thoughts to the lunch he had had with Kristina the previous day at Kervansary. There had been nothing remarkable about it really and yet he had found her charming, if a little distant, but he liked that; at least it was a good indication that she was not the pushy, calculating, husband-hunting kind. Like Natalie. Kristina hadn't even asked whether he was married. Sam took another mouthful of the malt whisky as doubt seeped inevitably into his head. Perhaps she wasn't interested. He pressed the thought down, but it came back stubborn and unkind; it would explain her initial coolness towards him. Yet she had agreed to see him again – for lunch. For lunch, because she had successfully avoided his offer of dinner.

He swallowed the last of the whisky and reluctantly placed the bottle back in its familiar place in his drinks cabinet. It wouldn't solve anything if he got drunk, and he had some notes to go through for a meeting first thing in the morning. He would think of Kristina later, or tomorrow, but even as he turned to his desk and the open briefcase he was aware of a vague feeling of bleak sadness which was beginning to spread through him in a wave. What did it matter anyway, he hardly knew her. Sam sighed heavily as he reached into the open mouth of his briefcase for his working papers. Sometimes he wondered whether he really knew himself at all and sometimes what he knew he didn't like too much. You're a weak schmuck, Sam, a push-over – 'a good ol' boy' as his almost ex-wife would have said.

Genevieve placed the receiver gently back in its cradle. Elizabeth Thornton had been so kind, so understanding about the portrait of her son which Sophia had agreed to sketch. It wouldn't happen now, of course, or ever. She moved over to the fire which burned so greedily in the grate, watched the flames rise and fall as sparks soared into the chimney. Even now she still did not understand how things had happened so fast, how her life had taken such a turn. Genevieve sat down in one of the wing chairs and leaned closer to the fire. For the first time in her married life she had been prepared to stand up to Felix, and it was also the first time she had ever admitted to herself that she had always avoided doing so. After the weekend at the castle she had found it hard even to speak to him, but she had, because of Sophia. A hideous row had followed on their return and she had wept, ultimately, in her weakness because he had beaten her down with his acid tongue, humiliating her and taking away her pride, but she had not given way, she had stood her ground – for Sophia.

Her thoughts turned inevitably to the painful scenario she had had with her daughter in the evening of the following day, and once again she examined the carefully composed face of Sophia as it formed in her head, examined the round eyes, the pale cheeks, the pretty mouth which quavered. And only she, her mother who knew her, saw that it quavered, that it was not Sophia's mouth at that moment, but someone else's who had shut her out so that her beloved daughter was now heartbreakingly locked away.

'Your father seems to think that you and Oskar . . .' she had said and felt a burning flood of blood surge into her face as her words faltered.

'Uncle Oskar?' Sophia had queried and had turned the full force of her now careful gaze on her mother.

'That you could be . . .' She swallowed. 'Of course, the idea is preposterous . . .'

'What idea?'

Genevieve pushed back her hair in a gesture of anguish. 'You should marry whom you wish,' she gushed.

Sophia's eyes opened wide in bewilderment, unable to comprehend immediately. 'Father suggested that I should marry Uncle Oskar?' she asked almost in a whisper.

'It was just an idea . . . I don't think he could have thought it through . . . we quarrelled.'

'I heard you,' Sophia said quietly.

'Oh, my dear.'

She had moved instantly to Sophia's side and taken her hand and in return her daughter smiled, but it was a strange smile, a smile that made her stomach churn, and then they seemed to sit there a long time as the silence became minutes and the minutes stretched and stretched.

'What does Uncle Oskar say about this?' Sophia asked at last.

'I don't know, I am not even sure your father has even mentioned it to him yet.'

Sophia looked down at her hands and the two thumbs which were nail-bitten, at the fingertips which were stained with charcoal.

'I have always liked Uncle Oskar.'

'I know, he has been very good to you,' Genevieve said. 'But he is no husband for you, even your father must come to realize that.'

Sophia made no answer.

'It will be all right,' Genevieve offered. 'I promise you.'

'And Father does not want me to study art – does he?'

Sophia's eyes gave her an odd, desolate look and Genevieve was touched by shame and guilt, as if she had betrayed her.

'No.'

'I think I knew, all along.'

'He does not realize how talented you are,' Genevieve said feebly.

'It doesn't matter.'

'But it *does* matter – very much,' she protested, and then Sophia stood up and walked over to the window.

'I think I would like to go away, Mama. After all I'm nearly eighteen, hardly a child any longer.'

'What do you mean – *go away*?' Her heart had begun to race then, and the breath to catch and hold in her throat.

'I have some savings . . . enough to see me through six months at an art school.'

'No.'

'*Yes*. Mama.'

'But why? Why must you go?'

'Because I want to, because it is the right time.'

'No. I don't want you to.'

She turned back from the window and the pretty mouth was tight, the lips pressed together almost white. 'Mama, it is for the best.'

'Because of this thoughtless idea of your father's?'

'No. Not just that.'

'What, then?'

And there was something in the look of Sophia's calm, set face which made Genevieve's insides draw together.

'Let me do this, Mama.'

Sophia seemed so adult then, so suddenly grown, and Genevieve stared at her for a long moment knowing that whatever she might say, her daughter would go anyway.

'What school did you have in mind?' she said quietly, and almost wanted to smile at the catch in Sophia's breath, the sigh of relief.

'I thought I might go to Munich.'

'Munich? But why?' she exclaimed. 'Why not Vienna?'

'I spoke to Uncle Oskar the weekend at the castle – he recommended one there.'

'No,' Genevieve said. 'It's too far.'

'I have already registered, Mama,' Sophia replied. 'And Uncle Oskar has said that I may stay in his house until I find some rooms.'

'On your own?!'

'Contrary to what Father might say, I do not believe Uncle Oskar has designs on me.' She smiled then, a small taut smile before adding, 'And it is a very large house.'

The sudden bitterness in Sophia's voice stung her, and across the room the girl's over-bright eyes slid away from hers and turned to the window and the garden beyond.

'Will you let me give you some money?' Genevieve said finally, her voice quiet, still filled with disbelief.

'I thought I might get a job . . . in the evenings.'

'Please, Sophia.'

'I want to do this on my own.'

'It is from *me*.' She swallowed hard, as if her throat were closing up. 'Sophia?'

'Oh, Mama . . .'

'What *is* it?'

'Nothing, nothing,' she said. 'I just want to go.'

And her room would be empty, the bed made up, the little things gone. A sense of bleak sadness had begun to spread through Genevieve.

'If that is what you wish.'

There had been little more to say after that and she had let Sophia go to her room and pack whilst she was left alone with the doubts and the fears and the strange air of unreality. She remembered a dog barking furiously amongst the background noises; the calm tick-ticking of the clock; Felix's face grinning at her from its silver frame, and then a strange picture of her brother Heinrich had formed in her head as she had seen him on that last day: teasing, running, his feet heavy and over-large in big, brutal sandals.

Andrew was coming. Laura sat in the Central Café and waited for Ralf. But Andrew was coming. He had telephoned her office today and Fate had decreed she should be absent, going through a cable with her ambassador, and she had had little chance since to call him back. When she had finally got through there had been the familiar, eternal ringing of his telephone as if he was playing games with her. Her lips pulled into a tight, pensive smile as she stared into the cream mountain which floated serenely on the skin of her coffee. Perhaps if she had known that he really had intended coming, that he was trying to meet her halfway, she would not have gone on seeing Ralf, would not have decided to sleep with him, and gone on sleeping with him. She shivered just a little as a vision of his powerful, naked body poured into her brain. She had given herself to him, literally, and in the giving she had made herself forget the words he had said and the way he had used her, made herself forget for a brief moment how she had been swept away by the terrible ecstasy he could give her with frightening ease. Andrew had never done that to her, Andrew had been an average lover, she supposed, but there had been no guilt afterwards, no disquieting echoes to disturb her everyday existence as Ralf's intimacy had done. She lifted her eyes to the doorway of the café as if she had sensed his presence and watched him beneath lowered lids as he walked across the crowded room towards her.

'You seem preoccupied.' He sat down. 'I thought you hadn't seen me.'

Laura gave him a searching look and wondered how she could have misjudged him so badly; perhaps because she had wanted to. Ralf knew all about women, he was a master, as if he had received an Honours in some kind of sexual degree. An expert, yet he was and would remain curiously aloof. In the deepest part of her heart she knew now that he did not and would not love her, that women were merely part of his landscape and that he would never pretend otherwise because that was the way he was. She wondered whether he even *liked* women at all. And she did not love him, but he fascinated her. But she had loved Andrew. She wondered which was the lesser of two evils.

'I'm sorry.'

He reached across the table and let his fingers caress her hand.

'I've missed you.'

But she didn't believe him.

'Have you?'

'You doubt me, don't you, Laura?'

'I didn't know that you could also read minds.'

'There are many things you don't know about me.'

'You play with me, don't you, Ralf?'

His eyes narrowed very slightly. 'Sometimes.' He smiled. 'But I thought you liked me playing with you.'

She swallowed slowly, felt her face grow hot with sudden, unexpected desire. 'I hardly know anything about you.'

'What do you want to know?'

She sighed, suddenly feeling foolish. 'It doesn't matter.'

'I want to be here, with you – isn't that enough?'

She pulled her hand away from beneath his and lifted her coffee cup to her mouth.

'I don't know.' She shook her head.

'Will you come back tonight?'

She felt herself stiffen and she lowered her eyes, but there was a rush inside, like white heat.

'I'm not sure . . .'

'Laura.' His voice was soft, coaxing, and he said her name again. 'Laura.'

The coffee cup was empty as she placed it back on the shining metal tray.

'You know I'll come back.'

He leaned back in his chair and she thought she saw a gleam of triumph in his eyes.

'Would you like to spend the weekend in Hungary?'

She pressed down her eagerness and looked back at him carefully. 'I've heard Budapest is very beautiful.'

'It is.' His mouth turned up at the edges. 'Will you come?'

'When?'

'Three weeks – the first weekend in March.'

'It might be difficult, it's generally frowned upon for British diplomats to go tourist in the Eastern Bloc.'

'Yes, of course, I understand that.' He smiled and opened his hands wide. 'But now? With all the barriers literally crumbling?'

'Even now.'

'But your uncle – isn't he ambassador to Budapest?'

She frowned, puzzled. 'How did you know? I don't think I've mentioned it.'

'No, but one of your colleagues did – at the Opera Ball . . .' he said deliberately vaguely.

'Well, I suppose that might help.'

'It's worth a try.'

'It will have to be cleared with my ambassador.'

'Of course.'

She felt her mood beginning to change as if his physical presence alone had finally banished all the doubts which crept up on her when he was not there, when she was on her own and her uneasy thoughts would seep out around the edges. She smiled back at him and he touched her hand once more. Laura watched him as he lifted the tips of her fingers to his lips and pressed them just a little too hard, just a little too long, and she felt the muscles in her legs go limp as his brown eyes met hers and the black core at their centre grew larger, wider as serenity changed to desire.

Gurney wanted the US to take the lead on environmental issues at the talks by pressing hard and fast. Karl inhaled sharply with exasperation and wondered once again why he in particular had been selected for Vienna; after all, he had no real experience or knowledge on the issues concerned, but then neither did most of the diplomats present. Impatiently he pushed away his notes on a debate Gurney had in mind: 'Tropical forests and their use on a sustainable basis'. He sighed and moved over to the glass wall of his balcony. It was freezing, black and miserable. What the hell was he doing here? He couldn't really give a damn about the rain forests, or the garbage which seemed to spurt from every mouth on the goddamn ozone layer. He'd be long dead before the world finally gave its last, choking, shit-filled breath.

But even as his harsh, grudging thoughts began to recede his mind was switching to Africa and its wild, brutal beauty and the fabulous time he had spent there. He had taken trip after trip, soaking up the panorama of the plains and the sudden, soaring peaks, the endless wilderness where life simply lived and died, never progressing, turning over on itself in the hard and unfeeling cycle which was only Africa. It was out of character, this love, this rash eagerness for something which he did not, really, understand. He picked up one of the tiny ivory figurines he had bought in Nairobi – a wild boar and its young; the others he had picked up in Paris and Hong Kong and they were less crude, more exotic, like the grinning fat buddha and a naked geisha curled up, hair carved loose in a torrent, running over thighs, buttocks, feet. He frowned softly, turning each one carefully over in his hand as if he had never seen them before. He sighed because he had hoped that tonight she could have stayed longer, but she had telephoned to say that she was not going to come at all, that it was 'impossible'. But then, slowly, surely he had persuaded her and she had agreed to come for an hour. An hour. He should have known. Karl looked out beyond the window and placed the piece of ivory held in his hand back on the table. He wanted very badly to make love to Elizabeth, but he did not want the first time to be rushed, not now. Perhaps she did not expect him to seduce her, here, in the small unlooked-for hour they would have together.

His mind somersaulted backwards to the week he had come to know her in London, a week he had let slide into a dusty corner of his memory.

She had been an interesting, immensely enjoyable diversion and he supposed that he must have loved her a little, but all the same he had gone and not looked back. Now, inexplicably, things had changed and she had become much more than just a challenge, because suddenly he really wanted her. Karl wasn't sure what his wanting would mean, but it disturbed him, like Africa disturbed him; he was no longer skimming happily above the surface of life, avoiding its complexities, he was involved, and the knowledge was somehow unnerving. There had been more than just simple pleasure in having her in his arms and feeling her undoubted response to his persistence, there had been a slow dawning, a slow, insistent hunger for more of her even as his mouth had raked her face and neck: there had been loss of control. And it had been *he* who had agonizingly reduced the heat between them and not taken her there, amongst the dying carnations and the aching shadows.

He shook his head very carefully and looked back to his neglected papers. Maybe he would make this his last posting. Diplomacy was getting him down, he wanted to run his own life, have his own goals, not be steered by some faceless Washington bureaucrat who hardly knew who he was, but at the moment it was highly unlikely that he could afford to give his career up. Not like John Thornton.

Karl's eyes drifted back to the ivory figurines. His dealings with Claude were coming to an end, they had to, all the markets were beginning to close up and the price of keeping the long line of corrupt officials happy had already begun to soar. And there had been a death, and a death that mattered, which would mean more trouble eventually. His jaw tensed as he thought of the young journalist who had died. For Chrissakes, he had even gone to Ifakara, a mean, stinking cesspit of a town where no sane white man would go alone; the poor bastard hadn't even had a gun. Karl closed his eyes. But it had had nothing to do with him. Nothing. He walked across the room to the cognac bottle which waited, and poured himself a long drink. Besides, the ass-holes were beginning to chase their own tails in their greed. His eyes drifted to the other side of the room and came to settle on the ivory figurines. After all, Africa would not be Africa without the elephant. He would have to think of something else.

'I'm sorry you had to cancel the table.'

'That's okay.' But it wasn't.

Kristina looked back at Sam and waited for him to suggest another time, another place. She had already prepared a careful little speech rejecting any such suggestion. But Sam remained mute, his face unhappily preoccupied, and suddenly she felt awkward and strange standing watching him in the middle of the corridor.

'Is there something wrong?'

He gave a small start. 'Oh, not really,' Sam lied.

'Perhaps we could talk over coffee?' she offered unwillingly. 'I have ten minutes.' It had been difficult to telephone him and break their lunch date and now his anxious face was calling her back.

'I'd like that.' And his eyes darted too eagerly to meet her own.

They walked in silence to the restaurant area and waited as a waitress, her lips painted too red, to served them. For a fleeting second Kristina saw herself in the woman and she winced inwardly, wishing she had gone to the Kärntner Strasse after all, and bought herself something to take her mind off life's little thorns and pinpricks. She had had enough of those lately.

'What is it?' She studied his face carefully.

'I'm just letting an old problem get me down.' He stirred his coffee and smiled with obvious effort.

'What sort of problem?' she asked. Was he ill?

'No, it's okay – you've probably got enough of your own.'

'That might be true, but if you just want to talk . . .'

He sighed. 'It's my wife.'

She caught a weary breath.

'Doesn't she understand you?' she said dryly. It still surprised her how many men still used that old, worn-out phrase to get a woman's sympathy and ultimately the hot novelty of sex with a different partner.

Sam laughed and the bitterness in his laugher startled her a little.

'I don't think the word "understand" has any meaning for Natalie.' He looked away from her eyes, his voice remote and too low. 'I thought she was the most beautiful thing I had ever seen, but it's different, you know . . .' His eyes slid back to her face '. . . living with someone day after day, seeing their face, hearing their voice – really learning about them. It didn't take me too long to learn about Natalie.' Sam looked into his coffee cup. 'She saw me coming a long, long way off.'

Kristina gave him a searching look. 'Why don't you divorce her?' she asked. 'If things are so bad.'

'I am.'

'You are?'

'That's why she's in New York and I'm here – we're separated.'

Her fingers straightened the angle of her coffee spoon unnecessarily.

'Is she being difficult?'

'She's planning to come over – and I don't want her to.'

'Can't you put her off?'

'You don't know Natalie, and in any case she says she wants to see Joanna.'

'Joanna?'

'My daughter.' She was *his* daughter, somehow, she was never Natalie's.

'You have custody?'

Sam nodded. 'Natalie wasn't a fit mother.' To put it mildly.

'Oh.' Kristina's gaze fell to his clenched hands and the whitening knuckles. 'I'm sorry, Sam.'

He snorted softly. 'What the hell – I suppose the worst is over. It's just that sometimes when she phones I get this tight, sick feeling in my stomach and then afterwards . . .' Afterwards he usually vomited. 'And then afterwards all the old scenes start playing over in my head again like a bad movie.'

'Are you still in love with her?'

'No, I'm not in love with her . . .' he said slowly, carefully, as if he were reciting a charm. 'That was over a long time ago.'

They sat in silence, feeling awkward and exposed.

'How long is she staying?'

'Three days.' His eyes lifted. 'At the Imperial . . .' He knew he was answering her unspoken question, it seemed important just then.

'And you will *have* to see her?'

'If I don't she'll just force her way into my life – and Joanna's.' He sighed heavily. 'I don't want any scenes.' She was good at those, especially when she had had a drink. Towards the end of their relationship he had wondered which depressed him more – her aggression or the shallow, sweet highs she conjured when she was on coke; the highs that sickened him, sending a clinging despair through his veins like a noxious gas. There had been many, but the worst, the big one, had been at a White House party. He had been able to see from the black, swollen pupils of her eyes that she had been snorting; they were almost completely black, her eyes, big jet buttons – flat and expressionless. He had arranged to meet her at the party and she had taken his breath away, and no doubt a few other guys', in a flaming red sheath of silk which left little to the imagination. He remembered wincing when she had been dancing with Buster, one of the White House aides, the silk sheath had ridden up, exposing the brown curves of her almost naked ass. Hot stuff, his wife. And when, finally, he had managed to drag her away, they had returned to their apartment and found Joanna lying in her own vomit. The very English nanny wasn't there any longer, she had walked out that same evening and he had been able to guess why because she had been threatening to leave them for several weeks. And Natalie had left Joanna alone. Ten months old. Old enough to lean through the bars of her crib and to the small piece of tinfoil laced with coke which Natalie had so recklessly left on the little white chest of drawers as she kissed her darling daughter goodbye.

'Perhaps it won't be as bad as you think.'

Sam shook his head and smiled humourlessly. 'It will be bad . . . you can bet on it.'

Kristina said nothing, but her eyes watched him, pity seeping into her heart. It would be difficult not to feel sorry for Sam and to perceive how bewildered he still was by the shattered pieces of his marriage and by a woman he had never really known at all. And she believed him because he was the sort of person who couldn't lie, or at least couldn't lie very well, which was almost the same thing. Sam was a rarity, a man who knew little of deceit and who found it hard to believe it when he found it in others. Natalie was a fool. Kristina sighed inwardly with relief. Thank God for fools.

'You mentioned the English Theatre last week . . .'

Sam looked up. 'I can get tickets if you like?'

'Friday would be a good day.'

'We could have dinner afterwards. . .?'

Kristina smiled. 'I'd like that.'

Genevieve began setting the table for dinner, but each time her hand reached to the huge casket of silver cutlery she would find her attention drawn to the window and her thoughts would switch inevitably to Sophia' her mind running over and over, faster and faster, until she thought she might go mad. They had spoken briefly that morning on the telephone, and her daughter's voice had been high and brittle, almost remote, but then slowly the voice had grown warmer, less tense, and by the end of their conversation she was nearly the 'old Sophia' again. Apparently she was happy in Munich, in the big house, with Oskar who was 'behaving like a perfect gentleman'. Oskar of the long sallow face and heavy-lidded eyes. But Sophia was so far away. A long time ago it seemed she had dreamed of her daughter going to a Viennese art school and of how sometimes she would meet her after a lecture, or for lunch, to talk of her day and her work and the exhibitions they would attend together, but Munich was too far for coffees and lunches and exhibitions with her lovely daughter. And there was something wrong, wasn't there? She had sensed it, *seen* it in Sophia's face, but when she had asked yet again, she had been given the same answer – 'everything is fine'.

A door slammed somewhere in the house and Genevieve's eyes slid automatically to her watch, it was six forty-five. Felix always arrived home exactly forty-five minutes before their guests were due to arrive. She heard his clipped steps as he moved through the house, as he made his way up the marble stairwell and into his study, no doubt to pour himself his customary dry sherry. Felix always drank a dry sherry when he arrived home. She swallowed, her feet seeming to move of their own accord as she walked out of the dining room and into the outer hall. She stopped for a moment as the elaborate gilt mirror on the wall opposite confronted her and she was forced to study her reflection – the white, thin face, small grey pouches gathering beneath her eyes, the angry beginnings of a cold-sore on her upper lip.

'What are you doing?'

Felix's voice made her jump and she turned towards him.

'I wanted to talk to you.'

'This is hardly the time, Genevieve,' he said, glancing at his watch. 'We are expecting guests in only forty minutes. I have to shower and change and I have had a particularly tiring day.'

'I wanted to talk about Sophia, Felix.'

'We've already discussed it.'

'There is something wrong, Felix, I know it.'

'There is *nothing* wrong, Genevieve.' He sighed dramatically. 'Sophia has made her own choice – and with very little prompting on my part. I cannot say that I am pleased with this art school nonsense, as you know, but at least she is with someone who will take care of her well.' Of course, he did hope for rather more than that, but all in good time.

'But I know there is something wrong.'

'How *can* you know?'

'Because I love her – I know her,' she replied lamely, 'and why would she behave so strangely, so out of character? Felix, *why* would she suddenly decide to leave and go to Munich of all places?'

'Perhaps you don't know her as well as you think,' he said unkindly. 'Perhaps she has more common sense than either of us realize. Anyway, from what you told me yesterday she was not very taken with my idea of marriage to Oskar, and I still do not see why you felt the need to tell her ... but never mind that now.' He shook his head impatiently as if she were a fool. 'But possibly, after some thought, she decided to find out for herself. I am just disappointed that she will not be spending more time with him whilst she is indulging herself in this idea of learning how to paint.'

Genevieve made no answer.

'I am planning to visit her,' she said at last, breaking the awkward silence.

'*NO!*'

His voice was too shrill and he could see that he had startled her.

'Forgive me – I did not mean to raise my voice.' Felix walked towards his wife. 'Please, Genevieve.' He took her hands, 'I simply think that we should leave them in peace, at least for a few weeks. Won't you be guided by me in this?' He kissed the tips of her fingers, saw her eyes widen in surprise and wondered if he had gone too far. 'I want what is best for Sophia, my dear, and despite what you might think, Oskar is the best . . .' She seemed confused for a moment and Felix felt relief begin to filter through him.

'She has no intention of marrying Oskar, Felix – she is in Munich for her own sake.'

'If that is what you wish to think, my dear.'

'I only wanted to spend a day, perhaps two . . .'

'Not yet,' he responded quickly, gently, and then switched to another tack. 'I never told you that Sophia once confided in me that she had always admired Oskar, that she thought him . . . distinguished . . . did I?' he lied.

Genevieve shook her head. 'But that doesn't mean that she was thinking of him as a marriage partner, Felix,' she stammered quickly. 'And she is so young, far too young to marry anyone.'

'Well, well, we shall see,' he said. 'And have you thought, Genevieve, that perhaps you have been trying to live your own thwarted dreams through your daughter?' He took her arm and guided her into the study and began pouring her a sherry. 'It happens.'

It could not be true, what he was suggesting. Genevieve clasped the small, delicate glass between her hands and stared at her husband; she felt more confused than ever. Felix was unwillingly reminded of a woman he had seen once who had climbed out of a car smash unscathed, leaving a dead husband and child behind her. He swallowed slowly and refilled his glass.

'This will all pass, Genevieve,' he said with a guilty rush, 'and in a few months you will know that all this worry on your part was unnecessary.'

Her eyes began to waver beneath his.

'Perhaps we could go to Munich for her birthday,' she said in a small voice.

His eyebrows came together in a frown; Sophia's birthday was in March, that much he knew, but the actual date eluded him.

'The twenty-eighth,' she said, as if she had just read his mind.

'Yes, of course.' Almost five weeks away, time enough for Sophia to settle down, time enough for her to forget the little incident at the SAS Hotel. Well, perhaps not *entirely* forget. Felix drew a sharp breath. He did want Sophia to marry Oskar, naturally, von der Heyden was a byword for wealth in Europe – like Krupp, de Rothschild or Thyssen – only a fool would pass up such an opportunity! But the swiftness of her leaving had almost taken his breath away, it had never occurred to him that his daughter might actually leave home because of what had happened.

He reddened a little as his mind swept backwards to Eva and that fateful afternoon, and Sophia. He had practically swooned when he spotted his daughter sitting in the corner of the hotel foyer, surprised that his heart had not stopped in protest. And Sophia, Sophia had shrunk before his eyes and continued shrinking as she looked back at him. It was a day to forget, and already the remnants of panic from his initial reaction were finally beginning to filter tidily away. Even Sophia had been safely removed. For a few days he had been terrified that she might have told Genevieve, but instead she had gone to Munich to stay with Oskar, ostensibly to study art. So swift and yet so neat, he really couldn't have thought of a better solution himself, but somehow the swiftness and the neatness made him uneasy, and ultimately he was touched by shame. His daughter's empty room reproached him and her voice, Sophia's little broken voice reproached him because he knew that she knew he was no longer the father she had thought – that handsome paragon, righteous, stainless father – and the knowledge did not please Felix, it made him surprisingly unhappy. He took a long sip of his sherry and endeavoured to push his feelings of discomfort away. After all, there was nothing he could do about any of it now, and life had to go on, had to be lived to the full. A smile began to tip the edges of his mouth as he looked back at his wife.

'We'll go to the castle at the weekend if the weather holds, ask along some friends . . .'

'Yes, Felix.'

He drained his glass. 'I expect you have things to do . . .' He patted his wife's shoulder. 'And I shall take a nap for ten minutes and then shower and change, do try and not disturb me.'

Felix walked out of the wood-panelled study and towards their bedroom off the frescoed gallery which pleased him so much. The French ambassador and his wife were coming this evening and also, rather bravely, he had decided to invite the severely polite Japanese delegate and his wife. Hadn't someone somewhere told him once that when the Japanese say 'yes' they really mean 'no'? Something to do with harmony, apparently . . .? Felix's face pulled into puzzled lines and then he mentally made a note to tell Genevieve to avoid the subject of whales. And the

Turks – he of the huge nose and she of the massive girth. He smirked, making a mental note on place settings; they had roped in a tedious cousin of Genevieve's called Herbert to partner the almost freakishly ugly, die-hard bohemian Claudia Capucci, who was standing in for the Italian ambassador. Herbert was unmarried and Felix had deliberately made Claudia sound mysterious, if not desirable. He was looking forward to seeing the expression on Herbert's face when they were introduced. It would brighten up what would probably be a long and rather dull evening. But the smile on his lips died slowly as his thoughts turned to Eva; he would not see her for a week, perhaps even two – it would be a way of salving his conscience.

Elizabeth smoothed down her dress and studied her reflection again. It was a plain, but beautiful dress, black cashmere with simple blazer buttons from neck to knee. She wore no jewellery except a large pair of hooped earings in beaten gold. She met her own gaze tentatively in the glass of the mirror and then her eyes slid furtively away to the perfume bottle on the satinwood dressing table. The musky scent was slightly warm as she finger-touched the white skin behind her ears, her wrists, the pulse points at the back of her knees and finally, opening the two topmost buttons of her dress, the swellings of her breasts. The note she had already written to John lay on the small table in the hallway, he would see it immediately as he came through the door. Elizabeth inhaled deeply as she picked up her coat which was lying across the bed; she was afraid, she had almost telephoned Karl again, but had pressed the urging down. She heard her son's voice as she opened the bedroom door; Christopher was with Grace, but she would be back in time to see him to bed and read him a story in case John was late, because that was John's job, reading to Christopher, he had made it his job from the very beginning. She swallowed the tightness in her throat. It was an hour, only an hour. She closed the door softly behind her and began walking down the polished wood floor towards the entrance to their apartment. As she turned the heavy brass door knob her gaze switched reluctantly to the note, her note, her lie, but she closed her eyes for a second to shut out the vision and walked out of the apartment, despite her fear and despite the nerves which rippled and swam through her body as if they might, finally, forbid her.

It was already dark and the shops were closing, but people still milled and paused along the Kärntner Strasse and down the narrow rib-like cobbled roads leading from Vienna's famous street. Elizabeth cut across the shoppers and moved into the pedestrian precinct of the Graben, past the numerous jewellers and dress shops, past the gilded Plague Pillar in the centre and into the outer realms of the Hofburg. Her heart was beating painfully, resounding in her head, as she turned into a deep archway of pillared stone and each breath came quick and hard, a thin white mist forcing itself from between her dry lips and out into the cold night air. She had wanted the walk, telling herself that it would cut away the minutes from the time she would spend with Karl. Like a penance. Instead she found herself walking faster, her feet almost flying across the old cobbled streets and out into the wide, flat boulevard of the Ringstrasse. A vicious wind tore at her face, her hair, and she laughed soundlessly, mocking herself when she thought of the trouble she had taken with her appearance, all the loving little details, all the skill, but in the end it wouldn't matter because neither she nor Karl was interested in the careful face she had painted in the mirror of her apartment half an hour ago; they were only interested in the faces from the past and a room in a hotel called Blake's five years ago. Nothing had changed and it had been made patently clear to them both by their meeting at the Opera Ball. There had been a kind of desperation in the way they had clung to one another in the conspiratorial darkness and she had ultimately been damned by the fierce longing which had leapt inside her, damned by the terrible wanting which had swept unchecked through her limbs.

Sophia watched Oskar as he slept before the fire; they had had a long day in the city because he had insisted on showing her all the things that were of interest, all the things that might be of use to her once she started college. He was, indeed, a good, kind man and shy, very shy, but not a man she could marry. She leaned back in her chair and closed the book which had lain open and unread in her lap; her father would be very disappointed. Sophia stiffened as his handsome face formed in her mind and then there was that girl, that whore, slipping her hand inside his jacket, and a vivid picture of the unhappy meeting which had followed later, and his lies, and the odious secret they would have shared if she had stayed. And he had laughed. She would not marry Oskar von der Heyden if he were the last man on earth, no matter how kind, how rich, and her father could go on wishing and wanting the match for ever. Inside where the hurt was growing and spreading like a stain she wondered how her feelings could have changed so suddenly, so fast, because now she did not care if she ever saw him again. Gunther had told her that 'most men of any standing have a mistress . . .' that it was 'an accepted practice . . .' and 'all father's friends have mistresses . . .' Did they? Was there really another world being lived in some sordid shadow-land of which she was supposed to have no knowledge? Were her mother and others like her merely playing a part? And did she know – did Mother *really* know? Sophia squeezed her eyes tight shut. If that was the case, then she would never marry . . . never, never, never.

She opened her eyes and sighed heavily, her gaze drawn to Oskar and his gentle snoring. Mother had told her once that he had never looked at another woman, not since his wife had died years and years ago. She smiled sadly at the lolling head as it tipped forward on to his chest, each hand clinging to an arm of the chair, even in sleep. Automatically she found her fingers reaching for her sketch-pad and the pack of charcoal which lay beside her own chair. On her arrival he had kissed her on both cheeks and then said, 'At last I have a daughter . . .'. She wished her father had been there and *heard*, she wished suddenly and fiercely and helplessly that he would *change*, that he would give that dreadful girl up, and the others, because she knew in her heart that there had been others, that there would always be others, and that her wishes were wasted. After her journey from Vienna and the greetings and the smiles she had given Uncle Oskar she had gone to her room and finally allowed her smile to fade and her cheek muscles to relax as loneliness swept over her and warm, slow tears began to pour down her cheeks. And even as she had wept she had known that it was a sort of exorcism, her weeping; she had cried for what once was, for Vienna and the house she had loved near Schönbrunn, for the father she had quietly idolized . . . Gunther's voice and his unkind words had poured back into her head and in her misery she had thought that, perhaps, after all, she was 'ridiculous' and 'a baby', that he had learned long before her the stuff of disillusionment, indifference and gods with feet of clay, except that something of her fading innocence rose up inside in protest. Sophia stared down, unseeing, at the piece of charcoal held in her hand. And Mother? A huge surge of pity and love made her want to weep again because she had left her alone.

'I had to,' she whispered. 'I had to.'

The street was almost in darkness when Elizabeth finally found herself standing outside the white luxury of Karl's apartment block. One street lamp burned a few metres away, turning the black road to silver and the frozen, greying snow to melted jewels. She swallowed as his voice answered her finger-touch on the doorbell and the silence which followed was broken by a brief high buzz as the lock on the lower door was released and she made her way inside to the icy cold of a marble walkway and the lift. Time seemed to slow as she moved higher and higher inside the building and inevitably she found herself looking at her face in the dark glass of the lift. She could see only an ebony silhouette, the features lost without light or shade, and she thought of all the times, countless times, she had longed for such an opportunity; but not like this. Her eyes flew open as the lift stopped abruptly and the doors slid soundlessly back and real warmth hit her. She sighed softly and moved left as he had directed, down a burgundy and white corridor to the door of his apartment. He was standing in the doorway and the sight of him made her stomach leap, made her limbs feel impossibly heavy as she walked towards the open door. She felt, quite suddenly, that she was crippled by the need for him and was certain in the knowledge that without the thought of seeing him again she would only be half alive, and the pain and remorse for John which she had kept fiercely at bay stole silently and irrevocably away.

'You're late . . . I thought you had changed your mind.'
She moved past him, not answering.
He followed her with his eyes and softly closed the door.
'Are you all right?' he asked gently.
She looked back at him, surprised at the gentleness, and then nodded.
'What would you like to drink?'
'A gin and tonic, please.' She slipped off her coat and let it fall across a chair. Her eyes inspected the wide, pale room in silence and painful curiosity because all this was his, this *was* Karl. Her hungry gaze swept across the deep, soft leather furniture, Chinese Canton vases, Baccarat glass, superb sketches by Dorian Ker, splashes of African wood and exquisite pieces of ivory lovingly placed about the room.
'You have beautiful and expensive taste, Karl.'
'What did you expect?' he said carefully. 'I haven't changed.'
'No, you haven't changed,' she said softly in response and turned towards the wall of glass which preceded the terrace. 'May I see the view?'
'It's freezing out there, Elizabeth.'
But she took no notice and he watched her unlock the sliding doors and step out on to the glittering balcony. For a few long moments his eyes lingered on the black outline of her body as she stood away from him, as she hugged herself with her arms, her hair lacerated and made wild by the bitter wind. He knew what she was thinking, his Elizabeth, she was uselessly weighing it all up in her head: all the duty, all the cost, all the desire, all the longing, all the passion and the conflict; except that there was no choice, no way to stop, not now.
'Come in . . .'
She did not move and he reached out to pull her into the warmth of the room. She let him lead her, let him take her into his arms as he shut out the freezing cold. And he thought that she could be like so much tissue

paper, the way she cringed as he drew close, as if he might crush her between his hands. He brought her head into his shoulder, felt her cold, cold skin against his cheek and began stroking the thick windswept hair and unpinning the final, stubborn strands until it fell loose and free around her face which he tilted slowly upwards so that he could take it in his hands. He kissed the closed eyes, the broad white brow, the cheekbones, his mouth following the line of her jaw to the hairline, and for a long moment he buried his face in the fragrance of her hair. And he whispered her name over and over as if he had never said it before, as if he had never caressed her before, and somewhere in the deepest part of his heart he wondered how he had come to let her go, how he had let her slip away so easily, out of his life. Five years. He looked back into her face.

'Don't . . .' The tears standing in her eyes made him ashamed. 'Don't . . .' His arms enclosed her tightly and there was a weight trapped in his chest, a heaviness which wrenched at his insides, aching. His mouth began to move quickly, greedily across her jaw, her neck as if it needed to taste that sweet, searing skin which burned, and as he kissed the soft pink mouth he felt dizzy, amazed, out of control. His fingers reached for the buttons of her dress and she did not protest as each one was undone, releasing her. He felt her hands in his hair, her nails clasp the brown, warm flesh at the back of his neck as he undressed her, heard a small sound, like a sob, break free from her mouth when finally he pulled her against him and they both were free. He thought her perfect, as he had never found any woman perfect, and with great deliberation he let his mouth and tongue steal lingeringly along her shoulders to the warm, velvet baby skin of her underarms, down down to her breasts, staying there, raking the tender-sweet nipples until she cried out, until she pulled him away and her hot, joyful mouth closed over his. He was conscious only of a desire to please, to make happy, to atone. There was for him then brief, searing rapture, a thinning of the darkness which had plagued him all the years of his life. Each moment was slowed, each finger-touch soft, softer, each kiss long, longer until there was no more control, no time left and she lay before him round-eyed, flushed, lovely and ready. He possessed her quickly, suddenly, thrusting deeply inside and her arms came up and over, clawing at his back, her body arching, her mouth open as she moved beneath him and he was aware only of the raw scent of their coupling as slow, excruciating delight began to burn and spread through his limbs, could hear only her voice rising higher and higher and his own words coming from somewhere far away '. . . Elizabeth, Elizabeth, Elizabeth . . .' The life force rushed from him to her, draining, emptying. And Karl knew that he loved, knew what he had never known and that it would never come again.

John was reading the paper before the open fire when he heard her key in the door and then the steady clicking of her heels as she walked along the corridor towards him.

'Sorry I'm late ...'

For a moment she stood framed in the doorway and he thought she had never looked more lovely, and for that reason alone little butterflies of apprehension began to flutter and spin deep down in the pit of his stomach.

'Clare kept me talking.' She looked away from him and moved close to the fire, rubbing her hands together, her voice too casual, almost nervous. 'Oliver's working late again, sometimes I wonder how she puts up with it.'

Her lie was like a blow and the little butterflies began to grow large and fearful now, twisting and turning, making his heart panic.

'I came home early,' he said at last.

She shot a glance at him.

'Oh.' She adjusted a framed photograph unnecessarily. 'And Christopher's asleep?'

'Yes.'

He watched her as she stood before the fire, as the light and shadow from the flames danced across her face. He had telephoned Clare on his arrival home to say that he would pick his wife up, but Elizabeth had not been there, there had been no arrangement to meet that night.

'Grace has left your supper warming in the oven.'

'I'm not hungry,' she said quickly.

'Are you all right?'

For a hopeful, fleeting second he thought she might be ill, that that might be the answer to the dread which waited just out of sight.

'I'm fine ... just a bit of a headache.' She switched her gaze back to him. 'I think I'll go to bed – have an early night.' There was wariness in her face and it nearly broke his heart. She began to walk away from him.

'There's nothing wrong, is there?' He had to ask, had to quieten the cold sour dread.

Elizabeth stopped abruptly and turned back, her face only half illuminated by the rose red of the fire.

'Of course not.' She came to his side and said the words of no comfort again. 'Of course not.' She leaned downwards and for a moment he thought she would kiss his lips and then somehow, everything would be all right again, but her mouth came to settle on his brow, her hand smoothing back his hair, and he was suddenly conscious of the white streaks beneath her fingers as her soft voice touched his ear. 'I'm sorry.'

For a split second they looked back at each other.

'You don't have to be sorry...'

He felt the tenseness come over her as she shook her head and smiled and the news he had wanted to tell her since she had arrived home remained muted behind his lips. Now wasn't the time, and suddenly he felt enormously sad because he couldn't share this one important thing with her when he wished, when he wanted, because she had successfully castrated his happiness by a lie, and a few empty words and a look on her face which told him everything. Because she could do that, his wife, his very lovely wife. And now there was a barrier between them which nothing, not even good news, could pass without falling flat and lifeless at his feet. Like a sick joke. His eyes followed her as she walked slowly across the room and disappeared from view, staying there as the sound of her steps lessened and died away. He supposed there would be another, more appropriate time to tell her, but it would not be the same, and she had said that she had wanted this for him so much: Ambassador to Washington – the plum, the pearl, the most sought-after of diplomatic postings. John swallowed; it was what he had worked for and hoped for, and now his likely triumph seemed to shrink and fold in upon itself as he sat in the empty room, because it was empty without her, without Elizabeth. John shifted his gaze to the fire, wishing he had not seen, had not heard, had not rung Clare Carter. But Elizabeth's face had said it all; the flush in her cheeks, the brilliance of her eyes – soft with pity as she looked back at him.

5

'Who is this man?'

'His name is Sam, Mother . . .' Kristina caught a sharp, weary breath. 'I've already told you.'

'And he's married.'

'He's getting a divorce.'

'That's what he says.'

'That's the truth.'

'You're such a fool, Kristina.'

'I *have* been a fool, Mother.'

'I see – so you've suddenly changed – overnight.'

'People can change.'

Her mother snorted with contempt. 'You should go to church.'

'How would that help?'

'God will guide you.'

Kristina shook her head in exasperation, her eyes automatically taking her to the carved figure of the Virgin standing beneath the window.

'He hasn't guided me very well so far, Mother.'

'And whose fault is that?'

Kristina looked back at the old woman sitting amongst the fat cushions of the fading Biedermeier sofa, saw her puckered, bird-like throat, the white hair, the liver spots on her decaying face and hands, the swollen legs in thick, brutal stockings. Her mother was nearly eighty-two, she had been born when the world was a very different place, when Austria and thus Vienna was still a byword for worldly splendour and the Habsburgs were still considered to be the instruments of God on earth. She and her sister, Theresa-Marie, were groomed for that world, for the sole purpose of making the most successful of bourgeois marriages. They had to be educated of course, but not too much; curious, yet shy, silly and unworldly and pretty, in a coy, girlish way.

Kristina smiled with a touch of sadness as she remembered the stories her mother had told her years ago about 'being grown' and 'a woman', and particularly 'a married woman'. Sex was naturally a taboo subject, improper even to mention, and for a woman to actually *enjoy* sex was considered quite shocking, if not abnormal. Once she recalled her aunt, who had never married, telling her that a woman must be 'noble' and practise piety, and that her sacred duty was to be a 'dedicated, pure and obedient wife'. *Pure* being the operative word.

She had always wondered why Aunt Theresa had never married and had presumed it was because she had no looks to speak of, but when she had asked her mother once, a long time ago, she had received a sharp slap across her legs and was told never to talk of it again. But she had found out one night years after when her mother had had a glass of cognac too many; there had been a scandal, of course, Aunt Theresa had been mistakenly raped by Uncle Franzie, their father's brother, mistakenly because Uncle Franzie had thought that Aunt Theresa was one of the maids he had arranged to meet in the dim shadows of the library. Poor Aunt Theresa had only been looking for a book to read. Uncle Franzie had subsequently shot himself and Aunt Theresa had had a child, but no one would talk about the child, it was as if it had never been born. Much later her mother had denied the whole story, but it was true, there was no doubt because Kristina had found the child's birth certificate. It had been a boy. Poor baby. It was ironic that her mother, the pretty, lucky daughter, had then seemed unable to have children to please her authoritarian and extremely successful husband until it had been almost too late and then the child had unfortunately been a girl, herself. An only child, born to Habsburg parents who could not reconcile themselves to the loss of empire and monarchy, could not reconcile themselves to an Austria that was no longer the centre of the world. Kristina blinked. And now there is only Mother and me.

'My fault, Mother – and yours,' she said finally.

The grey, rheumy eyes narrowed. 'Mine . . . mine?' she shrilled.

'You know why, don't you?' Kristina's eyes glittered as she met her mother's outraged gaze. 'You know why.'

'You will go to the Ruprechtskirche and make your confession.'

Kristina shook her head.

'We really *can't* talk, can we?' Kristina pleaded. 'We have never really talked.'

'You are making no sense this evening.' Her mother's gaze slipped away, unable to meet the plea in her daughter's face. 'The priest, Boeckl, is a good man – speak to him.'

'I have not made a confession in years, you know that, why do we pretend?!'

'Stop it! Stop it, Kristina!' She waved her hand to ward off any contradiction. 'And enough, I am tired.'

Kristina gave her mother a long, searching look and then walked across the room to the door.

'Will you be late?'
'Perhaps.'
'What is his name again?'
'Sam.'
'Sam what?'
Kristina stiffened. 'Sam Cohen.'
The silence dragged them down.
'A Jew.' She heard the sharp intake of her mother's breath. '*Gott im Himmel.*'
Kristina opened the door.
'You are not serious . . . Kristina?' The voice followed her. 'Kristina?' There was a moment's strange little silence. 'I'm sorry . . . Kristina? Do not go – do not go and meet this . . . Sam Cohen . . .'
But the door had closed and the old woman and her voice were shut behind it.

Laura felt tears start in her eyes.
'That wasn't the message I received, Andrew.'
'I'm sorry, Laura, I can't help that.'
The disappointment, the sadness which lay in wait was almost too much for her to bear because she hadn't expected it. And now, curiously, she wanted very much to see him.
'When *can* you come?'
'I don't know – it's difficult to say at the moment.'
'Obviously.'
'I didn't meant that the way it sounded.' He sighed. 'Anyway, why can't you make it to Brussels? After all, you could say we're meeting halfway.'
'Brussels is hardly halfway to Vienna, Andrew.'
'I didn't think it was such a bad idea.'
'It's not a *bad* idea, just not a very practical one – it's all very well for you, you'll be there on business, I'd have to give a good reason to my ambassador for taking time off in the middle of a busy week.'
'For God's sake, Laura – you can't be *that* busy.'
She drew a breath as the tears dissolved into anger. 'Why not, Andrew? There happen to be major talks on straightening out the environment here, in case you'd forgotten. And although I might not be *directly* involved, it has meant a lot of extra work here at the embassy.'
'All right, all right, point taken.'
Silence fell between them before he spoke again.
'How is it?' he asked quietly.

She sighed. 'Difficult, fine, interesting, lonely.' She thought reluctantly of Ralf.
'Are you still sure you made the right decision?'
'Are you?'
'It was your choice, Laura, ultimately.'
'Don't you get bored repeating the same old line?'
'It happens to be true.'
'That you insisted on putting your career before mine.'
'I can't help being male.'
'God, Andrew! These are the glorious, liberated 1990s!'
'I didn't call you for an argument.'
'Well, I suppose I'm lucky you called at all.'
'What the hell's that supposed to mean?'
'It means that you're hardly ever at home when I telephone . . .'
'I've been busy too, actually,' he said defensively. 'I don't usually leave my desk until well after seven.'
She said nothing.
'And after seven I generally have a bite with Keith, or one of the other guys.'
Did he really expect her to believe that? Then she swallowed helplessly because she had betrayed him, after all, and somehow hearing his voice swept her backwards to London, to the familiar safe memories of his flat, to the good times they had shared and which now seemed so far off, so unreachable. And she wanted to cry, to go back and start again. To tell him.
'You don't believe me, do you, Laura?'
'Yes, I suppose so,' she answered in a small voice.
'God, you must really have a low opinion of me.'
'Well, you haven't exactly made things easy, have you?' she responded defensively. If he had been different, if he had come even some way to meeting her and understanding, she would not be here in Vienna, or trying to stave off misery and loneliness with someone called Ralf Müller, someone, she realized, she was suddenly not sure of at all.
'And you have, of course?'
'You could have tried to understand, Andrew, and just for once seen things from my point of view.'
'I was angry,' he said slowly, guiltily. 'You know I didn't want you to go.'
She heard him sigh and wanted so much to be able to reach out and touch and make everything right again.
'Can't you come, just for a weekend?' If he came she would put Ralf behind her, they could make a fresh start.

'I don't think so, Laura, I'm sorry.' He sighed again. 'I really am. Perhaps after Easter.' He forced a laugh. 'It would make a damned expensive weekend.'

Andrew never had any money.

But Easter seemed weeks away, and so much could happen in those weeks, so much could change. Didn't he care? Couldn't he tell that she needed him? Ralf's fathomless face stole into her mind and once again she wondered why it was that that feeling of unease would creep up on her at odd times of the day. Laura closed her eyes and pushed away the vague sensation that something was going badly wrong somewhere, somehow, and that she was losing control.

'Laura?'

'Sorry . . .'

'Look, I'll call you on Monday.'

'Okay.'

'Don't sound so enthusiastic.'

'I just wish . . .'

'What?'

'Nothing – nothing.'

'Cheer up,' he said. 'I'll even try and write you a decent letter.'

'And I'll ask my ambassador about Brussels.' She had already asked Sir Nigel for an extra day in Hungary, with Ralf, but he had yet to grant her permission.

'Great.' He paused. 'I miss you, Laura.'

She swallowed. 'I miss you, too.' And she did, too much, and she had buried it all neatly and safely because he had wounded her damned pride.

'I'll call you Monday.'

And he was gone.

She sat wrapped in silence for long seconds and then her hand reached for the telephone and she dialled Ralf's number, but only got the irritating sound of the engaged signal. Her eyes drifted to the window. The afternoon was drawing to a close, but it was dry and not quite so cold as it had been. She would walk to his apartment and see him and say that she couldn't make it to Hungary, after all, say that she and Andrew had healed the breach in their relationship, that she would not see him any more.

There was a faint smell of mist as she walked through the Volksgarten and its lifeless rose gardens, but the sun was shining, slanting pink on the frozen snow, and the sky was stunningly clear. Laura took a deep breath and realized that she felt relieved. After all, she and Ralf were really worlds apart, she told herself easily, and she would never really mean anything to him; there was something remote, something indefinable about him which she had never been able to touch. Like looking at someone through a pane of glass. But she hated the telling, hated the thought of confronting him, and yet it seemed the right thing to do after her conversation with Andrew, and the sooner she told him the better; if she left it until tomorrow or the day after she might lose her nerve. Laura lifted her eyes upwards towards the deepening blue of the fading afternoon skyline. It made it easier that the day should be so beautiful, that there was nothing ugly or sharp-edged about this quiet Saturday. And there were few people about, they would be either in one of the coffee houses, or safe in their apartments, away from the seeping damp of this sudden thaw.

She felt a little breathless as she crossed the Ringstrasse and the Rathaus came into view. Tiny, unlooked for fears began fluttering inside her, tiny doubts which remained unformed and out of reach. She tried to swallow the tightness in her throat as stark, furtive pictures of her lovemaking with Ralf climbed into her head and she wished with all her heart that she could call them back and purge herself of the bewildering shame which she had carefully pressed down. Because Ralf could do that, could make her submerge her pride, her shame, her self-respect even as she begged him to finish the piercing, paralysing pleasure he gave her. And she did beg. Laura closed her eyes for a brief, agonizing second as if she would shut out the vision, but then she was turning into the street she had begun to know so well and her eyes were automatically searching for his car, but Ralf's car was not parked outside the apartment building, there was an empty space where his Alfa Romeo normally stood. With a sinking heart she approached the heavy wooden doors and pressed the bell of his apartment, but there was no reply. An image of the white, empty rooms slipped unwillingly into her head and for a curious moment she thought of Greece and his love of its culture, and a beautiful girl he had loved for her innocence and purity. She could not imagine that, not Ralf and purity, not Ralf and a love of innocence. Laura sighed heavily and shivered as dusk began creeping into the sky. She would call him tonight, or tomorrow. She would tell him then.

Elizabeth looked at John at the head of the table. He seemed less tense, but then she never knew with him, he played his part so well it was difficult to tell. She caught a quick, silent breath and tried to interest herself in the baked salmon which she had prepared herself with such care, but somehow the succulent slab of orangey-red fish bathed in soy sauce had lost any attraction for her. Instead she let her gaze drift back to her husband – he could not know, she had covered her tracks very carefully, but even as she acknowledged her deceit she knew that he would surely find out; John had a way of looking into her that was unnerving. John. Elizabeth pushed down the panic as a wave of guilt washed over her again. She was not good at this, not designed for deception, it weighed too heavily, cost too much. She tried to lose her thoughts for a moment, but once more her mind began skilfully to uncoil the time she had spent with Karl as searing echoes of the pleasure and the heat and the love began to build and build, becoming trapped in her chest so that she thought she could not breathe. And it seemed in that brief, heady moment that she did not belong here, in her own home, with these people and John – faithful John being good and perfect, playing the faultless diplomatic host. In that brief moment she did not feel guilt at all.

'Are you all right, Elizabeth?'

She turned abruptly.

'Absolutely – just for a second my thoughts were elsewhere.' And she felt that they must all know, suddenly, by the flush of her skin, the pounding, pounding of the blood racing through her veins; that she was different.

'The colour seemed to drain from your face . . .'

Elizabeth's eyes dropped to Count Dhoryány's hand, which was busy covering her own.

'I'm fine, really.' She withdrew her hand to the safety of a wine glass.

'My wife is like you, she loses her colour very easily, often over silly things.'

Elizabeth looked into Felix's bland, handsome face and was not surprised.

'How is Sophia?' she asked, changing the subject.

'Very well.'

'How are her studies going?'

'Her studies?' He chuckled as if she had made a joke. 'They very much take second place to the real reason she is there.'

Elizabeth frowned. 'What is the real reason?'

'Of course, nothing has been settled yet . . .' he parried. 'But it is our hope that she may be married some time in the not too distant future.'

'Married – isn't she a little young?'

'My dear . . . not for *this* sort of marriage.'

She looked back at him carefully, disliking the emphasis on 'my dear', disliking instinctively his smirk of triumph.

'How many *sorts* are there?' she asked dryly.

'She is staying with Oskar von der Heyden.'

It was as if that should explain everything.

'Yes?'

He sighed. 'As I said, it is our hope that she should marry . . .'

'Oskar von der Heyden?'

'Yes, I know, I can see your surprise, but it has come as somewhat of a surprise to us all,' he lied. 'And, of course, Oskar is not exactly young.' A shadow seemed to move behind his eyes.

She became very still as Felix's voice ran on.

'But nevertheless, an excellent catch. You have, naturally, heard of von der Heyden Chemicals, von der Heyden Pharmaceuticals, von der Heyden Fertilizers?'

'Yes.' She wanted to add that she could not see lovely, unspoilt Sophia amongst chemicals and fertilizers, could not see her married to the sallow, dry husk of Oskar von der Heyden.

'My wife and I are naturally very pleased.'

'Naturally.' Elizabeth stared at Felix and forced a smile and then turned back to her plate and made a feeble attempt at eating the salmon, which was almost cold.

'There's a von der Heyden Chemical plant in Buenos Aires, isn't there, Felix?'

Felix shifted his gaze to Dan Gurney who was sitting just a little further down the table.

'Yes, yes – I believe Oskar may have mentioned that he had plants in South America.'

'Quite a few companies do that,' Dan said too casually.

'Do what, Daniel?'

'Build new factories in the Third World or, shall we say, less regulated markets.'

'I'm not sure I understand you.'

'To escape the strict environmental controls in the West, or in their own country.'

Elizabeth longed to smile.

'Oh, really.'

'Yes, really,' Dan continued. 'Von der Heyden, along with many other Western companies, and I include the US in this –'

'I'm so glad . . .' Felix interjected dryly.

'– also ship their toxic waste to the Third World for disposal for the same reasons. Not the healthiest of exports.'

'And not the healthiest of topics to discuss over dinner.'

'I just thought you might like to know, Felix.'

'Thank you.'

Dan longed to laugh. Felix was like many people who worshipped money: the more you had the better, no matter what poor bastard suffered in the process.

'My apologies, Elizabeth,' Dan said. 'Talking shop yet again.'

'There's no need to apologize,' she replied quickly. 'Actually, I'm finding these Talks extremely interesting and for once John's work and the issues at stake are easily understood and easily applicable to everyday life. I feel more involved.'

'Yes, I see.'

'And apart from obvious self-interest,' she continued. 'I have a young son and I don't want him or other sons and daughters waiting to be born to inherit a dying or irreparably damaged world.'

'A pretty speech, Elizabeth,' Felix said, giving her a winning smile.

Dan raised his eyebrows.

'It's not just a pretty speech, Felix – I mean every word.'

'Oh, of course, naturally.'

'We all have to mean it, if these talks are going to achieve anything worthwhile,' Dan said slowly.

'Austria has always taken environmental considerations seriously . . .'

'And that's very encouraging . . .'

'I would certainly say that it is more than encouraging,' he said tautly. 'After all . . .' He turned to Elizabeth, patted her hand and added a little sadly, 'If we were all as unenthusiastic and parochial as some of the countries represented around the table we would all very soon be wearing gas masks and filling in the last of the world's green belts with concrete . . .'

Elizabeth gave Felix a small, tight smile. 'The UK is very committed to the Talks, Felix, otherwise we would not be here.'

'Of course.' Felix reached for his wine. 'It just seems to take some governments so much longer to come to terms with ceding a little of their national sovereignty . . . for the sake of higher principles, shall we say.'

Elizabeth found her eyes focusing on a tear of wine caught in the corner of Felix's mouth.

'And my dear Elizabeth –'

She winced.

'– we must suppose that turning a pallid sort of green is better than not turning green at all!' Felix guffawed.

'Perhaps we must,' Dan added and Felix's lips fell abruptly. He should have been a comic, Dan thought with amusement, the expressions on his face have the pliability of a rubber band, and if he has one more drink he might even fall off his chair. Not very aristocratic.

Elizabeth sighed inwardly and turned her attention to the rest of the table as a further helping of the salmon began to circulate; it was becoming a long, long evening. She focused on Genevieve and the almost untouched food on her plate and the wine glass her nervous fingers touched which had hardly been tasted. Felix's wife would be thinking of their daughter and her new life and the miles separating them, she would be wondering if Sophia was happy, and she would be missing her. The strange, unsettling scenario in the garden room of the castle came back to her and Genevieve's small tightly clenched fists, white, as if she were hurting; she would not want this marriage for Sophia. Suddenly the large brown eyes were looking back at her and Elizabeth smiled automatically, but wondered anew at the pale face, the features somehow pinched and withdrawn, the unhappiness vivid like gloss on her skin.

She forced her gaze to the man opposite, Ruloph Crommelin, a quiet Dutchman, a nice man, tall and rangy like so many of his race, and unmarried. 'I am not gay . . .' he had said with a grin over pre-dinner drinks '. . . just unmarriageable.' She had laughed and was glad that she had placed him next to the doll-like delegate from Singapore, Moy, who was not the greatest of talkers, but looked as if she had just stepped out of a performance of *Madame Butterfly* with her helmet of black lacquered hair and thickly powdered skin. Elizabeth's eyes were drawn to the tiny lips, like a gash in her face, which had been painted and outlined in lipstick the colour of blood.

The Talks had brought together so many of the nations of the world, and the variety of peoples gathered here – their cultures, their colour, their ideas, their often undisputed intelligence, and stupidity – continued to fascinate her. Elizabeth was not only fascinated, but amazed that such a group could be assembled, in Vienna, at all. That had to mean something, surely? And she had come here like all the other wives, with their husbands, as support and friend and wife and mother and tireless hostess. Always looking good, always being good, always there.

Her eyes slipped unwillingly back to John, and the fright began washing over her again. Five years ago she had risked nothing but shattered illusions, now she risked everything – her son, her husband, the rich life they led together. She should stop now before the world began crashing down around her ears; limit the damage. She looked down at her fingers, at the slim fingers which trembled, but the damage had already been done. And she was in love with Karl, there was no doubt about that now, perhaps she had always been in love with Karl.

*

'You weren't serious about taking a trip to London?'

They were alone now, the guests gone, the apartment virtually empty.

'I was – actually,' her calm voice said.

John poured himself a whisky.

'But why?' He drank quickly, the heat burning.

'Just for a break, John – that's all.'

He sighed softly. 'And that's all?'

'Of course.' She looked back at him for an instant. 'Should there be another reason?'

He lifted the glass again to his mouth. 'No, it just seems a little odd, this sudden desire.'

'In Madrid I went home for a break every few months, you know that.'

'I like you here,' he said slowly, 'with me.'

'It will only be for ten days.'

'Ten days,' he repeated and searched the carefully composed face of his wife. 'You just don't seem yourself, that's all.'

'I'm fine – really,' she said gently.

'Really?'

Would she be alone? But he could not ask, could not diminish himself any more. He closed his eyes for a fleeting, dread-filled moment because he knew that this was no figment of his imagination, that there was no mistaking the lie she had told him and what it implied, because he had never seen her like this before. He wondered if she realized that he knew her better than she did herself, that it had been like this always. And he would say nothing and do nothing because then he could pretend that everything was as it had been and she would not be forced to choose and therefore leave him with nothing. And Elizabeth would choose the other man, he was sure of that, but he banished the knowledge into a deep, dark corner of his mind because he could not bear it, could not bear examining this love of hers and holding it up to the light like a dazzling, golden orb – blinding him.

'Yes.' She looked at him for an instant, fenced in by regret and confusion and giddying panic. It was idiotic, this running away, and in her heart she knew that it would never be long enough – ten days, ten weeks, ten years, would make no difference, it was only evasion and a poor penance for what she had done and for what would come later.

John scrutinized the carefully bowed head as she turned away from him and thought again of the news of his likely posting to Washington. He had told himself that she would be delighted, that they would celebrate and then make slow, deliberate love later in the great Viennese bed which waited. But he had not told her and now she was going to London and he was a little afraid. John swallowed and thought of all the times and the future times he had only seen himself with Elizabeth by his side because that was the way it was and would always be. But there could be no Washington without Elizabeth. He caught her kind glance as she looked quickly back at him as if she had sensed his eyes, but he did not want that, did not want to evoke that look she seemed to save only for him, that tender, soulful glance as if he deserved her pity, as if her heart bled. John stared into the whisky-stained glass, his lips pressed together, almost white. It was not Elizabeth's heart that was bleeding, but his own, as surely as if she had driven a knife through his chest.

Sam whistled, he didn't know exactly *what* he whistled, but it suited his mood. He had taken Kristina out for dinner the second time that week and it seemed to him that each time he saw her he liked her a little more. The evening at the English Theatre had been a great success and tonight she was taking him to the opera; she had insisted and finally he had found it difficult to refuse.

Sam turned into the Johannesgasse where his apartment building was and smiled softly to himself – it was a sort of celebration, too, because Natalie had telephoned yesterday and told him that she would not be coming to Vienna, after all, she had a 'personal problem' which needed straightening out. Sam almost laughed; he could imagine what sort of 'personal problem' it was, she'd probably run out of dope, and she could stay away just as long as she liked because he didn't want to see her. Ever. He licked his lips as he walked through the great double doors into the building and continued whistling as he searched his pockets for a schilling to insert into the ornate turn-of-the-century lift, a procedure which normally drove him crazy, but today amused and entertained as if all the dark pressures which had tormented him for months had fled and left him free at last. He glanced at his watch as he approached the door to his apartment. He had half an hour before he met Kristina outside the Opera House.

The key slipped easily into the lock and the door handle turned with customary slickness, but it was only when he had closed the door behind him that his heart jumped, that he thought he heard *her* voice coming from the sacred inner sanctum of his den. He rubbed his forehead as if he were hearing things, as if the panic mounting inside was not real, like something half imagined. He walked down the hall, drawn inexorably by the sound of the voice, and found himself standing on the threshold watching his almost ex-wife. Natalie.

'Hello, Sam.'

Time seemed very slow then as he looked back at her and the moment had a dreamlike quality as if he had been taken back to another place, long forgotten, because she had not changed at all. It was the same Natalie he had seen that first dizzying time at the UN, it was the Natalie who had so flatteringly pursued him, who had finally seduced him. She was wearing the same dress. Clever Natalie. Sweet, searing memory.

'I thought I'd surprise you.'

His heart was beating very fast, fighting the disbelief.

'You've surprised me, Natalie – you said you weren't coming.'

'Like I said, I wanted to surprise you.'

He shook his head slowly as if he still couldn't believe that she was sitting there, for real.

'You look good, Sam.'

The blood began seeping into his face and he was suddenly aware of Clara standing awkwardly on the other side of the room.

'Is Joanna in bed, Clara?'

The Filipino woman nodded and lowered her eyes.

'That will be all for now . . .' Sam said, and forced a smile. He waited until she had gone before he turned back to his wife, relieved that some of the panic was sliding away.

'Why are you here, Natalie?'

'I told you – I want to see JoJo.'

'I know that. But you didn't have to come *here*, to my home, presumably you're staying at the Imperial?'

'I wanted to come.'

'You should have called first.'

'That's not very friendly . . . I thought a surprise was a great idea, I thought being here when you got home would be a great idea.'

'Oh, cut it out, Natalie.'

She looked away from him, her honey-blonde hair swinging as her head turned.

'*All right*, Sam.' She switched her gaze back to him and he thought he saw tears standing in her eyes and then she spoke, her voice almost a whisper. 'But you can't blame me for trying.'

His mouth fell open just a little. He wasn't any good at games and she usually won every time. That was what made him nervous, that was what made him think she always held the winning hand.

'I had to see you.' She sighed heavily. 'I *wanted* to, Sam.'

'It's over, Natalie, how many times do I have to tell you?'

There was a bottle of Scotch standing on the bookcase.

'Do you want a drink?'

'No, thanks.'

He glanced at her sharply. 'Nothing?'

'Nothing.' She gave him a humourless smile. 'I've given it up, Sam.'

He laughed.

'I knew you wouldn't believe me, but I also knew that if I had any chance of retrieving what we had, I would have to.'

He shook his head as he poured his Scotch.

'You must really take me for a sucker, Natalie – a real A1 sucker.'

'It's true, Sam.'

'This time.'

'This time, and for always.' She stood up.

He hated himself for the way his eyes were immediately drawn to the thinly disguised body beneath the carefully sculptured dress. He had always loved that dress, the way it clung, the way the soft, soft peach tones mimicked her skin, the way it teased the mind into thinking of flesh – warm, willing woman flesh. He wanted to tell her to sit down, to stay there and not move, but he knew he would sound ridiculous.

'I see you still like playing with model planes . . .' She began stroking the old Baltimore standing on a miniature pedestal in the corner of the room. 'Same old Sam.'

'Why don't you go back to your hotel?'

'Don't worry, I plan to.'

She moved closer to him so that they stood only inches apart.

'How long will you be staying?' he asked unnecessarily. He already knew, didn't he? Sam swallowed and met her cool stare, but found his eyes beginning to waver as he looked back at her.

'Three days, like I told you.' She smiled. 'And I didn't come all this way to yell at you, Sam.'

The smile widened into a grin and he could see small, white, perfect teeth.

'I was a fool, Sam, a smart-ass . . . I thought I could have it all.'

'Stop it, Natalie . . . we've been through this.'

She lowered her eyes and drew a sharp, shuddering breath as if he had slapped her.

'I just wanted to tell you that I've grown up a bit, that I'm really trying to get myself together.' She opened her eyes wide and looked into his face. 'I don't expect you to believe me, or to change your mind about the divorce, that would be too much to hope for, I just wanted you to see that all the pain I put you through wasn't a waste of time.' She paused. 'I know what I've lost, Sam.'

He tried to rid himself of the tightness in his throat, tried to ignore the deep rise and fall of her breasts beneath the sheer material. He took a gulp of Scotch and stepped back as if he was suddenly interested in the mail lying on a nearby table.

'You won't be able to see Joanna until tomorrow.'

'I managed to see her before she went to bed . . . I read her a story.'

For a brief second he was angry, but before he could speak her voice had stopped him.

'It was only a little story, Sam – I promise I didn't upset her.' Her eyes seemed to widen even more and he forced himself to look away. 'Clara was there all the time.'

'I don't know what you're trying to pull, but it won't work.'

'I'm not trying to pull anything, Sam.' Her words were laced with softness and tinged with skilful bewilderment and he thought he could almost believe her.

'You didn't have to come all the way to Europe to tell me this.'

'I think I did, Sam. You would never have believed me from the other end of a phone.'

'Well,' he said quickly, 'it doesn't really matter now, does it? The divorce is going through smoothly and soon it won't make any difference.'

'I know, I know.' Her voice was very small now. Sad. 'I'd hoped that if you saw that I was really making an effort – really changing – you wouldn't be so difficult about visiting rights to JoJo.'

He frowned a little, caught off guard by this new tack.

'She's your daughter, Natalie, as well as mine, you will have some rights.'

'I didn't want you to worry, that's all.'

He gave her a dry smile. 'Am I supposed to believe this?'

She sighed again and shook her head. 'I shouldn't have come . . .' She sat down. 'I knew you wouldn't believe me . . . if only you knew how hard it's been . . . if only you knew what it's like to have dope as your best friend, your family – your lover.' A sound broke free from her mouth like a sob. 'And then to give it up, Sam.'

He fought the doubt and the sympathy, tried to shrug off the spectre that she might, finally, be telling the truth. Slowly she lifted her head and looked into his face; big, fat tears were coursing down her cheeks.

'I'm sorry. I didn't mean to make a scene . . . that was the last thing on my mind.'

Tears always unmanned him; he felt useless, his hands tied – not knowing what he was supposed to do, or say.

'It's okay,' he said tentatively and removed the white cotton handkerchief from his pocket. 'Here, take this . . .'

Natalie smiled back at him gratefully; he was not used to gratefulness, not from her. He found himself studying her closely, curiously, as the little sobs began to die in her throat and her hands were reaching up to wipe the tears away.

'You're not really mad, are you, Sam? About me coming?' Her eyelids batted weakly over the green orbs he thought he knew so well. 'If I hadn't come – you see – I would never have forgiven myself.' She lowered her gaze and caught a quick, ragged breath. 'Not after all I put you and JoJo through. I had to try.'

He remained standing, watching the lovely, tear-stained face, his thoughts sweeping backwards, going over all the moments that made his stomach churn, even now. All the pain, all the anguish and shattered illusions, the hatred of her and the need of her and the emptiness which followed, sucking him dry.

'You had to try, Natalie.'

'You still don't believe me, do you, Sam?' Her voice was soft and slow. Like a stroking finger.

'I can't.'

'I understand.'

He blinked, taken aback by her response. 'I don't think you can.'

She smiled. 'Oh, yes.' She stood up. 'Because if I had been you – and I have tried being you – I would have walked out six weeks after our wedding – after you found the smack. You're too good, Sam, you let me get away with too much.'

'So it's my fault.'

'Not your fault.' She turned towards the door. 'My fault because I found a nice guy, a really nice guy. I should have found a son-of-a-bitch who knocked me around.'

'That's stupid.'

'No, Sam.' Tears were forming in her eyes again. 'It's what I deserve.' She shook her head helplessly. 'Look – I'd better go.' She took a step away from him.

'Not like this.'

'It's for the best.'

'I . . .'

He caught her arm and her musky perfume filled his nostrils and the cat-like green eyes grew round and voluptuous, as if they would claim him, but then he drew back with a start as the telephone rang, as if he had been stung.

'Hello . . .?'

'Sam – it's Kristina – aren't you coming?'

'Kristina.' He closed his eyes; he had forgotten. 'Christ! Sorry . . . something turned up, I'll be with you as soon as I can.' He put the telephone down.

'I have to go, Natalie.'

'A girlfriend?'

He blushed. 'I suppose she is. Yes.' He was back in control now, but inside he wondered what would have happened if the phone had not rung or if he had arranged to see Kristina some other time and not tonight.

'Well, it's been nice, our little talk,' Natalie said smoothly. 'Maybe tomorrow we could have lunch – if it's convenient, of course.'

'Maybe.'

'I mean – if you have other plans, I wouldn't want to get in the way.'

'If I have other plans I'll let you know.'

She studied him for a moment, knowing that any further overtures would be wasted now, the shriek of the telephone had seen to that. But for one sweet, beautiful second back there she had nearly had him! Natalie smiled. Poor Sam, you're really still mine, you don't know it and you'll fight a teensie weensie bit, but Natalie will have you back in the end. She laughed soundlessly. And he hasn't realized yet that if that girl, that woman, had really meant anything he would never have 'forgotten' her for his sexy visiting wifey. She slipped on her gloves and watched him as he checked his wallet. Anyway, healthy competition made her instincts razor sharp and it had never stopped her getting her man, ever – only Donahue, but that was different, his sour-faced hag of a wife had held the purse strings and he had been scared shitless by the press. She hadn't liked him much, anyway, no sense of humour. Her eyes narrowed to slivers of green glass as they followed Sam across the room. Oh, Sam . . . little Sammy, Natalie will eat you for breakfast, just like she always did.

Genevieve moved across the pillared hall to the Italian Room, her mother's favourite, her only favourite in the austere grandeur of the castle. She had not visited the beautiful room since the previous spring, but it had not changed, of course, except for the fresh flowers, primroses and early daffodils, standing on a brass-bound chest. Automatically she found her hand reaching out to touch the yellow heads and take in the tenuous, fragile smell before she walked slowly back across the black ceramic floor to look out beyond the leaded window to the grounds which were still partly sheathed in snow. Felix was standing by the octagonal fountain, no doubt convincing their guests of its uniqueness, and it was unique, she supposed wearily, if rather ugly. She had never seen so many fantastical heads, so many grotesques spewing forth water from vulgar open mouths. It made her tired, this place, this monolith, as if it drained her spirits, but not Felix. Schloss Bletz was his because he loved it, probably more than anything else, she realized with sudden clarity, and the knowledge did not really hurt, not any more.

She turned back into the room and looked towards the portrait of her mother hanging over the white marble of the monumental fireplace. She had been perhaps Sophia's age when the painting had been completed and there was a likeness between grandmother and granddaughter – that same fragility which seemed to pass through the female line, the same sensitivity of the eye, the shape of the mouth and gentle pale hands folded carefully across lavender silk. She shifted her gaze to the antique spinet which she had been allowed to play as a child. It was old now, very old, the keys paralysed with age because no one had touched it since her mother's death. Her father's wish, and a wish she had kept because there had been no others for her to keep, not since her brother had gone, because she knew that her father had wished that it had been she who had died and not Heinrich.

But he had been ill with grief, she told herself again, he had not known what he said. Her eyes darted back to her mother's face and the kind eyes and the careful hands. Sometimes she had wondered if things might have been different if Mother had lived and sometimes she longed for her to be here, now, with her; to calm and cool that wild, lost feeling trapped in her chest. Genevieve swallowed slowly and lifted her eyes to the deeply coved and sculptured ceiling in white and gold. The family crest with a crown above it wreathed in laurel stared back at her. Sophia loved this room, she had always said that it was 'peaceful', 'a good room'.

Genevieve felt a strange flicker of panic, knowing that the fatal trembling of her mouth heralded tears and therefore disaster. She had promised herself that she would not weep any more, and in three weeks she would see Sophia and all the panic and the fears would be quashed, eliminated, and everything would be all right again. Wouldn't it? She sighed heavily. Perhaps she was ill. Perhaps it was to do with the terrible heaviness which seemed to drag at her feet and her limbs, weighing her down like a world sadness. She looked quickly back at the silent portrait, at the spinet, and walked carefully out of the room; Felix would be wondering where she was.

Ralf's gaze beat her down and Laura switched her attention uneasily to the waiter who had begun pouring purple wine into her glass.

'You said you had something to tell me?'

She took a mouthful of the wine and looked back at him. She had left a brief message on his answer-phone on Sunday and he had not called her back until Wednesday, which had surprised her because he had always been so prompt at responding to her calls, but he had been away on business apparently. She had planned to tell him that their affair was over, as she had told herself she would, but Andrew's promised call had not materialized on Monday evening, in fact he had not telephoned her at all since their conversation the previous weekend. He had let her down again. There had been no letter either and she wondered why she had bothered to believe him; for a moment she had loved him again and the future had suddenly burned brightly with hope she had not felt in weeks. And now he had smothered all her carefully woven dreams and all the hope and she was left with the task of erecting all the barriers again and telling Ralf that she no longer cared to see him, except that now she wasn't so sure. After all, she hardly knew a soul in Vienna, she hadn't been here long enough to make a real friend. Her life, she realized, had begun to revolve around Ralf. And she had been willing to give that up for Andrew.

'It was about Hungary,' she lied.

'You can come?'

She was flattered by the eagerness in his voice.

'Yes.'

'Wonderful.' He took her hand. 'So you've cleared it with your ambassador?'

'Yes,' she said. 'He gave me special clearance. It was very good of him.'

'I know you will not regret it.' He kissed the tips of her fingers. 'Budapest is waiting to be rediscovered by the West.'

'You know it very well?'

'My company was one of the first to make links in the early seventies.'

'What *is* your company's name?'

'It's privately owned – Maier.'

'Maier,' she repeated.

She wondered why she had never asked before.

'Were you in Hungary when I called at the weekend?'

'No.' He removed a tiny speck from the sleeve of his jacket. 'I haven't been there for several months. I was in Frankfurt.'

But the telephone had been engaged, hadn't it? She had just missed him, hadn't she?

'What's the matter?'

'Nothing – I was just thinking about visas.' She must have been mistaken, perhaps she had dialled the wrong number.

'I'll take care of those.'

'Where will we stay in Budapest?'

'Usually I stay at the Hyatt. It sits on one side of the Danube, facing the old palace.'

'Sounds wonderful.'

'Have you managed to get the extra day?'

'Friday?'

'Yes. My ambassador was very generous, considering I shouldn't really be going at all. It's lucky my mother's brother happens to be ambassador there.' Wasn't that why she had gone into diplomacy in the first place, because it was a family thing? Uncle Phillip's success had practically been drilled into her.

'He's got an excellent reputation – Phillip Rowse, isn't it?'

'That's right . . . I didn't realize you took such an interest.'

'I take an interest in everything, Laura, especially when it concerns you.'

The smile she returned was dry, sardonic, but her cheeks still filled with blood.

'That line sounds as if it came out of some old picture, or a Barbara Cartland novel . . .'

'Barbara Cartland is a very rich, very famous old lady.'

'You don't have to quote her.'

'I didn't.' His face became serious, the eyes unblinking as he looked into her face. 'I meant every word.' He lifted a glass of wine to his lips. 'Why do I make you uneasy, Laura?'

'I don't know.' She smiled weakly. 'You just do.'

'I've always had this effect on women, perhaps that's why I've never married.' It wasn't true, not really; he *did* make them uneasy, but it didn't stop them from wanting to climb into bed with him, and once there the rest was easy. Why would he need to get married at all? He enjoyed his own company more, and besides, a wife or permanent lover would hardly fit in with his work. The thought almost made him want to laugh out loud.

'I had wondered.'

'It's difficult to fit in a worthwhile relationship when I travel so much.'

'Don't you want children?'

'Actually, I've always thought that four would be a nice number – four lusty sons.' It always reassured women if you started talking about children. To want children must mean that you were 'a nice guy', a decent sort, reliable, sincere, etcetera, etcetera. Beautiful.

'I think four is exceeding my limit – I'd rather settle for two.' She gave him a small smile. 'But somehow I don't think that will be happening for a long while – a career and a family don't seem to mix very well.'

'I wouldn't put it out of your mind altogether.'

Her eyes darted to his face. 'Good relationships don't grow on trees,' she responded carefully.

'I know, Laura.' He took another sip of wine. 'But I don't think we're doing too badly so far . . .'

She felt awkward, confused as he took her hand. What was he saying? What did he mean? He kissed the inside of her fingers, the soft flesh of her palm, and somehow the gesture seemed frighteningly suggestive.

'I will give you a weekend in Hungary you will never forget.'

The faintest of smiles tipped the edges of his mouth as he looked back at her. And it would be just as he had said, nothing would be left to chance because he had waited long enough. The timing always had to be right and he had developed a fail-safe means of making his victims eat invariably out of his hand. Women were always victims in some way and generally victims of their husbands or lovers, who were generally mediocre lovers who had not taken either the time or the trouble to find out what their woman wanted, or needed. How many times had he heard the women he had seduced tell him that they did not enjoy sex, that their partner never knew how often they 'faked it', just to get *it* over with as quickly as possible. Until they met him. Sad, really, tragic. Ralf laughed soundlessly, it was a sort of exquisite joke. And then, once they were hooked, there would be conditions. They never seemed to know how or why it had happened, except that they had allowed themselves little caution, little intuition, little moral strength once he had found out their special weakness. He never hurried, and now he was getting bored.

'Why don't we go back to my apartment?'

She nodded.

Ralf signalled to the waiter for the bill. It was almost too easy.

Dan sifted through the papers which the British ambassador, Sir Nigel Howard, had forwarded to him, confidentially, of course. His mouth grew thin as the implications of Howard's covering memo began to sink in and he found himself trying to remember the appropriate quotation which was just on the tip of his tongue, something about stirring up a hornets' nest . . . It did not make pretty reading, though there was very little in the documents which passed over his desk lately that did. But the slaughter of the African elephant, along with the black rhino, and the illegal export of threatened species, was a very hot issue and still showed no real signs of abating, particularly when there was so much money and so many 'respectable' individuals involved in the syndicates which ran the ivory trade and which gleaned so many lovely dollars from the 'white gold' which eventually made its way into the homes of ignorant, thoughtless, but ironically decent people as expensive souvenirs. $150 million a year meant 100,000 rotting carcases. Dan sighed; nothing would stand a hope in hell under that sort of pressure. But the death of the British journalist, Peter Brandt, had created quite a stir, and he supposed that was why Howard had passed him the interesting information his government's own sources had managed to dig up and put together: an American import and export business operating near the Mozambique border, apparently dealing in cheap costume jewellery and African artefacts, but it was only a cover and not a very good one at that, and yet it would probably have passed unnoticed if not for the death of the British Home Secretary's nephew and the subsequent intensive investigations. Dan's eyes travelled over the name again and he frowned – if there was any truth, any tiny speck of truth in what Howard was implying . . .

The airport was not very busy and for once Elizabeth was able to find a trolley on which to put her bags. She pushed back her hair and sighed heavily; she was glad John had been unable to get away and that she had had to bring herself to the airport. She would have hated the awkwardness of saying goodbye when her nerves were in such shreds and a vague note of hysteria not very far away – she was afraid she would cry suddenly, or crumble in his big, open arms. Maybe it would all end then, there, in John's safe embrace, because he would make it all right somehow and the burden and the pressures would be gone. But she was thinking like a fool and a very emotional one at that. There was no going back now, no running to John's arms and hoping the anguish and the longing would miraculously go away. It had been there too long. She was like a child wishing for the moon. Karl would still be in Vienna when she returned and she knew that she would see him again, that they would make love again, that she would not want to leave him – again. That was what she was afraid of, that dreadful longing, that knife edge which was making her choose. And she didn't want to choose, she didn't know how.

Elizabeth lifted her head and realized that she had been moving in the wrong direction. Cursing softly she turned back the way she had come and at the same time her eyes glanced at the airport clock. She was much too early, but she had had no desire to hang around the apartment any longer because she was afraid Karl would call. She had left an appropriate message telling him that she was going away for a short vacation. She sighed, perhaps she should have said nothing at all. She didn't know, she didn't know anything any more. But his face, his beautiful face soared helplessly into her mind and her stomach leapt, her heart knocking crazily, and she wondered what she was doing and why she felt so bewildered and sad. But there was happiness, too, she thought guiltily – a tortured sort of happiness which never left her.

The voice of the check-in clerk snapped her out of her reverie and mechanically she gave up her bags and took her boarding card. She felt free, suddenly, idiotically free, and she walked away into the stark white booking hall, past the endless wall of glass doors, her heels click-clicking on the white marble floor. The smell of coffee beckoned and she moved into the small restaurant/cafeteria, walking through the people at the small sets of tables, unaware of the envious glances and stares of appreciation she received as she made her way to a seat at the back. Her hands lifted up the glossy colourful menu and then put it down again – she only wanted coffee – and as she looked up her eyes met his face and she wondered how long he had been standing there, watching her.

'May I sit down?'

She smiled at Karl in a slow, weary fashion, as if the conflict inside her had ebbed away at last; there was something about the way he looked at her which struck straight at the heart, weakening her resistance and her resolve to be strong, to end it.

'You're running away.' He shook his head. 'Why didn't you *say* something instead of letting me find out through the help?'

'I'm sorry,' she said. 'But I have to go – just for a little while.'

'You can't run from it, Elizabeth – you, of all people, should know that.'

'I can try.'

'I don't want you to go.' And he didn't; he couldn't bear the thought of her being out of reach, away from him.

Her eyes travelled over his face, over the beautifully proportioned features, the soft asking curves of his mouth and the dark grey eyes which always seemed to say so much with such skill that she was made breathless, wanting . . . always.

'There are other considerations.'

'Your husband.'

She didn't want him to talk about John.

'And your son.'

'Please, Karl, not now.'

'When?'

'I don't know when – at this moment I don't know anything.'

He took her hand and she did not try to withdraw it from his grip, she wanted to close her eyes suddenly just to feel the warmth and closeness of his fingers and his palm as they wrapped themselves so surely around her open hand. She found her vision swimming slightly as her gaze moved back to his face.

'You love me, Elizabeth,' he said slowly.
'Yes.'
'What will we do?'
'I don't know,' she said softly. 'I don't know.'
'Will you leave him?'

An image of John soared immediately into her head and she felt her throat tighten.

'You're pushing too hard, Karl.' She sighed heavily. 'Don't, please, don't.'

He looked away from her and she felt his fingers tighten around her hand, as if they would not let her go. Karl swallowed and tried to rid himself of the strange feeling of panic which was growing in his chest; this was not like him, not this fierce desperation, this need. At first he had been able to smile at himself, sure that the longing would not last, would die and fade like all the other times, but his love for Elizabeth had not foundered, it had taken shape, deepened, increased, grown, flourished like some impossible, burgeoning flower. There was no control.

'You don't seem to realize that I can't help myself.'
'Five years ago . . .' she said softly.
'Five years ago I was someone else.'

'Life plays tricks, doesn't it?' Now her voice was sad and he winced inwardly because for the first time in his life he would have given anything to have the power to go back, to turn time on itself and to have her, finally, to himself.

'The tricks are not always funny, Elizabeth.'
'I have to go, Karl.'
'I want to make love to you.'

She laughed and he was glad that she had laughed, glad that he had broken the mood.

'Not here – not now.'
'When you get back.'
She didn't answer.
'Elizabeth?'
'I have to go, Karl.' She stood up and he took her arm. 'Someone will see us,' she said quickly.
'I don't care.'
'Karl – please.'
He let go and looked into her face. 'Let me call you.'
'No.'
He smiled.
'No, Karl.'

They walked the short distance to passport control in silence and as she turned to go he caught her hand again.

'I love you, Elizabeth.'

She smiled, but the smile wrenched at his heart.

'You've said that many times, haven't you, Karl?'

He stiffened just a little as he looked back at her. Oh, yes, he had said it many times to get what he wanted, to get the deed over and done with, to please, to satisfy his woman of the moment. It was, after all, what women wanted to hear. But not this time.

'And only meant it once.'

Her eyes examined him, searching the tanned, handsome face.

'You can't doubt me now?' His voice was almost a whisper.

She shook her head. 'No, Karl – I don't doubt you.' She looked down at his hand still holding hers and she thought that it belonged to him, somehow, that slim, elegant hand which rested so lightly in his palm. 'I have to go.'

'I'll call you.'

But she could not answer him and neither did she look back as she moved away from him and disappeared through the stark whiteness of the sliding doors.

People bustled past him and John's eyes looked beyond them, unseeing. He had accepted the invitation to this first night at the English Theatre because he had had nothing better to do and he did not want to remain in the apartment with only his thoughts for company, but now he regretted his decision because he suddenly felt so alone without Elizabeth, because she should *be here*. He took a sip of his gin and tonic and looked around him and would have smiled if his mood had not made that impossible – another evening with the cream of Viennese society. His glance caught the gaze of a woman standing amongst the gilded crowd, a gaze that was long and soulful, deliberate and practised. He let his eyes travel over her face and her body and was vaguely amused at the way her breasts rose deeply from her dress towards him as if she was telling him that he could have them, have her, later at some self-appointed place and time. She was very attractive, he supposed disinterestedly, but there was too much gold, too much tan, too much of the Viennese love of self to draw him, even if he had been free.

'John!'

He recognized the voice immediately and sighed softly.

'Madeleine – I didn't realize you were here.'

'Obviously, but please, come over and join Olaf and me – we are with some Austrian friends, I am sure they would love to meet you.'

'No, thanks, Madeleine. I'm just going to finish my drink and then I'll get back to my seat – the interval is nearly over.'

'Where's Elizabeth?' she asked, looking around. 'Isn't she here?'

He sighed again. 'In London.'

'Really?' she said. 'I had no idea – and she told me that she so wanted to see *Dangerous Obsession*.' Madeleine chuckled suddenly. 'Adultery is always such an interesting subject . . .'

'It was rather spur-of-the-moment . . .' he said, ignoring her remark and draining his glass.

'Has Christopher gone with her?'

'No – it's only a short trip.'

'How long will she be away?'

'Ten days, two weeks . . .'

'Really.' Her fiercely plucked eyebrows lifted ominously.

'Well, I think I'll get back to my seat.'

Madeleine touched his arm, as if she did not want him to go. 'It's such a small world, isn't it, John?'

He frowned.

'I mean diplomacy –'

'I suppose it is,' he replied.

'Not really extraordinary that Elizabeth should meet an old friend here . . .'

He watched her face intently for a moment and then deliberately switched his gaze to the open doors behind him.

'You know, John, the American . . . Karl Nielsen.'

'Yes, I know, Madeleine.' But he did not know and suddenly the air seemed sickeningly hot.

The bell for the interval sounded, piercing and too harsh.

'I saw them in Do & Co together and later Elizabeth explained that he had had a rather involved affair with one of her closest friends.' She giggled girlishly. 'Such a small world.'

'If you say so.' He was visibly battling against a desire to look away from her because then she would know. 'My best to Olaf, I shall probably see you at the end of the play . . .'

John walked away leaving a no doubt curious Madeleine behind him; he wondered briefly why she was such a cold-blooded bitch and why a nice man like Olaf had found her good enough to marry. It wasn't only a small world, but a strange, strange one. He swallowed slowly as he made his way into the foyer. Karl Nielsen, the smooth, sophisticated American – Nielsen of the film star good looks, Nielsen of the impressively perfect dress, Nielsen of the careful, softly spoken word. Of course there had been no 'involved affair with one of her closest friends', that was only the second lie; Elizabeth had met Nielsen at Heathrow Airport some years before, apparently; but that was obviously the first lie.

His mind swept backwards to the opening reception of the conference when Nielsen had been introduced to them, even then Elizabeth had not been herself, she had tensed like a frightened rabbit and then walked away. He had been puzzled at the time, but put it down to a mood, to tiredness. But never this – not this relentless passion which had risen like some vengeful phoenix from the flames. John felt hot rage and the silent, searing blade of jealousy pierce him and he wondered how he would endure it as a picture of them together, Nielsen and Elizabeth in bed, making love, having sex, slid agonizingly into his head – and his hands, Nielsen's hands touching, invading all the tender, soft places that he loved so much. Nielsen fucking his wife.

6

'Hi...'

Kristina looked up at Sam as he sat down. He was pale and there were dark smudges beneath his eyes.

'Has she gone?'

'Tonight – I'm taking her to the airport.'

'Why do you have to do that?'

He sighed. 'Because I think I should.'

'You don't owe her anything.'

'I know that.'

He looked away from her for a moment, his eyes reaching out beyond the window. Natalie had been good, almost too good, and it unnerved him. She had persuaded him to accompany her with Joanna on a walk on Saturday which had turned out to be a major success with their daughter. On Sunday he had taken her out for lunch – not dinner – he had avoided any chance of that because he was afraid of this sudden goodness in her character, this sudden change which had started blurring all the badness around the edges. What if it all *had* been the coke and the booze? What if he had never really known her before and that now he was sort of meeting her for the first time? He didn't know, he just didn't know.

'I'm sorry, Sam.'

His gaze shifted back to Kristina's face. 'It's okay, I know what you're thinking.'

'She's clever, Sam.'

'I know that too.'

'I'm not being very helpful, am I?'

'Kristina – relax. I am not going to do anything stupid. Okay?'

She looked back at him carefully. 'Okay.'

But she was afraid because she could see his confusion. At the opera he had been agitated, almost uncomfortable, and although the evening had not exactly been a failure, it had not been a success either. The following day she had tried to take a long walk so that she would not have to sit in the suffocating confines of the apartment and endure her mother's acid remarks, but he had picked her up on Saturday evening just as he had said he would. They had not been much better, those few hours, and she had returned home in a despondent mood and gone straight to bed. She had been unable to sleep and had lain in the darkness with her eyes open and tired, wishing and thinking and wondering, torturing herself with images of him with her – walking together, talking about old times, good times (because there must have been some good times) and then naturally she had imagined the high point, 'the finale' and Natalie's studied and brilliant seduction of Sam... The weekend had been a nightmare of garish, painful visions of him and her in various poses of growing closeness and reawakenings. But now, at last, it was over and Natalie was leaving, and yet even as the thought took shape and fled away she knew she was fooling herself, that this was only the beginning, and she wondered whether she had the strength or the hope to continue with him because she did not think she could endure another disappointment. Sam had told her almost everything, but her gut feeling was telling her that beautiful, mind-blowing Natalie was simply determined to get him back no matter what, and that she had plenty of tricks up her sleeve to accomplish just that. But the most powerful weapon she had, and Sam knew it, was the fact that she was the mother of his child. And Sam was soft, a big soft romantic fool. Kristina looked into his face. And yet that foolishness, that softness, was what endeared him to her most of all.

'Shall I order you some more coffee?'

She nodded and he turned away from her to look for a waitress.

'How was she with Joanna?' But she knew what the answer was because Natalie would have left nothing to chance, making absolutely sure that her daughter would be left adoring the mother who lived so far away, out of reach.

'What do you think?' He smiled wryly, once again awed by the skill of his wife, because she *was* still his wife, for better or worse, and she had been amazing with Joanna. By the end of Saturday his daughter seemed only able to say 'Mommy, Mommy, Mommy' and it had brought a lump to his throat. He had taken them to the Prater and the commotion of the fairground where Joanna had ridden on a merry-go-round and Natalie had persuaded him to take a ride on the giant Ferris wheel which he had hated, but during that ride he had caught his wife looking at him and he had felt his stomach lurch as the world turned around him. They had finished the dusky, cold afternoon by taking a walk through one of the leafy narrow lanes away from the fairground and he had thought that if someone had seen them then and not known, they would think that they were happy, a happy united family and what a lucky man he was to have such a lovely daughter and such a lovely wife. And she *had* looked lovely – Natalie – with her cheeks turned feverish red and her eyes bright and clear from the exercise, lean legs striding in the soft calfskin of long leather boots.

'Do you still want to have dinner this evening?' Kristina asked. It had crept up on her, this strong liking for Sam, and inside herself she would only say the word 'liking' because all the uncertainty made her feel helpless and empty and now there was panic jostling in her chest because she might lose him.

'Of course,' he said. 'What time should I pick you up? I'll be back from the airport just after eight.'

'That'll be fine.'

'Good.' And he smiled and her eyes were drawn to his lips and she wondered what he would do if she were to reach out and trace a finger along their soft outline, because that was what she wanted now, to touch Sam, to feel the firm, damp warmth of his skin and his arms circling her naked waist before they made love. Because then, she knew, everything would be all right.

Genevieve slammed the door behind her and walked left, along the grey marble floor to the kitchen. A soft drizzle had softened her hair into tiny curls and a few tenuous strands stuck to her cheeks and would have given an observer the vague impression of an impudent street urchin if only she had smiled, but instead she sighed heavily as she placed two over-loaded carrier bags of shopping on the white kitchen table and then looked at her watch; she called Sophia every day now. At first she had meant to be patient and not intrude too much, but she had been unable to help herself and now it had become a habit which she could not break, and at the very least she had gleaned that Sophia was well, if not happy.

Felix had eventually told her that they could not travel to Munich for Sophia's birthday, which meant that they had missed a family celebration and a reunion after all, so now the longed for visit was postponed again and she wondered if she could bear it.

Genevieve caught a tired breath as she approached the bulging carrier bags and began unpacking the various tedious items which had somehow managed to weigh so heavily. There was an egg stain on the table and a trail of yellow spots which ran away from it, across the floor, to the kitchen draining-board. Her eyes darted to the sink and saw the breakfast things still waiting to be washed, a tower of coffee cups from the night before and the large casserole dish with the grisly remains of the stroganoff she had cooked for dinner and which Felix had declined because his stomach was 'acidic'. She frowned and swallowed hard; Hilde had not been and she had promised. Now there would be dirty ashtrays to clean, hoovering, dusting, replacing the cutlery, cleaning the silver, polishing the coffee tables and making sure there would be clean towels and fresh soap in the cloakrooms . . . All the things that should have been done, she would now have to do because Hilde had let her down again. If only the girl had let her know she would not have attended the meeting at the American Women's Association which had only succeeded in giving her a headache anyway; all those women with their loud, shrill voices bobbing up and down, up and down, as they took it in turns to speak, and then she had hopelessly lost the thread of the whole occasion halfway through because they all seemed to speak so fast and her English had got lost somewhere, somehow along the way.

Genevieve felt the telltale prick of tears as she looked around the kitchen. She also had a five course meal to prepare because she had foolishly promised Felix that this time she would cook herself and impress their guests. What a fool she was! What a fool to rely on the fickle promises of Hilde . . . and the plump, lazy girl knew that she would not have the courage to sack her. She wondered suddenly whether it was only she who suffered at the hands of the hired help – before it had been a sallow-faced Yugoslav who had had a fondness for her napkins, her towels and her husband's Dutch gin. The girl before that had been a good girl except for the long-distance calls she had made to her parents in the Philippines. Felix had sacked her on the spot. Now Hilde, but at least Hilde was honest.

She sighed softly and walked out of the kitchen and up to the first floor to survey what would immediately need to be done. The door to Felix's study stood a little ajar and she pushed it gently open and was startled to find Gunther standing silhouetted against the window.

'Gunther?'

He jumped and the photographs in his hands tumbled to the floor.

'What are you doing?' But one glance told her what Gunther had been doing. Genevieve bent down and picked up one of the photographs. 'Where did you get this?'

Gunther stared at his mother's white face, not wanting to reply.

'If you don't tell me, I shall tell your father.'

He wanted to laugh then because he had found them in one of the drawers of his father's desk.

'This is no laughing matter, Gunther.'

'No, Mother.' But he would not tell her, of course.

'Where did you get them?'

'A friend.'

'What friend?'

'You don't know him.' And she didn't, not really.

Her eyes were drawn back to the ugly photograph: the girl was scantily clad in cheap black underwear. She was sitting down and her body seemed to spread out before her – vast and shiny, a meaty lump of dimpled fattened flesh, but whoever had taken the picture had focused on her breasts which protruded, shelf-like, just beyond the roll of her stomach – blue veined, coarse, slack, held up by the bones of a cheap black basque. There was a spot on her face.

'Do you know this person?'

'No, Mother.'

Soundlessly Genevieve breathed a sigh of relief. 'Does your friend?'

'I suppose so.'

Her eyes reproached him, but then her gaze was drawn irrevocably back to the picture.

'Is she a prostitute?'

'I don't know ... but she looks like a prostitute, doesn't she?'

Genevieve felt herself blushing. She couldn't imagine how, or why anyone would want ... 'That's enough, Gunther.'

'I think you'd better give it back to me now, please, Mother.'

'And I think your father should see it.'

'That's not a good idea.'

'Please keep your opinion to yourself, Gunther.' She swallowed. 'You may return the rest to your ... friend ...' She paused and then added quickly '... and please tell him that his taste in women leaves a great deal to be desired, and perhaps you should also tell him that it might be wise to visit his doctor.' She blushed again and darted a glance at her son up through her eyelashes. 'I think you understand my meaning, Gunther.'

'Oh, yes, Mother.' He smirked.

'As I said, this is no laughing matter.'

'Of course not.' But it was, and he couldn't control the smile that broadened into a grin as he looked back into the wounded face of his mother.

'Gunther!'

'I can't help it.'

'What is wrong with you?!'

'It just seems funny, that's all.' How he longed to be there this evening, when his father came home, to see his face as his mother produced the photograph.

'It is *not* funny.' Genevieve realized that she was trembling and that her son was getting the better of her. There was that old familiar look of scorn, of derision in his face, and her eyes were beginning to smart with frustration and hurt. 'Go to your room, Gunther ...'

'Go to your room ...' he mimicked. '*Gott im Himmel*, Mother, I'm twenty-one years old in a matter of months!' He shook his head quickly, mockingly, as if she were an imbecile.

She made no answer, but struggled with the persistent tears; hating him and hating the hopelessness of everything suddenly, violently. 'You are not . . . a good boy . . .' she stammered and then walked out of the room.

Gunther went on shaking his head for a moment and then his eyes returned to the photographs still clutched in his hand. He was still smiling. But he frowned a little as he surveyed each one with careful, curious scrutiny – they were all pretty dreadful, all tarts, or at least they looked like tarts, certainly not what he would expect of his father because his standards were usually impeccable, but even *he* had discovered that some people had very peculiar leanings, or perversions, or whatever. However, it certainly did not do to let the world know – to be careless – not when it was something gross like *this*, that was downright stupid, if not suicidal. Gunther was suddenly disappointed, he had thought his father would have more taste and above all, would be more careful about such things. He shuffled them back together until they made a reasonably neat pile and then slipped them into the large brown envelope which also housed some magazines, a video and a book. He had already glanced at the magazines, but realized he had seen similar versions before. The video he could see later, but he would take the book, it would probably make rather interesting reading once he had closeted himself in the lavatory. Gunther grinned to himself. But now he didn't really need to bother with secrecy, after all, his mother knew and his father would soon know, and he could hardly afford to make a fuss when his son was only borrowing some of his own literature – what difference could it possibly make? In any case, Father wouldn't dare, he just wouldn't dare.

There was a mist ghosting up from the turf, and the grass was deep green, but covered with dew so that it glittered like a sheet of crystal in the chill of the morning sun. Elizabeth looked towards the horizon as she walked and thought that the white fields could stretch away for ever, only broken by hedges and fences and trees, so that there would be no buildings, no people, nothing to disturb this tranquil time-capsule she had returned to, because it had not changed, this treasured monument to her childhood. Thank God.

Her parents' house sat on a small rise in several acres of land overlooking the undulating fields of Kent and in the distance, beyond the first copse of trees, lay the quiet little castle of Hever, once home of the famed Bullen family and 'Anne of a thousand days', Henry VIII's infamous second wife for whom he had mortgaged his soul – and the soul of England itself – all to get himself a son. Elizabeth lifted her gaze to the clear April sky and wondered, as she had wondered countless times before, what that strange, wilful girl had felt when Henry had tired of her and his disappointment had become rage and then revenge, and how ironic that the surviving child of that union should have been a girl and not the stillborn son. Yet the girl had triumphed ultimately because she had been the great and mighty, the cunning and the wise, Elizabeth I. A bird screeched and Elizabeth followed its path as it twisted against the sky, watched its black flight as it plummeted to earth – a hawk, a hunter.

She sighed. But she was no great and cunning queen, she was a woman of lesser stature and even less strength because Karl was tearing her in two and she was letting him do it with frightening ease. She walked on, her mother's wellington boots pinching her toes, but she did not care, she was only glad that she had come and that she might, finally, clear her mind of all the floss and the cobwebs which seemed to hinder rational thought. And it was easier in one way that Karl was not here, and John. And John. She swallowed and pushed her way past an outgrowth of lifeless blackberry bush and into the lane which would take her to the small Norman church which somone, somewhere had apparently said should be closed and shut up because people did not go to it any more. She went – albeit infrequently and not always to the services – just to look and visit. But she hadn't 'visited' in a long while, over four years, because she hadn't had the courage. There was a breeze and it tore at her hair as she moved up the lane and with a soft gesture of anguish she pulled it free and shook her head so that it fell about her face screening her features from the cold April sun.

There had been something about that first meeting with Karl which now seemed so far off, an instant spark or power surge, an air of tension which had cut them off from all the laughter and conversation of the party, something which had made the breath catch and hold in her throat and her heart pound, pound. She had never forgotten. He had taken her hand then, as if he had known, and they had danced, slowly, and he had not left her, and when he did it was as though she was only half alive.

A sense of bleak sadness spread through her as she turned into the gateway of the church, pushing back the rusting hinges so that they creaked and complained at her touch. But before the leaving, before the sadness, there had been Blake's and seven long, long days of delight when she thought she was discovering not only him, but herself. They had walked through the streets of London like tourists, visited almost every art gallery because he loved art and paintings and sculpture. They had slipped inside Westminster Abbey and walked carefully down the huge, hushed aisles to Poets' Corner and been suitably impressed and awed. They had taken a boat down the Thames to Hampton Court and she had been sure that she had felt the presence of Henry's infamous Anne in a high, cold room. They had gone to the theatre and seen *West Side Story* and she had wanted to cry, but he had smiled and shaken his head and kissed her long, long, long. They had made love every day, every night, through the night, and had been exhausted, lying breathless in each other's embrace. They had loved – hadn't they?

But then her thoughts tumbled over all the other moments after he had gone and stepped so quickly out of her life, all the moments of desolation, desire, anguish, fear even, and hate. She squeezed her eyes tight shut for a brief second as she recalled the one telephone call she had made to Washington and then, finally, to his home, and the sound of the soft woman's voice who had asked who she was. A long time ago, a far-off time which had broken her spirit, if not her heart.

Elizabeth's feet moved down the narrow path between the gravestones, most of them old, old stones with the lettering and numbers weathered and gone, or covered with mouldering lichen and no longer loved. The one she was looking for filled a very small space; they had squeezed it in between a family plot with once neat black railings and a long-dead man who had been born in 1806. Her steps slowed as she came to the well-remembered spot and as her eyes swept over the grave and its headstone she realized that her mother must come often because the folded, drooping flowers could only be a few days old. Susan Victoria, four weeks and six days old, born 9 November 1985. With love.

She had been a tiny little thing, so tiny that Elizabeth had wondered how she had survived the trauma of the birth at all. The contractions had started suddenly and with a vengeance and nothing the doctors or anyone had been able to do could stop Susan being born sixteen weeks early; but she had lived for nearly five weeks. Elizabeth leaned her head back, her mind freezing the memory and the despair and the emptiness: five painful, pitiful weeks when her life had stood still and she had hated Karl. Susan had died of a lung infection, and when her dying was finally over they had released her from the rubber tubing and the glass bottles and the plastic sterile unit and she had held her in her arms for the first time. Pretty baby; poor, pretty baby. But Susan had left her safe, hadn't she? Susan had left her free to start again as if she, the baby, had never existed, as if Karl had never happened, and Elizabeth had despised that secret part of her deep inside which felt only relief because her burden had gone.

Elizabeth took a long shuddering breath and pushed her hands deeper into the pockets of her jacket, suddenly cold. And no one knew, no one except her parents – not John, and certainly not Karl, but how she had wanted to tell him! How she had wanted to pour out all that grief, all that mournful legacy he had left her, but she had not, and even now she was not sure why the words had stayed locked and silent behind her lips. But now he loved her, really loved her and it was as if they were to be given a second chance. She shivered as a vast shadow ran unheeding across the earth and she looked up – a cloud was passing across the face of the sun and in the distance there were more: huge galleons of milky, pearly white, floating across the sky. Soon there would be rain, probably a great deal of rain, but her father had said 'that's what we need'. She frowned softly and her eyes came back to rest on the headstone and then the dying flowers. She had brought nothing, but she would come back later, perhaps tomorrow morning after the rain, when this sadness, this dull refrain had receded a little and she was herself again.

'I thought you had given up smoking?'
Kristina turned to her mother with barely concealed impatience.
'It's just one cigarette, Mother.'
'That's all it needs, or so I am told.'
Kristina snorted softly with contempt and wondered who on earth had *told* her – not Vater Boeckl, or old Tante Lilibet, or any of the other very old, very decrepit favourites of her mother's. Kristina sighed inwardly. She has probably read it in one of my 'decadent magazines'.
'Would you like some wine, Mother?'
'No, thank you.'
'But you like a glass before dinner . . .' She poured herself another glass, willing Sam to come, wondering why he was late. Wondering endlessly. 'It's the German Mosel you like so much.'
'The Bernkastel?'
'Yes.'
'Well . . . just a small glass.'
A glass of wine always softened her mother even though she would protest that she did not drink. Sometimes, sometimes if she had had enough to drink she had even been known to call her *liebling*, and that usually brought a reluctant lump to Kristina's throat.
'He is late.'
'Who?'
'Don't act the fool . . . you know who I mean.'
Kristina swallowed a mouthful of wine and glanced at her mother. 'He said some time after eight.'
'It is almost nine o'clock.'

'I know, Mother.'
'Perhaps he is not coming.'
'Perhaps.'
'You like him very much, don't you?'
'He is a nice man.'
'There are lots of nice men . . .'
Kristina made no answer.
'Is his wife pretty?'
'I've never met her.'
'He will go back to her – mark my words.'
Kristina looked into her wine glass. 'I think sometimes that you like to hurt me, Mother.'
'That is not true.'
Kristina took another mouthful of wine.
'That is not true, Kristina . . .' the old woman repeated. 'But certainly I do not like to see you throwing your affections at a man who will only leave you alone in the end.'
'Why – do you have a crystal ball?'
Her mother shook her head in a knowing fashion and was about to speak again when the doorbell rang and Kristina jumped, but inside her heart leapt. Thank God, thank God, thank God.
Sam stood in the doorway, nose slightly red with the cold night air. He smiled and handed her a superb box of miniature chocolates in apology for his lateness.
She grinned and kissed him lightly on the cheek. 'I'll just get my coat.'
Sam watched her as she flew up the stairs and then his gaze swept through the hall, taking in the dark, old paintings in thick, gilded frames, the fading persian carpet on the floor, the heavy flock wallpaper in deep, depressing burgundy. Like a museum.
'Come in.'
He blinked as Kristina's mother emerged from an open door, one of her ancient hands reaching out carefully so that her body could lean with sureness on the thick stick of oak, its handle curling back into her stiff, bony fist.
'Thank you.' He stepped into the light and warmth of the hall, his eyes travelling over the old, old lady who was looking at him with barely concealed disdain.
'She will not be long . . . I can assure you,' she said with a biting edge of sarcasm. 'She is like this with all her men . . . enthusiastic.'
'Really.' Sam swallowed. What a hag.
'You are American?'

'Yes.'

'Jewish–American.'

Ah. He smiled tightly. 'Yes.'

She nodded, and the nodding seemed to go on and on.

'Well, actually German–Jewish–American . . .' Let her chew on that.

'What part of Germany?'

'Berlin, but then my mother and her husband moved to Vienna.'

'When did they leave Vienna?'

'In 1945 – at least my mother.'

She was staring at him fiercely, her underlip trembling and thrust forward.

'In 1945?' she repeated and there was a trace of disbelief in her voice. '*Where* in 1945?'

'Where – what?'

She shook her head impatiently. 'Where was she living in Vienna?'

'She wasn't living in Vienna by then, she was living in Mauthausen concentration camp – if "living" is what you want to call it.'

The old woman visibly stiffened as the words dropped like stones into that dark, stifling hallway, and now he longed for her to turn away and leave him alone so that this unlooked for interrogation could be over. He sighed softly with relief as he heard Kristina's steps coming down the stairs.

'Mother?' Her heart froze for a moment. 'You should have stayed by the fire, you will catch cold.' How long had she been there? What had she said to Sam . . . what had she said? It was not enough to have his damned lovely wife here, her mother had to have her say as well, and as Kristina's eyes flicked quickly to Sam's face she could imagine what sort of conversation had just passed.

'Will you be late?' the old woman asked finally as Sam helped Kristina into her coat.

'Mother – *please*!'

'I hope you are a good driver.' She turned her withering gaze on Sam.

'Oh, we Jews are pretty much good at everything . . .' He smiled and there was mockery as he looked back at her. '. . . that's what gets us into so much trouble.'

Kristina looked at his face in bewilderment, smiled with an effort at her mother and quickly closed the door on the old woman who still stood watching them.

Once she was sure that their footsteps had disappeared into the night air Augustina limped to the bottom of the stairs, her old head shaking, her hands trembling as she began climbing the wide wooden staircase. For a helpless, fleeting second she wondered whether she would die this night when Kristina was out with this man, enjoying herself, so that she would die alone – after all every day was a distinct possibility and every day she grew old, and older; a shrinking husk. But she had been a beauty once, a real, sought-after beauty, and even after the Emperor had gone – God rest his soul – and the hard years had come there was still fun, still parties and wonderful, wonderful dresses to be worn. But then she had married Klaus and the joy had dwindled just a little, but the richness, the splendour of old Vienna had been there still . . . she was sure.

The old woman caught a sharp, ragged breath as she pulled herself up another step, suddenly aware that her death would make very little difference really to anyone and least of all to herself, because her world, this confused old-young Vienna, disturbed her and no longer made her happy. She had no desire to spend her good days sitting in the Stadtpark with all the other old ones talking about their aching bones and grandchildren she did not have and now probably never *would* have. Or, of course, there were the glories of the past to talk of, always that distant, golden past which still scented the air of the old Habsburg city like a heavy, fading perfume. But it had all changed so much and so painfully that she was no longer sure whether her life was worth living in such a time, such a bewildering, chaotic time where things were no longer black or white, but a jumbled collection of greys. It had been so much easier, before, in the old days when everyone knew their place, when people did not presume to cross boundaries where they did not belong anyway. She thought of Sam.

Augustina reached the top of the staircase and found herself smiling; if she should die tonight, then she would die eating Kristina's miniature sweets from Altmann & Kuhne – at least the Jew had spared no expense and, after all, they were her favourite. She stood for a moment, catching her breath, and then moved slowly into her daughter's bedroom where the long narrow box of chocolates lay provocatively on the silk coverlet. There was a large red ribbon wound around the box, tied into a huge bow. Her eyes drifted covetously across the room. On the bedside table was a pile of magazines. Old Augustina smiled again, it would not be such a bad evening, even if God did decide to take her, but then her eyes lifted quickly to the ceiling in panic, her right hand flying to her chest to make the sign of the cross, as if he might strike her down there and then for her reckless thought. '*Mein Gott . . . mein Gott, nicht nun . . . noch nicht, noch nicht, nicht allein.*'*

*'Not now . . . not yet, not yet – not alone.'

Kristina could not concentrate on the enormous white and gold menu. Her eyes slid back to Sam.

'What did she say?'

'Who?'

'My mother.' She sighed inwardly. 'I know she said *something*, so you might as well tell me.'

'She doesn't seem very keen on me.'

'What did she *say*, Sam?'

He smiled, surprisingly relieved that their attention had switched from Natalie.

'I don't think she approves of my religion.'

'Oh, God . . .'

'It's okay, it's okay.'

'It is *not* okay.' She closed her eyes for a burning moment. 'She's not happy . . .' She struggled to find the right words. 'I disappointed her, I think everything and everyone has disappointed her.' But mostly me. 'So she blames the world.'

'She can't be easy to live with.'

Kristina smiled wryly. 'No.'

'Just you and her?'

'Yes.' She looked at her hands. 'My father died over twenty years ago. I was the only child, and rather unexpected at that, my mother conceived me when she was forty-four.'

'And they wanted a son, of course.'

'Of course.' She smiled with a trace of sadness. 'In those days, like everything else, it was expected – even after the war in a family such as ours.'

'How old is your mother?'

'Eighty-two.'

'A real Viennese.'

'What do you mean?'

'Born in the days of the Empire.'

'It was decaying badly then, Sam.' Almost before their eyes and those of the aging autocratic Emperor Franz Joseph. But the Opera House had still been full night after night; the carriages had still drawn fine ladies and fine gentlemen in their splendid uniforms of the Imperial Army. Husbands and lovers. The golden people had still sat in the elegant café houses beneath the gilding and the candelabra as if their world would last for ever, as if the glittering façade would never crack and crumble because they owned the world and because they were the envy of the world. But that brittle superiority had turned in on itself, finally, had turned the face of the beautiful city into something hard, something cruel. Lost.

'Oh, sure, I know – but to be born into that atmosphere must be quite something – and then to see it all fade and die. It would make anyone bitter.'

'Sam, Sam . . .' She shook her head in gentle exasperation. 'You are too kind.'

'Well, it must be part of it.'

'Part of it, yes.' But only a part.

'You're very hard on your own people,' he said curiously.

'I think it's healthy in light of the past.'

'Yes.' He thought of his mother and felt that familiar turn of his stomach. And the others, and the others, and the others. 'Of course, you're right.'

She searched his face and was touched by the sadness there, wanting to lean across the white and silver of the table and brush the lines from his brow as if they would disappear at her touch. Sam was so nice, so kind – too nice, too kind – because it made him vulnerable, and naturally Natalie knew that only too well. Kristina withdrew her gaze and turned her attention back to the menu, afraid, all at once, of what she might say, because suddenly there was a weight in her heart, heavy with meaning, and she did not want to examine it now, not here in the glare of the crystal lights and Sam's knowing, kindly eyes.

'Budapest is coming alive again, Laura.' Ralf glanced at her as they drove through the centre of the city to the hotel and then he reached quickly for her hand so that he could kiss the tips of her fingers.

'And that means a great deal to you?' It obviously did by his reaction on entering the city.

'It should mean a great deal to most people,' he said a little sharply. What did *she* know of repression, or hunger, or fear?

'But your reaction has a personal edge to it somehow.'

'I don't think so.' He had been born here, a long, long time ago. The rest of Eastern Europe could go to hell, but not Hungary.

He suddenly released her hand and she was startled, not sure how she could have offended him.

They turned a corner and she sat in silence until the Hyatt rose up to greet them, a modern high-rise hotel overlooking the Danube. She felt hurt and ill at ease, but then he leaned towards her as he finished parking the car, kissing her nose and then covering her mouth with his own.

'I'm sorry, I didn't mean to upset you.'

'What did I say?'

'*You* said nothing, it's me – and old memories.' He kissed her again and was relieved to see that she had considerably brightened. It was as well he had brought her now because she was beginning to ask real questions and he wasn't the sort of person to ask such questions and in return give her the sort of reassuring answers she so obviously needed. Moreover, her irritating little probings only served to make him impatient and even angry. He felt himself stiffen because the surges of anger were like white heat. The Americans would say his temper was like a short fuse, but as far as Laura was concerned he had kept it under control and at least all the pretence wouldn't be for much longer now.

'I'm sorry,' she said softly, mistaking his tense expression for sadness.

'Don't be sorry – it was my fault.' He smiled. 'Forget it. Let's book ourselves in, I've arranged everything.' He began to get out of the car. 'You do, of course, still plan to visit your uncle?'

'Yes, I must, otherwise my ambassador may check, he's already been in touch with Uncle Phillip.' She sighed. 'And I can't say I'm exactly thrilled at the prospect – not only is he a bore, but a pompous bore at that. I haven't seen him for nearly seven years.'

'All the more reason to see him, then,' Ralf responded, with relief. 'And I'm sure he will approve of what he sees.' He grinned and she found herself blushing like a schoolgirl. There was something about Ralf's smile which made her a little breathless, made her anxious, suddenly, to get to their room in the hotel and close the door, but he stopped her as they emerged from the underground car park and took her arm, guiding her across the narrow road to the embankment of the river.

'That is the west flank of the Danube . . .' He pointed to the other side of the river. 'And the old capital of Buda. We stand on the east flank and in Pest, marking the edge of the vast Great Plain.'

She followed his gaze, curiously proud, to the old city on the hill with its fairy-tale skyline of church spires.

'Can we walk there?'

'Yes, perhaps tomorrow, across the Chain Bridge, just beyond our hotel,' he said, but then snorted abruptly with disgust.

'What is it?'

'I am looking at the incongruous outline of the Hilton hotel, across the river, on the west side.' He shook his head. 'Yet another American hotel, another monstrosity of glass and concrete, and built around the ruins of a thirteenth-century Dominican monastery. Are these people mad?'

His face had darkened and he stood quite still, the muscles in his neck and jaw bunching and tight, as if the skin might break.

*

The Hyatt was a fabulous hotel, as far as Eastern Bloc standards were concerned, and Laura gasped a little as the glass lift raced higher and higher and the people in the foyer retreated, growing smaller and smaller, almost dizzying as she was taken ever upwards, but once the doors of the lift slid open her attention was taken by the atrium-style interior and the balconies of plants which hung floor after floor, floor after floor, so that the whole atmosphere was that of a rather exotic and exclusive garden.

'What do you think?' Ralf walked into the middle of the suite and spread out his arms.

'It's wonderful...' Her gaze travelled swiftly over the luxurious furniture, fat cushions, bowls of sweets and fruit, a bottle of champagne waiting to be opened on the distinctly ostentatious bar; flowers in cellophane, a huge bunch of red roses.

'Oh, Ralf – really, you shouldn't have.'

'I wanted to, let's leave it at that.'

She looked back at him as he stood in the centre of the beige room, sensing that he was tense and that somehow, once again, she had been the cause of his unease. She crossed to the enormous picture window and stood silently staring out at the grey-brown Danube and the magnificent royal palace which faced her from the hill across the river, wondering why she should suddenly feel so lonely, so out of place.

'Sorry... I'm sorry, Laura,' he whispered. His hands slid up her arms and then ran sleekly across her shoulders and down to slip neatly inside her jacket to cup her breasts. 'Forgive me, Laura. I'm tired, that's all...' He began to kiss her neck, the soft cushion of her earlobe, probing with his tongue until he heard a soft moan escape her lips and she turned to him at last.

'I planned to take you for a cocktail...' he murmured as she pressed against him and despite himself he could feel the beginnings of his own arousal. 'But perhaps I will give you a little foretaste of what is to come.' He pressed her against the glass and lifted her skirts so that his hands could slide more easily across her thighs and then he turned her roughly so that she was looking back across the river, her hands pressed against the window.

'It's a beautiful view, isn't it Laura...?' he breathed. His hands began to slide down, down... Beautiful.'

'Not here, Ralf, not against the glass... please.' It seemed to her then that they would make love in public, against the sky and the palace and the river and the people moving far below in the busy street.

'Ssssh... leave it to me, leave it to me,' his voice said over and over.

'Relax, Laura, relax.' And she would, of course, because he always got his way in the end, time after time. Women obeyed him, women did as they were told. Always.

'Not against the glass . . .' she repeated feebly, but already she knew that it was too late and she cried out in shock and then searing pleasure as his fingers began to play expertly with the soft, sweet flesh as he pulled her thighs apart. Laura bit her lip as she felt him position himself behind her and waited for the pain and the pleasure. And the pleasure – because Ralf did not take her then, he merely continued stroking, stroking, faster, faster until the expectation and the slow delight began to burn its way through every fibre of her being, but still he did not enter because this was a game, played by his rules and his alone, and she was unable to do anything else but give herself to the shuddering rhythm which was building and building, climbing higher and higher, growing larger and larger as if it would engulf her mind as well as her body. Her mouth came open as a scream rose into her throat and Ralf forced her abruptly against the window so that the scream was stifled and gagged and she took her climax alone and in silence, her nose and cheek flattened and turned white, ugly, from the pressure of his hands as he pushed her up against the slick, cold glass.

'Where are my gold cufflinks, Genevieve?' Felix swept his silk handkerchiefs to one side, piled a small mountain of leather and suede boxes on his dresser. 'Genevieve?!'

'Which gold cufflinks?' she asked and stood nervously on the threshold of their bedroom watching him as he rifled through several drawers.

'The ones I bought when I was in New York – the Tiffany set with the tiny ruby stones . . .'

'I'm sorry, Felix, I really don't know – when did you wear them last?'

'Good God, how am I supposed to remember that?!'

'Can't you wear another pair?'

'No!' he hissed. 'The colour of the ruby almost matches exactly the red silk tie I plan to wear this evening.'

'Let me look,' she offered.

He nodded curtly and moved to the mirror as she brushed past him.

'We must be running late.'

'We still have half an hour, Felix.'

'Yes, but we must allow for the traffic and parking, of course.'

'I have allowed for that and we still have half an hour.'

'Good.' He pulled down his jacket sharply and studied his reflection. 'What opera is it again?'

'*Salome.*'

'Well, I hope it has a little more zest than the last production we saw.' He sighed heavily. 'But at least it's Strauss and at least it has a certain shock element.' He was thinking of the last *Salome* production they had seen, perhaps two years ago; the female lead had been exceptionally attractive and had even performed the Dance of the Seven Veils herself rather than use a stand-in; she had had practically nothing on. Felix had secretly been delighted.

'Here are your cufflinks, Felix.' Genevieve picked them out from their tiny purse of kid leather. 'You must have slipped them in the larger purse by mistake . . .'

'Will Gunther be at home this evening?' he asked, ignoring her remark.

'Yes, I think so.'

'Good, I don't like the house lying empty, it is too much of a temptation for burglars.'

Genevieve thought of Sophia because Sophia had always been here and they had never had to worry before. But she sighed softly because her thoughts were turning to her son and the matter of the photographs; she had not told Felix.

'Felix . . .' She felt nervous suddenly, a little foolish.

'Yes, what is it?'

She drew a large breath. 'I found Gunther with some photographs . . .'

'Photographs?' Felix said vaguely, busy with his cufflinks.

'Yes.' She smoothed down her dress unnecessarily. 'They were not nice photographs.'

'What do you mean?' He turned towards her and her eyes wavered beneath his.

'They were of girls – girls with very little on.'

Felix smirked. 'Boys will be boys, my dear, we must expect Gunther to have an interest in such things.' He paused and looked carefully back at her. 'It is healthy, Genevieve, believe me.'

'But surely . . .' she stammered '. . . not like this.' She pulled the photograph out from its hiding place behind a picture of the castle taken in high summer and handed it to her husband. Felix gasped and his cheeks filled with colour as the pasty face of the girl stared back at him.

'Where did he get this?' he said at last and Genevieve was relieved to note that he seemed as shocked as she was.

'He was standing in your study when I discovered him.'

'What was he doing there?' Felix asked carefully.

'I don't know, but he was standing by the window, I presume because of the light.' She looked down at her hands. 'There were more, Felix – most of them like *this*.' She emphasized the word 'this' as if it were something distasteful, untouchable.

'Of course, I shall talk to him.' Felix closed his eyes for an agonizing moment. It was Doris. He had had a brief fling with her, the last time, perhaps two months ago. She was a catering assistant with a local company, Viktors, and he had spotted her large bulk emerging from the kitchen as he was passing through the hall at one of their friends' parties; Doris had simply smiled and he had smiled back. She was a particularly willing girl, willing almost to do anything he asked of her, including posing for photographs. She thought he was in love with her, the poor girl had even written him severely passionate love letters, but the letters were often a bright spot in a dull day. He realized that he was probably one of the few men who would take notice of such a creature, but that really did not matter very much, she was grateful for his attention, he was doing her a service. Of course, she was not like Eva, but Doris had a crude charm of her own – like a naughty secret, something bad for you which you should not touch, something socially unacceptable which made their sex all the more exciting. And she was such a very willing girl. He did not call her often, or even see her very much, but she was always *there*. And now Gunther knew. Felix swore soundlessly and wondered if the gods on high were trying to tell him something.

But the telephone rang and snapped his thoughts and his cursing.

'I'll go, Felix,' Genevieve said, thankful to get away.

It was Sophia.

'My darling! What a surprise . . . but are you well?' Immediately she thought there must be something wrong because her daughter was not ringing at their scheduled time.

'Yes, of course, of course . . .' But Sophia paused then.

'What is it, Sophia?' Genevieve asked sharply. 'Tell me, there is something wrong, isn't there?'

'No, no, Mama – nothing wrong.' She paused again. 'I've been offered a scholarship.'

'But that's wonderful.'

'Only three of us were accepted.'

'You must be so pleased . . .'

'And it involves travel, Mama . . .'

'Travel,' she repeated uselessly. 'Where?'

'To the United States.'

Genevieve became very still. 'When, Sophia?'

'September.'

'As soon as that,' she said thickly.

'It's only for a year,' Sophia said. 'Just a year . . . and Mama, they will give me five thousand dollars to help with expenses, and Uncle Oskar has promised to act as my sponsor for whatever else I may need.'

Genevieve made no answer, afraid to speak. Munich was bad enough, but America. It seemed like the other end of the world.

'Do you want to speak to your father?' Genevieve asked, suddenly aware of Felix breathing over her shoulder.

'No . . . no, you tell him, Mama,' Sophia said quickly.

'Yes . . .' she stammered. 'Of course.'

'But I will call you tomorrow, in the morning, for a long talk,' she said softly. 'Try and be pleased for me.'

'I do not need to try,' Genevieve lied. 'And I am very, very proud.'

'Thank you,' she said slowly. 'I have to go now, I'm seeing a girlfriend to celebrate and I'm already late.'

'Of course, of course.'

'And, Mama . . .'

'Yes?'

'I love you.'

And she was gone.

For a long moment Genevieve stood by the telephone and then slowly she replaced the receiver and turned to her husband.

'Sophia's been offered a scholarship.'

'I gathered it was something of that nature.' Glad, at least, that his wife's attention had been diverted from the photograph of Doris. 'I suppose I am meant to be pleased.'

'She has done very well.'

'It will all be a waste of time,' he said irritably. 'Even if I decide to let her go she will only meet the wrong man and make a mess of her life.'

'She has already accepted, Felix.'

'But she has no money.'

'She will receive money from the scholarship.'

'Not enough, I'm sure.'

'Oskar has offered to act as her sponsor.'

'I see.' He stared back at her white face and then his mouth moved into a smile. 'Well, at least he is showing an interest, so there will be a substantial tie between them.'

Genevieve made no answer because she knew that it was useless to argue, and besides she felt so weary suddenly that his voice began to grow small and distant as she thought of Sophia and America and the miles which would stretch and stretch dividing them even further. She rubbed her forehead as the headache which had been lurking all day seemed to grow big and cruel all at once. An ache climbed into her throat and her eyes brimmed because she had an overwhelming desire to weep and weep and weep. It was happening too much, the tears, almost every day – and the little fears without foundation, and the apprehension which seemed to sit in her stomach like cold, sour dread.

'That was a wonderful meal,' Kristina said as Sam signed the bill. 'Thank you.'

'You deserved it.'

'I'd ask you to come back to my apartment for some coffee, but my mother . . .'

'Actually, I was going to ask you back to mine.'

She smiled back at him, relief swimming through her.

They were the last to leave the restaurant, but the streets were still busy as they stepped out on to a flagstoned path.

'Tourists,' Sam remarked.

'Vienna will be full of them very soon.'

'Well, it's a beautiful city.'

'Yes it is,' she said almost to herself; but somehow she had always had a sort of love-hate relationship with the city. She wondered fleetingly whether it was simply the past, her own past which followed her like some unwelcome shadow.

'Hey . . . smile!' Sam said and put his arm around her shoulder. 'We can walk from here and when we get back I will make you the most delicious coffee you have ever had the pleasure to drink!'

She leaned against him as they walked down the street and she thought that this was the first time, in a very long while, that she had felt so comfortable with a man, that it felt right, that it should continue and go on and on. But she pressed the thought down because the future promised nothing, not now, not yet.

Sam's apartment was wide and high, one wall soaring upwards, the great white space filled by an enormous map of the world. There were several bookcases and an old mahogany dining table at one end of the room which, she knew instinctively, was rarely used. A small terrace grew from this main room, but it was empty of any ornament and what view there might have been was obscured by the high grey sides of metal from the sloping roof. A few magazines and some mail lay across an octagonal glass coffee table, along with a child's beaker, a bib and a glove puppet of a green crocodile with one of its eyes missing. It was quite easy to see that there was no soft, comforting touch here, no real woman's touch to take away the edges from this wide, spartan room. But Sam's den was warm and cosy, the two sofas well worn but half filled with deep, plump cushions. There were more books here, lining the walls, and she wondered when he found the time to read them. A model aeroplane stood on a narrow pedestal in the corner.

'I'm afraid I haven't made the best of this place,' Sam said.

'I don't suppose you've had the time.'

'Or the inclination,' he said with honesty. 'Would you prefer coffee or perhaps a liqueur?'

'A cognac would be lovely – after the delicious coffee you promised to make me.'

'Coming right up.' He disappeared from the doorway and she walked over to the fireplace and the framed photographs standing on the mantelshelf. Two were of his daughter at various stages, a delightful, pretty child with dark hair and unusual eyes – green. They were not Sam's eyes, she realized instantly and with a tiny shrinking, no doubt Natalie's; she stared at the eyes for a long moment and then slowly put the picture down. The other photograph was of his parents, with a separate miniature of his mother slipped into the thick silver fame.

'My family . . .' Sam said, walking into the room bearing a tray.

'Very nice.'

'I think so.' He put the tray down and began pouring hot steaming coffee into two mugs. 'But my parents are dead. Mom died a few years back and my father followed only a few months later.'

'Must have been rather a shock – the two, happening so close.'

'It was.' He smiled gently. 'But I think of them, particularly my Mom, a great deal; she was that sort of person.'

'So she never met Joanna.'

'No,' he sighed. 'But she did meet Natalie.'

'And . . .'

'My mother said an awful lot with her eyes . . . do you know what I mean? One glance, one little glance could say much more than "I don't like her".' He looked at the face in the photograph. 'I didn't take any notice – I thought I was in love, really in love for the first time in my life.'

'Well, as the saying goes, we all make mistakes.' And it was a *mistake*, Sam, she said silently.

He nodded and as she looked back at him she wondered how she was going to bridge the gulf of this polite conversation and the coffee tray which separated them. It seemed very important to her then that their relationship should now develop in a physical way. She felt the need to draw closer to Sam and gain his confidence in every respect because every instinct told her that was one of Natalie's winning cards – her body, sex – the way she had kept such a hold over Sam for so long. Like a lamb to the slaughter. What would she do when she was old, when the beauty, the sensuality, withered and became something sad, something obscene? Kristina crushed the thought because it bore too many painful, disquieting echoes of the life she led – had led, before Sam. And if Sam were to make a choice, the wrong choice . . . what then? What would there be for her any longer, because she was afraid that the day would come when she would be reduced to the attentions of a fat Greek diplomat who made passes at conference attendants. But not that, never that, she had some pride. She was simply afraid of being alone, of the future, alone. I am not a very brave person, she thought with a touch of shame.

'The plane,' she said quickly, 'is it a hobby?'

'Since I was a small boy.'

'Do you have many?' She brought the glass of cognac to her lips and let the warmth sink slowly into her belly, driving the flutterings of cold despair slowly away.

'I have a few hanging in my study, but most of them are still packed away. Would you like to see what I have?'

'Yes, very much.'

The study was just as she had imagined, simple but functional – except for the planes which were hung by almost invisible pieces of nylon thread from the ceiling.

'I'm afraid my knowledge of planes is rather limited.'

'Well, if you really want to know . . .'

'Please, Sam.' And she didn't really, but she did want him to relax and wind down, and wind down enough for her to break through that barrier of respectability which still lay between them.

'Do you want to know the story behind this one?' he said brightly and pointed upwards, turning his face towards her.

'All right, Sam.'

'It's a B25 North American Mitchell – the first aircraft to make a very perilous flight from a carrier to bomb Japan . . .' He looked back at her and smiled and she nodded in response. Reassured, Sam continued, 'You might recognize this one, the Messerschmidt 109E, it took part in the Battle of Britain . . . and this little beauty is almost my favourite, the Vickers Supermarine Spitfire Mark One, a bit limited in performance, but gave excellent service at a bad time . . .' He started to speak again, his gaze fixed on the plane in question, but then abruptly he turned towards her.

'You're just being polite, you don't really want me to talk, right?'

'No, no – really.' But then she smiled and felt a small giggle tickling her throat. 'Oh, Sam . . .'

'What is it?'

He has a nice face, she thought, not an entirely handsome face, but intelligent, peaceful, young, as if there was something yet in him that remained unspoilt.

'I don't want you to talk, Sam, I want you to make love to me.'

He stood very still and then cleared his throat as if there was something large and uncomfortable there, but then his mouth took over and he was smiling.

'Really?'

'Really.'

'I thought men were supposed to say that sort of thing?'

'Well, I think, perhaps, you are a little out of practice.'

He blushed. 'How can you tell?'

'Oh, Sam . . .' She sighed softly.

'I'm talking too much, aren't I?'

She nodded.

Their eyes locked and there was a peculiar sensation in his stomach as his gaze became fixed on her face and he wondered why he had not noticed how lovely her red, red mouth was, and her skin, lovely dusky skin which would be darker underneath, dark hair, dark nipples . . . He blushed again.

'My room is on the other side of the apartment leading off one side of the balcony, well away from Joanna . . .' And he had put himself there deliberately, hopefully, but he didn't want to tell her that.

She lay in the cool sheets, eyes fixed on the ceiling, waiting for Sam. Kristina turned her head so that she could look at the night sky through the glass door of the balcony. There were no stars to be seen in the heavens, only a rolling mass of blackened clouds which would be gone by morning. There was no moon. Sam was taking too long and she was beginning to feel nervous and the ardour was slipping, slipping away, but then, finally, he was standing in the shaft of light from the hallway, a blue towelling bathrobe tied loosely about his waist. She said nothing as he removed it and placed it across a chair, nor did she speak as he climbed into bed. She swallowed slowly. This was something she had wanted, something she was sure would work well for them both, but now, suddenly, she had no idea what to do, what expression to wear, or whether she should move towards him or remain still. Her instincts seemed dead and she thought inevitably of Natalie, because Natalie would have known what to do.

'Are you okay?' Sam's voice whispered.

'Fine,' she lied.

'Shall I leave the light on?'

Oh, Sam, Sam.

'Yes.' She wanted to see him, wanted to know that it was him and not one of the other, empty embraces she had so often received in the past. She thought of Manolo; he had used her body, but he had promised her the moon, the stars and the sun, he had even said that he would divorce his wife and she had believed him. Liar, liar, liar. And what of his wife? What of the woman who waited at home? Probably an ordinary woman, probably a nice woman who had hopes and dreams of her own. Kristina shivered a little and wondered at herself, wondered why she had never thought of that woman, because she had been too busy thinking about herself. What a sad mess she made of everything.

'What is it?' Sam asked gently.

She squeezed her eyes tight shut for a moment. 'I don't know . . . but it's nothing to do with you.'

He looked down into her face, not liking the sadness there, wanting to wipe it, push it away.

'I love your mouth, Kristina. Has anyone told you that you have a lovely mouth?'

Suddenly she wanted to cry because he was being kind and she didn't want him to be kind, didn't want him to see the fat tears coursing down her cheeks because this was not how she had planned her monumental, unforgettable seduction of Sam.

'Hey, it's okay . . .' He began stroking her hair as if she were a child. 'It's okay.'

And then Sam kissed her. It was a hesitant kiss to begin with, then exploratory as her lips parted, no longer tense, and their tongues touched with more and more determination, twisting, probing. The long, long seconds turned into minutes as he kissed her again and again until he had her drawing quick, inadequate breaths and soft, soft whimpers, and her arms came up, slowly, possessively to crush him against her. She was aware of his hands – warm, seeking hands tracing the outline of her shoulder, her breast, the roundness of her belly. She was aware of utter delight as her nipples rose to his lips and her hands dug and pulled at his hair because she was not sure she could bear it. She was aware of his mouth and his kisses travelling down the damp perfumed skin of her body to the soft fur at the apex of her thighs. And she was aware of his tongue, like a spear, piercing, paralysing so that her pelvis jerked up towards him, to take her. Because it was Sam, only Sam, and all the other brutal, empty and desperate unions began to retreat and fade until they were no longer there at all.

Christopher was sitting up in bed as John walked into his room.

'It's late, Chris, you're supposed to be asleep,' he said gently. 'What's up?'

'Where's Mummy?'

John swallowed. 'In England.'

'But why isn't she here?'

'You know why, we've been through this before, she needed a little holiday.'

'But I always go with her – home, to Granma and Grandpapa.'

'You have school now – even if it is only in the mornings.'

The little boy frowned and then looked up at his father.

'I don't like it when she's not here.'

'Neither do I.' John sat down. 'Would you like a story?'

'When is she coming back?' he said, brushing his father's question aside.

'Next week, you know that too.'

'Can we meet her at the airport?'

'I don't know, yet,' John sighed. 'But we can try.'

'I want to.'

'We'll see, Chris.'

'When you say "we'll see", that means no.'

His son was getting too smart for his own good, but at this stage John didn't even know what *day* Elizabeth was flying back, let alone what flight.

'Not always.'

'Nearly always.'

There was silence again and John found himself scrutinizing the small, vital face which, for him, was neither like Elizabeth nor himself, although she constantly said that he was the image of his father. John's eyebrows drew together in a frown; like me? He couldn't see himself in Christopher at all. And Elizabeth loved their son, there was no doubt of that. And he's like me. John closed his eyes for a fleeting, pain-filled moment.

'Daddy?'

John's eyes flew open. 'Yes?'

'What's the matter?'

'Nothing, Chris.'

'You don't smile very much now.'

'Don't I?'

'No.'

'I'm working very hard at the conference.' That much was true. 'And, like you, I miss your mother.'

'When I speak to her next I shall tell her to come back very soon.'

John smiled. 'Yes, perhaps that will do the trick.' Because if *he* asked her to come back it would have no effect at all, as he seemed unable to touch any inner chord that sounded right with his wife. But Christopher was her Achilles' heel, she could not leave him for long, and that was his only safeguard; his son. 'Do you want that story now?'

Christopher looked into his father's face, examining him too sharply so that John found himself visibly battling to look away from him. And he *is* like me, he thought with a trace of wonder; I have seen that confusion, that touch of bewilderment when I have looked back at my own reflection in a mirror, and automatically his hand reached out to touch the perfect skin and the boyish jawline which was his own.

'Jason and the Argonauts, please . . .'

John nodded and picked up the large red and gold book lying on the bedside table. He always liked this part, reading his son a story, but he blinked suddenly as realization began to filter through, burning, like biting acid rain: Nielsen would take all this away from him – not only his wife, but his son, because Elizabeth would never be parted from Christopher. His guts seemed to twist; there would be no joy then, no purpose, without them. A shadow dimmed his eyes as he looked back at his son. No joy.

7

'The final document *must* state that the ultimate goal is to eliminate the use of all CFCs, not just fifty per cent as some countries would prefer...' Dan said aloud. He was alone in the sitting room of his apartment surrounded by a sea of papers, and a headache threatened. The talks were costing thousands of dollars per day and now it was nearly May and very little *real* agreement had been reached among the 124. Oh, sure, they all *recognized* the need for a new international authority with new powers, new standards *and* legal backing, but at the moment that was as far as it went. Someone had even called the proposal of such a body 'showboat diplomacy'. Idiot. And in March the European Community governments had agreed to outlaw CFCs by the end of 1999 – too late. Dan took a gulp of the Scotch waiting at his elbow. He was trying to press for 1995 latest; as he had said during his speech at the Hofburg yesterday morning, companies in Sweden had been obliged by law to stop using the damned chemicals by 1994 and already they had proved remarkably ingenious in discovering substitutes. There had been a few agreeable mutterings, a few nods of the head, but that was it. If, by the end of July, no real progress had been made, the whole thing would be a mockery, a tiger with no teeth... Of course, it all came down to money, as Felix Dhoryány constantly reminded him, which came back to a worldwide environmental fund. But even his own government was wary of moves to adopt broad new spending programmes or create new institutions for protecting the environment, just like the Brits. Dan sighed; it was, he supposed, an achievement to get the 124 nations here at all and at least they were *talking*, which was something. And they did have another three months, another three months of bickering and sidestepping until the last two weeks and then they would all probably pull themselves together and pull something out of the hat because the world was watching and 'the world' expected their immediate governments to really *do* something about the poisoning of the planet and not just use the talks as a vote-catching exercise.

Dan took another mouthful of Scotch and switched his attention to the other matter which awaited. He had heard nothing further from Sir Nigel Howard, and indeed, would have been surprised if the British ambassador had involved himself any more. Sir Nigel had given him enough information to make his own inquiries, which was what was intended, and the picture which had begun to take shape was not a pretty one. To all intents and purposes there was an all-out ban on the ivory trade, but pockets of poaching were still going on and the stockpile of tusks which had accumulated before the ban was finding its way into the markets of China and the Middle East; the trade was dying, but it was not dead yet. The American import and export business in Mtwara near the Mozambique border which Sir Nigel had drawn his attention to not only traded in ivory, but also black rhino horn, which apparently the Yemenis valued highly for dagger handles, and other phallic-conscious males prized as a sexual stimulant . . . Dan shook his head sadly and wondered at their sanity. This same company also dealt in a smaller way with the illegal export of protected species like the pygmy chimpanzee, the bushy-tailed mongoose and Hunter's antelope, as well as the skins of the leopard, the cheetah and the crocodile. Dan's eyebrows drew together in a sad frown . . . shoes, handbags, briefcases – and not forgetting the status symbol of the fur coat. He'd seen a brilliant advertisement somewhere once which had summed it up for him rather well – a beautiful model was walking along a catwalk languidly trailing a fur coat behind her, but the coat had been 'crying', crying tears of blood and the caption had said something like: 'It takes a dozen dumb animals to make this coat, but only one to wear it . . .' Shocking, upsetting, but nevertheless absolutely brilliant.

Judy had managed to obtain a copy of the ad from the agency concerned, Yellow Hammer, and had had it framed to hang over her desk. She had been ill, dying even then, and her interest in conservation had become a handhold, a last passionate grip on life, as if she would pour every last drop of feeling, power, love into this, her final endeavour. Dan stared out beyond the window at the darkness, the quiet sky, the black roofs of old Vienna; missing her, always missing her.

His gaze drifted slowly back to the papers, the documents, the information and the distasteful investigations which the British ambassador had kindly slipped his way. If it was proved beyond reasonable doubt that the man in his delegation knew that this company in which he was ostensibly a 'sleeping partner' was trading illegally behind a legal façade then he would not only fire him, but bring a legal action against him and ruin his career. Dan lifted his eyes to heaven in exasperation, knowing that there was no way he could allow such a scandal to surface. He smiled humourlessly – that one of the US delegates to major talks on the environment was a trader in ivory and protected species, there would be hell to pay! He had no choice but to keep it well under wraps. But he could still ruin his career – silently and with infinite skill. Nielsen wouldn't know what hit him. An image of Karl slid into his mind and he supposed, if it had had to be anyone, Nielsen fitted the bill rather well somehow – there was something a little clinical about his attitude to life, unemotional, as if he was able to pass over life's tragedies without knowing they existed. As if his handsome, unlined face had never felt deep pain or known insecurity, or anguish, or loss.

Dan frowned; there was something else, too, but the details had to be put together and a picture formed, something the security people had picked up when he had put them on to Nielsen. He wondered if Howard had any idea and that was why he was being so damned helpful. After all, it could hardly be good news to find out that there was every indication to suggest that the wife of a top British delegate in Vienna was having an affair with a US diplomat who was also a suspected ivory trader. Dan closed his eyes in exasperated fury.

'Jeeesus Christ...' he swore at the empty room. And he liked John Thornton very much – an excellent diplomat with a fine reputation, and a beautiful wife. He found it difficult to believe of Elizabeth, that someone of her integrity and intelligence would be so easily seduced by someone as obvious as Karl Nielsen, but then he chided himself gently: when did integrity and intelligence have anything to do with something as complicated as love or infatuation? Poor John, poor bastard. Did he know? If he did, he would hardly know about Nielsen's suspected connection with ivory, which would turn another knife in the wound. Dan shook his head with misgiving; John wanted Washington and from what he had heard there was a good chance of him getting it, but not if this came out, not if the world discovered that his wife was having an affair with a disgraced US diplomat and a trader in something as sick as ivory; the consequences would be ruinous, he could just imagine the hot, hot headlines in the newspapers, and John's career would never recover. There would definitely be no Washington for him, and in all probability he would be pushed away, as far out of sight as possible so that people and the world could forget he existed. Sir Nigel had left him holding a potential time bomb. Dan swallowed. But perhaps it wasn't a time bomb at all, maybe there was a mistake somewhere along the line. He frowned, but he knew everything was pointing in that direction and only a fool could think otherwise, and once the final part of the investigation was placed neatly on his desk it would just be a matter of confirming and tying up all the details into a readable report and sending it on to Washington. He sighed heavily. Maybe, just maybe, he could make sure that it didn't get that far. For John Thornton's sake, he hoped to God that it didn't.

Ralf knew that the video camera had worked, but he always liked to be sure because generally he wouldn't be allowed another opportunity. Only one woman had cooperated more than once and that had been an American, Suzanna, a lonely, unattractive divorcee who had needed him more than she did her job. She had driven him crazy in the end and he had persuaded her, finally, to defect because she had been little use anyway, and she had agreed when he assured her that Czechoslovakia was where his 'other' base was. Ralf laughed soundlessly, he didn't really have 'a base' anywhere, at least not for long, and even if he had, one of the last places on earth he would have chosen would be the grey, haunted Czech Republic, but he had 'friends' there and the friends were naturally very useful, particularly when it had come to the problem of Suzanna. There had been some little scandal, but it had died down fairly quickly and he had arranged for her to live in Ostrava in the eastern part of the country, with a job working in a clothes factory where she would live and die and hopefully be forgotten. He had never seen her again.

Ralf clipped the mirror back over the hole in the wall where the camera was fitted – the glass was two-way, of course, and it had not failed him yet. He used this room in the Hyatt infrequently, but one of the assistant managers in the hotel was a colleague and always made sure that everything was in working order. He was sure that last night he had got some fairly lively shots, but Laura had not been as cooperative as he had hoped, there had been a sullenness about her which had made things difficult and he had had to use all his efforts of persuasion to make her do as he wished. Tonight would be different, he had something which he could slip into a drink and that would make her much more pliable; there was no question of it sending her to sleep, he didn't want that, he needed her awake, needed her to respond in a totally realistic manner, so that there would be no mistake.

Ralf fished in his pocket for a handkerchief to wipe the telltale finger marks from the mirror and as he did so the palms of his hands lay flat against the glass for a moment, the network of lines which were supposed to tell the past, the present and the future spread wide and turned a livid red. He blinked as memory shook him and then slowly turned first one hand and then the other over, scrutinizing them very carefully; they were big hands, large hands, the fingers rising out of the square palms seeming to resemble small tree trunks. Like his father.

A garish, ugly picture of the man he had loved and then hated lying mangled in an alleyway burst across his brain: his father lying in the blood and the glass and the urine and the excrement, the stench which had filled his nostrils and his mouth like a noxious, fetid gas until his own belly revolted and he had vomited in the gutter beside the body, amongst the tears and the rain and the thin, filthy laughter of the whores in the nightclub. Hamburg, a long time ago. But he had never meant to kill him, it was a mistake, he had just lost control.

Ralf looked at his hands again and brought them up close to his face so that he could smell them, as if there was still that stench, that sickening, impossible-to-forget smell that always seemed to cling to his skin. He wiped them quickly, abruptly, on his trousers and then walked into the bathroom, and in the back of his mind he vaguely knew why he did what he did, but then the blackness, the saving blackness would come down over all of it and he would be left alone, in peace for a year, maybe two or three if he was lucky, before the remembering would come back.

The sound of the water running into the basin broke through his thoughts, and anger like scalding heat took control of his fingers so that the soap in his hands shot out into the white enamel bowl, hitting one side and then another, sliding with incredible and surprising speed until it slowed, rolling softly, rhythmically until it came to a gentle halt. Ralf shook his head. He would take a break soon, go back to Greece, see Georgios, rest up and walk through the hills and down to the tiny beach where the water was so clear that each grain of sand was visible, each grain, each minuscule speck as if some awesomely inspired creature had placed them there, each one, with gentle, loving hands. But Ralf did not believe in God, any god.

He picked up a towel and began to dry his hands. Laura would be back from having lunch with her uncle at his residence shortly and at least he had managed to disengage himself from the invitation by pleading a stomach upset which would miraculously be cleared up by dinner this evening. He had insisted that she go to lunch despite her protests because that was part of the deal with her ambassador – part of the reason she was allowed to be in Hungary at all – and if she did not see her uncle she would only find herself 'in trouble' and that would spoil everything; they would check up, they always did. Ralf smiled to himself. After all, there would be trouble enough later for Laura after her performance tonight and once she'd been given the grim pleasure of seeing this, his latest, most creative, production.

The lights were dim. Dim. She stretched her arms up over her head and strained her body luxuriously. Laura could not see Ralf, he had disappeared and she thought she was alone in the room because the quiet was heavy, almost torpid, so that she wanted to sleep. But all at once her mouth tilted upwards as if she were remembering something funny, something amusing which had surfaced from her memory, and she lay across the bed, naked, with her eyes half closed, smiling, smiling and languishing in the strange, dreamlike state which seemed to lie oppressively over everything so that to move an arm, a leg, or raise her head seemed to take the greatest of efforts. But then there was his mouth on her mouth, his hands clasping her hands, his thighs lying against her thighs. She felt him move abruptly so that she was lying alone again, but she could smell him, beautiful heady smell; he was behind her and she was amazed at the intensity of the smell as if her senses had suddenly been heightened and every sound, every touch had the potential to drive her slowly, gloriously out of her mind. He was speaking to her: very low, very husky – bad things, things that made her head swim, and she turned to find him because he was teasing her and she was confronted by his kneeling torso, massive, breathtaking, and her mouth went dry. But she started to giggle as he pushed her back, twisting her body expertly so that she was lying on her stomach and he was leaning over her, parting her thighs, and she thought she heard him laugh, thought she heard him call out, but she was never sure. Only when she was suddenly taken, when she was filled, did she lift her head and find herself staring back at her own reflection in the mirror. And she saw Ralf, felt Ralf's mouth on her mouth, but he was sitting beneath her on the floor, his hands thrust under her – the other man, the man who sat astride her was fat and bearded, grinning, a gap in his teeth so that blackness showed through . . . but when she blinked, when she squeezed her eyes tight shut and opened them again he had gone and there was only relief and laughter and a sudden hunger for the pleasure, black frenzied pleasure which went on and on and on making her body shudder and jerk, her throat to open, begging; making her scream . . . 'Oh God, oh God, oh God . . .'

The telephone seemed to ring and ring, a shrill empty blast against his ear, but Karl waited patiently until the receiver was picked up and a woman's voice answered. But it wasn't *her* voice.

'Could I speak to Elizabeth, please?' Instantly he was sweating and he hated himself. He could hear the sound of someone's feet, someone calling and then more feet drawing closer and closer.

'Hello.'

'Elizabeth.'

'How did you get my number?'

'I told your son's nurse that it was urgent and that you were expecting me to call.'

'This is my parents' home, Karl.'

'I know.' He swallowed. 'I wanted to speak to you.' No, he *needed* to speak to her.

'What is it?' she asked gently.

'It's crazy . . . crazy . . . but I just wanted to hear your voice . . .' And say your name, out loud, your name.

'Karl, Karl . . .'

'I know, it *is* crazy, but I can't help myself.' He shifted restlessly, pressing his jaw against the mouthpiece of the telephone, wondering if he was going mad. 'When are you coming back?'

'Next week.'

'When, next week?'

'I'm not sure, I haven't decided.'

'Let me meet you.'

He heard her sigh.

'No, Karl.'

'Why?' he demanded. 'Why, Elizabeth?'

'Don't push so hard, Karl, you haven't the right.'

The words were said almost in a whisper, but he was surprised at the way his heart jumped, the way his hand tightened around the white receiver so that the knuckles showed through as if the skin might break.

'Okay, okay.'

'I'll call you when I've seen my husband and my son.'

'They come first . . .' That was a dumb thing to say – stupid, careless, but he couldn't call it back.

'Yes, Karl, they come first and you can't expect anything else.'

'I know – and I'm sorry, I shouldn't have said that.' He inhaled deeply. 'I can't stop thinking about you, that's all. I have to see you . . . you understand, don't you, you know what I'm feeling, don't you?'

There was an odd, unsettling kind of silence then, and for a tense, unhappy moment he thought that she would not answer him, that something had changed for her.

'Yes.'

'And you will come to me when you can, when you get back?'

'Yes.'

'I will try and not push, I promise, and I will also try and keep this great big mouth of mine under control because it seems to be running away all by itself.' He forced the lightness into his words because there was something about this space between them which was strangely fragile, as if by taking this step away from him she was able to examine him carefully and in perspective, turning him over and over in her hand as if he was an object to be considered, valued, accepted or rejected. And he did not like that, it made him afraid. Karl felt irritation begin to bite because if she was close, if she was here, he would not allow her to keep him at arm's length and he would quash all the doubts, all the uncertainty by just holding her. He was sure of that much, and so was she, wasn't that why she had gone?

'I think I'd better go now, Karl.'

'Okay. I'll see you when you get back.' He shook his head with exasperation. 'Won't I?' For Chrissakes what was happening to him?

'Yes.'

'And you'll call me?'

'Yes.'

'Sorry, sorry . . . I'm just not used to this.'

'I know.'

He sighed heavily, helplessly. 'Why am I saying the wrong things now, when you're not here, when I can't put them right?' He gritted his teeth. 'I love you.' But he wondered if that would ever be enough.

There was silence and he felt the panic crawling closer again.

'And I you . . .'

He closed his eyes and a painfully vivid picture of her soared into his mind and he wanted to reach out and touch and take and take. Elizabeth.

The click of the receiver being put down made him blink and he pushed a weary hand through his hair as his eyes strayed, finally, to the window. He could see the Ringstrasse from his office window and the late afternoon traffic racing onwards to the outer realms of the city. The days were growing longer now and the sky was still light, people had even begun to sit in the parks again: the old ladies on wooden benches, the students and the tourists with their papers and cameras, there were even signs of the revival of the concerts in the pavilion in the Stadtpark – the leaves had been brushed away and stacks of metal chairs and tables stood waiting to be moved into place for the first Strauss waltz. But Karl did not want to be here, and now there was only one reason he stayed, and she was in England.

A door slammed and he heard the voice of his ambassador, Gurney, along the corridor. Not now, Dan, don't bother me now with climatic consequences, waste disposal and the undoubted virtues of the rain forest, I just can't take it; go see Sam, he's your little pet puppy dog, your ever-enthusiastic pupil. The whole conference was driving him crazy and he couldn't concentrate, not really, and he wasn't interested, not enough for Gurney, anyway, and it was beginning to show. And he was tired, tired of this goddamned circus and the endless round of meetings and arguments and half truths and the squalid little successes which meant basically nothing at all and yet had to be greeted with the right amount of eager heartiness. It would lead them all precisely nowhere, except to some half-hearted final document which would actually achieve very little in real terms. It bored him, they bored him and he wanted to get the hell out, but he couldn't, not without her, not without Elizabeth.

The faintest of smiles tipped the edges of Karl's mouth, a tight small smile, and he leaned his head back in exasperation and disbelief because he had allowed himself to get involved, to love, to sacrifice himself a little for someone else. A joke, big bad joke, but it had happened all the same ... and she was *his*, and she would come with him when he left Vienna, he would make sure of that.

'I hate this trip,' Felix said suddenly. Visiting his aging, senile father always made him uneasy because the old man was no longer a man but a white bag of bones, a dribbling slack-jawed old fool who didn't even know who he was. It reminded Felix of what could be, of the insistent passing of the years and his own mortality.

'I'm sure he appreciates our visits, even if he can't say so,' Genevieve replied quietly.

'You must be a complete fool if you believe that, my dear,' he guffawed. 'The addled, pickled brain of my father is beyond appreciating anything.'

She lapsed into silence because Felix in this mood was impossible and she was too weary to make an effort at reasonable conversation.

'And if it wasn't for the fact that he is likely to die at any moment ...' he persisted '... I would transfer him to a home in Carinthia or Salzburg, somewhere I find pleasant, but *not* Burgenland and *not on* the edge of the Neusiedler See, I feel like one of the proletariat every time I drive down here.' He sighed. 'The place swarms with screaming children and beer-swilling louts and murderous mosquitoes ...'

'A great deal of people seem to like it, Felix,' Genevieve remarked, finally drawn.

'The opinion of a great deal of people – what does that signify? Nothing.'

'Your mother thought he would like it.'

'My mother,' Felix repeated. 'My mother was a fool.'

'Felix ...'

'I was lucky that there was any fortune to inherit by the time she had finished indulging my idiot father's whims. If the trustees had not finally allowed me to take over the estate early, a great deal would have been lost and I would have been a much poorer man.' There was another sigh before he spoke again. 'And we would never have married, my dear, and your father would have been forced to sell Schloss Bletz, and you ...'

'Yes?' she asked.

'I suppose you would have remained a spinster.' He placed a patronizing hand on her knee. 'After all, we must be realistic ...'

She made no answer and turned her face to the window and the flat, treeless grassland. She could still see the lake in the distance as they drew farther and farther away, a grey sliver of glass which seemed to go on for ever and yet was only a few feet deep. There was mud at the bottom, thick, black heavy mud which clung to feet and skin. Many years ago she had taken Sophia and Gunther boating there; the sky had been startlingly blue and the sun bright and strong, but it had seemed deceptively cool because of the constant breeze, and yet later they had all suffered sunburn and she had spent half the night rubbing ointment on to her children's shoulders. But it had still been a beautiful, good day somehow. And she remembered the laughter, like crystal, cutting across her memory. Sophia and Gunther. Felix had been away somewhere.

'Simone is organizing a party to attend one of the operettas at Mörbisch . . .'

'Oh, God.'

'Please, Felix – it will be *Grafin Mariza* – you know how you enjoyed it last time. I thought we could ask Sophia and Oskar to join us . . .'

'We don't have to make it an annual event.' He had enjoyed it because he had just started his fling with Simone. 'And besides I'm not sure I could endure being eaten alive by the mosquitoes, you know how the place is full of them.' He sighed heavily. 'It's all very well having a theatre built into the lake, but considerations like the local insect-life should be taken into account. I remember distinctly having to bribe a man behind me with one hundred schillings to give me his mosquito repellent.'

'But it is I who got bitten, Felix, not you.'

'Not so, Genevieve.' He frowned. 'Anyway, it's not a good idea at the moment.'

'But why not?' She wanted to go, very much.

'Next year,' he said finally, and in a voice which encouraged no further discourse.

Genevieve turned her face to the window, sensing defeat, knowing that it had been inevitable all along.

But Felix patted her knee again. 'There is always another time, and besides I thought we might make some special arrangements for Gunther's birthday which will fall at about the same time.'

She did not want to talk of Gunther's birthday, sure that she would find it difficult to summon any real enthusiasm and that her son would no doubt find her wanting.

'Did you speak to him about the photographs?'

Felix coloured slightly. 'Of course, of course.'

'Was he suitably chastened?' Gunther would never be chastened, she supposed, he was not the type and she did not understand that, not that coldbloodedness, that lack of conscience. Where had he got it from?

'Yes,' Felix replied quickly. 'Yes, I believe he was.' The boy had practically laughed at him, but it had ended amicably enough, even to the extent that he had offered him a cognac. After all, Gunther was almost twenty-one, hardly a child, hardly a silly teenager, and what harm could a look at a few photographs do? 'I think, somehow, that Gunther will one day be a great credit to this family.'

She shot a sideways glance at her husband and wished she held such a belief in their son, but he was not like her son at all. Inevitably her tired thoughts came back to Sophia, her darling, her sweet daughter, so far away. It had all gone wrong somewhere and even now she was still bewildered by the course of events which had followed one another so fast over the past few months.

'What is the name of this Belgian colonel?' Felix asked abruptly so that all thoughts of Sophia were immediately swept away.

'Oh . . . Wyninx, Hermann Wyninx,' she said. 'We met him and his wife at the Danish dinner last week.'

'I wish we could have got out of this evening.'

'It will only be for a couple of hours, Felix.'

'Two excruciating hours spent in the company of an ostentatious military bore with ideas above his station.'

'His wife seems a charming woman,' Genevieve offered. 'I believe she studies oriental art and Mandarin.'

Felix chuckled unkindly. 'I think she would be a wiser woman if she studied herself more closely in the mirror.'

'Felix . . .'

'Come, come Genevieve, I am only stating a fact. And what good will Mandarin do her, for God's sake? I really do not see our precious Colonel Wyninx going on parade in Peking.'

'I found her charming.'

'Perhaps, perhaps,' he said impatiently and blasted his horn at a woman on a zebra crossing. 'I am just rather tired, that's all, seeing my father always makes me tired and the last thing I feel like now is yet another cocktail party.'

'We have a free night tomorrow.'

'Thank God.'

They drove on in silence until he spoke again.

'We shall have Gunther's birthday celebrations at the castle – make it a really big affair.' He smiled to himself, pleased at the thought.

Genevieve made no answer, only letting her gaze reach out beyond the windows of the car into the passing streets and the faces of the people. She would make all the arrangements as Felix directed and act the hostess for this special day of Gunther's because Sophia would be there, and this time there could be no excuse for her non-attendance. She brightened visibly as a picture of them shopping together in the Kärntner Strasse formed in her head, because she would persuade Sophia to spend some extra days with her buying clothes and other things she might need for America. But even as the picture faded Genevieve caught a breath and wondered yet again why her daughter seemed loath to come home, even for a visit. Surely it was not because of this wish of Felix for her to marry Oskar – not now? But she would come – for Gunther's birthday she *must* come – and the prospect of the birthday celebrations suddenly began to take on a pleasant edge, even if they did take place at Schloss Bletz and even if Gunther did not like her . . . because she was sure of that now. Her own son; she felt a surge of despair. Gunther thought she was a fool, and as much as she tried to analyse or look into herself at all the failings and weaknesses, she could not think why.

It was a glorious afternoon, a glorious April day, and the sky was clear except for a few sluggish clouds. Kristina took in a mouthful of the still cold air and stopped for a moment to touch Sam's arm and make him turn around so that he would see the distant hills of the Wienerwald.

'This place is fantastic.' He bent down towards his tiny daughter. 'Can you see the hills, honey?' Joanna nodded obediently and Kristina smiled at Sam's concern. 'Doesn't the word Belvedere actually mean beautiful view?' he asked, switching his attention back to her. She nodded and he smiled in response. 'I can see why. And the Emperor lived here – right?'

'I think his heir did, Franz Ferdinand, but the Belvedere was originally built for Prince Eugene of Savoy about three hundred years ago.'

'It hasn't aged much . . .' Sam laughed.

'I suppose it's a masterpiece in its way,' she said quietly.

They stood at the crown of a small hill on which the Upper Belvedere had been built. Sam's eyes swept over the sumptuous ornamentation of the baroque palace and then down the paths, steps, cascades and fountains which connected to the lower building.

'It's quite something – really, quite something.'

'I was afraid you might find all this pomp a little dull.'

'No way.' He took her hand and then glanced at Joanna.

'Won't she get confused?'

'Confused?'

'With the sudden appearance of women in your life . . .'

'Or do you mean the fact that I'm holding your hand?'
She felt her cheeks grow pink.
'I didn't hold Natalie's hand, Kristina.'
'It's not really any of my business.'
'Now, I think we can both agree that that was a dumb thing to say.'
She said nothing and he too lapsed into silence as they walked slowly to the other side of the building and a large lake reflecting the magnificence of the palace like a mirror.
'It's just a little unsettling, that's all.'
'Because she's coming again?'
Natalie.
'I suppose so.'
'She wants to see Joanna.'
Kristina darted a glance at his face, but there was nothing to read, no shadow of expression which might say something to her. His wife wanted him back and even if Sam couldn't see that, it was all too clear for her to see, and it terrified her. They saw each other almost every day now, made small plans from week to week, and they made love whenever they could and it was good, *so good* between them – everything. She swallowed and her eyes drifted to the small dark head who walked beside them; Joanna was the pawn in the game. Such a little thing to have such a big part in this play, this performance which seemed to have no obvious ending.
'She wants you back, Sam.'
'I don't think so,' he said slowly.
'I just know that she does.'
He drew a sharp, weary breath. 'Maybe.'
There was a seagull, flying low, almost skimming the lake, and she watched its flight before it soared upwards again to disappear over a wall and some trees and the city. If this chapter in her life went wrong she would pack up and leave, go away, somewhere, anywhere, but not stay here in Vienna with her mother and that tomb of an apartment overlooking the Stadtpark.
'When is she arriving?'
'Two weeks.'
'Will she be staying long?' The words slipped out. She knew what they sounded like – predictable, weak – but she just couldn't help herself.
'Kristina . . .' He stopped and turned her towards him, putting his hands on her shoulders. 'Natalie will be staying another three days, like last time, no more, no less. I asked her not to come, but she insisted and I can't really stop her, can I? If she *is* up to something it doesn't really

matter, because I hold all the cards and she has none. None.' He kissed her lightly on the lips. 'Okay?'

She nodded helplessly and they began walking again. The day before she had met a young diplomat from the US embassy and the subject of Sam had somehow slid into their conversation; he had met Natalie briefly at a White House party. Kristina's lips stiffened as she recalled the way his eyes had widened in excitement, and his words: 'What a body, what a woman... I don't know how Sam could have let her slip away.' He had even walked away from her shaking his head in disbelief.

'Don't go quiet on me, Kristina.'

'I'm sorry.'

'It will be okay, I promise.'

And she wanted to believe him, she really did.

Laura read the letter again and realized her hands were shaking. Andrew's father had had a stroke and it was a letter of apology explaining why he had not rung when he had promised, why he had not written since their telephone conversation, although he had tried to call her several times with no luck. He was still in Bournemouth with his mother who had not taken his father's illness very well, so he didn't expect to be back in London until next week, the end of April. He hoped she wouldn't be angry about his neglect under the circumstances. How was she?

Laura clamped her eyes shut and then opened them quickly as if she expected to see Ralf coming towards her across the busy room, weaving his powerful body between the tables, drawing closer and closer until he reached her and looked into her face, as if he would know. Even if she hadn't received this letter from Andrew she would still have gone through with her plan to finish her relationship with Ralf. Finally.

Inevitably her thoughts tumbled uneasily backwards to Hungary, to the hotel, to the giddying, shameful nights – and days. It had been too much, all of it, like getting drunk on too much wine, except that the aftereffects still clung to her like an unpleasant skin. Laura looked down at her hands, at the white fingers and the carefully manicured nails, nails which had dug into his flesh too hard because he had cried out and in that hazy blur of lovemaking she had tasted blood, his blood; but in the morning his skin had been unmarked, there had been no nail marks, no blood. She remembered stumbling to the bathroom to vomit as dawn was breaking and then staring at her pale face in the mirror, shaken by the deep smudges beneath her eyes and the bruises under her arms and between her thighs. There was a big anxious question mark in her head and she found her mind dragging her back to the scenario and living it all again, except that there was almost a blank spot the last night, a hazy uncomfortable blur from which unbeautiful shapes would emerge to frighten her and make her shiver as if she were reliving a nightmare. She supposed she had drunk too much wine, but she had known, hadn't she, what Ralf was capable of?

'I think I'm disturbing you . . .'

Laura jumped, her hands fanning abruptly outwards, knocking her coffee across the small metal tray and across the marble table where it began to form a small seeking trickle which found the edge and dripped, dripped down to the polished wooden floor.

Ralf laughed.

'Do I make you so nervous?' But he knew that he did; when she looked at him now the pupils of her eyes grew wide and black, like fish eyes.

'You simply took me unawares,' she said quickly, trying to keep her voice steady.

'I'll call a waitress. Would you like some more coffee?'

'Yes, thank you.'

'You look tired.' He sat down.

'I haven't been sleeping terribly well.'

'That's a pity.'

He didn't mean it and she wondered why he pretended.

'I've been thinking . . .'

'Have you?' He grinned, as if she had made a joke.

'About everything.' She faltered, like a frightened child, as if she might lose her nerve.

'Everything?'

'But mostly,' she continued quickly, 'about the relationship I had in England.'

'You mean your chauvinistic diplomatic friend?'

'He's not so bad – really,' she said feebly.

'That's not what you said a few months ago.'

The waitress came with a cloth and began cleaning the table, dividing them.

'We're going to try and make it work again.'

He said nothing for a long moment and sat watching her carefully, making her more nervous.

'And us?'

She took a deep breath. 'We don't really work do we, Ralf?'

'Don't we?' He smiled, but it was not a nice smile somehow. 'I thought we "worked" together rather well.'

She felt the hot blood rise up from her neck. 'I don't mean that.'

'What *do* you mean?'

'I want a relationship that might go somewhere, ultimately,' she said.

'Explain.'

'I think you know what I mean.'

'No.'

She swallowed. 'We have, I suppose, what you might call . . . a physical relationship.'

'*Very* physical.' He almost wanted to laugh at the flush in her face, at the hands which fidgeted, tying her fingers in knots.

'I don't want just that,' she said awkwardly, not meeting his eyes.

'And I do?'

She shook her head. 'I don't know what you want, Ralf.' The coffee steamed as it was placed on the table and she looked back at him through the steam. 'Sometimes you *say* the right things, but . . .'

'But what?'

'They don't really go very deep, do they?' Her voice had grown very small.

He smiled. 'You think about these things too much.'

'Shouldn't they be thought about?'

'Not if thinking about them makes you nervous about me.'

'So I'm wrong?'

'Yes, you're wrong,' he lied, 'but it doesn't really matter now, does it, because you've obviously made up your mind?'

Her eyes fled into the enormous room of the Café Central, to the other people drinking their coffee, or hot chocolate, or biting red wine – to the real lovers who sat and talked, to an old man playing chess, alone.

'Yes.'

He reached across the table and took her hand, and she forced herself not to withdraw it, not to shrink away from him now.

'I'm sorry, Laura,' he sighed. 'You don't know how sorry.'

'These things happen, Ralf, it wasn't anyone's fault.'

'Are you sure, absolutely sure?'

He was squeezing her hand very hard, hurting.

'Yes, yes.'

He let go and she forced a smile.

'I'd like to take you for dinner – just one last time.'

'I don't think that's a good idea.' She wanted to leave now, to get away from him.

'Come, come, Laura.' His voice was low, coaxing.

'No, Ralf.' And she meant it, never again.

Their gazes locked for a moment. His eyes were flat and expressionless and she wanted to look away because he suddenly made her afraid.

'As you wish.'

She swallowed. 'I'd better go, I'm already late and I have a long cable to write for my ambassador this afternoon.'

'Of course.'

'Goodbye, Ralf.' She stood up.

'Goodbye, Laura.' He pushed his chair back and slowly rose to join her. 'And good luck.' He took her reluctant hand and brought it to his lips and let his mouth linger, too long.

She smiled with an effort as she withdrew her hand and then she was picking up her coat and walking away. And he watched her, his eyes scrutinizing her carefully, as if for the last time – except that it wasn't the last time. He had played along with her juvenile decision because it suited him for the time being, but in two or three weeks he would call her again, when she was more calm and any unpleasant echoes of Hungary which might remain had died away to imaginings. After all, there was plenty of time.

Ralf frowned slightly as he returned to his seat because that final look she had given him, when he could have crushed her fingers between his hands, had wounded him, injured him, mocking his vanity because her eyes had said 'distasteful, un-nice, offensive', as if touching his hand alone had made her gorge rise, her flesh creep. Ralf switched his attention to the window, to the people walking in the streets, little people: little people walking in the streets with their little dreams of little things. His mouth set into a thin line, his eyes narrow and watchful, and beneath the table his hands clenched into big marble fists as the little people went by.

'You have hardly touched your supper . . .'

Kristina lifted her head from the dry Wienerschnitzel and looked into her mother's old-woman face.

'I'm not very hungry.'

Her mother sighed loudly. 'It's this Jew, this man . . .' She shook her head. 'I knew he would disappoint you.'

'He hasn't disappointed me,' she said, 'and he's a man before he's a Jew, Mother.'

The old woman went on shaking her head. 'Tante Lilibet says that Hans Wittig's wife has left him – now *there* is a nice man!'

'I am not interested in Hans Wittig in the least, Mother, and in case you had forgotten he must be at least seventy.'

She waved a hand impatiently. 'Sixty-five. And what of it? What is sixty-five, I ask you, what difference does it make? Hans is rich, rich, Kristina and can *still do it*, so Tante Lilibet tells me . . .'

'How would Tante Lilibet know?'

'His wife told her.'

'Perhaps that is why she left him.'

'Now you are deliberately being difficult.'

Kristina stared at the cooling carrots on her plate and the huge pile of steaming potatoes her mother had served her.

'No.'

'No, what?'

'No, I am not being difficult, and no I am not the slightest – not the slightest bit – interested in Hans Wittig or his money or whether he can still *do it* or not.'

They lapsed into silence and the silence turned into long minutes whilst her mother ate and Kristina listened to the slurping and the shovelling of the food as it was pushed into the old trembling mouth.

'It is still the Jew, then,' she said finally, wiping her mouth with a pink napkin. The pink napkins were almost as old as she was and they were only fraying around the edges.

'Don't call him that.'

'But that is what he is.'

'You are not kind, you know that, don't you?'

'Nonsense,' she replied. 'What is wrong in stating facts?'

'Then what is wrong with saying that "you are not kind"? Because that is a fact, and it is also a fact that you still live in the past and that you intend to stay there with all your ancient, twisted ideals.'

'*Gott im Himmel*, Kristina, can I not say what I please in my own home!?'

'I love Sam, Mother.'

The old woman began folding her napkin very carefully and then placed it back on the table.

'You have loved a lot of men.'

'Not like this.'

'Will he marry you?'

'I don't know.'

'You don't know.' She sighed again. 'What good is "I don't know"?'

Kristina made no answer, but she felt the ominous prick of tears because her mother was getting horribly close to her own fears.

'Would you like some more wine, Mother?'

'No, I need a clear head, as you don't seem to have one.'

Kristina poured the chilled wine into her glass and picked it up, letting it cool the warmth of her hands, keeping her eyes down so that her mother would not see her distress.

'I suppose it is his wife,' her mother said at last.

Kristina said nothing.

'Isn't it?'

'Yes.'

'She is coming again?'

'Yes.'

'So you are afraid?'

Kristina took a long gulp of wine and turned her face to the fire, which needed more wood and would die, soon, if she did not feed it.

'They share a daughter,' she whispered almost to herself.

'And the woman is using the daughter to get at the husband?'

Kristina nodded.

'An obvious tactic.' Augustina watched her daughter and then followed her gaze to the fire. 'I almost lost your father that way.'

Kristina looked up. 'Father?'

'He had a mistress, of course.'

'I didn't know.'

'Of course you didn't know,' she said irritably. 'You were not even born. It was more the fashion then, although I don't think times have changed very much. She was a widow, quite lovely I suppose, but no bosom – your father liked boyish figures . . .'

'She had his child?' Kristina asked with disbelief.

'Yes.' Augustina's mouth grew tight. 'A boy. And for several years your father spent more time with her and the child than he did with me.' He had practically lived with the woman and she had despised him, hated him and the happiness which had radiated from him most of all; she had even thought deliriously of killing the damned woman, but she was not that much of a fool, instead she had waited and waited, and waited. 'A divorce would have been a scandal, even then, and I did not want it known that my husband preferred the arms of another woman to my own, that she had borne his child where I had failed.' But all her friends had known, the whole of Vienna had known, even during the giddying times of the early war years when there had been other, greater, considerations.

'What happened?'

'I took a lover for a while.'

Kristina could not believe it. Her mother?

'I was beautiful then . . .' She looked at her daughter suddenly as if Kristina might dare contradict her. 'Walther was in the Luftwaffe – a German officer, naturally. He was killed on a flying mission over

Yugoslavia – Belgrade. His plane finally came down in the mountains,' she said softly, 'the people there – in the village nearby, and the partisans – tore him to pieces ... they had taken photographs at the last and sent them back to his unit "as a warning", but the warning had come too late because Belgrade, as Hitler had ordered, was razed to the ground.' Her mouth tilted into a small, unhappy smile. 'But, of course, Walther had died for the Fatherland, which was supposed to make his death beautiful. But death is not beautiful ... not like that, not like that.' Augustina paused and looked at her hands as if she could not believe that the stiff, discoloured fingers were her own.

'I did not take another lover after that, and besides, even after everything, I still wanted your father – he was *my* husband. Mine.' She touched her hair gently, carefully. 'He was often a dull man, often severe, but *so* handsome, so big – magnificent – just to look at him sometimes would make my heart beat a little faster. But he was hers, then.' She turned to Kristina. 'Do you think that because I am old I cannot remember such things? Do you think that because I am eighty-two I am beyond all of that heady excitement? Nature is cruel, she allows the outside to decay, but the inside, the inside is always young, always remembering the dizzying moments, the bitter-sweet moments that made life beautiful and possible to bear.' She shook her head. 'You can fill my glass now.'

Augustina drank slowly and her fingers rose to her throat, tracing the sinews in her old neck as they moved up and down and the wine slipped into her belly. 'At the end, during that last hideous year, we were bombed badly and during one of the first bad raids she, his mistress, and her *two* children – for he had fathered another by then – were killed when their building caught fire. Afterwards I heard that the bodies were hardly recognizable, and I was glad.' She made the sign of the cross and drank some more wine.

'And Father came back?'

'Oh, yes, he came back.' She lifted the glass again to her lips. 'He had nowhere else to go, and he wanted me then, even wanted my sympathy, which I gave him.'

Kristina watched her mother carefully, in amazement, unable to believe. 'I don't think I could have done that.'

'No,' she said. 'But there was no one else in either of our lives and not likely to be. You see your father was not a womanizer, not a Don Juan. I couldn't have borne that, not such fickleness, not such disloyalty, for I was a good wife – he simply *fell in love* with someone else. It was not a passing fling, as you say today, and I knew that and somehow it made living our lives together easier because I knew that she was dead, and I am not afraid of ghosts.'

'And then I was born.'

'Yes.'

They sat in silence for a moment, mother and daughter, looking into the small, yellow flames which were fading now.

'But this does not help you, Kristina, not with this woman.'

'No, perhaps not, but nevertheless I am glad you told me.'

The old woman sat silhouetted against the fire, quite still, and then she lifted her arm and held out her glass in silent command and Kristina reached for the bottle of Mosel and poured her some more wine.

Christopher was asleep. Elizabeth left the carefully wrapped present at the end of his bed and walked back into the sitting room. The apartment was very quiet, Grace was in her room and John was in Salzburg on a weekend briefing; she had told him to expect her tomorrow, Monday, on his return, but she had pre-empted him because she had wanted to come home alone, without any drama, and see her son alone because she just wanted to be selfish. There had been several messages for her, though none from Karl. Elizabeth looked at the telephone and closed her eyes. She would call him and tell him that it was over, that there could be no future because of her child, because of Christopher. But it could never be so easy, never be so simple, and she was a fool to even play with such an idea; Karl would never leave it like that and she knew that he would come here if she did not go to him because he was not afraid of John or the consequences of his actions any longer, if he ever had been.

She sat down and locked her hands together in a tight knot, felt the pressure of a headache because of the panic and the confusion and the burden of it all. She lifted her head and stared at the large carriage clock which ticked, ticked away; there were faraway voices coming from the street and it made the room seem isolated, made her feel withdrawn from reality and the outside world. And she wanted him. Elizabeth swallowed deep in her throat as Karl's face stole, unasked, into her mind and she made a soft, despairing sound as if he were there, as if his fingers stroked, stroked her spine, taking her will away. She stood up and walked out into the hallway and picked up her coat which was still lying across the old Edwardian chest. It was not really cold outside, but there was a wind which, when it blew, seemed to cut right through to the bone.

Karl stood at the window, his eyes staring out across the patchwork quilt roofs of old Vienna. He could see the spire of St Stephen's, massive and slender at the same time, a great slab of gothic in the centre of the city. He recalled an enthusiastic delegate telling him that there was a crypt beneath the cathedral filled with bones upon bones, but he was not interested in bones. He turned back into the room and his gaze drifted to the coffee table which was covered with the usual array of papers, documents and letters. But the doorbell rang and his eyebrows drew together in a frown. He moved slowly, casually towards the door and as he did so he automatically lifted his hand up and pushed his hair back, smoothing it down, making himself more presentable. When he pulled back the lock and opened the door she was standing directly in front of him and he thought: she has come to me, to me. As he looked back at her face, at its lostness and vulnerability, at the deep eyes fenced in by regret, he could only secretly rejoice because she was here, she had come, to him.

'I had to see you,' she said.

Karl stood back and let her pass into the apartment.

'Would you like a drink?'

'No, no thank you.' Elizabeth pushed her hands deeper inside the pockets of her coat. 'I won't be staying.'

He felt a thickness gather in his throat, felt a tiny shrinking as she turned to look at him.

'I can't see you any more.' She shook her head. 'It's impossible . . . the situation, everything, it's hopeless, but I knew if I didn't come myself you wouldn't give up.'

'And so this is the momentous decision you have come to after running away?' he asked softly, his voice deceptively calm. 'And you were right to think that I wouldn't give up and wrong to think that you could persuade me in any way. Do you think I am so easily swayed? For Chrissakes, Elizabeth.'

'It wasn't – isn't – easy . . .'

He watched her for a long moment until her eyes wavered beneath his. 'Elizabeth . . .'

'No, Karl.'

'You don't mean this, not really, you know you don't.' He took the few steps towards her which separated them and then waited for her to lift her eyes back to his face.

'I must go.'

'No.' His voice was almost hushed. He brought his hand up to her cheek and traced the gentle curve with a finger, then drew an invisible line down to her mouth and followed the edge of her softly swollen lips so that she closed her eyes.

She shook her head, but he knew the gesture was meaningless, empty because she would not leave him now, it was too late.

'Why are you doing this?' She opened her eyes. 'Don't you see, it can't lead anywhere.' And it couldn't, could it?

'Why not?' he said softly. But he did not want to talk now, they could talk later, now he wanted to make love to her because that was all he had been able to think about since she had left him, the only weapon he felt sure of.

'You know why,' she said helplessly, uselessly.

His hands were on her neck, caressing hands, stroking the pulsing vein and the creamy hollows and she thought she would swoon, fade from the pressing, the stroking, the touching. And finally, when his mouth found hers she was ready and open, her lips eager and hot and sweet beyond belief. He unbuttoned her coat and let it fall to the floor and then he lifted her into his arms before she realized what was happening and carried her up the few steps into his bedroom. And there she became quiet, waiting, as he undressed her and then himself and as the silence deepened and he moved towards her she wondered why she had bothered to protest, why she had pretended, because that was all it had been – pretence, because in all the world, in all her life there was nothing she had ever wanted more than this moment in time with him. His face said nothing as he slid over her, as his mouth opened and closed over her own and she lifted her body instinctively to meet his thrust because that was all there was for them then – no prelude, no tender foretaste, nothing, except the joining. And as he moved, as he took her, she could not believe that his body, his flesh, could drown everything, could take her beyond the fear and the longing and the loneliness and the pain. That the searing pleasure which crashed out could only be right, good, glorious and theirs alone.

'You don't have to go back.'

He had pulled her into his arms so that she lay across his chest.

'I have to.'

'Leave John.'

She made no answer.

'Leave John,' he whispered. 'For me, for us.'

When Karl said her husband's name it was only a word, not like the John she knew and the man who loved her, the man who would hate it if she said that he was 'good and sweet and kind'.

'Don't push me, Karl, please.' It was a weak answer, a nothing answer, but she couldn't say anything else, not yet.

'What can I say then? What the hell am I supposed to do?' he said softly, pleading. 'I want you – I want to spend the rest of my life with you, if that doesn't sound too dramatic.' He tugged gently at her hair, ran his fingers through the thick curtain which screened her face from him. 'We love, don't we? We love each other – nothing else should matter.'

'It's much easier for you, Karl.'

'I know,' he sighed. 'I know.'

'And I have a son.'

'I haven't forgotten that.'

She sat up and his gaze was immediately drawn to the beautiful flushed face and the grey eyes which looked back at him carefully.

'Sometimes, sometimes . . . even before Vienna . . . I would wake up aching for you, wanting you, tasting your skin on my lips . . .'

There was a pounding in his ears, a wild feeling trapped in his chest as she spoke.

'Don't . . .'

'I have to.' And she wanted him now, again, and she took his hands and pressed them against her breasts. 'Do you think I could let you walk out of my life once more? Do you think that is what I want?'

Her head went back in silent agony as he bent his head to take her tender nipple into his mouth and her arms moved possessively across his back, his shoulders, up to his warm, beautiful neck and in a dark, lost corner at the back of her mind she wondered how she could tell John. John. She closed her eyes, pushing the thought aside, out of sight, as Karl pushed her down, away, and she gave herself up.

'Actually, it was simply chance that I called,' Madeleine said. 'And how was London?'

'I was in Kent, Madeleine, with my parents.'

'Is everything all right?'

'What do you mean?'

'Oh, nothing, of course,' she said, too quickly. 'It just seemed a little odd – you sneaking off like that.'

'I didn't sneak off, Madeleine, I felt like a little break, that's all.'

'John looked distinctly lost without you, I must say.'

'John manages very well without me.' But she knew that wasn't true, not really, and she swallowed slowly, willing the woman to go away.

'You know, you're quite wrong,' Madeleine persisted. 'John is like Olaf, the sort of man who needs a wife to be *with him*, the sort of man who is incomplete without his wife.' She laughed. 'Extraordinary.'

'I didn't know you went in for do-it-yourself analysis, Madeleine.' And yet she was surprised by her perception because it was true and she didn't want to think about it.

'I go in for a great deal of things you don't know about, Elizabeth,' she chuckled. 'And by the way, how is your friend?'

'My friend?'

'Yes, your "friend", Karl,' she said too casually. 'Karl Nielsen.'

'I think he is well, as far as I know.' Elizabeth closed her eyes tightly. 'I have been away, Madeleine.'

'Oh, yes – yes, of course,' she said quickly. 'Silly of me. Such a very good-looking man, reminds me a little of that American film star, Robert Reynolds, but with dark hair.'

'You mean Redford.'

'Of course, yes.'

'I'm rather tired, Madeleine.'

'Actually, I did try and call earlier, but your girl told me that you had gone out . . .'

'As I said, I'm rather tired,' Elizabeth responded, ignoring the barbed remark. 'And I'm expecting a call from John,' she lied.

'So you really can't join us tonight?'

'I don't feel like a game of bridge so late, Madeleine,' she said wearily. 'And as I have often told you, bridge is really not my game, anyway.'

'Come, come, there is always the chance that I might convert you. And the night is yet young and I have arranged a sumptuous buffet.'

The woman must have the hide of an elephant.

'No, really. I still have to unpack.'

'Just for a little while, then?'

'No, thank you, Madeleine.' A little while would certainly mean until one a.m., Madeleine's bridge nights often went on until the early hours of the morning. 'I really don't think so.'

'Oh, you are a spoilsport, Elizabeth,' she said, barely able to keep the irritation out of her voice. 'After all, you've been out of circulation and everyone has missed you.'

'I'm sure they haven't even noticed that I've been gone.'

'You are too modest, my dear.'

'I'm sure you will manage without me.'

'I have a number of interesting guests coming a little later – that darkly handsome Italian ambassador and his dazzling wife; the male lead from *Salome* who has promised to sing, some wonderful Austrian musicians and a Russian prince who apparently has a rather eccentric collection of Victorian erotica, he's promised to bring along some amusing examples.'

'No, Madeleine.'

'I've even asked that dreadfully entertaining drunk from the Swedish embassy . . .'

'Please, Madeleine.'

'Just a joke, my dear . . .' She sighed dramatically and then added softly, intimately, 'You really are beyond temptation, aren't you, Elizabeth?'

Elizabeth felt blood seep into her face.

'Goodnight, Madeleine.'

'Goodnight, Elizabeth.'

8

Genevieve paused and looked up from her desk. It was going to be a long letter and she had probably said things she shouldn't have, asked questions which were not supposed to be her business any longer. Yet Sophia was *still* her child, even if she felt able to take a momentous decision such as accepting a scholarship in a country halfway across the world on her own. Genevieve looked down at the carefully written words which she had struggled over because she hated writing letters, even to her own daughter. Soft panic began to flutter inside as those odd, disquieting echoes from the past made her stomach churn just as if she were a child again. Until the age of ten, when it was discovered she suffered from a mild form of dyslexia, everyone had thought that she was simply stupid, but somehow the feeling of being 'stupid' had stuck and she was never happy or confident about her spelling, could never look at a letter in her own hand and be pleased or sure without being tortured by feelings of inadequacy. Always. She swallowed slowly and tried to push the memory down and concentrate on finishing the letter, and it was, after all, a silly letter, she decided a little sadly, just a letter asking for reassurance and details of the scholarship and where and who Sophia would be staying with, and would she come home for the holidays? A mother's letter.

She let go of her pen and stood up wearily; there were some stamps in Felix's desk, she was sure, he was always so much more organized than she was about such things. Tonight he would be late and Gunther was out so she would have the house to herself, an unlooked-for luxury. She walked out into the marbled gallery and down the small stairwell to his study. A key was in the lock, but the door just stood ajar and she pushed it gently so that her arms still brushed the door frame and the heavy wooden door as she walked through.

A man's room, a room for Felix. The walls were panelled in walnut and on one side there was a rack of shotguns and hunting rifles locked behind glass. On the wall facing the gun rack were several trophies – two magnificent red deer, their antlers dusted and polished, the grim head of a wild boar and three pheasants with long brilliant tails. She didn't like those faces looking back at her, beautiful, proud faces cut down to adorn a wall. Between them stood an eighteenth-century candle-stand Felix had retrieved from the castle, a huge object almost as tall as herself with carved skeletal branches supporting the sconces and tiny pointed stalactites, like teeth, fringing the small platforms at the top; around the stem, as thick as a man's fist, two Chinese serpents writhed and hissed with open mouths. She turned her face away and brushed a lock of hair from her eyes. The room smelt of polish, old leather and gun oil and a little of Felix and his delicate, but somehow clinging, sweet toilet water which she had never come to like.

Genevieve walked over to the rolltop desk which stood against the window, opened the top drawer and found nothing but envelopes and writing paper. The second housed a battery of files, from several on the children to electricity bills which went back over five years. Felix was very good at filing paper and writing letters and hoarding; he never threw anything away. In the lower drawer there was only a bulky brown envelope, bulging and splitting down one side so that a plastic case poked through. She frowned and reached into the envelope, pulling out the plastic case and turning it over in her hand only to discover that it was a video, not a case – a Dutch video with nude and semi-nude women on the lush, lewd cover, except that they were not like normal women, a vague voice said in her head, they were sexual caricatures, cartoon women with vast bosoms and breathless, pouting mouths which shone slick and wet and red.

Her heart seemed to be beating very slowly as she put the video on Felix's rolltop desk and her hand found a book, in German, with more cartoon women, but these were sad creatures in black and white, grinning, with over-used faces. She paused helplessly for a brief, burning moment, unable to comprehend immediately as a letter fell out from between the pages, a letter to Felix, a letter beginning '*Mein geliebter, mein liebling*', a letter saying many things about their apparent love, and how much she missed him, how much she longed to see, listen, touch and *love* him again and how sad she was that he was unhappy, 'that he had so many burdens to bear' . . . it was signed '*your* Doris'.

Genevieve stood quite still; nothing in her seemed to be functioning, nothing except the slow, loud beat of her heart like a dismal, miserable echo. There was another letter, from another girl, someone called Eva who would 'never forget the beautiful hours' they had spent together; she had even written a poem, a love sonnet, to Felix, her husband.

Genevieve tried to swallow the bile which had crept up into her throat like sour dread; she wondered whether this girl, this Eva knew that he was married, that he had two children, and that there were other women – because that was obvious and he was not loyal to any of them, not one. He used them and there was a sort of arrogance in that use, as if it was not good enough that they should merely want to sleep with him, but that they should come to adore and love this other Felix who did not really exist. And that was cruel. She sat very still for a moment and then her small pink tongue split the white line of her mouth as it passed over dry, broken lips.

Beneath the book and the letters were the photographs, lots of photographs, and she knew that they were of women, or girls, in provocative poses because, of course, she had seen them already when she had walked in and surprised Gunther. And he had laughed at her, and no wonder, because he knew that they belonged to his father and that therefore there would be no repercussions, no reprimand, no punishment – he had found his father out, not the reverse. His face, Gunther's face, soared painfully into her head and that look of his as he had gazed back at her, contemptuous and scathing. No wonder, no wonder. What a fool he thought her, what a fool!

She sat down in Felix's ornate, high-backed chair, her hands resting on the thick carved arms of vines and grapes and cherubs, her mind whirling, her thoughts dazed and yet tumbling slowly backwards over all the times he had been late, all the times he had gone out on one of his 'long walks' around the city, leaving her hours alone, and the times he had been separated from her on business and for one reason or another had been unable to leave a telephone number so that she could not contact him. No wonder. Genevieve leaned her head back and closed her eyes as bleak sadness began to spread through her.

And what was *she* to him? Not a woman, not in the *real* sense; she could not remember the last time he had touched her, intimately, could not remember the last time Felix had made love to *her*. These days she deliberately forgot that part of her body and she had not minded that forgetting because it had never played a large part in her life; there had never been much pleasure and she could barely remember desire, let alone passion or fire – nothing like the stuff of romantic novels or the chapters that filled the lives of other, no doubt, beautiful women. She had built her life around her family, around Felix and Gunther and Sophia – and now, suddenly, it had all gone. She stood up and moved to the window, her eyes taking her beyond the glass to the garden and the trees which were in bud now because it was spring and because the sun was shining, sure and strong and brilliant. May would be glorious, there was that little promise in the air, that gentleness which would probably be given up to a heady, heat-filled summer, and the narrow pavements of Vienna would burst with coffee tables and umbrellas and people: languid people with sunglasses, and jackets slung across their shoulders. Just then she was aware of no feeling at all, only a curious emptiness, a void, a wilderness where all the love had been. Genevieve blinked at the unpleasant prickling in her cheeks, as tears began to brim and cascade silently down her face and the grief began to grow and grow.

'We chose this house because it is so spacious, so free . . . so, so Viennese.' The Brazilian ambassador's wife gesticulated extravagantly with one arm, as if she could embrace the enormous room with one grasp of her impeccably manicured hand. She gave Elizabeth a dazzling smile and turned her attention to the brilliant artworks which illuminated the walls and furnishings of their new home. 'Traditional Brazilian themes, Mrs Thornton. I thought they would blend in very well with the art nouveau feel of this glorious apartment.'

'It's a very interesting combination,' Elizabeth remarked carefully. And it was interesting, if a little over the top.

'But Klimt – now he is my favourite, and Lalique – for different reasons, of course.' She sighed wistfully, her syrupy voice quickly adding, 'Klimt was one of the few art nouveau artists who painted women with, shall we say, *disturbing* sensuality.' She sighed again. 'I am so glad to be here at last, so very glad. After Cairo, Vienna seems so civilized, so cultured, and one can get so tired of perpetual sunshine and the constant problems of unreliable and dishonest servants.' She laughed in a little-girl sort of way. 'At least in this beautiful city my poor husband has been able to fend for himself in a reasonable fashion all these months, and I do hope that these talks do not end too quickly, so that I may not only be at his side to pamper him, but also reap an artistic harvest before I leave.'

Elizabeth swallowed and wondered how she could get away. Maria Marajo was typical of a certain type of diplomatic wife, too posed, over-cultivated and the sort of woman likely to use her status for trivial and personal purposes, something which John called 'abuses of their position' and something Elizabeth studiously avoided. There was an expression, an old expression – 'woe betide His Excellency the day he thinks he actually *is* excellent . . .' Their own ambassadress, Lilian, was an old hand, a perfect eccentric with a razor wit and a penchant for too much sherry, smoking the occasional cigar and worrying, usually unnecessarily, about her teenage children who were at school in England. She did literally 'everything' for her husband, from paying the bills to discussing his speeches and coaching him on his languages – something she had a natural talent for. Lilian was wonderful, Lilian was someone Elizabeth knew, with a surprising trace of envy, that she could never be.

'I'm afraid most people are hoping quite the opposite – for a quick and decisive ending.'

'Oh, yes, yes, of course. We are all, naturally, concerned about escalating environmental problems.' The Brazilian ambassadress said carefully.

Elizabeth responded with an automatic and practised smile. And Brazil had a big role to play in these talks, that was why there was such a large turn-out for this particular cocktail party, this 'housewarming' for the Brazilian ambassador to the conference, because Brazil and the future of its tropical rain forests was a delicate and pressing issue. John called it 'wooing' and there was much wooing to be done before the Brazilian government really began to change its attitude and policy towards the small-scale, land-hungry cultivators who were left with little choice but to slash and burn the forest because they were denied scope and land elsewhere. An élite and often corrupt one per cent of the people owned ninety per cent of the land and were prepared to murder migrants who dared to squat on their property. There were the loggers, too, and the cattle ranchers who set light to massive tracts of forest for grazing to feed the lucrative beef export market. Dan Gurney had privately suggested that the Western world should 'stop glutting itself on red meat, cease wanting more precious hardwoods like mahogany and ebony, and last, but by no means least, persuade the Pope, among others, to reconsider the birth control question.'

'My husband has often said that concern is not enough.'

The Brazilian ambassadress smiled tightly. 'Your husband is right, of course.'

Of course. Elizabeth sighed softly, her gaze drifting away from the face of Maria Marajo and across the small sea of people, searching for John who was standing near the open door on the other side of the room, and as she watched him he turned towards her as if he had felt her eyes. Their gazes locked for a split second and she felt the muscles of her stomach contract as he looked back at her, as realization flooded in. John knew. Her heart jumped in sudden panic and the blood drained from her face. There was no mistaking that look, that expression of bewilderment and the desolation and the sorrow which seemed to reach out and claim her. She found her vision swimming slightly and then his mouth moved into a smile, a small smile, tilted on one side, which seemed to hang there fixed and alone.

'Elizabeth!'

She jumped and then turned automatically, and it was Clare, only Clare.

'How are you?'

Elizabeth forced a smile and tried to concentrate as Clare's bright, innocent face looked into her own.

'Oh, fine – fine,' she said. 'I've been away.'

'So I understand.' Clare caught a breath. 'I envy you, I long for home sometimes, but at least the weather here is beginning to be wonderful. Oliver says we might take a trip to one of the lakes soon, we can just about scrape up the funds for that.' She laughed and then added quickly, 'We might even receive reimbursement of our VAT expenses by the end of the talks, if we're lucky...' Clare smiled ruefully. 'Poor Oliver's been nagging personnel for simply ages, with no joy as usual, and I really don't like to keep asking him if he's heard anything because he hardly seems able to find the time to stop working as it is.'

'John tells me Oliver works almost too hard.'

'I know.' She sighed. 'Sometimes I wonder if it's worth it – after all, he was inexplicably overlooked for promotion, *again*.'

'Have you heard any more on Brussels?'

'Not a thing,' Clare replied. 'I try not to think about it.'

'I suppose it really depends on when the talks wind up.'

'Yes.' She shook her head and grinned broadly. 'At least you have very little to worry about.'

Elizabeth frowned, puzzled.

'Well,' Clare prompted, 'John's next posting seems almost in the bag – although, of course, I'm not supposed to know anything.'

'Is it?'

'Oh, Elizabeth, don't pretend... I'm sure everyone knows that John is almost certain to get Washington.'

Elizabeth swallowed.

'I'm sorry,' Clare said, 'I really didn't mean to probe.'

'No, no – it's all right,' Elizabeth stammered, 'I just didn't realize that you had any idea...'

'Well, I'm not really supposed to have any idea, but you know how these things get out.'

'Yes, yes, of course.' Elizabeth shifted her gaze away from Clare and back to her husband, but he had moved, gone, swept away by the tide of people into another room. Why hadn't he told her? Why? He had wanted this of all things: Washington, possibly the pinnacle of his career. She stared into the glass in her hand and the bubbles of Perrier which were rising, rising; John hadn't told her because he had known about Karl. Once he would have told her everything. There had been no silences, no secrets – only on her side, but she had not liked herself for that. She felt sick, suddenly, with uncertainty and guilt.

'Are you all right?'

She smiled quickly. 'Yes, yes. I haven't eaten anything, that's all.'

'Let's dig in to some of those smoked salmon canapés, they look wonderful.'

Elizabeth feigned interest and picked up one of the tiny, delicate rolls of fish between her fingers.

'Try the asparagus tips . . .' Clare said enthusiastically, 'so sweet.'

'Yes, I might, in a moment,' Elizabeth replied, but the food tasted like cardboard in her dry mouth.

'I do hope Oliver's tucking in because he came straight from the embassy as usual . . . he'll make himself ill, Elizabeth, with all this pressure, that's what really worries me.'

'Would you like me to ask John to have a word?' The response was automatic because John was not only senior in rank to Oliver, but a friend; they had known each other in Helsinki, before she had met him and long before their marriage. Even as the suggestion slipped from her mouth she wondered how she could ever ask anything of John again.

'I'd be so grateful . . .' Clare said.

'It's the least I can do, Clare.' Another automatic response, another silky acccepted phrase to cover yet another situation, but this was Clare, wasn't it? Not a stranger or Maria Marajo, and Clare did not deserve 'automatic responses'. Elizabeth drew a sharp, silent breath and wondered what was happening to her that she should suddenly be so angry and yet so sad, so cynical and yet so in love that she was prepared to turn her own life upside down because she thought it was worth the cost. But she hadn't asked this to happen, she and John had been happy. She forced her thoughts backwards: there had always been Karl between herself and John, because she had wanted it that way; she had permitted it. Her gaze slid restlesly from Clare's face and she saw him. Karl.

'I wonder if you would excuse me, Clare.'

'Of course.'

She wove slowly, carefully, around the groups of people and individuals and all the time he was watching her, all the time he looked at her and all the doubts and all the fears seemed to slide stealthily away.

'I hoped you'd be here,' he said.

'We'll just talk for a few minutes.'

'Elizabeth,' he said with exasperation. 'Everyone will know, soon.' What did it matter, now?

'Please, Karl,' she said. 'I would never embarrass John deliberately.'

'Sometimes I think you don't know yourself.'

She shot a glance at him. 'What do you mean?'

'Nothing – it doesn't matter.' It had been a stupid thing to say and he did not want to press her now because she was nervous and it showed in her lovely face. And he was afraid to press her because she was walking between them now; John was his rival and she was not even aware of the fact. And he was not used to rivals, not used to feeling wild, jostling panic.

'We'll be leaving shortly, we have a dinner immediately afterwards.'

'When can I see you?'

'I'm not sure.'

'Don't say that, not to me.'

She looked up into his face and felt her stomach lurch, felt that familiar terrible longing and wondered anew why she bothered to pretend when it was beyond her control.

'Tomorrow.'

'I can get away by five.'

'All right.'

He looked away from her for a fleeting moment, across the room at the endless faces and the endless nodding and shaking of hands and then abruptly his gaze returned to settle on her eyes.

'I'd like to take you now – and run – in front of all these clowns,' he whispered, and then smiled as the blood soared into her cheeks. 'You are all to me, Elizabeth, all I have ever wanted.' He had never said that before. Never.

'Don't.'

'Sssssh . . .' And he lifted his hand and put a finger on her lips as if he would quieten any words, any protests, for ever.

The gesture happened in a split second and she flinched instantly, but she knew that it was too late, that someone would have *seen* and wondered and begun to draw their own conclusions. She sighed unhappily and began to move away as he turned to a couple at his side, resuming his normal role. She could hear his silky American voice introducing himself, drifting across the room as the gap between them widened until his words became lost in the other voices and the conversation and the laughter.

Kristina stood at the edge of the enormous duckpond. There were scores of the brown, waddling birds now that the weather was warmer, and she had brought some bread to feed them. She smiled to herself as a woman with a young child jostled past her because she was one of many feeding the already fat, sleek creatures whose home was the Stadtpark. Behind her the renaissance-style loveliness of the Kursalon was abandoning itself to the sounds of Strauss in the pavilion and as she turned her head she could just see the familiar sight of the peacocks roving freely across the ornate terrace. Sometimes at dusk, and in the early morning if she was sleeping badly, they could wake her with their high shrieking cries and she would get up and go to the window and sometimes, if she was lucky, she would see the offending bird walking through the deserted grounds, always alone, and feel a strange empathy, a warming, and then she would usually make her way down to the kitchen for some coffee and her mother would hear her and then the two of them would sit in the kitchen drinking steaming hot coffee as dawn broke.

Kristina walked back to the path rubbing her hands together, sprinkling the ground with the crumbling remains of the bread. Sam was supposed to be meeting her here in half an hour with Joanna and they would have a walk and then take her to one of the cafés for a huge ice, or a lavish cream pastry. Kristina lifted her head as a bird screamed and wondered how she could keep off the subject of Natalie's coming visit; she knew it irritated Sam if she mentioned it because it would somehow betray this tenuous peace they had together, this little oasis of contentment which his wife seemed able to destroy with such ease, and she knew his own peace, his own confidence was at stake, too. It only needed her to glance at him suddenly and take him unawares to see his confusion and the conflict which haunted his features when he thought he was unobserved. Next week Natalie would be in Vienna for three days, just like the last time, but this time Natlie would be playing for keeps because that was the sort of person she was, and she would know that if she left it too long now the distance between her and Sam would make winning him back so impracticable as to be impossible.

'I would do the same,' Kristina murmured to herself, except that she would never have lost Sam in the first place, that was the difference. Did Sam realize it? After all, he was hardly a fool. She pushed her hair back from her face as the wind caught it, and stared back into the brown water. But Natalie was, by all accounts, stunning, and Natalie could be charming and clever when it suited her, particularly where Joanna was concerned, because Joanna was naturally Sam's weak spot. If she was able to convince Sam that she no longer touched drugs and booze, that he had never really seen the 'real' Natalie, she would win the game simply because of Joanna. Endless, endless thoughts, endless imaginings, endless anguish.

Kristina stopped walking to watch a group of pigeons fighting for some crumbs of bread, her hands plunged deep in her pockets, her teeth clenched. She had lost weight and it suited her and she hadn't even been trying, she smiled wryly to herself, even worry could have its advantages, but not like this, not because of Sam. She had simply liked him to begin with, but the liking had changed to something deeper. Sam made her laugh, Sam was kind, Sam was tender. She loved him, but had never told him because that would be foolish, really foolish, like opening herself up, like giving away a part of herself, one of the mistakes she had made in the past. But this time she had been deliberately more careful, she had not rushed in, she had not expected too much and now for all her pains she stood on this precipice, this edge, and she didn't know if she could stand another disappointment, or how much longer she could bear the suspense of not knowing.

Perhaps she should just go, now, and leave Sam to Natalie, because she was not at all sure whether she had the strength to go on with it. Only yesterday Monika had looked at her with big, knowing eyes and said how good the salaries were for interpreters at the UN in New York – meaning, naturally, that she was wasting her time in Vienna with Sam and that she should make a fresh start somewhere else, and preferably far away. She sighed heavily and returned her gaze to the pigeons as they brushed against each other, battling against a flurry of feathers and beaks, but then they moved, parted, as a raven appeared from some bushes, a great black creature which strutted towards them disinterestedly. His beak was vicious, his body powerful and he passed through the grey cluster of birds as if they did not exist and they, in their turn, waited until he had gone. Kristina smiled without humour because she was reminded of Natalie.

Laura stepped out of the lift and turned right into the burgundy and white corridor; it was cool here, pleasant after the unusually warm day. Ralf had telephoned and asked her if she would like to see some mementoes of their trip to Hungary over some coffee at his apartment and at first she had hesitated, but he had seemed so easy, so natural, that finally she had agreed. After all, it had been over three weeks since she had seen him last and some of the curious and unpleasant echoes of their weekend had faded, and she wondered if she had not overreacted. Perhaps they could become friends, because there was no going back for her now. She had intimated as much to him on the telephone and he seemed to understand, even to the extent of saying 'for old times' sake', as you say in England'. She had been reassured and even touched by shame at his generosity and the shabby way she had treated him, but she and Andrew had grown closer again, and particularly since his father's death. He was already planning to visit her at the end of July and she had begun to tick off the weeks in her head. True, there had been no renewed talk of wedding plans, but that was still a difficult and touchy subject because of their opposing career paths. She shrugged a little sadly, perhaps one day. At least things were better between them, immeasurably, and that thought alone made her feel happier than she had in months. Laura paused outside the door of Ralf's apartment and pressed the bell before drawing a swift, deep breath because her heart had begun to race irritatingly fast and because suddenly she wished she had not come at all.

'Laura, you look wonderful!'

Ralf kissed her hand lightly and gave her a broad grin, and once again she was struck by the difference this made to his broad handsome features and understood all at once what the phrase 'lit up his face' really meant.

'Thank you,' she responded easily, 'you look very good too.' Her heart was slowing now and she thought how often she had got this man wrong, how ready she was to think ill of him.

'Come in, come in,' he said and began helping her off with her jacket and ushering her into the living room. 'Would you like a drink, rather than coffee? I have some superb madeira, or why not champagne?'

'Champagne?' she asked. 'What are we celebrating?'

'A little triumph of mine.' He guided her to a seat. 'Please.'

Directly in front of her, on a low oriental table Ralf had set an exquisite selection of dishes; the champagne was already cooling in an ice bucket.

'And caviar . . .' She looked up at him.

'Royal beluga,' he said, 'should always be light grey, almost pearl-white. It has the most delicate flavour.' He picked up a tiny silver spoon, piled it high with caviar and brought it to her mouth. 'Let me offer you the first mouthful . . .'

'Ralf . . . what is this all about?'

'Later – for the moment, just taste this.'

And she did, and it was wonderful. He began filling her glass with champagne.

'A toast – to the loveliest lady in Vienna.'

She began to feel slightly uneasy. 'Ralf – what *is* this?'

'I told you, to celebrate a little triumph of mine.'

'Why don't you tell me?'

'Because I want to surprise you.'

The unease began to grow and she lifted the glass of champagne to her lips.

'I'm afraid I can't stay very long.'

'Why, is your *boyfriend* here?' He did not attempt to hide the sneer in his voice.

'No, of course not,' she said. 'I have a dinner engagement this evening.'

She looked nervously into her glass and then darted a glance at him, eyes lowered. 'Perhaps this wasn't such a good idea.'

'No, no,' he said quickly, 'forgive me, I am only jealous.'

'You said you had some mementoes to show me . . .?' She wanted to go, to get this over with, and now she wondered why she had allowed herself to be persuaded to come.

'Oh, yes, the mementoes,' he said as the grin came back to take over his face. 'I had almost forgotten.' He moved closer to her so that he stood looking down into her eyes, so that his hands which were clenched into fists were on a level with her face. 'Let me give you some more champagne and then we shall go into the next room where I have set up a little film show.'

'A film show?'

'I thought I would surprise you, Laura.' He shook his head sadly as he filled her glass. 'I had meant to tell you whilst we were in Budapest, but somehow it slipped my mind.'

She frowned, not understanding him.

'Come . . .' He offered her his hand and for a moment she just sat there staring at his thick, powerful fingers which were reaching out to her.

'No, Ralf . . . I think I'd like to go home.'

'Not now, surely, when I have prepared such a surprise.' He grinned even more broadly as he took the champagne from her hand and pulled her to her feet. 'It won't take long.'

The light was muted in the small room, which was almost totally empty except for the large blank screen of a television set and two chairs which had been placed directly in front of it.

'Sit down, Laura.'

But instead she turned to him, baffled and confused.

'Sit.'

Ralf closed the door behind her and then crossed the room to the television; underneath there was a video machine and he pressed 'play' and the blank screen became a live blur of black and white until the numbers erupted into her vision . . . five, four, three, two, one. Almost immediately she recognized the hotel room they had occupied at the Hyatt and she swallowed slowly, deep in her throat, as a wave of fear cruised upwards over her body. For a few deceitful seconds there seemed to be no one in the room and then she saw herself appear from one side of the screen, almost naked except for a man's shirt which was completely unbuttoned, Ralf's shirt. She saw herself lift a glass to her lips, drain it and then fall leisurely across the bed. She saw herself remove the shirt as if it were an irritant and throw it to the floor. She saw herself stretch her arms above her head and arch her back, opening her legs . . .

Laura closed her eyes tight shut with disbelief and horror, felt Ralf standing behind her, and opened her eyes again to see him with her on the screen, kneeling behind her, his hands moving down her body, turning her over, smiling into the camera. She winced as he brought her buttocks into full view, as his fingers pulled them apart, felt her nails digging painfully into her palms and tears of shame standing in her eyes. But he had planned it well, superbly, in all its sordid, ugly detail and her hand came up to her mouth as she saw the other man, the man she thought she had imagined, the man who had haunted her waking hours for days afterwards. In the moments that followed she thought she would die because the horror seemed to suffocate her heart and bile rose up into her throat so that she wanted to retch, but her eyes would not leave the screen and Ralf's hands were on her shoulders, thick powerful fingers massaging her neck like ever tightening coils, forcing her back into her seat. And she saw herself smiling, saw herself giggling as the man spread himself above her on all fours like a crab, his bearded face disappearing between her thighs as her mouth began opening, wide, wider as he forced himself into her throat, her body jerking, jerking as Ralf came to lie alongside her on the bed, as he pushed the man to one side so that she lay between them and the bodies, the arms and legs, the fingers and tongues seemed to work as one predatory creature in a constant black rhythm and she saw her nails rake across the man's back, saw blood, saw her head snap backwards as she abandoned herself to him and Ralf, saw Ralf smiling, smiling, saw the man's tongue slide out from behind the black gap in his teeth, down, down . . . She could feel her head shaking slowly from side to side as if she could not believe what she saw, that it was not her on the screen, not her who was silently opening her arms and legs so eagerly to a stranger, a man she had never met, and Ralf. And Ralf. The screen went blank.

'Enough, I think,' he said. 'After all, I have seen it before, of course, but it is quite long, another twenty-five minutes in fact.'

She made no answer.

'Quite a performance.' A smile tipped the edges of his mouth. 'I don't think a professional could have been more convincing than you, Laura.'

The silence was long then, strange and taut.

'Why?' she whispered, and lifted her eyes to his face.

'You mean you haven't guessed yet?' He laughed. 'It's my job, dear Laura, my job.'

'I don't understand.'

'And you are supposed to be so bright – a bright, pretty British diplomat, alone in Vienna.' He laughed again. 'Need I say more?'

'I see,' she said slowly.

'And it was so easy, my dear, so very easy.'

'You are a spy?'

'That word always sounds faintly ridiculous, don't you think?' He shook his head. 'But I suppose it will do.'

She should never have come, but it wouldn't have made any difference in the end, because he would have sent the tape to her, or used some other means. The day had started so well, she thought vaguely, so well, and now everything had changed, irrevocably.

'Even in these days of *perestroika* and *glasnost* we are not so foolish as to believe that people really change, that my sort of job will *ever* go out of fashion, and there is always something to learn from other countries, other nations, always little secrets that need to be shared and discussed and thought through.' He sighed dramatically. 'And the world won't change, Laura, not really, there are always those "dark" people waiting on the sidelines to exchange one power for another. Just waiting for their time to come.'

'I want to go home.'

'Of course. But you realize that now we have a bargain, that you will be a good, cooperative girl.' He smiled meanly into her white face. 'And don't think that I shall need your services immediately, that may not be the case at all. Nothing may be asked of you for months, even years, until you are in the right place at the right time, and then perhaps . . .'

'I want to go home.' Suddenly Andrew's face slipped unhappily into her head and she wanted to cry.

'You will meet me again, in three weeks, perhaps at the Central Café, and I will discuss things a little more thoroughly, but I won't bother you with details now, you would probably not remember them anyway.'

'You are disgusting,' she said softly.

'Not really disgusting, Laura,' he replied. 'You were very willing.'

'You put something in my drink.'

'Did I?'

'You *know* you did.'

'And who will believe that?' His mouth opened a little and she could see his beautiful teeth. 'You seemed to enjoy every minute, every second. Didn't you? Perhaps we could do it again some time, Hans would be very willing, I can assure you.' He had brought his face lower, closer to hers, and she reacted instinctively and her hand came up to slap him. He caught her wrist instantly as if he had anticipated what she might do, as if he had wanted it, and then his own arm was coming up and with one carefully aimed blow his fist caught her on the side of her jaw and she was knocked sideways, the chair falling with her, the noise raking the awful silence as she gasped and rolled to the floor. Fear made her crawl away from him, fear made her hands reach frantically to the door handle, but instead Ralf pulled her up by her hair and pressed her face against the thick dark wood.

'Silly, silly girl,' he said softly. 'Not disgusting, not Ralf. Don't *ever* say that.' He sighed. 'And don't think of telling anyone, it would be much, much wiser not to.' He gripped her hair tighter, tighter. 'You won't, will you?'

She shook her head numbly.

'Will you?'

'No.'

The lift was too warm and Elizabeth brought her hand up and felt beads of perspiration on her neck. She was late and he would be waiting, worrying, wondering, she knew that much about him now. And as she stood there, the lift rising higher and higher, the same questions soared inevitably into her head, the same uncertainties, except that once she saw him, once he took her in his arms, they would recede again and there would only be the four walls of his apartment and him. And him. But her thoughts began to swim backwards to the Brazilian reception and John's naked, desolate face. Nothing had been said afterwards and they had had their normal nightcap in the drawing room, made a few desultory remarks about the people and the conversation and gone to bed, though there had been no touching, no pretence at lovemaking, no goodnight kiss. Yet he knew, and his silence seemed worse than any words. There was a pressure in her chest, hard, like a fist, and as the doors of the lift opened she took a long breath and wiped the perspiration from beneath her eyes. The girl who was standing in front of her, waiting, seemed familiar and for a moment Elizabeth was puzzled, but as the girl slipped quickly past and into the lift the swathe of dark hair which had been covering her face fell backwards and revealed the beginnings of a massive bruise on the left side of her face and the swollen, pink lid of one eye which was trying to close; as if she had been struck very forcefully. There was misery in the face too, and desperation, and as the doors slid shut Elizabeth turned and found herself staring at stark white metal where the girl had been and gone. She frowned, but then remembered the dark hair and the pretty face and a beautiful burgundy velvet dress which Laura had worn to the Opera Ball. She was from the embassy, Elizabeth recalled, John had introduced her. If she had realized even a few seconds earlier she could have stopped her, found out what was wrong, but she knew instinctively that Laura had not wanted that. In any event, it was not really any of her business, but perhaps she should mention it to John, later. Elizabeth closed her eyes as she saw his face again, hating herself suddenly.

'I thought you weren't coming . . .' Karl was standing in the doorway of his apartment. 'But I heard the elevator and hoped it was you.'

She smiled with an effort and tried to lose her thoughts.

'You look as if you need a drink.'

She nodded and moved past him into the safety of the apartment and the room she had come to know so well.

'A large gin and tonic please, Karl.'

'Ah, I see.'

'I'm just not very good at all this,' she offered apologetically.

He took a step towards her and brought his face close to hers, pressing his mouth against her own for a long, lingering moment, and immediately felt her begin to relax.

'It's not for much longer.'

She looked back at him, searching his face. 'You're so sure of yourself, aren't you?' she said softly as he poured the drinks.

'I just don't like hanging around, you know that.'

'I don't think we're "just hanging around", it's not that simple.'

'I know, I know,' he said, trying to reassure her, trying to take her mind off her husband, her son, anything but him. 'But there's only another nine weeks until the official close of the Talks, we have to start making plans.'

She took a mouthful of the gin and tonic. And he was right, wasn't he? They did need to make plans, or what had all this been for?

'I'm pretty sure that I'll be sent back to Washington . . .' He watched her face carefully. Or maybe he wouldn't be sent back at all. Gurney had been too cool with him over the last week, almost hostile on one or two occasions; if it was his work he would have said something by now. Karl blinked as he thought of his last conversation with Claude, two, maybe three months ago? The deals were over, Gurney couldn't really get anything on him, he had covered his tracks too well. 'You'll come with me.'

She blinked. 'I'm taking Christopher to his grandparents.'

'Can't John do that?'

A shadow seemed to fall behind her eyes and he knew, instantly, that he had said the wrong thing.

'John will be tying things up here, arranging the removal of our things, you know that.'

'Yeah, yeah – of course.' He was pushing too hard, but somehow he couldn't help himself. 'I'm just scared you'll change your mind.' He looked at her. 'You won't, will you, Elizabeth?'

She shook her head in response.

'Say it . . .'

He took her glass away and placed it on the table, circled her waist with his arms. 'Say it . . .'

'I won't change my mind, Karl.'

He leaned his forehead against hers and closed his eyes with relief.

'Sometimes I don't believe this is really me, saying these things, wanting you like I do, looking at a future with only you.' He smiled dryly. 'Now that really is something – for Karl Nielsen, that really is something.'

She smiled at last, for real, and he kissed her as if she had given him a prize.

'I was crazy to leave you five years ago.' He shook his head. 'Crazy.'

His lips brushed her hair and he crushed her against him as if she might slip away, and all the while she was remembering, all the while she was thinking of the time after he had gone, the first time, when he had left her alone, when she had found out that she was pregnant. Elizabeth squeezed her eyes tight shut at the strength of the memory and how she had thought, then, that he would surely come back, that he had not just forgotten her, that he had really meant it when he had said that he loved her. And now she wanted to tell him about her baby, her first child, Susan, and about her loneliness and the terrible longing day after day which had crept up on her, even eclipsing the love for her husband. But then his mouth was tracing her jawline, his hands were reaching into her hair to expose her neck and he was pressing against her, and the desire and the need were beginning to blot out the memory and the pain and the doubts which had begun to gnaw and gnaw.

'Hilde told me, Mama,' Sophia said. She had called her mother earlier only to be told by the girl who cleaned that 'Madam has gone out on urgent business to see the notary.'

'It was only a little business I had to attend to, and certainly not urgent as Hilde said – silly girl – that was all,' Genevieve replied. There was no point in saying any more, Sophia would only get alarmed at the mention of wills and other such things, but it had been done now and she could forget all about it. Herr Lechner, the old family notary, had been very kind.

'I was surprised, I suppose,' Sophia persisted gently. 'I cannot remember the last time you undertook family business, you usually leave that to Papa.'

And she did, but this business was something she did not want Felix to know of.

'It was nothing, Sophia,' she responded firmly. 'Now let us talk of more important things like you, and if you are getting enough rest and all those other things which a mother like me worries about.'

'I am very well, Mama.' Sophia smiled to herself as her mother spoke.

'Really?'

'Yes, really.'

'And Oskar . . .' she said hesitantly '. . . does he . . .'

'Mama,' Sophia interjected wearily, 'Uncle Oskar treats me like a daughter. He is a very kind man.' And she realized quite suddenly that he was probably one of the kindest people she had ever met, apart from her own mother, and that there was nothing he would not be prepared to do to make her more comfortable or more happy.

'Good. I'm so glad.'

'You do not need to worry about him, Mama.'

'I know your father spoke to him . . .' Genevieve's words trailed off.

'Mama – nothing has changed and, after all, I shall be leaving here at the end of August,' she said. 'The scholarship.'

'Oh, yes, of course.' Genevieve sighed softly and then abruptly changed the subject because she could hardly bear the thought of her daughter going. 'Will you be able to come a few days earlier for Gunther's birthday?'

'Only a day, I'm afraid, I have a tutorial at college which I must attend.'

'Oh, I see.'

'But I shall stay on a few days afterwards, Mama,' Sophia offered quickly, and frowned as she imagined the sadness in her mother's face. She would try and endure her father for three short days for *her* sake; it had been selfish of her to stay away so long. 'In the meantime, couldn't you come to Munich and spend a weekend here? I know Uncle Oskar wouldn't mind.'

'No. I don't think so. Your father has so many engagements as we lead up to the final weeks of these Talks . . .' She closed her eyes and gripped the telephone a little tighter as an unhappy picture of the bulky brown envelope with its sordid contents poured into her mind. She had said nothing to him, somehow she was still loath to bring the fragile walls of the only life she knew crashing down around them, because that was what would happen, or else he would lie and through all the lying he would somehow talk her into dreadful, mocking silence. And she could not bear that, that sort of terrible quiet pretence day after day, month after month, year after year, knowing what he would be doing behind her back, the other life he would surely be leading even though he would no doubt tell her that it would never happen again. Lies.

'Mama?'

'Yes.'

'What is it?'

Genevieve swallowed. 'Nothing. Why?'

'You just sound – well, you don't sound yourself,' Sophia said lamely. 'Are you well – there is nothing wrong?'

'No, no,' she lied. 'I'm only tired.' And she was tired, enormously tired. 'There have been so many functions this week, and this evening we have a *Heuriger* in Sievering and I had hoped I would have at least one early night to bed.'

'Do you *have* to attend?'

'Your father thinks so.' And as he had stood before her that morning tightening the knot of his silk tie she had wondered what he would do if she had suddenly produced the letters and the photographs and the filthy magazines and faced him with his infidelity but, of course, she had said nothing. He had not even noticed her red-rimmed eyes, or the fact that she had been up since dawn unable to sleep. But that was Felix, wasn't it? She had learned not to expect anything else from him, and hadn't she also come to expect little for herself? Handicapped as she was by irritating timidity and an inexplicable desire to please and please, like a homeless waif or a stray dog. She shuddered. Perhaps she was to blame for this unhappy turn in her life, this shattering of any illusion she might have had left. Where had it all gone – her life? Lost, piece by piece, in the debris of the years. So, she had said nothing to Felix, not one word, but it had all been in her eyes if he had cared to look.

'After July, then, for a holiday?'

'That would be wonderful,' Genevieve said quietly, lying.

'I shall write you a long letter today, after this call,' Sophia said. 'You write such beautiful letters to me.'

'Do I?'

'Oh, yes. I keep them all.'

'That is very sweet of you.'

'I like to, it's just nice to know they're there.'

'Thank you, Sophia.'

'For what?'

'For what you've just said.'

'Oh, Mama . . .'

'And now I must go,' Genevieve said thickly because the tears were coming back. 'I can hear Hilde calling.'

'And you are really all right?'

'Yes, yes – just tired, that is all.' She swallowed. 'Tomorrow morning I will stay in bed for a while, perhaps I shall even have breakfast there and read the papers.' But she wouldn't, not now, because the effort would be wasted. It seemed so difficult to relax these days, to close her eyes and let blissful sleep wash over her. No morning seemed to pass without her waking to that anxious, panic feeling trapped deep in her chest, as if her body was warning her that something out of her control, something bad, was going to happen that day.

'Goodbye, Mama.'

'Goodbye, my darling.'

So, it had all turned out better than she had dared hope, because Sophia might even come to know real happiness, and ironically it had all happened because of Felix's grandiose ideas for their daughter's future – and something else too, something within Sophia, as if she had suddenly grown up overnight, and that still puzzled her, but nevertheless she was happy and doing, above all, what she really wanted in life. Genevieve shook her head gently, surprised at the sad, furtive envy which was creeping slowly into her heart. She replaced the receiver back in its cradle, her hand lingering on the ivory plastic, and then patted it once, twice, before lifting her head to the picture of her husband framed in silver, sitting on the seventeenth-century cabinet; yet another item retrieved from the castle. The castle, Schloss Bletz, which meant more to Felix than anything else in the world.

'The picture's new, isn't it Sam?' Natalie asked sweetly as her gaze swept across his den and then back to the black and white print on the wall.

'It's the Belvedere, one of Vienna's historic palaces. Beautiful.'

She brushed past him, too closely, and his eyes were unwillingly drawn to the roundness of her buttocks moving beneath the careful cut of her skirt.

'I didn't know you went in for sightseeing.' She leaned forwards as if she studied the picture and thought: Dull, dull, dull.

'I took Joanna,' he said quietly, and added as an afterthought, 'with a friend.'

'A friend?' She turned and looked at him. 'The girl you were seeing last time?'

'Yes, Kristina.'

'Pretty name.'

Clara came into the room and shot a glance at Natalie before speaking to Sam.

'Dinner is ready, sir.'

Sam smiled. 'Thanks, Clara.' He had thought of trying to avoid dinner with Natalie, but in the end it had proved too difficult, too much like running away. He had finally settled on having dinner served at home with Clara safely and comfortably installed in the kitchen. Usually he saw Kristina on Friday evenings after both of them had finished a hard week at the Hofburg, it had become a sort of ritual, and her face had grown wary and tense when he had told her of his intended plans. But Natalie was only here for three days, and the visit would be over before she knew it.

'You shouldn't have gone to all this trouble, Sam', Natalie said. 'I could have arranged for us to have dinner at my hotel.'

'Clara's a very good cook and I don't give her enough opportunity to show off her expertise; she was looking forward to it.' In fact, he had no idea whether Clara liked cooking or not, he had just told her to 'fix something'. They sat down and immediately the Filipino woman appeared like magic from the kitchen bearing a mouthwatering platter of langoustines and small spiny lobsters served on a bed of light fluffy rice, celery hearts in rings of chives and carrots in courgette rings. Sam gulped in surprise because he had not really known what to expect, but this was clearly beyond any expectations.

'Wow . . . you really have got yourself a little jewel there, Sam!' Natalie lifted her eyes to the broad, brown face of the woman who was leaning over her, filling her plate with the luscious food from the platter, and for a fleeting, furtive moment their gazes locked. The woman's eyes were almost black, Natalie realized, piercing as they looked back at her, and she stiffened as if that look went deep inside and saw all the shadows, all the dark corners, as if Clara knew what she was. She reached for the glass of wine Sam had poured her and brought it quickly to her mouth.

'Hey, slow down . . .' Sam said, 'you're supposed to savour that.'

'What is it?' she said, pressing the beginnings of her hot, erratic temper down.

'It's a white Piedmont.'

'Oh.'

He laughed, knowing that she didn't have any idea what he was talking about.

'Piedmont is mostly known for red wines.'

'You're a real education, Sam,' she said dryly. 'Still trying to blind me with science.'

'No, Natalie, you always get me wrong – I'm just interested, that's all.'

'Can't we talk about something else?'

'Sure – go ahead.'

'When are you coming back to the States?'

'In the summer, after the Talks are over.'

'You said you were coming at Easter and you changed your mind.'

'Well, I hardly thought a trip was necessary then when you'd decided to come here instead.'

'And what if the Talks don't end as neatly as you think?'

'We'll have to think again.' He sighed. 'But they will, they will, everything looks as if it's heading that way.'

'Some gink spat on my chinchilla in Fifth Avenue.' She frowned. 'If that's where all this green stuff is heading, you can forget it.'

'Natalie,' he said, 'when people see a fur now they see a lot of little animals all sewn up together to look pretty.'

'So after these terrific, mind-blowing Talks furs will be out, smoking will be out, maybe even breathing will be out . . .'

'That's up to you, you know that.'

She watched his face and saw how serious he was and knew she had said the wrong thing.

'Joke, Sam . . . I know how important all this is, I've even started using recycled Tampax.' She started to laugh and Sam tried to press down the beginnings of a smile. Coarse, but funny. 'But I know it really is important, Sam, despite the gag.' His face softened and she drank some more wine. 'All this stuff on rain forests, CFCs and pollution, I mean, it's really bad . . . right?'

'Really bad, Natalie.'

'The *Washington Post* said that things were going to get worse before they got better.'

Sam raised his eyebrows just a little – Natalie reading the *Washington Post*?

'Maybe – it means changing a lot of things and people; and countries don't like change.'

'Like?'

'Like reducing the burning of fossil fuels – oil and particularly coal – like stopping the burning of tropical forests.'

'What will happen if we don't?'

'Climatic change – rainfall patterns will be disrupted, sea levels will rise, places like Florida, the Netherlands, Bengal and other low-lying areas will be flooded; some islands, like the Maldives, might disappear altogether. The US grain belt will probably suffer a decline . . . shall I go on?' He sighed. 'These are estimates, good guesses. Really long term, who can tell what might happen?'

'It sounds such a *drag* . . .'

'If it wasn't 'such a drag' I wouldn't be here.'

'The last time I was in LA I had to wear my Hermes scarf in front of my mouth . . .'

'Atmospheric pollution – or smog, to you – LA being particularly vulnerable because geographically it sits in a basin.'

She took another mouthful of wine and wondered how long she would have to keep her interest up. This was all getting just too much and anyway, it wasn't really her problem because somehow, someway, the world would go on turning, Sam and people like him would see to that, even if she did have to put up with the odd gink gobbing over her chinchilla. Now that really *was* a drag.

'Perhaps we'd better talk about something else – I can get boring once I get on the subject.'

She smiled carefully – you sure can – it was almost as if he had read her mind. Natalie looked down at her plate and the watermelon fruit which was sitting there; she hadn't even noticed Clara flitting in and out, which was probably just as well. She didn't like her. But she switched her attention back to Sam as the cool, refreshing fruit slipped down her throat and watched him from beneath lowered lids. He had loosened his tie and there was a touch of pink in his cheeks as if the wine was getting to him. Very casually she undid the buttons of her bolero jacket, it was beautiful, a great buy: black velvet studded with tiny jet beads, and underneath was another beauty, a matching black velvet dress with a low, low scoop neck. With studied indifference she placed the neat little jacket on the back of her chair and without so much as a glance at Sam continued eating the watermelon. He didn't say a word.

'Could we have coffee in the den, Sam?' she asked. 'My back's still stiff from the flight.'

He looked at her for a moment and then nodded. 'Sure, I'll just tell Clara.'

'Why don't you tell her that she can go off duty and I'll make the coffee? The poor woman's been stuck in that kitchen all night spoiling us with that terrific meal.'

He stood up and seemed to hesitate for a moment.

'Go on, Sam . . .'

It was difficult to refuse.

Natalie looked at the carefully prepared coffee tray and then began smoothing her dress, pulling it down sharply so that her cleavage rose up above the cut of the neck. 'Beautiful, honey,' she whispered to herself and then reached for the tray. 'Oh, Sam, Sam, we're going to have such a good time . . .' As she walked into the living area she set the tray down again and turned off all the lights, so only the light from the den could be seen and that coming from Clara's rooms just below. 'We won't be needing your services tonight, sunshine . . .' And she brought her hand up abruptly into the dark empty air with the thick middle finger thrust upwards, a crude, vicious gesture because somehow the woman had known her.

When she walked into the den Sam was standing in front of the fireplace and she could tell immediately that he was tense even as he tried to hide the eyes that had travelled instantly over her body.

'I'll have to leave pretty soon, I'm expecting a call back at the hotel.' Of course, it wasn't true, but it had the desired effect, she could almost see the relief pouring out of Sam.

'That's a pity.'

Sam had always been a bad liar.

'Well, it seemed a good idea at the time – I knew you wouldn't want me to stay too late.'

He blushed. 'At least join me in a liqueur before you go.'

'These days I don't like drinking alone.'

'Okay, okay.' He smiled.

They both drank cognacs out of massive brandy balloons and she snuggled into a corner of a couch and carefully crossed her legs so that he could see that nothing had changed, that her thighs were still firm, the warm flesh still lightly tanned.

'How are things generally?' he asked casually, feeling the clinging heat of the day draining down his back.

'Not what they were, better, really – I try to read more and I do a lot of riding, particularly at weekends.' She wanted to laugh then, Donahue was back on the scene and he liked to ride *a lot*.

'What about the parties?'

'Maybe I've grown up, I just don't seem to find them so interesting any more.'

'Really?' He gave her a wry smile.

'Really, Sam.' She uncrossed her legs and leaned towards him so that he would see her breasts.

'I suppose people change,' he said weakly and wondered why he had said that.

'Could I have another brandy before I go?' she asked and stood up as if she would pour it herself.

'Oh . . . sure.'

She walked slowly to the bookcase where he had left the bottle, knowing that he watched, and then filled her glass and made to fill his.

'No – Natalie.'

'Just one for the road, Sam – and then you'd better call me a cab.'

He looked up at her and nodded reluctantly.

'Do you still have that album by Feliciano?'

'Somewhere.'

'Play it, Sam.'

'It's late, Natalie.'

'And I'm leaving in ten minutes . . . come on . . .'

He sighed and then began searching through his CD collection until he found it. He switched the stereo on and prepared the disc to play and then took a mouthful of brandy. As the warmth of the liquid hit his belly the low, heady notes of 'Light my Fire' began to ooze out of the speakers.

'It speaks to you, don't you think, Sam?'

'I know it's good music, Natalie,' he said neutrally.

'Oh, sure – but it *says* things . . .' She stood up and moved over to him. 'Why don't we dance, just once?'

'Because it's not a good idea.'

'For Chrissakes, Sam, I won't bite you,' she sighed dramatically, 'it's only a goddamned dance.' She took his hand and pulled him into the middle of the floor. 'Just a dance, Sam.'

He closed his eyes as she put his arms around her waist, as her hands came up around his neck.

'Relax, just relax,' she whispered.

But he couldn't, he was too aware of her body, of her breasts, of her legs, of her hair, of her perfume and the moist curve of her mouth as it played softly against his ear.

'Ssssh – sssh – no more thinking, Sam, just listen to the music, it's so, so beautiful.'

And it was true; the words, the guitar, the burning voice asking so much, making him dizzy with terrible possibilities. And then her arms were sliding down over his back, her cheek pressing against his face, her thighs pushing, pushing against his own. He knew what would happen next because it had happened so many times before and he was suddenly powerless to stop it because he wanted, hungered, and as her lips found his own he abandoned himself to the succulence of her searching tongue as it forced itself into his mouth, lost himself in the tasting of her skin. Natalie.

She stood in front of the mirror, slightly shaky on her feet, and began unwrapping the carefully hoarded tin foil. As the powder began to flake out Natalie licked it greedily before placing a small, neat pile on the back of her hand and inhaling sharply through her nose, snorting the deadly snow and breathing deeply as it penetrated into the tiny veins in her nostrils. 'Oh, better – much, much bet*ter*.' She shook her head and began examining her face in the mirror: her skin was looking an unhealthy yellow beneath the artificial tan and her eyes were bloodshot, but she smiled, knowing that in a few minutes, after a shower and some make-up, she would look good again. It had been a long night, she had made sure of that, and now she was paying the cost, but it had been worth it because Sam had, finally, given in and played the game her way. And it had been so goddamn *easy*, now it would only be a question of time before they made arrangements for the future, and there was no way she was going to let him slip away again. Her gaze shifted to the piece of tin foil; Sam need never know if she was careful and discreet and as long as she acted the good wife – and Joanna would have another nanny, not that Filipino bitch. Natalie stepped into the shower and let hot, hot water cascade down over her body. It wouldn't be so much of a sacrifice getting back with Sam, after all she had to be realistic; she was over thirty now and her reputation in Washington and New York precluded a decent match with some other guy. Her hands came up to her throat to feel the soft skin there, then she let them trail down to her breasts which she touched carefully, lovingly and then to the flat stomach and round to her buttocks which were almost hard from the riding – she smiled then – and the burns she did at the gym every day. 'Lovely ass,' she whispered. She switched off the shower, stepped out into Sam's white and blue bathroom, slipped possessively into his bathrobe, looked back at herself in the mirror and said, 'Mine'. The coke was already making her feel *really* good and she began brushing her hair vigorously as if there was electricity at her fingertips, but then she pinned it up quickly and let a few, studied tendrils hang tantalizingly to caress her neck; a touch of rouge, lipstick and mascara and she was almost ready, but the telephone rang. Tentatively she stepped out into the hallway. She could see the receiver vibrating with the shrieking, rhythmic sound; Sam was asleep and Clara . . . where the hell was Clara? Natalie padded out into the living room and walked over to the phone.

'Hello.'
Silence.
'Hello.'
'Is Sam there, please?'
Natalie smiled.
'You mean Sam Cohen?'
'Yes.'
'He's in bed, all tucked up.' She wanted to laugh then and would have given just *anything* to see this woman's face. Kristina?
'Oh, I see.'

'Who shall I say called?'
'Kristina.'
'Kristeeeena,' Natalie drawled. 'Oh, yeah, Kristina. Sam told me about you.'
'He did?'
Poor cow.
'He said that you'd been really good to him.'
'Really.'
'Oh, yeah, said that he'd always be grateful to you.'
Silence again.
'I couldn't speak to him, could I?'
'Sorry, Kristina, but he really is all tucked up in bed and I'm going to be joining him there just as soon as we finish talking.' She sighed. 'You see, that's how it is with us, just one of those things . . . I knew we'd get back together, it was only a matter of time – I'm real sorry that you got caught up in all of this.' Natalie brought a fist up to her mouth as if she would stop herself from laughing out loud.
'Perhaps you would tell him I called.'
'Oh – sure.' Like hell she would. There was a sharp click as Kristina put the receiver down. Natalie looked into the mouthpiece and pulled her lips into a sneer, letting her tongue slip out long and pink and wet as she blew a raspberry.

She pulled the belt of Sam's robe tighter and turned back to go into the bedroom, but as she did so her eyes caught a glimpse of black and white standing in the doorway of the kitchen. Natalie gave a small inward start as she focused on Clara's wide, contemptuous eyes and her face fell into a sullen frown that for all her beauty made her suddenly ugly and unpleasant to look at. The Filipino would have to go . . . def-in-ite-ly.

'I didn't realize you were home, John.'
'The meeting wound up earlier than expected.' He loosened his tie and then glanced at the leather-topped desk against the wall to see what mail there was; it was a safe, everyday habit. Elizabeth remained sitting, a magazine lying unread in her lap. He watched her for a painful moment, longing to ask whether she had seen *him* that day, or whether she would make some lame excuse to go out this evening. But he was afraid of himself, afraid of the person inside who he was forcing to be calm and cool, the person who was meeting and talking and walking and being 'John' as if his world was not falling apart.

'How are things going?'
'There's a good chance we may finish.'

'At the end of July?'

'Probably.' He didn't want to ask the inevitable question – why her sudden interest? That was also something he was saving, something he couldn't say. 'Would you like a drink?'

'Please.' She watched his broad back as he moved to the table and the silver tray with its array of decanters. 'I think I saw a colleague of yours the other day.'

'Who?'

'You introduced us at the Opera Ball – a dark-haired, pretty girl. Laura?'

'Laura Drummond.' He turned back into the room, drinks in hand. 'Why do you "think" you saw her?'

'Sorry . . . I don't "think" I saw her, I *know* I did, but it was all rather odd and she seemed to be in a bit of of state.'

'What do you mean?'

'We actually bumped into each other . . .' she swallowed, trying to avoid mentioning the meeting place '. . . and it seemed to me that not only had she been crying, but there was a huge bruise on her face – almost like a black eye.'

John's eyebrows drew together in a frown. 'Where was this?'

Elizabeth's gaze was inevitably drawn to his face. 'Near the Rathaus.'

'In the street?'

'Not exactly.'

He looked back at her knowing instantly that she had been seeing *him*.

'Where?' He knew where Nielsen lived, yet somehow he wanted her to tell him.

'An apartment building.'

'I see.' It was enough.

She flushed but didn't look away from him, and he felt a curious twinge of admiration. Elizabeth could do that to him, even now, even now. He put his drink down.

'I'd better see Christopher to sleep, he'll be waiting for his story.'

'Let me, John,' she said softly. 'I want to.'

There was that look again and he felt a flutter of panic. She stood up and moved across the room to the shadow of the open door, but then seemed to hesitate before looking back at him.

'You may get Washington . . .'

'Yes.'

'It's very good news.'

But it didn't seem to matter any longer, there was no joy or great expectation in looking at a future without her, no matter how grand, no matter how prestigious. She had taken that away from him.

'What will you do?' he asked quietly, amazed at the calmness in his voice, amazed that the words had slipped out so easily.

'I don't know, John.' She lowered her eyes and then looked back at him and whispered, 'I don't know.' And then she turned her head and moved from the doorway and he heard her slow, sure footsteps taking her to their son's room, and away from him.

9

'You've got some beautiful things, Karl.' Dan watched his counsellor as he poured coffee from a sleek glass jug. He had arranged a private meeting with Karl because he was curious, wanting to see the man at home, where he lived, how he lived.

'Just some stuff I've been collecting along the way,' he responded carefully. 'Like everyone in this business.'

'Yes, and naturally I have a few nice things myself.' Dan paused. 'But I don't have any ivory.'

Karl sighed silently with resignation; so that was it.

'I like African artefacts, I became a collector while I was out there – it's a fantastic place.'

'Well, it was, and might be again, given a chance.'

Karl looked into his ambassador's impassive face and felt the first stirrings of anger.

'Cut the lecture, Dan, and get to the point.'

'All right, Karl.' He smiled without humour. 'The point is ivory and rhino horn and the illegal export of certain endangered species.'

'What's that got to do with me?'

'Come *on*, Karl, don't insult my intelligence.' Dan shook his head with disgust. 'I happen to have quite a few facts in my possession about a certain import and export company operating in Mtwara, a port near the Mozambique border.'

'So?' Suddenly it didn't matter any more, the pretence, the lies, let Gurney do his damnedest, he wouldn't get very far.

'It's yours, isn't it? Or at least a good part of it.'

'I don't think you'll find my name anywhere.' He had always been ruthlessly careful, and besides, his whole interest in ivory trading was over; it had just got too hot.

Dan nodded. 'Oh, yes, you're right, but the guy who runs it for you – who *ran* it for you – mentioned your name. He mentioned a lot of things.' His eyes examined the man opposite very sharply. 'There's a German priest involved too, they call him the King of Mtwara – supposed to be a good friend of yours – and my sources tell me that you've both done a pretty good job at buying the local police and party officials.'

'I didn't know they had a king in Mtwara.'

'Don't get smart.'

Karl smiled.

'Your name does happen to appear on some import documents with regard to a nice line in videos, TVs, radios, ice-boxes and even a number of Mercedes.' Dan sighed.

'Apart from breaking sacred diplomatic rules, I don't see what you're getting at.'

'Well, you aren't – weren't – selling the stuff out there, that much I know, you were giving it away, I think it's called unsophisticated bribery, isn't it? The natives go ape-shit for garbage like videos, like ice-boxes, like Mercedes in exchange for a few illegal tusks. I'd say that there must be at least one Mercedes for every dead elephant by now.'

'I've never counted, Dan.' He was enjoying this, enjoying sending Gurney up.

'You cheap son-of-a-bitch.'

'You can call me all the names you like, but you don't have any real evidence, *Dan*, and even if you did I doubt, somehow, that you would use it. After all, the publicity would almost kill these talks stone dead.' He tasted his coffee. 'And you really don't want that, certainly at this stage when it looks like everything might be all wrapped up nice and neat.'

Dan made no answer, but stood up and prowled slowly about the room, glancing at books, at glass, at the masks on the wall, picking up the exquisite pieces of ivory and turning them over in his fingers.

'Haven't you ever felt dirty about all this . . . have you ever felt *anything* at all?' He had to ask, he had to try and understand.

'You mean guilty? No,' he said, slowly. 'I needed the money.' There *had* been doubt, sometimes, sliding stealthily into his mind, but he had blinked it away. 'For the record I went into this business before it became such a popular, political issue and I have since pulled out.'

'Oh, sure – because it got too hot to handle.' Dan shook his head. 'Don't try and tell me you had an unnatural attack of conscience, because I don't believe you have one.'

'You're getting personal, Dan. Not very professional.'

'How much did you make, Karl – how much?'

'I don't think you really want to know.'

'How much?'

'About four million dollars.'

Dan swallowed, deep in his throat.

'I told you you wouldn't want to know. And did you really think I'd risk my neck for peanuts, Dan?' The corners of his mouth moved upwards into a sardonic smile. 'You surprise me . . . aren't you the man with all the facts at his fingertips?' Karl sighed with exaggerated patience. 'Did you know, for instance, that a mere kilo of raw tusks alone can instantly rocket to one hundred dollars if the circumstances are right, or a single rare parrot or orchid in good condition can fetch somewhere in the region of five thousand dollars?' He shook his head. 'I do a great line in crocodile skins, Dan . . .'

'You bastard.'

'*Oh, come on* . . . I'm chickenfeed to some of the big boys we're brushing elbows with around the conference table. You know and I know that all these treaties and conventions are so much bullshit when people like the Japs sign them and then turn a blind eye to illicit trading, but the great governments of the world are too busy doing business with them to have the guts to do anything worthwhile about it . . .'

'No one sane could call four million dollars chickenfeed.'

Karl shrugged his shoulders.

'You will have to resign, of course.'

'Naturally.' Karl began pouring himself another coffee. 'Presumably at the end of the talks.'

'Yes.' Dan looked at him with weary contempt. 'I would prefer it otherwise, of course, but I am forced to be practical.' He wanted to fire him there and then, get him out of his sight.

Karl stared back at the implacable profile, but said nothing.

'There is another alternative, one I find rather distasteful.'

Karl wanted to smile.

'If you were to cooperate with names, places . . . it might be possible to find you a position somewhere, but obviously not in the State.' He said the words without expression because they were not his to say.

'This wasn't your idea, was it, Dan?' He shook his head as his mouth began to tilt upwards. 'Must really stick in your gullet.'

'I can see the benefits,' he said quietly.

'Oh, sure.' Karl stood up and moved over to his drinks cabinet. 'I think I need something stronger – join me?'

'No.' Dan watched him as he poured himself a large cognac.

'You know what this reminds me of? Those Nazi war criminals who were given the seal of approval by person or persons unknown, in the State Department, so long as they "cooperated". Some of them are still alive, aren't they, Dan? You know, the doctors, the scientists, the really top guys who could give the good old US a helping hand with new knowledge and information by *cooperating* . . .' He lifted his eyes and frowned as if he were concentrating deeply. 'If I'm not mistaken one of those nice, cooperative scientists who had a hand in murdering hundreds, maybe thousands, of innocent people was given some kind of medal, or did he have a memorial built . . . yeah, that was it . . .'

'Enough.'

'And you really think that I'd "cooperate", as you so sweetly suggest?' Karl said. 'You must be crazy – I'm no Nazi war criminal with nothing to lose, I'd like to think that I've still got the rest of my life ahead of me and if I "cooperate", as you so nicely put it, I'm likely to have my balls hacked off.' He swallowed a mouthful of the thick, treacly cognac. 'This is an international illegal network we're talking about, and like everywhere else, it has its hard-liners who have no pity, no remorse, no scruples.' He shook his head. 'You think I'm not a nice guy, but you ain't seen nothin', Dan, as the saying goes.'

'So. What will you do? Somehow I don't see four million dollars lasting very long with someone like you.'

Dan lifted his arm up and gestured extravagantly at the contents of the room. 'Apart from the fact that I haven't thought about it much, it's none of your business.' But it was true, half of it was gone already and he could hardly account for it; money had a habit of trickling right through his fingers like sand.

'There's always the drugs trade, Karl, something I don't doubt you'd be good at.'

'Very funny, Dan.' But it was a possibility, in fact Claude had even implied that much and Claude seemed to have his finger in most of the juicy illicit trades; after all whatever trade it was they probably all travelled the same routes in the same, illicit way – like in packing crates, false floors in vehicles, inside tubing, even diplomatic bags depending on the article to be smuggled, and the beauty of drugs was that they were so mobile, so compact, so easy to hide and the pickings were almost too good, too easy as long as you were reasonably careful. Thousands and thousands of no-hopers out there just waiting to pop pills or snort the little white line. Like pieces of broken glass. If it wasn't him, it would be someone else, wouldn't it? Even as the thought took shape and faded there was that little seed of doubt, that thinning of the darkness as if he had just missed something, as if whatever it was had just slipped disturbingly out of sight.

'I'd better get back.'

Karl looked up, snapped suddenly out of his reverie.

'Well, look on the bright side, Dan, you won't have to endure my company for much longer.'

'True,' Dan said as they walked to the door. 'Just one last thing . . .' The only real card he had to play.

'What is it?'

'I really don't think Elizabeth Thornton would approve of your lesser-known activities.'

There was a moment's strange little silence as Karl met the eyes of his ambassador.

'You didn't think I was ignorant of the situation, did you, Karl?' He thought with gratitude of Sir Nigel Howard. 'I try not to miss the finer details of the lives of my staff.'

'She knows.'

'No. I don't see someone like Elizabeth Thornton going along with something as sordid as your nasty little deals, Karl.' He gave his counsellor a long, searching look. 'I don't think she really knows you at all, does she?'

'My private life isn't your concern.'

'Oh, but it is, Karl, very much so. I happen to like John Thornton.'

'I knew Elizabeth long before he came into her life.'

So that was it.

'I couldn't give a horse's ass whether you knew her before, you had your chance and you lost it. Give her up, or I'll make sure she gives you up – one way or another.' The anger was coming back now and Dan thrust his face forward and hissed. 'And do you really think that you'll be any good to a woman like that? *You?* Don't make me laugh.' He sighed heavily, impatiently, so that his hot breath touched Karl's face. 'People like you don't change, Karl, they don't have it in them to do so. You see, you don't really *feel*, not deep down where it matters ... there's no room for sacrifice in that murky hole you call a soul, no room for anyone else but Karl Nielsen, ivory trader extraordinaire.'

'Fuck off, Dan,' he said quietly.

'Be careful, Karl, the diplomatic veneer is slipping and, don't worry, I'm going.' He opened the door and gave him a sardonic smile. 'But naturally I expect to see you at the delegation office in the morning because as far as anyone else is concerned this conversation never took place.' Dan stepped out into the corridor and added, finally, 'I do believe that, as I speak, you have approximately forty-five working days left to look forward to – but maybe I can do something about that, after all.'

Karl watched him go and then closed the door of his apartment and walked back into the empty room. He wouldn't put it past Gurney – telling Elizabeth – that was his only weapon. Smart. Karl poured himself another drink and sat down and found his thoughts sweeping backwards over the past few months, over his first meeting with her and the times which came after; remembering the hesitancy, the smiles, the torment, the lovemaking; remembering. He leaned his head back and closed his eyes as a picture of her formed in his mind. But it was true, what Gurney had said. Elizabeth didn't know him. And if she did, what then? His eyelids flickered open and he looked across the room at the masks on the stark, white wall; the man and the woman. A shadow momentarily dimmed his eyes and there was that uneasiness again, that furtive shrinking inside, and he wondered where she was, what she was doing.

She seemed to have lost her taste for café life, Laura realized sadly, and she knew that whatever the future might hold she would always look back on her time in Vienna with regret and shame, as if a blackness lay over it. The shock of Ralf's revelations had not receded, if anything they had grown into something monstrous as her mind whirled with endless unendurable possibilities. She had waited for his call day after nerve-racking day: her concentration had gone, she was not eating or sleeping properly and on one particularly nightmarish evening she had even gone to bed mercifully drunk to shut the horror out. She did not know what to do.

Laura looked across the room at a couple sitting at one of the round marble tables, they were holding hands, oblivious to anyone else in the café, and she felt her eyes brim. Even now she could hardly believe that such a thing had happened to her, that her life had taken such a bewildering and ugly turn; it seemed astonishing to her then that she had had no inkling, no idea of what was to come, only her instincts had touched on something intangible from time to time which she had been unable to grasp and which she had allowed inevitably to slip away.

The irony of it all was that she and Andrew had probably never been closer and he had naturally sensed her distress, but she had merely said that she was overtired, that she had been doing too much. If only he knew, and if he did what would he think of her then? Their relationship, she presumed, would be over. And her career? How she had fought for the right to come here to pursue her own glittering path in the world of diplomacy! Ultimately she had been incredibly naïve and extremely foolish, not the sort of qualities to earn her respect or advancement.

She looked up, her eyes drawn unwillingly to the glass doors of the Central Café; Ralf was late, but then he could afford to be late now because he knew that she would still be waiting, whatever time he decided to come. And now she was afraid of him, really afraid. When his fist had struck her face she had been able to feel the muted power behind the blow even as her body had hit the floor – he had controlled himself and she wondered for a brief fearful moment what Ralf Müller, or whatever his real name was, could do with those fists when he really lost his temper.

And the video, the video . . . misery spread through her like a gross, seeping stain and she thought she would never recover from this, never get over this squalid chapter in her life because it would always be there like a filthy blot on her memory. Never clean again. It was stupid, irrational, but since that last time at his apartment she had scrubbed and scrubbed her body almost raw as if she would somehow remove the past and his hands and the other man's touch from her skin. But not inside, never inside.

She saw him then, moving slowly towards her; he was smiling. Laura swallowed and her hand began to play nervously with the handle of her coffee cup.

'You look quite pale, Laura.' He sat down. 'I thought you might at least have taken advantage of this lovely weather we've been having.'

'I've been busy.'

'Ah – you've been busy.'

He looked around and snapped his fingers at the nearest waitress; he had never done that before.

'More coffee, or perhaps something a little stronger?'

'No, thank you.'

'You're so *English*, Laura, do you realize that?' He was smiling again. 'The English hardly ever drink during the day unless it's wine with a meal. Very boring.'

'What have you come to say?'

'You *will* have a drink with me,' he said, ignoring her remark, 'I insist.'

A large carafe of red wine and two glasses were brought to the table and he pushed one towards her and filled the glass to the brim.

'That will bring a little colour to your cheeks, Laura.'

'I don't want colour brought to my cheeks.'

'No?' He shook his head. 'Have I misjudged you yet again?'

'A few minutes ago I asked you what you had come to say.'

'Oh, yes, so you did.' Ralf brought his hands together so that the fingertips touched and he began flexing his knuckles. 'I suppose I simply want to be reassured that I may rely on your cooperation in the future.'

'I don't know what you mean.' Oh, but she did, she did.

'Silly girl.' He shook his head. 'Shall I repeat myself – "I simply want to be reassured that I may rely on your cooperation in the future."'

'And if I don't reassure you?'

'I'm sure I don't have to explain in great detail what I might do with that rather colourful video I have in my possession – there are photographs too. I wonder what your colleagues, your ambassador, even your parents or your precious boyfriend might make of those?' He shook his head again in mock sorrow. 'It could ruin your life, Laura.'

She looked back at him, her eyes flat and expressionless. But he had done that already.

'I just need to know that when it is necessary you will be very helpful.' He brought the glass of wine to his lips. 'That is all.'

'I do not have access to very secret material.'

'Oh, but you might, Laura, you might very well in the future once your career really takes off and you are no longer merely the lowly rank of second secretary.' He looked at his hands, at the square, flesh-pink nails. 'Indeed, I am sure that, even now, an interesting document or two must slip through your lovely hands.'

'Not really.'

He sighed. 'Laura, Laura . . .' he said with feigned exasperation. 'I know, I just know, so don't treat me like a fool.'

She turned her face to the window, to the people and the shops and the world beyond the glass, wishing she was anywhere, anywhere but here. She jumped as his hand closed tightly over her own and the blood shot through her veins.

'This city is full of spies, Laura, didn't you know that? Didn't anyone tell you at your precious Foreign Office before you arrived in this City of Dreams?' He snorted with quiet laughter. 'You take a photocopy, Laura, that is all.' He let go of her hand. 'I will call you, shall we say, in a month? It would be nice if you had something, even something small, to show me so that I will know that you have taken our little conversation seriously.'

He stood up and walked away.

Her eyes drifted back to the carafe of wine which was still half full and she wondered vaguely why he had ordered it at all if he had only planned to stay for such a short time. Perhaps he expected her to drink alone and get herself drunk, as she had done a few nights previously, the day he had called. But she wasn't a great drinker and alcohol only dulled the pain, or mercifully blotted it out altogether for a few fleeting hours. He was right, of course, because her life would be ruined, disgraced, dishonoured, tainted if she did not do as he asked; but equally she knew that she would never have an easy moment if she agreed to cooperate, there would never be peace for her, anywhere. Laura looked back to the window and the people and the faces and the warm blue sky overhead and tried to imagine Ralf's square, handsome face once he found out what she intended to do, but it would be too late then. It was ironic really that he had taken all that time and trouble to seduce her, degrade her, blackmail her only to discover that it was *he* who had misjudged, not her, *he* who had picked the wrong victim, after all. Her gaze drifted wearily from the window and was drawn back to the couple across the room; they were still there, still holding hands. Her stomach began to churn as she thought of Andrew, and his blond hair and his slanting smile, and what he would say when she told him.

Sam walked briskly up the thick stone steps to Kristina's apartment; he had tried to call her several times as promised, but each time her mother had answered and each time she had told him that Kristina was out and that there was no need to leave a message. She had been rude, of course, but then Kristina's mother did not like him. Sam rang the doorbell. From within he could hear the gradual opening of a door and the shuffling and the sound of the old woman's stick as she moved ponderously towards the door.

'You.'
'Yes, me. Could I speak to Kristina?'
'I told you on the telephone, she isn't here.'
'Where is she?'
'Salzburg.'
'Salzburg?!'
'She felt she needed a change – a weekend away.'
'But I told her I'd call.'
'Perhaps she misunderstood.'
'I don't think so,' he said dryly, confused and exasperated at the same time. There was no question of a misunderstanding, he had definitely told her that he would call today, this morning in fact; now it was well into the afternoon. Natalie was in the Stadtpark with Joanna and he had made an excuse to leave them for a few minutes. 'Is there a number I can call her at?'
'No.'
He took a deep breath. 'I would really like to call her, Frau Heidl.'
'I told you, no.'
He looked into the old face, criss-crossed with lines and liver spots, and almost wanted to smile. She was tough, this old lady, and he had to admire that.
'I know you don't like me, Frau Heidl, but I believe that Kristina does and I would like to talk to her.'
'My daughter has never been a good judge of character, she has always allowed herself to be taken in by strangers, foreigners, and suffered for her impulsiveness.' She began to close the door.
'I haven't finished.'
'You make her unhappy, Herr Cohen, that is enough.'
'I don't understand.'

'She should find a good, Austrian man, not a . . .'

'I've got red blood flowing through my veins, Frau Heidl, just like you.' He drew a sharp, weary breath before adding quickly, 'Maybe you do this all the time.'

She stopped closing the door, her pinched, ancient features a cameo in the space between door and frame.

'What do you mean?'

'Humiliate her, make her life difficult.'

'You know nothing, Herr Cohen – about me or my daughter.'

'I'm not talking about Kristina, I'm talking about *you*.' He swallowed. 'It must be quite something living with someone as ill-tempered and ungrateful as you day after day, week after week, year after year. And, sure, I bet you're really terrified that she might meet a *foreigner*; I can understand that, because then she would have to leave your gilt-edged Vienna and you as well – all alone. That's it, isn't it, Frau Heidl? That's what this is all about.'

'Go away, Herr Cohen, go back where you came from.'

'Do you mean America, or my roots which bring me back here to Europe and Berlin and even good old Vienna? *Where*, exactly, Frau Heidl?'

The door slammed shut and he was left looking at deep brown wood and a small spy hole which he didn't doubt she was looking through. Sam sighed heavily and walked back down the curving staircase. He had taken too long, Natalie would be wondering and he didn't need that, he wanted some peace to think. Last night had been a mistake, he could see that now, but he had allowed her to seduce him in the end and she had been very clever about it, very cool; she had not even suggested seeing him tonight, a suggestion he would have refused anyway. Natalie was being very good, very convincing, and Kristina had been right, of course, his wife wanted him back. And she *was* Joanna's mother.

What if she had really changed? Was that possible? Natalie? His mind swept back to the night before and her slick performance, because even through the hypnotic sounds of Feliciano and the taste of the last cognac in his mouth he had known that that was what it was. But she was dizzying, his wife, superb with her body and her hands and her tongue. Dizzying. And as a searing, provocative picture of her soared into his head he wondered at the power of her skill to leave the sensation and the images almost reverberating beneath his skin, his fingertips, his eyes. She had sat astride him ultimately, her mouth open, her teeth laughing at him, the tongue licking greedily across the red lips as she had moved her hips, her pelvis in hot, frantic rhythm. Every man's fantasy, his wife.

And as he waited at the kerb for the lights to change and the traffic to stop, he was back in New York and the UN seeing Natalie for the first time. The most beautiful thing he had ever seen, at least that is what he had thought at the time, but he'd grown up a bit since then. He crossed the Ring to the Stadtpark and saw her sitting on one of the white wooden benches, and she cut quite a picture with the tan and the golden hair and the big black sunglasses and the lush red, beckoning mouth. He squinted as he came out of the shade of some trees and the sun dazzled his eyes and for a moment he thought he saw Kristina, but she was in Salzburg, wasn't she? He frowned softly as his vision cleared and he realized his mistake. It was weird the way she had suddenly decided to take a trip, but maybe she *did* need a change and maybe all this business with Natalie had finally got to her because her damned mother had said that 'she was unhappy', and somehow he didn't think the old crone had made that up. That, anyway. He would call her again, perhaps she would be back tomorrow, because he had made a promise to her that he would call, and he owed her that much, at least.

Augustina shuffled awkwardly back into the sitting room where her chocolates were and her port wine and her magazines. There was a fire in the grate because she still seemed to feel the cold even when the sun was shining outside and today her bones seemed to be aching more than usual – hateful, despised, brittle old bones that were of no use any longer. She sat down with an exhausted sigh and thought of her daughter. It was true what she had said, she was unhappy, but Kristina had not confided in her, she had just packed a bag and left, mumbling something about Salzburg through a haze of tears. Oh, yes, she had seen the tears, just as in the past she had heard sobs from the bedroom above and seen the make-up plastered over the red-rimmed eyes the next morning. And this morning she had looked unwell, her face had been almost frighteningly white when she had come down to share some hot rolls with her, but in the end Kristina had not eaten a thing.

It had been a pity about her husband, Frederico, and the divorce, although privately she had always thought him a sallow, unappetizing man with that round fat face and effeminate slender hands, but there had been something refined about him, something definitely aristocratic. These things told in the end, she tried to convince herself, but it wasn't true. Augustina took a large mouthful of the port wine. Frederico had behaved disgracefully all those years ago and poor, naïve Kristina had been left with nothing.

And since then nothing had really changed for her daughter, only the men – and the faces; face after face after face and now, finally, Sam Cohen. And she was such an emotional girl, always falling in love with almost any man who seemed kind. But they were not always kind, not really, not beneath that veneer of sophistication Kristina believed meant a passport to a better, fuller life. Augustina looked into the depleted remains in the glass and poured herself some more wine – and what good would he be to her, with that wife of his, that *whore* by all accounts? She shook her head at the empty room. And yet he had come here all the same to see Kristina. His face slipped unwillingly into her head, it was not a *bad* face, if a little weak, but Jewish. She sighed again. And he had been right, she supposed with a surge of self-pity, she did not want Kristina to leave her and Vienna and Austria – to leave her alone, that would be too much to bear. That had been astute of him, that observation, she thought with a twinge of reluctant admiration, but not so astute, to stay married to a whore.

Karl had found them a cool, shady inn near the top of the Kahlenberg hill, and they sat quietly on a wooden bench drinking new wine, looking out over Vienna, at the vineyards and the lush meadows and the city itself lying in the curve of the hills. It was a clear day, crystal clear, and it seemed to Elizabeth that she could see every tree, every leaf, every blade of grass, and she knew that this was one of those times in her life that she would remember, always, that she would not forget this view, this other Vienna which she had never seen before.

'Beautiful, isn't it?' he said softly.

She nodded.

'Are you okay?' He lifted her hand to his lips.

'Yes.' She smiled back at him. 'I'm just enjoying the peace and the quiet.'

'You didn't mind me bringing you out here?'

'Oh, no.'

They fell into silence again and then he shot a glance at her. Somehow he had come to think of her as *his*, it seemed that simple. Even when John Thornton had asked him into his office at the Hofburg it had not perturbed him, not shaken his determination to have Elizabeth, and it did not seem to matter that she was someone else's wife. After all, what was John Thornton to him? The man was nice enough and he had spoken quietly, carefully, as if he had thought out every word because it had cost him so much. But he had betrayed himself by the fear in his eyes and the way his hands had clenched and unclenched, admitting the pain. Thornton had tried to be casual, had tried the gentle approach, but finally he had become angry, finally he had said that Karl wasn't good enough for Elizabeth. Karl had given him a small, knowing smile and simply said that his wife was obviously of a different opinion. For a moment there he had thought that he had gone just a little too far, but Thornton had surprised him by retaining his cool and then indicating the door as if the interview was over. His parting words had been: 'But you won't have my son as well.' And of course, he didn't really want his son – her son – but that, unfortunately, was part of the deal.

'I'm flying to the Mediterranean on Tuesday.'

'Why?' She pulled her gaze away and looked at him.

'Gurney has arranged an independent analysis on all the notorious ocean pollution black spots and he wants me to pick them up personally, which means a round tour of Barcelona, Marseilles, Genoa, Piraeus and Naples – not forgetting Libya and Tunisia.'

'Good God . . . Couldn't someone else do it?'

'Apparently not.' No way. Dan had arranged it all so that he would be away from Vienna for at least ten days, literally killing two birds with one stone: he would be out of Dan's sight, and out of Elizabeth's. Neat.

'So, I won't see you.'

'No.' He smiled wryly. 'And naturally, you won't come with me?'

She closed her eyes and he wished he hadn't asked.

'You know I can't.'

He took a deep breath. 'But you will come with me when the Talks end.'

'And Christopher?'

'He could stay with John until we found a place,' he said quickly. Later he knew that that had been his first error. 'And although I am not exactly rich, I have enough cash to keep us going.' He paused for a moment as if he were picking his words very carefully. 'In any case, as to the future I know John is the sort of man who would be generous when it came to supporting you and Christopher.' That was the other, much bigger error.

'Yes, he would be generous,' she said without expression, because John still loved her and because he *was* that sort of a man.

They sat there for a long moment, a strange empty moment as if the life had been sucked out of the air.

'I suppose that was a sort of clumsy thing to say . . .' he said lamely. 'I'm not always good at this.' He took hold of her hand and as she did not withdraw it he thought that everything was all right. He thought back to Gurney and his visit and wondered if he would dare tell Elizabeth. It was a bluff and somehow it seemed unlikely now, in the cold light of day.

'Who was the girl – in Washington?' she said suddenly and he blinked with surprise, not, at first, understanding.

'What girl?'

She cleared her throat, gently, as if she might disturb the heavy quiet. 'I phoned you once, at your home in Washington, a long time ago, five years I suppose, and a girl answered.'

His eyes gave her an odd look. 'Gabrielle,' he said softly, suddenly remembering. 'Why?'

'Did you love her?'

'A little . . . I don't know . . . yeah, a little.'

'Like you loved me – then.'

He looked into her face. 'You were different.'

'Not then, Karl.' She shifted her gaze back to the city lying at their feet.

'Even then.' But he couldn't really remember, it was all vague, that time before he met Claude and his life had begun to turn round.

'Sometimes it's hard to remember, isn't it?' she said as if she had just read his mind.

He swallowed. 'Hey – what is all this?' He tilted her face back to him so that she would look into his eyes. 'Don't you believe me?'

She smiled, tremulously, and he thought she was going to cry.

'Yes, I do.'

'You just needed my reassurance – right?'

Elizabeth lifted up her hand and began to trace his fine mouth with one finger, her eyes all the time studying his face as if she had never seen it before.

'Yes, that's right,' she said at last.

The doorbell rang and Sam motioned Clara to answer it, then walked back into his den to pour himself a drink and found his eyes drifting to the black and white print of the Belevedere Palace hanging on the wall. He heard the sound of the door opening and closing and the sound of her footsteps drawing closer and closer and then her breathing as if she had been running.

'Hi, Sam.'

'Hi.'

Her eyes travelled quickly over him as he stood casually sipping a Scotch.

'You're not ready – we'll be late.'

'I'm not going.'

'But you said the table was booked . . . everything.'

'Oh, it is, but I'm feeling tired, I've asked a friend to stand in for me.' He smiled. 'You'll like him.' And Natalie probably would, that's why he'd chosen a member of the Italian delegation, Carlo, a real Don Juan; it was just a pity he wouldn't be there to see who finally seduced who.

'I don't get it.'
'Simple. I'm tired.'
Her face seemed to narrow, the features to sharpen.
'What *is* this, Sam?' She had looked forward to tonight, everything seemed to be going so well – okay, he had said that he needed to work last night so they had not seen each other and she had allowed him that, allowed him the time he might need to think things through about their future. But now, this.
'I've just told you, Natalie.'
'That's not good enough.'
'Well, I'm sorry, but it's going to have to be.'
'Are you seeing *her*?'
'Who?'
'You know who . . . the mystery lady . . . Kristeeena,' she sneered.
'There's no mystery about Kristina, she's a nice, nice lady.'
'I'll bet.' Her anger was beginning to slip out. 'Well, are you?'
'What?'
'Seeing her tonight?'
'No.'
'Liar.'
'I might have seen her tonight if I'd been allowed to speak to her yesterday morning, or if you'd been adult enough to tell me she'd called.'
'So that Filipino bitch tells tales as well.'
'Don't talk like that – Clara simply wanted to ensure that I got the message.'
'Oh, sure. And she'll get another message pretty soon – I'll see to that.'
'Enough, Natalie, you're the one who made the mistake, you're the one who goofed.' And he had almost, almost, begun to believe that she might have changed, had allowed himself to be gently lulled along with her illusions, but she wasn't patient enough or clever enough to keep the illusions up. He had let her seduce him with a strange mixture of curiosity and reluctance, but it had amused him too. Yet in the end it had been a performance, a very erotic performance which had produced the ultimate physical response, but there had been no love, no affection in the act, merely cold calculation and barely concealed triumph in the glitter of her eyes. And he supposed with a trace of sadness that that was how it had always been. No love; at least not from Natalie, but he had been unable or unwilling to see it. And now, even the fascination she had held for him had gone and it was like looking at a memory.
'I did it for us, Sam, us – and Joanna.'
He had to admire her perseverance.

'You did it for yourself, good ol' Natalie Majors.'
'You're wrong, Sam.'
'You never have known when to quit, have you?'
'I'll never quit on you, Sam,' she gushed.
'Oh, cut it, Natalie,' he said wearily, 'it doesn't work.'
'You haven't given me a chance!'
'You seem to have a very convenient memory, because I've given you plenty of chances.'
'But I've really tried, this time, really I have – you even admitted that yourself.'
'Did I?' he said. 'That was before yesterday, before you let everything begin to show.'
'Okay, so I put your precious girlfriend off, that was all – and for God's sake I was human about it.'
'I doubt that.'
Her eyes darkened.
'And you're back on coke, aren't you?'
She shook her head.
'Oh, come clean for once in your life.'
'The only thing I've taken since leaving the States is an aspirin, a goddamned aspirin, Sam!'
'Not true,' he sighed. 'You left the tin foil in the waste disposal, I looked for it.' He looked at her mouth which had grown small and tight. 'And I could see it in your eyes, it always shows – don't you know that yet? But you're so damned busy getting high you don't even notice. Like all the times before.'
'You bastard.'
'I'm not a bastard, I'm just an ordinary guy who wants a nice ordinary wife and a nice ordinary life. I don't want some glittering disco queen who doesn't know how to keep her knickers on, I don't want some panting blow-up doll who snorts so much that her nose is likely to disintegrate.'
'There's nothing wrong with my goddamned nose.'
He found himself laughing.
'Don't laugh at me, Sam.'
'I should have done it before.'
'That was a cheap shot.'
'And you should know all about those.' He shook his head, suddenly bored, suddenly tired. 'Look, Natalie, let's forget all this, we're not getting anywhere and there's a nice Italian guy waiting for you at Steirereck which is supposed to be just about the best restaurant in Vienna.'
'I don't care about any goddamned greasy wop,' she said quietly, and the green eyes seemed to ice up momentarily.

He had seen her like this before, but it had been a long time and he wondered how he had been able to forget the ability her features had to distort and change just by a tilt of her mouth, or the narrowing of her flat, unsmiling eyes – how the coy little girl melted into the seductive grown woman melted into someone with a mask for a face. He looked back at the picture on the wall.

'I've written you a cheque,' he said finally, 'it's in my study.'

'I don't want your goddamned money, Sam.'

'I owe you,' he sighed. 'After all, you've had extra expenses with the air fares and the hotel . . .' He walked out of the room.

She followed slowly, staring at the back of his head, hating him, and wondering how things had changed so much, so badly. Natalie swallowed hard as resentment began spreading through her like a stain. She had planned this for weeks – what she would wear, what she would say and what she would *do* most of all, and he had thrown it right back in her face. Her eyes lifted automatically as she walked into his study, caught by the model planes which floated serenely above them, and she thought for a vague moment that if she closed her eyes just a little they could almost seem real.

'Hold it,' Sam said abruptly, 'there's something else. I'll be back in a moment.'

She frowned sullenly as he moved past her and then stood awkwardly, waiting, her bored gaze sweeping across the study, the desk, the papers, the books, and then upwards, to the planes. The planes: Sam's other babies. Natalie stretched out her arm and gave the Messerschmidt hanging just above her head a hard knock. 'Now you're really flying, buster . . .' she said meanly. It began to rock back and forth and each time it swung towards her she hit it harder until the fragile model shattered against the ceiling. She moved over and began giving the same treatment to another and another and another until the air above her head was full of sad, broken things, spinning and spinning, ragged and lost, and beyond healing. Natalie picked up the cheque and walked quickly out of the study. She could hear Sam somewhere down the hall and her feet began to move faster. On the hall table just inside the door was her bag. She pushed the cheque inside, opened the door and walked out, slamming it hard behind her.

Sam winced as the noise echoed through the apartment and his eyebrows drew together in puzzlement. He made his way out of Joanna's room and back into the study. Natalie had gone. For a long moment he stood on the threshold and watched the crippled remnants of his plane collection swinging listlessly backwards and forwards, backwards and forwards until gradually, one by one, all movement ceased and they became utterly still. There was a thickness in his throat, a lump like grief and he looked down at the delicate picture frame held in his hand and the photograph of Joanna he had saved for Natalie. What a fool he was, what a goddamned schmuck.

'Sophia and Oskar will be arriving later, then?' Felix snapped and slipped a finger inside his collar as if it were too tight.

'Yes,' Genevieve said and turned her face to the window of the car.

'I spoke to Oskar yesterday morning and he said how proud I must be of Sophia's success...' Felix continued with barely suppressed anger. 'Obviously none of the hints I have given him have made any impression at all.' He sighed heavily. 'Perhaps I misjudged him.'

'Perhaps he realizes he is not the right man for Sophia,' Genevieve responded quietly.

'Please, Genevieve...' he said wearily.

'Sophia tells me that he treats her like a daughter.'

'Such a waste,' he said. 'After all, Sophia is very pretty, surely he can see that...'

Genevieve caught a sharp breath. 'She also has feelings – and a mind, Felix, as well as a pretty face.'

He flashed a glance at her. 'Of course. I didn't mean...'

'Perhaps he sees her as a person as well...' she said awkwardly, and then opened her mouth to speak again. 'I am a person, Felix, I feel...'

His eyes widened in surprise and irritation. 'Good God, Genevieve – what a strange thing to say. Are you ill?'

She shook her head and as they drove in uneasy silence she looked down at her hands which had grown clammy with sweat, until she lifted her head as he took yet another turning in the road and she was able to see the grey mass of Schloss Bletz through the trees.

'I found your letters...'

'My letters?' What was she talking about?

'And the photographs and the video and the magazines...'

He swallowed. 'I don't know what you mean.'

'They are in the drawer of your desk.'

'Ah,' he said, his heart suddenly an annoyingly hard lump in his chest. 'Why, Felix?'

'They are old mementoes, Genevieve – souvenirs, if you like,' he said quickly.

'The letters are dated this year, one as recent as a month ago.'

His hands tightened around the steering wheel. Why had he not put them in a safer place, like the cellar?

'Why were you looking through my desk?' he asked sharply, suddenly on the attack.

'I needed a stamp – for a letter.'

'Anyway . . .' he said impatiently, as if she had not spoken, 'they mean nothing.'

'They mean nothing?' she repeated softly.

'Of course not.' He patted her knee. 'You are my wife, after all.' As if that was enough. There was something unpleasant and smug in the foolish grin on his face.

'Didn't you care that I, or the children, might find out?'

He blushed then as he thought of Sophia.

'Yes, yes – of course,' he stammered uneasily. 'I didn't think.'

She was surprised at the bitter laugh which rose up into her throat.

'It was wrong, I agree,' he said glibly, but he had not thought that he would be found out and there was something exciting and challenging in the secrecy. And he had never felt guilty, never. He had been brought up to believe that he had a right to do what he wanted, that he was able to do as he pleased, no matter what the cost to anyone else – wasn't he one of the élite?

'One of them said that she loves you to the point of madness . . .'

'Silly – and over-emotional,' he said. 'I certainly have never said any such thing to her, or anyone else. You can be assured of that.'

'I don't need your reassurance, Felix,' she said quietly.

'Good, good . . .' he said easily and with a sigh of relief, not realizing that he had misunderstood.

They drove on wrapped in silence as the car drew closer to the castle.

'But I think I would like to go away after the birthday celebrations, somewhere quiet, somewhere peaceful.'

'Of course, of course. I quite understand, and when you come back we shall put this behind us and start afresh.' He had expected a scene, tears at least, instead she had taken it all very well; Felix could hardly believe his luck.

She blinked and turned back to the window because all at once she was tired of his shallow words, his voice, his face, the arrogant hands that gripped the wheel of the car, the smell of him. She found her vision dimming slightly as she looked at the trees and the grass verge and the road which was taking them to Schloss Bletz and the weekend she had been too busy to dread and which now seemed to loom up large and relentless, except for Sophia. Genevieve made a soft, despairing sound: but Sophia was going away. Inside there was a tiny shrinking, a seepage at her very core which she could neither stem nor control, and a thought came into her bewildered mind unbidden, odd, and she wondered what was happening to her.

Elizabeth stepped out through the double doors and into the grounds of the castle. Against the hum of conversation in the garden room she could hear the sound of water falling in the fountain and could just glimpse the enormous ornament from the terrace, an extravaganza of mythical heads and round cherubic bodies spouting cascades of silver water. She moved over to the long, low wall which ran the length of the lake-side of the immense building and sat down. It had been a surprise, this invitation to Gunther Dhoryány's birthday celebration, but it had been difficult to refuse and now she was glad John had accepted because the weather was so glorious and she was away from the sweltering confines of Vienna. Up here, on this rocky spit of land in a cleft of the hills the air was fresher, lighter; she could breathe.

Elizabeth shifted her gaze to the massive castellated walls of Schloss Bletz which rose up like soaring granite peaks; there were two main towers, a round tower on the eastern side and a baroque tower with the familiar bulbous, onion-like spire on the western side. Within the walls the main body of the castle had been made virtually impenetrable except, apparently, to the Turks, led by one Suleiman the Magnificent, almost five hundred years previously, and there still was an exotic, Eastern feel about certain parts of the castle as if the invaders had determinedly left their mark. Elizabeth took a deep breath, stood up and was about to rejoin the party when John walked out and gave her a careful, wary smile.

'Felix has hired a magician – he keeps drawing champagne cocktails out of his hat . . .'

'I thought I'd come out for some air, it was getting so stuffy inside.' She turned her head and he followed her glance to the rich, deeply forested hills which lay on all sides. 'I like it better this time; it seemed so grim, so sombre when we came before.'

John studied her soft profile and was touched by regret and bitter sadness because he remembered their time here, those months ago, when they had been happy, when she had looked at him and known that he had simply wanted her and they had made abrupt and earthy love before dinner and she had still been wearing her dress, lovely black velvet dress which had almost made him giddy. Even as he watched she looked back at him as if she had sensed his eyes and his thoughts, and the blood in her face seemed like so much guilt, so much remorse.

'It's the sunshine, of course . . .' she continued awkwardly, wishing she could call back her words.

And he wanted to walk away and forget and not see that pity in her eyes any more.

'Elizabeth! There you are.' Felix Dhoryány appeared from the garden room. 'We are about to go in to dinner, I thought perhaps, your husband might give me the honour of escorting you.' His eyes swept over her and he grinned greedily.

'But where is Genevieve?' Elizabeth asked, slightly alarmed.

'Oh, somewhere being busy, busy, as usual – she won't mind in the least.'

She looked into his face, at the show of gleaming white teeth, at the carefully oiled hair which had been sleekly brushed back so that not one hair lay out of place. It would not occur to him to wonder whether his wife might mind or not.

'John?' Elizabeth turned to her husband and knew what his answer would be. After all Felix was their host.

'Of course.' He nodded.

John sighed inwardly as Felix guided Elizabeth back inside and then drained the glass held in his hand. He wished that in some way he could come to dislike her, or that her attraction for him might wane and then he would be set free from the burden of loving her. And surely she would have to choose soon because the Talks were coming to a close, for better or worse, and Nielsen was leaving and going back to the States, at least that was what he had said during that brief, unhappy meeting at the Hofburg. Even as he had invited the man into his office he had regretted it, but he had been unable to help himself, and finally nothing had passed between them which had given him any hope, any cause to think that she might remain his. Sometimes he tried to force himself to think of a future without her and Christopher, as if imagining such a scenario might make the bearing of it easier, but he could not think of it or imagine a life without them because a blackness seemed to come down over all of it and there would be that sucking, empty feeling deep in the pit of his stomach. Nielsen's face drifted reluctantly into his head; handsome, tanned, chiselled like a damned film star. He had given the man a feeble threat with regard to Christopher as he had left, but why would Nielsen be worried about *his* son, it was Elizabeth he wanted. For a few painful minutes after the man had gone he had toyed with the idea of fighting for Christopher if it became necessary, but then knew that he could never do that to his son, not put him through the confusion and the bewilderment and the anguish. Not Christopher.

John caught a breath and remembered the anger which had almost slipped out, the anger which had made him wonder what Nielsen would do if he had smashed his head through the glass panel of his office door. Instead he had indicated that Nielsen should go and the man had nodded and walked out, leaving him feeling humiliated and helpless, dragged down by a sense of overbearing loss which was beginning to seep into his bones. The thwarting of all his hopes, all his dreams.

For a fleeting second his gaze strayed to the fountain and the pyramid of gargoyles all vomiting water from wide open mouths, and he wondered how such a monstrous folly could be permitted here in this lovely garden beneath the dour magnificence of the castle. But there was no telling with Felix Dhoryány, he seemed to be a man of extreme conventionalism and yet there was a curious touch of the vulgar about him – he recalled Elizabeth's remark last time they were here and the crude remark Dhoryány had whispered in John's ear about one of the conference attendants after a plenary meeting at the Hofburg. And now he was taking Elizabeth in to dinner – a man, he mused, who always seemed to get what he wanted.

John smiled wryly and with sadness, but then the sudden quiet broke into his reverie and he realized he had spent too long on the terrace because the hum of voices had died. With a heavy sigh he placed the empty glass he was still holding on the long, low wall and began making his way back to the rest of the party.

From her seat Elizabeth could just see Sophia Dhoryány and despite her misgivings she thought the young girl looked quite radiant. Her eyes travelled down the length of their table, one of three trestle tables placed side by side in the enormous dining hall to accommodate the one hundred and twenty guests invited, she was looking for the hostess, Genevieve, and finally saw her, almost running, as she appeared from an outer corridor. She was at such a distance that it was difficult for Elizabeth to see if she looked well, except that her eyes seemed even larger, even more doe-like set in the thin pale face. She turned to Felix.

'Your wife is well?'

'My wife is always well – she thrives on this sort of occasion,' he chuckled. 'I believe she has been planning this for weeks, just to make sure that every detail is exactly as it should be.' He covered Elizabeth's hand with his own before she could remove it. 'But naturally I had a hand in the finer points which make a special day such as this remembered as a day apart, a day extraordinaire.' He finished by concluding in an intimate tone, 'I am very good at such things, my dear Elizabeth.'

'I wonder if you would pour me some water, please,' she said and sighed inwardly with relief as he was forced to remove his hand to fill her glass. As she lifted the cool water to her lips, her eyes looked across the rim of the glass instinctively searching for John, but she could not see him and she realized that he must be sitting behind her on the next table. It was odd not being able to see him, not being able merely to lift her head and see him somewhere about a room as she was used to. She found herself looking at the white orchid which had been placed for each of the ladies at the sides of their plates. John had bought her two dozen when Christopher had been born and a long, long string of exquisite creamy pearls he had ordered from Hong Kong because she had seen them there on their honeymoon. She blinked as the sweet, searing echo faded and wondered if he hated her for what she had done to him.

'We have had the carvings and the tapestries carefully polished and renovated just for the celebration of Gunther's birthday – it seemed little enough,' Felix broke in. 'After all, twenty-one is quite an age to reach.'

'Yes, of course, it is,' Elizabeth replied, glad to switch her attention elsewhere, and it was difficult not to admire the workmanship of the carvings, the skill of the tapestries, the three fabulous rock-crystal chandeliers hanging above the central aisle like clusters of stars.

'I hope you have also noticed one of the most lovely of the family icons which stands in an alcove just inside the door. It is of the Virgin, naturally, and a particularly good one – thickly adorned with gilt and semi-precious stones and over four hundred years old.'

Elizabeth wondered that Felix's head did not swell visibly.

'It was blessed by Pope Pius VI in 1782, actually.'

She drew a soft, tired breath and realized with relief that they were about to be served with some oysters and Felix would be forced to concentrate on his plate, but then she closed her eyes in exasperation because this was no ordinary dinner, Felix had intimated 'a banquet' which would probably mean ten or twelve courses including coffee. All night next to Felix and the small, seedy little man on her right who seemed loath to say a word, but who apparently owned half of Styria. And later there would be dancing and fireworks on the terrace. They had even arranged a schedule for tomorrow morning: breakfast, followed by a walk around the lake or clay-pigeon shooting and then back for lunch. The evening would probably not be as painfully long as she anticipated, she told herself, and if the weather held, tomorrow could be glorious. Elizabeth tasted the wine which was magnificent and tried to think of Karl in the incongruous setting of Naples collecting pollution data, but instead her mind jumped ahead to the end of the evening, to the room and the bed she would share with John. It was the same room with the heavy furniture and the velvet and the gilt, overlooking the lake and the gardens, the same room where they had made passionate and happy love, and the same room where the passion and the happiness and the love had twisted in on itself, shrinking, and she had lost something there, hadn't she, in that room?

Genevieve took a short-cut to the upper floors, an ancient spiral staircase which wound up through Schloss Bletz like a funnel of air. People were still on the terrace, still drinking coffee and liqueurs and watching the fireworks which threatened to go on for several more hours. She would have to wait until the very last guest decided to go to their bed, unless she could persuade Felix to make an excuse for her, and yet she did not really feel tired, even after all the exertion and the worry and the stress of the day, because tomorrow it would all be different. It would be a new day, a fresh day, and the thought made her unusually happy. Some eighty or so of the guests would be leaving after breakfast, though the rest would be staying until after lunch, but during the morning the castle would be virtually empty. The company who had hired them the twenty or so wall partitions to create more bedrooms would not be arriving until Monday morning.

Genevieve gained the first floor and thought of her daughter, her darling, her baby; that was the hardest part of all, but Sophia was busy now with her new life and a blossoming career – safe and happy in Munich, and then she would go to America. Just too far. She moved quietly through the deep shadows cast by the bronze lamps which stood at intervals along the stone-walled corridor; Sophia's room was just up ahead, out of sight around a corner because Genevieve had wanted peace and tranquillity for her to rest in and the best of the linen and in front of the open window fresh, fresh flowers which she had picked and arranged herself.

She shut her eyes tight for a brief, burning moment as the headache which had been hovering just out of sight all day began to make itself felt; there had been too many of those lately, making her dizzy, making her head feel as if it would split wide open. But she gripped the brass door handle, as if for support, and stepped into her daughter's carefully prepared room; for a long moment she stood there, her eyes travelling over the bed and the lace coverlet, the pretty Chinese boxes on the rosewood table and the sweet irresistible scent from the summer flowers in the window. She walked over to the side of the bed, and ran her fingers gently across soft white linen and lace. She turned once, twice, scanning the room for any fault, any minor imperfection, and then walked to the door and closed it soundlessly behind her before walking back down the corridor. There was a small bathroom to the left of the staircase and a large linen cupboard which adjoined, and as she moved quietly past she stopped because she realized that there was someone inside.

Genevieve frowned softly and began opening the door, forced to narrow her eyes because the naked light bulb was too brilliant. At first she saw nothing but shelves of crisp white sheets, towels and bathrobes, but as her vision cleared she could see a man with his back to her, just in front of the far wall and behind several cylindrical wicker baskets. The man was Felix, and sitting on one of the wicker baskets was a woman with her thighs spread apart; she was wearing black fish-net stockings which barely came up above her wide, fleshy knees, and a white overall which was unbuttoned revealing a tiny red and black brassiere which seemed to have difficulty in supporting the massive prow-like proportions of her bosom. It seemed strange to Genevieve then that she had not recognized the girl before when she had been supervising the catering staff, but the girl's hair had been tightly pinned back into a ridiculously small white hat and, of course, she had had her clothes on. It was the girl from the photograph.

Genevieve tried to swallow the tight thickness which had climbed into her throat, but there was a sick feeling in her stomach and her legs suddenly felt weak as if they might buckle beneath her. Even as she moved a step back the girl seemed to sense her presence and the half-closed eyes opened wide and looked at her from over her husband's shoulder, out of the pudgy face. Later Genevieve thought that the girl from the photograph had smiled, that the smile had seemed like a leer of triumph as she had pulled Felix closer, harder against her – before he had cried out, before he had panted and gasped, and shuddered and shuddered and shuddered. And Genevieve had closed the door and vomited carefully into a huge ornate Indonesian urn which stood outside, before walking away and back down to the terrace and the party and the people and the fireworks.

Sophia slipped away from the crowd of people and back into the garden room, but her mother had disappeared. She walked out into the hall and waited for a moment and was about to go to the kitchens to see if she was there when she heard her familiar step. In the shadow of the staircase her mother did not see her, did not know that her daughter watched and saw the ashen face and the small white hand which was still clasped against her mouth. Genevieve leaned against the door frame of the ground floor cloakroom and then opened the door and made her way inside.

Sophia drew a quick, anxious breath and was about to cross the wide flagstoned floor to her mother when she heard her father's voice above her and instinctively froze as he came down the stairs. In the half light he did not see her, he was too busy straightening his tie and pulling down the cuff of his shirt to notice. She frowned at his retreating back and then made her body move and even as she did so she almost came face to face with one of the catering assistants who was standing hesitantly at the bottom of the staircase because Sophia was barring her path. The girl's hair had partially fallen around the plump, unappetizing face and her white cap was now clutched tightly in one of her hands. The top button of her overall was undone. Sophia felt her mouth tighten and then closed her eyes in disgust as the girl brushed nervously past her.

Her thoughts inevitably swept backward to that sad, dreadful day when she had seen her father at the SAS Hotel, to that pathetic meeting with him later when he had tried to persuade her to believe him and, oh, how she had wanted to! She had even hoped in her naïvety that he might change because she, his daughter, had found him out. She shook her head in anguish. All those moments of disillusionment and disbelief and resentment and hatred which had driven her to leave, and then to leave her mother alone. He had betrayed them all, even Gunther, because Gunther could not know any better. She swallowed, deep in her throat, as a fierce urge to protect her mother made her eyes burn – perhaps she could persuade her to leave, to go away somewhere – but even as the thought took shape and fled away she approached the door where her mother was cowering with trepidation and a bitter, sinking heart.

Elizabeth turned on her side and then opened her eyes. She had only dozed because the illuminated dial on the clock still told her it was not yet four o'clock. There was no light in the room, but occasionally the dark shapes and shadows would retreat momentarily as a firework exploded outside and she would turn again, knowing that there would be little sleep for her tonight. John had not come to bed and she had no idea where he might be. For a brief moment of disbelief she wondered if he had found solace with someone else, but he would not do that, would he? She felt a mocking blade of jealousy pierce her, and even if he had, she would have no right to say a word, not after what she had done.

She tried to lose her thoughts and let her mind sweep back to the long evening and all the little bits of conversation, the little isolated things which seemed to cling to her memory, like the talk she had had with Sophia in a quiet corner of the garden room and the surprise she had felt when Sophia had said she was going to the US, that there was nothing in the rumour that she was marrying Oskar von der Heyden. Then she had added quietly, 'I doubt if I shall ever marry,' and there had been something in the sweet, calmly arranged face that had startled Elizabeth as she had looked back into eyes that were now wary and careful, the youth gone. Finally she had said that perhaps, after all, she would have time to sketch Christopher before she left; and then Felix had joined them briefly as he had passed on his way through to the terrace and Sophia had winced, just perceptibly, as her father placed a hand on her shoulder. Strange.

   In the darkness Elizabeth swallowed and her eyebrows drew together in a frown as she realized how dry her mouth was and she reached for the glass of water beside the bed. There was no breeze in the room despite the wide-open window and the heat seemed to wind itself around her body like an extra skin so that she kicked the thin white sheet away with exasperation and lay naked and too warm in the empty room. She smiled bitterly because if John had been there she would have felt obliged to keep herself covered because of some peculiar false modesty which had developed between them, and yet before . . . before she had loved the way he had looked at her, loved the hunger in his eyes and the wonderful desperation when he had finally taken her. Regret washed over her because there had never been any desperation for her in their lovemaking, not with him. She forced herself to acknowledge the thought which she had pressed down all these weeks – that he would surely, at some point, ask her for a divorce. Wouldn't he? But the thought did not seem real somehow and she snapped her eyes shut because her life was out of control, running away at dizzying speed. For a moment her mind seemed to freeze up, tight and helpless, and she squirmed with self-loathing, turning to the window as yet another firework lit up the sky. She wondered sadly where he was – John – and suddenly she was crushed by loneliness and shame because she had driven him away.

It was only a small piece of luggage, almost tiny, but she did not intend taking very much with her. Genevieve locked the leather case carefully and then brought the well-worn straps over the lid and buckled them so that it looked neat and well cared for as it sat on the floor. She had not used that particular case in a long time, it had been Heinrich's, a present from their father, and he had used it for holidays and special outings. Her fingers moved to the initials on the lid edged in gold and she traced them delicately before standing up and smoothing down her skirt.

   It had been a wonderful party, but now it was over and the grounds and the castle seemed suddenly blissfully silent. It was a thick silence, she thought: heavy and languid with the heat and the smell of gunpowder still in the air. She picked up the old brown case and draped her favourite green felt jacket over her arm before moving quietly out of the room and into the corridor. Felix was asleep, she could even hear him snoring and he would probably sleep until well after nine o'clock. Sophia had been silly to think that she had been upset, there had been no need to be concerned about her father's behaviour, or his unbeautiful whore; she was perfectly all right now. It was nothing, Felix had said so.

Genevieve looked from right to left as she came to a crossroads in the corridor and then moved quickly to the staircase, not caring to notice the creaks and the groans of the wood as she passed. They were all asleep, weren't they? She stopped abruptly when she came to the hallway because there was someone there, someone sitting in a lone armchair in one of the alcoves. She watched the sleeping man for a long moment before putting down her jacket and case and walking to the mahogany chest which was full of cushions and several car blankets which were always used for picnics or long drives. With an anxious smile she draped a plaid blanket over John Thornton and then stepped back and examined him sharply; he should be with his wife, not here in the cold hallway, as if he had nowhere to go. Genevieve sighed, but moved away back to her case and her jacket and then drew back the bolt on the heavy doors before slipping out into the grounds.

Dawn was not far off, there was a lightening, a certain greyness far in the distance and already she could hear a few birds begin to stir and cry. She began to walk, but paused as she drew close to the formal terraced garden; along the borders the grass had begun to grow too high and there were wild red flowers amongst the green, with stiff, hairy stems – wanton pretty things. Genevieve shook her head, surprised that her father had not had them cut down because he was such a perfectionist when it came to the garden and the grounds; perhaps she would tell him when she got back – or mother, perhaps, but mother was ill, wasn't she? Genevieve pushed a tired hand through her hair, but smiled as the old scents from the garden invaded her nostrils and she had a sudden, compelling urge to lie down against the earth, amongst the flowers and the grass because they were solid, timeless, beautiful things which never changed, never became ugly. She began to walk again and as the light grew stronger it seemed to her then that she was seeing everything in astonishing detail, so that the clouds, the trees, the dank rich moss, the twisted buried roots of trees all took on a powerful life of their own which almost made her breathless.

There was an ache somewhere in her head and her vision swam a little as she lifted her face and looked at the shifting colours in the sky because she was trying to remember, but her mind seemed to play tricks as strange faces filtered out of dusty corners and she heard the laughter and the anger, saw the places and the smiles and the sweet, searing sound of melancholy so that when she put her hand to her face her fingers came away wet and salty. Remembering. But her feet came to a sudden halt and she stopped and tilted her head as if she were listening very carefully. There was someone in the water, she could hear them, but then the quiet descended again like a mantle over everything. She frowned with confusion, her thoughts switching immediately to Heinrich because often he would sneak out at this hour and go to the lake and swim before Mama and Papa awoke. Genevieve chuckled quietly and then began to hum because she was sure that it was him she could hear – Heinrich, in the water ahead of her.

The morning was glorious, the morning was probably one of the most beautiful Elizabeth had ever seen, or so it seemed to her then. As she walked through the grounds with some of the other guests she could still taste a trace of gunpowder in the air, that smell from her youth of bonfire night and Guy Fawkes which the previous night's fireworks had conjured. But she thought unhappily of the night before and her glance was pulled back to the garden and the clay-pigeon shoot well beyond where John was spending the morning with Felix and most of the other men. He had not returned to their room after the party and she had had no idea where he might have spent the night, neither did she have the courage to ask him, or even acknowledge that he had been away.

She sighed heavily and switched her attention back to the walk and the path they were about to take along the lake. The water was apparently very deep, it was also very black and seemed thick like oil and she shivered as they moved past out of the sun and into the trees so that momentarily the lake retreated and they were alone with only the birds and themselves for company. There were not many of the party left, as more than the allotted number had decided to return to Vienna, no doubt due to the effects of the mammoth celebrations which did not really end at all considering the time things apparently did come to a halt. Elizabeth's gaze slid back to the lake as they came out of the trees and the sun shone down warm and hot on the top of her head and her mind began tumbling backwards to that weekend in January, a lifetime ago, when the snow had been so thick, so white, and she and John had driven from Vienna to Schloss Bletz hoping that they would not be snowed in because they had promised Christopher that they would be back in time for dinner. A lifetime. Karl had intruded even then, because she had let him, and she had pushed John away because she had allowed herself little choice and because she wanted the man who had left her alone five years before.

She had once woven intricate dreams of the life she had planned to share with him, and the child which had grown from that passion, and the child which had died, finally. *Her* passion. It had only been her passion then, and now the tables were turned at last. Her gaze swept over the lake and the hillsides of dark green pine and she felt a heaviness, a bleakness behind her eyes as she thought of John and what she had done to him. She trailed listlessly behind the others as they made their way down a small rise and she could see the gate into the gardens through the trees. Elizabeth sighed with relief because she was in no mood for walking and there was something about the lake which depressed her. She blinked as the sun shot suddenly through the trees and her eyes hurt because they were sore with lack of sleep, and no amount of make-up had seemed able to disguise the dark rings which lay underneath.

They passed through the gate and back into the grounds, and she saw Sophia coming towards them. As Elizabeth scanned the white face she thought that the young girl had probably had as little sleep as she, but then Sophia drew closer and she could see that she was crying, that the large eyes had grown larger, luminous, rising out of her face wide and frightened. She clutched a green felt jacket close to her chest as if it might suddenly slip out of her grasp.

'You didn't see her . . .?' she pleaded.

'Who?' one of the women asked.

'My mother?'

The woman shook her head and then Sophia's terrified gaze was searching all the faces and Elizabeth felt fear stroke her spine as the young girl's mouth began to tremble again and she moved towards her. But already Sophia was turning her back and walking away, quickly, and then she was running, running, across the grass. They all looked at one another sensing disaster and started after her across the garden.

It was only much later that Elizabeth tried to make sense of what happened next, but failed dismally. When they reached the edge of the clay-pigeon shoot where Sophia had gone they saw her flaying wildly at her father, pulling at his clothes, her fists pounding against his chest as her voice rose higher and higher . . .

'It was you, you, you made her do it . . . I hate you, hate you, hate you . . .' And then she suddenly melted to the ground, sobbing pitifully until Oskar von der Heyden lifted her into his arms and took her back to the castle and the weeping faded, finally into emptiness.

They did not find Genevieve in the special place Heinrich had once swum, but at the edge of the water there was a pile of neatly folded clothes and an old brown leather suitcase with shining buckles and initials still edged in gold.

10

'How was Tante Maria?'

'She seemed well,' Kristina replied.

'I did not expect you to stay away so long.'

'I felt I needed a change, I told you.'

'Because of Sam Cohen.'

'Partly.'

The old woman looked at her daughter carefully, at the deep smudges beneath her eyes and the thin face; she had lost weight.

'He came here,' she said reluctantly.

Kristina's eyes leapt. 'When?'

'After you had left for Salzburg.'

'What did he say?'

'Pour me some more chocolate first, I have missed your chocolate, only you make it just the way I like it.' She sighed.

Kristina stiffened with impatience, but knew that the chocolate would have to come first as her mother had directed because it was useless to do otherwise, she had tried in the past and utterly failed; her mother always seemed to win.

'Well?' Kristina said as she settled her mother back into her chair.

'As I said, he came here.'

'I know that, Mother – what did he say?' Sometimes she wondered why she did not scream at her.

'He wanted to call you.'

'And you gave him Tante Maria's number?' But he hadn't called; she had asked every day if she had had any calls. Nothing.

'No, of course I did not.'

Kristina stared at her mother with disbelief. 'Why not?' she shrilled. 'Why not?'

'There is no need to shout at me – I only had your best interests at heart.'

Kristina shook her head back and forth, back and forth.

'You have never had my interests at heart – never!' Angry tears made her vision dance. 'You did not give him my number because you don't like him, because he is a Jew, because he is simply a man who *wants me*!' But she was no longer sure whether Sam wanted her; inside she grieved, inside there was no belief.

'Don't be a fool!' Her mother thumped the arm of her chair in temper. 'You never learn, do you? Never learn! His wife was waiting outside, in the park, I saw her and his little girl.'

'How do you know it was his wife, his child?' she pleaded. 'You have never seen them!'

'I watched him through the window as he crossed the Ring and into the park, I saw him walk up to his whore of a wife – with her too tight slacks and big white smile. I could see them from the window, Kristina!'

'All right, all right!' So it really was true, what Natalie had said. And she wanted to weep. But Sam, she would not have believed it of Sam.

'You didn't tell me what he said,' Kristina said at last in a small voice.

'Just that he had promised to call you.'

'Is that all?' And how much she wished now that she had not decided to call him on that fateful Saturday; perhaps if she had left him to telephone her as he had said, everything might have been different. Might, might.

'Yes.' Of course that was not true, but the rest didn't matter.

'Has he called since?'

'Kristina, Kristina, why do you do this to yourself?' Augustina shook her head. 'The man has obviously decided to stay with his wife. Let him go.'

'It's just not that simple, Mother.' And she thought she was dying inside.

'Of course it is, you knew all along the risk you ran.' She snorted in contempt. 'And anyway, what sort of man is he to stay with a woman like that? A weak man, a foolish man.'

'You don't know him.'

'And you do, I suppose?' She tapped her fingers impatiently. 'If you knew him so well, why did you not predict that he might go back to his wife? And why did you convince yourself, as usual, that here was another man who would throw up his world for you.'

'You are cruel and heartless – and sometimes I think I hate you.'

'I try to help, but you will not see it.'

'Help – me? You are merciless.' Kristina felt her mouth begin to tremble and the tears she had kept at bay to brim and fall.

Augustina looked at her daughter, at the misery and the despair and was touched, all at once, by shame. She thought surprisingly of Sam Cohen and what he had said – that such a man should say those things to her! But she flushed and lowered her eyes to her chocolate cup which was still half full of the sweet, milky drink.

'I do not mean to hurt you,' she said slowly.

Kristina swallowed, deeply as if the action might somehow stem the flow of tears that was becoming too heavy to hold back.

'But you do, you do . . . don't you?'

'I want the best for you, that is all.'

'I love Sam,' she said helplessly.

Her mother made no answer. Kristina stood up and moved to the window.

'I had thought, really thought, that this time . . .' she said, almost to herself.

'You will find another man . . .'

Kristina laughed bitterly, and the laugh was rough, raw like a sob. 'You don't understand, Mother, you really don't understand.'

Augustina had not seen her daughter like this in a long time and she did not like it, not the despair, the loss which laced every word, every gesture. And the white, white face.

'Have some port wine. Sit down.'

'I can't have alcohol.'

Augustina frowned. 'Why not? Are you ill?'

In the heavy quiet which followed, Kristina could hear the peacocks shrieking in the Stadtpark and see the tourists with their cameras, snapping, snapping at the Johann Strauss monument.

'No, I am not ill, Mother. I am pregnant.'

She heard a small sound issue from her mother's mouth, like a gasp.

'Are you sure?'

'I have never been more sure of anything.'

'And you have been to a doctor?'

'Of course.'

'There is no mistake?'

Kristina whirled around. 'No, Mother, *there is no mistake*!'

'All right, child, all right.'

She could not remember the last time her mother had called her 'child'.

'This changes everything,' her mother added after a pause.

'How?' Kristina asked bitterly.

'Well – he must marry you.'

Kristina closed her eyes with disbelief.

'Sam is already married, or have you forgotten?'

'He *must* marry you,' her mother repeated. 'You are having his child.'

Kristina looked back at her mother and wondered whether she should tell her everything, but at that moment she was too tired, too weary, and she had no heart.

*

Laura sat back in the plane, leaned her head against the seat and thought of London and Andrew and what she was returning to. She had felt only relief when she had decided, finally, to see her ambassador and tell him the whole story, there seemed to be no other choice because she was not the stuff spies were made of. She sighed inwardly, remembering the trembling of her fingers as they had reached for the door handle of his office, and the pound, pound, pound of her heart as she had approached his desk and sat down. But he had been so kind, even through her stammering and the humiliation of her tears, because she had been unable to hold back in the end. Sir Nigel had then ordered tea and even brandy and she had sat quietly for several minutes before he had spoken again.

But the tea and the brandy had quickly been followed by the switching on of a tape recorder and questions, questions, questions. Her ambassador called it 'an entrapment set-up' and had spared her the embarrassment of the gory details. She had been grateful for that, but nevertheless the experience and the almost minute by minute description of her encounters with Ralf had drained her, and when she had finally been allowed to return to her desk she was exhausted.

She smiled dryly when she recalled Sir Nigel's last comment which was to inform her that 'this sort of thing happens from time to time', he had even mentioned the case of a British ambassador who had been compromised by an attractive maid whose favours he had been unable to resist – he was photographed making love to the Russian maid in a laundry of his residence in Moscow of all places. Sir Nigel had tried to hide his amusement, adding finally that 'the misguided man was later retired on full pension'.

There was a further interview later with some security people and then she had been told that she was relieved of her duties, which she had expected. She had also been instructed to leave her apartment and move into an alloted hotel near the Schottentor and a small, featureless room overlooking a busy street; that had depressed her most. Yet, there was some solace in the way it had all been taken care of so quickly and with such effortless ease; the responsibility belonged to someone else now.

Laura looked up as a stewardess asked her if she would like another coffee and she nodded and realized that she felt relaxed at last, almost at ease because it was all over. Wasn't it? She turned her face to the window and the perfect mantle of cloud which lay beneath the sky. They had asked her to meet Ralf one last time, for the 'first exchange', and she had reluctantly agreed because she had felt obliged, as if she 'owed them' someone, something for her stupid naïvety.

But he had not come. Ralf had agreed, but he had not come. It was as if he *had known*. And she had sat in the Central Café for nearly four hours before 'they' had indicated she could leave and as she left through the double doors she had promised herself that she would never be persuaded to come here again, not to the Central Café, or Vienna, or even to Austria to ski as she had done several times. Never again. She shivered a little and wondered where he was, what he was doing. The security people had gone to his apartment, but it had been empty. Ralf had gone. She tried to imagine that stark white apartment with none of the Greek artefacts and the careful lighting, none of the artwork and the massive, deep leather furniture. Her imagination took her through each room, pacing in slow motion down the corridor into the kitchen and the enormous living room, out on to the wonderful terrace, but she found herself being pulled back to the one place where he had shown her the film, the room with two chairs and an enormous television. She closed her eyes. And his face: big, square handsome face slipped unhappily into her head and she saw his hands, like white marble fists, and the other man, the bearded man, and bile climbed into her throat.

Laura took a deep breath and made a feeble attempt at reading the book in her lap, but nothing worked. She had written to Andrew and told him everything as much as she could, but he had not replied and so she presumed that it was over, and she could not blame him; not after what she had said, not after what she had done. She felt a thickness in her throat, a sadness, and she tried to push it down, away. But her parents were another matter and she would have to tell them because there was the possibility that they might receive a 'little present' from Ralf – and he would do that, she knew it.

Blood began to seep into her face and Laura wondered if she would ever be rid of this ugly spectre, or whether it would haunt her for the rest of her life. And where was the video now, and the photographs and the negatives? What did these shadowy people do with such things when they were no longer useful? She cringed inwardly and then gave a start as a voice broke into her thoughts, a voice telling her to fasten her seat belt because the plane was about to land.

She looked back to the window and saw Heathrow airport looming up to greet her. London was appropriately grey and the tarmac was wet from the light drizzle which showered the glass with tiny specks of water so that the landscape blurred and she turned her face away.

There was a delay in the luggage bay because the automatic belt was not working properly, but gradually the fault was cleared and she was able to pick up her luggage and move swiftly through customs. Laura looked at her plastic bag proclaiming 'Duty Free' – two hundred cigarettes for her brother, a bottle of malt whisky for her father, and a silk scarf for her mother. Not much to show for her stay in Vienna, but she thought of the etching of Schönbrunn she had found at the Nashmarkt and a battered old German helmet she had bought in a mad moment and which her father would no doubt hang in his study. There was also a narrow bracelet of garnets, quite old, which she had picked up in one of the cobbled side streets. And a beautiful hand-crafted miniature chess set she had bought for Andrew in the Kärtner Strasse. He would like that, she thought, and she would give it to him anyway, or perhaps she would send it to him because she didn't know if she could face him just now, not with this shame, this bitter sadness which seemed to cloak everything.

Laura pushed her trolley through the automatic doors and tried to look away from the thick line of faces and people who stood by the barriers. She concentrated on keeping her trolley straight, on looking directly ahead because it was always slightly depressing to arrive at an airport to no welcome, no matter how illogical or irrational that feeling might be. She lifted her head and pushed her trolley with a little more determination and it was then that she saw him. Her heart began to beat painfully as she looked into his carefully composed face, her vision swimming slightly because her eyes had inexplicably filled with tears. But then Andrew was smiling, that small slanting smile which had always had the power to make her stomach lurch. It was as if her life had come full circle, as if nothing had changed, but even as the corners of her mouth began to tilt upwards she was stung by regret because nothing would ever be the same again.

'I came to thank you for your kindness,' Sophia said as Elizabeth led her into the drawing room.

'There is no need – and I really did very little.' Her mind swept backwards to that sad, lost weekend and the frantic efforts to find Genevieve, but they never had. Finally Felix had arranged for the lake to be dragged, but it was too deep and too dark and the bottom was thick with reeking black mud. Her own kindness had been a simple one, of sitting with Sophia as she retreated into a sedated sleep; it had been little enough.

'It meant a great deal to me at the time.'

Elizabeth looked into her face, at the hollow cheeks and the eyes which seemed to rise up out of pale features grown sharper and older.

'Come – have some tea,' Elizabeth offered and they sat down.

'I shall be in Vienna for at least another week and I thought I might begin the portrait of your son before I leave.'

'Are you sure.'

'Please. I would like very much to do this.' She forced a smile. 'I understand you will be returning to England in two or three weeks?'

'Yes, the conference will be ending very shortly.' Elizabeth swallowed. 'The time seems to have passed very quickly.'

'And you will be going back to England?'

'Yes, I think so.'

'You don't seem sure?'

Elizabeth picked up her tea. 'Nothing is certain at the moment.' She thought of John.

'And your next posting?'

'That will be confirmed very soon.' John was going to Washington, there was no doubt of that, but they had not discussed it because they did not really talk any longer. And tomorrow she would see Karl.

'Perhaps I could call on Wednesday or Thursday, to begin the portrait?' Sophia said quickly, sensing Elizabeth's unease.

'Are you really quite sure – ?' she repeated, and sighed inwardly, glad the subject had changed. 'You must have so much on your mind.'

'I am, really. It will do me good, take me out of myself, as you say. I need that.' Sophia looked down into her cup. 'We had the reading of Mother's will yesterday.'

'Oh, God, I'm so sorry.'

Sophia felt a lump gather like a tight knot in her throat. She needed to think of other things and other faces because otherwise she would find the white, fragile face of her mother slipping furtively into her head and she could not bear that, could not bear the fact that she was no longer there, that she could not pick up the telephone and speak to her. Her eyes lifted abruptly to the window and she thought that there must be something left, something indomitable and unyielding which would remain of her mother, a precious fragment of the person she had loved, who had told her stories, who had been her one true friend. She felt Elizabeth's hand close on her own.

'My father is furious,' she said suddenly, fighting the tears which waited just behind her eyes. 'Mother left the castle to me.' She shook her head. 'To me.'

He had gone mad – he had cursed and sworn because Schloss Bletz had been left to his daughter, not even his only son! And the lands and the lake. He had turned on her in his rage and asked her why she should want it – what would she do with it? But she did want it, very much, because that had been her mother's wish. Her father had raged again, saying that he would contest it – that her mother had been insane.

The notary had calmed him by showing him the will and the clause which had stated the reason quite clearly why she had left Felix nothing: 'I have made no provision in this, my Will, for my husband because of his adultery'. Her father had become very still suddenly, his mouth hanging open and a part of her mind was saying what a fool he looked. He had turned slowly towards her and their gazes locked and she had known then that he would never contest the will. And in that long, ugly moment when their eyes had met she knew that she hated him.

'What will you do?' elizabeth's calm voice broke into her thoughts.

'After I have sold Schloss Bletz I shall be taking up my scholarship in America.'

'You are selling the castle?'

'Yes. My mother never liked it.' She could do that much for her now. But in the darkest part of her heart she was twisting a knife in the wound of her father. After the reading of the will he had almost begged her to let him run the estate – 'manage it', he had said, and she had smiled, but the smile had been a lie – a bitter, poor thing which her father had been too blind to see. He was really a very stupid man. To sell Schloss Bletz out of the family would break him; she hoped that it would kill him.

'But you once told me that it was very dear to you,' Elizabeth said uneasily.

'Not now.'

There was a moment's odd little silence as they looked back at one another until she spoke again.

'Don't you see – I have to,' Sophia said, as if she desperately wanted the older woman to understand.

Elizabeth nodded slowly.

'She was not herself,' Sophia added, almost to herself, and she caught an unhappy breath. Inside, where her dreams and imaginings grew and flourished, she had invented a little picture of her mother slipping away – not stepping into that ominous stretch of water, just slipping away into the woods with another case, with other clothes.

'I wish I had known,' Elizabeth said lamely. 'Perhaps we could have talked.' But she had been too busy with her own affairs, busy dreaming of Karl, busy looking back.

'But she would have been glad that I have come to see you,' Sophia said. 'I know she liked you and I know she would be pleased that I intend to sketch your son.'

Elizabeth smiled, but her eyes were searching the young face with concern. Perhaps she had expected too much, too soon, but so much had changed in the face that looked back at her as if the soul had gone or withdrawn, as if the Sophia she had met only a few months before no longer existed, and even as her eyes scrutinized the desolate face the young girl slowly turned her head away as if she had sensed Elizabeth's regret, but no longer cared.

Sophia's gaze shifted back to the window; she was suddenly tired of talking, tired of it all, and the tiredness was heavy, like a burden, an ache. She closed her eyes as they began to prick and sting, as the grief began to twist and turn again, as if it might reach up and choke her, and she swallowed, desperately, sliding that pretty picture she had conjured into her head – the one of her mother, the one of Genevieve slipping quietly away through the trees. Free at last.

Kristina walked towards the music and the pavilion where a little orchestra was playing another Strauss waltz. She sat at one of the small round tables and ordered a mineral water and a pastry whilst she watched the antics of a group of young Italian tourists. There was a wind and clouds in the sky, but no threat of rain. For a brief moment she placed a hand on her stomach and tried to imagine the life inside. She had gone to a doctor in Salzburg, an old man due to retire, but he had been kind and efficient and had told her what she had guessed already. The pregnancy was a complete surprise because she had thought that she was not capable of bearing a child; all those years with Frederico had produced nothing and he had had a son from a previous marriage so she knew that the fault lay with her. She had said as much to the doctor and he had smiled, that old man, as if it was a great joke.

'At your age, Fräulein, the ovaries can have "a splurge", even inactive or lazy ones – a last furious drive to be fertilized, to create.' He had chuckled then and clucked her on the chin as if she had been a child who had done something mischievous instead of conceiving a baby out of wedlock.

The knowledge of her pregnancy had crept up on her; at first she had thought that she was ill and then she would have a good day and feel suddenly better, but then the bad days began to follow one another ominously; she lost weight and she was tired, tired, and then she had gone to Salzburg because of Sam and any thoughts of her health just didn't seem to matter any longer until Tante Maria had marched her down to Doktor Lueger and she had been forced to face the lurking truth which had been hiding in a dim corner of her mind.

And now she was sitting in the Stadtpark on a summer's day in Vienna having a mineral water and eating a pastry as if everything was just as it should be. Kristina patted her stomach again and thought inevitably of

Sam. She had told her mother that if he should call again to say that she was still in Salzburg and that she was likely to stay there for some time. After all, what good was an apology to her now, or the carefully designed phrases he would use to tell her that he was back with his wife, with Natalie. She did not even like the name, she realized suddenly and with bitter relish. But Sam . . . she would not think about Sam, nor would she tell him about the pregnancy, there was little point, and she did not want his pity or his money or his time. 'Let him go,' her mother had once said, and she was right.

She picked up the small pastry fork at the side of her plate and began eating the sweet sticky mountain before her and she smiled a little wistfully There was nothing wrong with her appetite now and she had regained the weight she had lost and more, and when she looked in the mirror she had the impression that she looked younger, that the lines which had begun to form around her eyes and mouth had been plumped out and made almost invisible. Sam had left her life, but he had given her something which made the leaving almost bearable.

She felt a slight fluttering of panic and caught a tight, ragged breath as her thoughts swept backwards – the pregnancy had been conceived in love, hadn't it? It had not been one of those dark, empty couplings when she had made love with a sinking heart, when she had awoken in the morning to regret and doubt and embarrassment. Kristina brought her glass up to her mouth and shivered as she let some of the too-cold water slide into her belly.

She shifted her gaze back to the pavilion and the small dancing area in front of it; there was an old woman twirling in the centre, her skirt lifted on one side as she stretched out her arm and pointed her toes, moving her feet in perfect time to the music; occasionally she would smile and nod as if there was a man, a partner dancing with her and then she would twirl again and again, oblivious of the people watching and the smirks and the giggles. All alone. Kristina looked away, her eyes travelling over the heads of the crowd to the terrace and the Kursalon and the peacocks.

There was a man leaning against the ornate railings, not too tall, dark hair, light suit. She shaded her eyes from the sun and suddenly felt drained of breath. Kristina stood up and began to weave her way through the tables and back on to the path, but he had seen her, of course, and caught up with her quickly, easily, taking her arm, and she wanted to tell him to go away, to leave her alone because she didn't need him.

'What *are* you doing?'

Sam looked back at her and she could see his anger.

'Are you crazy or something?'

'I just want to live my life in peace, that is all.'

'I didn't think you were the theatrical type, somehow.'

'Well, I don't suppose you really know that much about me.'

'What is that supposed to mean, for Chrissakes?'

She said nothing, trying to concentrate on the grass, the trees, old ladies on a bench.

'Why have you been avoiding me?' he asked with impatience, and tilted her chin towards him so that he could see her face.

'You're going back to the States soon.'

'That's right.'

She moved as if to shrug him off, to walk away.

'What the hell is the matter? I haven't been calling you every day and waiting around for my goddamn health.'

She twisted round suddenly. 'I don't need you to salve your conscience by coming here to *say* goodbye, Sam,' she said with too much emotion. 'You could have sent me a letter.' There was bitterness too, because she had had those letters before and the telephone calls – if she was lucky.

He watched her for a long moment before he spoke again.

'I haven't come to say goodbye.'

'Then why have you come?' And her voice began to break.

'Because I wanted to see you . . . you know, like I used to,' he said softly.

'But nothing is like it was, like it used to be.'

He frowned. 'You don't want to see me?'

She made no answer and wondered why it was so difficult to say that she didn't want to take any more risks, that she didn't want to be hurt any more.

'I thought . . .' He paused and swallowed hard. 'I've made a mistake, then . . .?' he said with disbelief, but then darted a glance at her face as if she might tell him otherwise. Sam looked down at his hands, waiting, in the long awkward silence which followed and then shrugged his shoulders helplessly, his eyes pleading and confused. Then slowly he began to move away.

She watched him go, watched his heavy steps and wondered if she was going mad as her voice broke free, shrill and bitter –

'*Why did you sleep with her?!*' Her mind froze up, tight and despairing. '*Why?!*'

Sam stopped dead in his tracks as if he had been struck hard by a massive blow between the shoulderblades. He turned slowly and looked at her sweet, contorted face, at the anguish which brought a thickness into his throat because of the damage he had unwittingly done to her. As he walked back he was aware of the old ladies on the benches muttering and nodding their heads, and their probing eyes most of all – this was a real field day for them, they would probably be talking about this for weeks, but what the hell did it matter? He sighed and then paused a step away, almost afraid to touch her.

'But she's gone, Kristina, back to the States.'

She shook her head again and again and then abruptly his arms were pulling her into his shoulder and she could smell his clothes, his skin.

'It's over – really and truly over,' he whispered. 'That's what I've been trying to tell you.' He chuckled with an effort, to try and cheer her as he spoke again. 'Oh, she's very good at seduction, my almost ex-wife, and it works sometimes, but not this time, it was all an act, a big dumb act.' He kissed the top of her head. 'I think I just had to prove that to myself, finally.' His hand was stroking her hair. 'I'm sorry, really sorry.'

And it seemed that they stood there for a long span of time, holding each other, on a path in the Stadtpark, before the Johann Strauss memorial, and she thought that she would never be able to separate herself from him, never leave the solid, safe feel of his arms again.

'There is something else,' she said, at last, but she did not move her head from his shoulder because she was afraid, now, to look into his face.

'Tell me,' he said gently.

'I'm pregnant.'

He did not make any reply immediately and she closed her eyes.

'Would you repeat that, please.'

'I'm pregnant.'

Very carefully, very slowly he uncoiled himself from her arms and took hold of her hands.

'Look at me, Kristina,' he said, and he waited until he could see her face properly. 'You're sure?'

She nodded.

He frowned and she thought she would die, but he caught her glance and said quickly, 'I'm not frowning because you're pregnant, I'm frowning because the divorce probably won't be through by the time the baby is born; I'm old-fashioned, I don't like the word illegitimate.' But he grinned broadly and she felt relief, fantastical, wonderful relief beginning to filter through her body.

'Bab-*ies*, Sam.'

'Babies?' he asked. 'You mean plural?'

'Twins.'

'Oh, my God.' He started to laugh. 'I don't believe it!'

'Apparently older mothers are more likely to have twins than younger ones.' She smiled sheepishly. 'My doctor in Salzburg called it "a splurge", a last-minute bid for creation.'

Sam shook his head in wonderment. 'I like that – "a splurge".' He grinned again, but then his face grew serious. 'And you won't mind waiting?'

'Waiting?'

'To get married.'

She shook her head and smiled. It didn't matter, not another year, or two, or three, because she realized quite suddenly and with searing clarity that the real waiting was finally over and that Sam had been there somewhere, somehow all the time. All her life – and she wanted to laugh, dance, as the relief began to take hold. But instead she took a few steps towards a bench where three old ladies had been sitting with avid, curious eyes – three old ladies who had been listening, but not really understanding because they were 'real Austrians' and spoke little English.

'*Ich bin so glucklich – weil ich eine unverheiratete Mutter sein werde...!*'

One of them was obviously deaf because the words were repeated loudly and in an appropriate tone of exaggerated horror, causing the old woman concerned to shrink away as if Kristina might be slightly mad.

'What did you say?'

Kristina grinned and took his arm. 'Oh, I simply told them I am very happy because I am going to be an unmarried mother...'

'Must be the best piece of gossip they've heard in years.'

And she supposed that it was, but it didn't matter in the least and she gripped Sam's arm a little tighter as they walked past the pavilion and the music and the people sitting at the tables. Kristina smiled a little sadly as two peacocks appeared from under the trees to stand tentatively in the warm sunshine; perhaps she would miss them most of all.

Augustina had lost sight of Sam beneath the trees and sighed with exasperation; now she would have to wait, but it would be all right, she felt certain of that in her heart. Kristina had proved difficult in the end, so she had had to take the initiative for her and telephone Sam Cohen. True, it had been a little awkward, but she had simply told him that her daughter had been ill and was now back from Salzburg and finally, and most important of all – when was he getting a divorce? She had never believed in prevarication, that was for fools. He had paused then and finally said, 'as soon as possible'. Now that had been a very good moment, almost like triumph, and that was when she had told him where Kristina was and she had just watched and waited at the window.

Augustina moved back to her seat by the fire and took up her glass of port wine. The match was not ideal, of course, but at least she had saved her grandchildren from being *bastards*, that would have been too much to bear, a scandal, whatever the modern thought was these days. There were some things in the ever-changing world which should stay sacred, and one of them was a child, or children. The old woman grinned with delight. Grandchildren! Twins! Augustina tapped the arms of her chair in silent rhythm; apparently Sam Cohen had a wonderful house in New England and it was supposed to be very beautiful there – not as beautiful as Vienna, or Austria, of course, but good enough. And naturally, Kristina would need a great deal of help once the babies were born, so naturally it was only logical that she should accompany her, be there, to give her the benefit of her experience and advice. They would see that, surely? She took a long sup of the port wine and looked into the fading flames of the fire. Sam Cohen was astute enough to see that and they would not leave her, would they, not in Vienna, quite alone? After all, it was she who had made the telephone call which had brought them together in the end, wasn't it? Augustina smiled to herself. She had orchestrated everything rather well, except for the fact that Sam was not Austrian, or even German, but unfortunately Jewish. She shook her head sadly with resignation. Yet, he *was* astute and she admired that, and she would try and forget his Jewishness, put it away somewhere ... so perhaps New England would not be so bad, not such a hardship, and it was beautiful, she had read that somewhere, in one of Kristina's magazines, she would look it up.

The old woman sighed heavily with contentment as the port wine began to have its customary pleasant effect, the warmth spreading slowly, languidly through her limbs, like floating. Her eyes strayed to the dark green glass of the bottle. She had been told that you could find anything in America, if you looked hard enough, even port wine.

'I thought we could have drinks on the terrace,' Karl said and watched her as she moved through the doorway and across to the white, curling railings and the magnificent view beyond.

'It's a lovely idea,' she replied quietly, and felt his curious gaze on her back. Sad, curious gaze.

'Gin and tonic?'

'Yes, please.'

They drank in silence for a few minutes and then he placed his glass back on the table with great deliberation and walked over to her. The sun was shining slanting light across her hair so that it looked as if it might be touched with gold; toffee and gold. Elizabeth's hair. Karl studied her for a long moment before bringing his hands up to her shoulders and sliding them down her arms so that he felt her shiver gently. He kissed her neck and his hands slid around her waist so that he could press her against him, smell her, bring her close as if the very closeness of her would make her his.

'No, Karl.'

Her voice was very soft, too soft and he wondered why he should suddenly feel afraid.

'I want to make love to you.'

He turned her around so that he could look into her face.

'No,' she said again.

'Not now, or not ever?'

She shook her head. 'It was over before you left.'

There was something about the wariness in her eyes, something in her face which struck straight at his heart.

'You mean that day on the Kahlenberg hill . . . you knew then?'

'I wasn't sure,' she said weakly, clumsily. And it was as if he had been growing farther and farther away, fading, slowly.

'How do you know that you are sure now?'

'I just know.' She locked his gaze. 'It's not something that you can measure or say when, or how, even, is it?' she pleaded. 'I just know.'

'I said the wrong things,' he said quickly. About John and his money; Christopher.

'Sometimes.' But that had not been all; it had been John, somehow. John growing inside her all the time and she had not known until it had nearly been too late. She felt her heart lurch because it might still be too late.

'So it's all gone,' he said quietly. 'All that goddamn passion, just drained away . . .' He tilted her chin towards him as if he might lean down and kiss her lips, but stopped a fraction away from her face. 'All gone?' he whispered and tasted her mouth again and again, felt her yield slightly, just slightly until her hands came up and pushed him oh, so softly away. That softness, frightening, and he wanted to laugh at the irony.

'Not all gone, Karl.' But it was going, and passion was not love, she thought sadly; it was dizzying chemistry, infatuation, a brief ecstatic flight to the gods.

'You're letting it go.' His words were careful and angry. 'It doesn't have to be like this – not after the past few months, not after all you've risked.'

'I didn't want this, or the risk, Karl. I didn't ask for any of it.' It had been a madness, a finishing of something which should have been forgotten and buried and put away somewhere.

'You said to me once that when you were alone, without me, it was as if you were only half alive . . .' He swallowed. 'You remember?'

'I remember.'

'And that's gone too?'

'Yes.'

'Where, Elizabeth?' he hissed. 'Where the hell has it all gone?' He took her shoulders in his hands again and pulled her against him. 'Where?'

'Don't, Karl.'

He closed his eyes in exasperation and pushed her gently away.

'I wanted you to come with me so that we could both start again.' It had been the one thing that was tangible in his life and the only thing that really mattered. All the times before when he could have had it all with someone else, some other girl, he had let them go, swiftly, through his fingers because he hadn't wanted them.

'I know – and I'm sorry.'

He shook his head and smiled dryly. 'I must have said that a few times, probably too many times,' he said, almost to himself.

'Perhaps we missed our chance, long before Vienna.'

He looked back at her, tense and unsmiling. 'You mean *I* missed our chance.' And wasn't that what Gurney had said – that he had had his chance and lost it . . .? He switched his gaze away from her to the blue, blue sky which seemed to mock him in all its glory.

'There was no one else then, Karl. I was free.' And as she watched his carefully composed profile she found herself wondering if that was not part of her attraction for him now, that she 'belonged' to someone else.

'It was different then,' he said defensively.

'No.' And he seemed to shrink a little, fading again.

'I had commitments, problems . . .'

A shadow seemed to fall between them and she placed her glass back on the table as if she would go.

'I don't want you to leave yet.' Not like this.

'I have to get back, Karl.'

'To John.'

'Yes.'

'Do you think he will want you now?' he asked meanly.

She made no answer and looked away from him.

'I'm sorry, I shouldn't have said that.' He grabbed her arm. 'I'm sorry.'

'It's best if I go now.'

She began to walk away, across the terrace, and he felt panic begin to crawl inside his chest.

'Do you love him?'

She stopped and looked back at him so that the sun shone directly into her eyes, blinding her, making him invisible.

'What do you want me to say?' She took a deep breath and stepped back into the apartment, knowing that he would follow.

'I want you to tell me that you love him.'

She paused, helplessly, not wanting to answer because, even now, she found it difficult to hurt him.

'Yes, I love John.'

He shook his head. 'After this, after us?' he said with disbelief.

'Yes, even after this.'

His lips were pressed together, almost white.

'But how? Why?' Fear was seeping into his heart, driving calmness out. 'You can't change so quickly, so fast – first one and then another. You're staying with him because of Christopher.'

'No, Karl,' Elizabeth said slowly, carefully, so that there would be no mistake. 'I do *love* John, and I don't think that I have ever stopped loving him. I was dazed for a while, I let him slip away, I let the past take over the present, call it what you will.'

He looked back at her for a long, weighted moment, stunned and staring.

'Dazed?' he repeated quietly. 'Dazed?' He could not believe what she had said. Inside the need of her was tearing him apart, and the losing and her indifference, because he had not loved before, not like this.

'Perhaps that was the wrong word. I'm sorry, I didn't mean to sound glib.'

'For Chrissakes, don't go polite on me.' He shook his head in bewilderment. 'I love you, Elizabeth, doesn't that mean anything any more?'

'It can't.'

'Back to John – it's all been switched back to good old John.'

'You really don't understand, do you?'

'Now, what don't I understand?'

She gave him a searching look as her mind swept inevitably back to that time, that place, all the places.

'That when you left me five years ago I still loved you, that you never gave me a chance to finish what you had started.'

'And you have now, I suppose. Is that what you're trying to tell me?'

'I think it's something like that.'

He felt blood soar into his face as if she had struck him.

'Is that all?'

'Don't make this more difficult than it need be.'

He squeezed his eyelids together, tight shut.

'You English are masters of the understatement, Elizabeth, but not with me – don't use it with me.'

'It's just over, Karl. Over.'

'It doesn't have to be like this.'

'You left me,' she said suddenly.

'I've told you all about that.'

'Not really.' Her voice was stubborn, a little angry.

'But that was five goddamn years ago – people change!'

'You didn't call or write once.'

'For Chrissakes . . .'

'You left me,' she repeated as the bitterness began to seep out around the edges.

'Elizabeth, Elizabeth . . .'

'I had your baby.' The words slipped from her mouth and she was surprised how easy it had been and at the sensation of release, at the laming heaviness which was suddenly no longer there.

'My baby?' he whispered.

'Yes,' she said.

'But . . .'

'She died – five weeks old; she was premature, weak.'

'For Chrissakes . . .' he said softly, 'why didn't you tell me?'

'You weren't there to tell.'

'So that's what this is all about.'

She shook her head. 'It's only part of it.' And she wanted to go then, wanted to close the door behind her and leave the past with him. She reached for the handle and began to push it down.

'Don't go,' he said. 'Please.'

'I must.'

He watched her as she stepped through the white frame of the doorway and away from him.

'John wouldn't have done that, would he?' he asked suddenly, but wishing he could call the question back because he knew what she would say.

'What?'

'Left you alone.'

Twisting the knife in the wound.

'No.'

The Foreign Ministers were all arriving for the 25th as planned and then would follow a week of speeches before the close of the Talks. Dan sighed heavily. Twelve minutes for each country and there were one hundred and twenty-four of them; it would take days. And the final speeches were important because they were not supposed to be just 'pretty words', they had to reflect what they had achieved which was not, of course, what he had hoped or dreamed. But the fact that the world would be watching and waiting was a massive plus, because this was not just an East–West concern, it was global – really, truly global and therefore a hot, hot issue. His eyebrows drew together in a frown as he recalled the final document which still sat on his desk waiting to be read, but he knew what it contained – too much compromise and not enough real action – which was what he had expected in the cold light of day. The hopes and the dreams would have to wait a while yet. However, there was still some time left for last-minute miracles and Judy, his Judy, would not be entirely disappointed because at least people, governments, countries were sitting around the tables and actually talking about what was happening every day, around them. He smiled with a trace of sadness; they were actually beginning to realize that the natural world was not just there to be exploited, ruthlessly plundered and domesticated, all for the advancement of the human race. He tried to remember the quote he had read somewhere in a book his son had sent him, an excellent quote, something sharp and neat enough to be inserted into the speech he was drafting for the Secretary of State:

Our response to natural environments has changed little for thousands of years – we dig them up, we chop them down, we burn them, we drain them, we pave them over, we poison them in order to mould them to our image.

Dan sighed because back at the State they would say it was too emotional, they would probably give each other patronizing, knowing glances and then suggest that they bring his retirement forward, or send him some place over the rainbow. There was only one more posting for him anyway. But where? Not London, his favourite place, or Paris, they were already accounted for, one of them being a controversial political appointment – an oil baron whose busy and very rich fingers had dug deep during the last presidential campaign – so he had been granted a handsome and prestigious favour for services rendered, something Dan had always found faintly distasteful. He shook his head and thought of Bonn, which would not be available for another year, and besides he had been there eight years ago. Brazil was free in January and after his experience at the talks he would probably make a likely candidate, although the Brazilian government might find him just a little 'too green', but *someone* had to take a stand and do something about the devastation of one million acres of rain forest *per week* . . . and he had nothing to lose now, he was getting old.

Dan shrugged and walked over to the window and mopped his brow with a handkerchief; it was hot and he was tired and just a little weary of the Talks and the constant bickering and sidestepping which had been taking place particularly over the past few weeks. Sometimes he realized how much progress, often in the way of discreet bargains, was made in the corridors of the Hofburg or at some of the cocktail parties, compared to the ritual exchanges taking place around the goddamned negotiating table. But they had achieved something, hadn't they? It seemed suddenly terribly important to him then that he had not wasted this first, God-given opportunity or otherwise, he chuckled softly, Judy might come back and haunt him, but he wouldn't mind that – *not at all*. He slipped on his jacket and straightened his tie ready for one of the final cocktail parties he would attend here, in Vienna.

The invitation from the Thorntons had been sitting above the marble fireplace for over two weeks and he had almost forgotten about it because he had been so engrossed in his work. He wondered if Nielsen would be there, wondered whether his talk with him had done any real good for John.

Wondering got no one anywhere, his mother had once said, but he had always been a wonderer, a dreamer, and sometimes it surprised him that he had gotten where he was because when he looked back it seemed to him that he had spent most of his life dreaming of what could be, what could happen, what might be. He had had endless conversations with Judy about the past, the present, what was to come. Endless conversations, endless talks that had sent his mind whirling into space and set Judy to laughing. She had always had her pretty feet firmly on the ground; she had been the one to march in demonstrations, which had made him blush, she had been the one to write letter upon letter about needless waste, pollution, child abuse, animal extinction, to anyone who would listen, and usually they hadn't, usually they had not replied at all. It was she who had so cleverly pinned the President into a corner at a White House reception with her usual charm and then began quoting Norman Myers:

We may achieve our aim, by eliminating every 'competitor' for living space on the crowded Earth. When the last creature has been accounted for, we shall have made ourselves masters of all creation. We shall look around, and we shall see nothing but each other. Alone at last.

Dan chuckled again as a vivid picture of the President formed in his mind. The man had visibly shuddered, but it had been a good moment, a moment to remember. He brushed his hair back quickly, knowing that he would be late, and darted a glance at himself in the mirror in the hallway as he passed. He stopped for a moment and looked into the big face that was looking back at him. It had once been a handsome face, and perhaps it still was in its way – for a man of his age, he supposed bleakly – but the cheeks were beginning to cave in just a bit, the skin beneath the cavities of his brows and his jaw was loose, white, sagging and the eyes were beginning to sink just a little too deeply – and yet they were eyes that were still alive, still alert. But the mind behind the eyes was beginning to be peopled by memories, old places, old friends, ghosts, and he sighed as he realized that at that moment they were just a little too bright, just a little too dewy, and there was a thickness in his throat.

'You old fool,' Dan muttered sadly and wished with all his heart that Judy would come back and haunt him.

'I'm so happy for you,' Elizabeth said.

'I still can't believe it,' Clare responded, her face glowing. 'We only heard yesterday and I had practically geared myself up for a trip back to London.'

'But now you don't have to.' Elizabeth smiled. 'You must be terribly relieved.'

'Yes, I am,' Clare said. 'And Brussels will be so convenient – literally an hour away.'

'Oliver must be pleased.'

'Oh, yes – he hasn't said much really, but that's not his way, he just walks around with a sort of smug look on his face!'

'We will have to keep in touch.'

'I'd like that – and you have Washington to look forward to.'

Elizabeth nodded, but her eyes drifted away, across the room to John.

'You do want to go, don't you, Elizabeth?'

'Oh, yes,' she said. 'Very much.'

Clare watched her friend's face closely and wondered if it was true what she had heard, that Elizabeth had been having an affair; Madeleine Lindahl had implied as much.

'Actually, we'd better be off, I think we've overstayed our welcome as it is.'

'Nonsense,' Elizabeth said automatically.

'No, really, we must go – the babysitter . . .'

'Oh, yes,' Elizabeth responded. 'But let me see you out.'

Clare signalled to Oliver as she made her way through the last few people remaining.

'Oh, by the way, did you know that Olaf and Madeleine are being sent to Prague?' Clare gave her a conspiratorial smile. 'She's absolutely furious.'

'I don't doubt it – hardly Madeleine's preferred sort of posting.'

'Well, at least things are changing there.'

'But not fast enough for Madeleine – I think she'll be spending most of her time here . . .' Elizabeth said, and then added, 'Poor Olaf.'

'It could have been worse – Colombia or Lagos or Cambodia!'

Elizabeth smiled with a twinge of memory, because Madeleine had said almost exactly the same thing of Clare, months ago, and now the tables had turned completely. Her mind somersaulted backwards to that opening reception in January when everything had been different and everything had changed.

'Well, we must go,' Clare said as Oliver came up to join her. 'Please try and come to my lunch party on Monday.'

Elizabeth nodded. 'I will.' She touched Oliver's arm as he passed. 'Congratulations on Brussels.'

'Thanks, Elizabeth.' And then he smiled a little sadly. 'I hope I can say the same about you and Washington . . .'

She nodded stupidly with mild shock as he walked through the open door after Clare; Oliver knew, and she wondered all at once if everyone knew. For a long, painful moment she stood woodenly in the glare of the hall light watching a night breeze billow some curtains inward. And she thought she had been so careful, so discreet. Her eyes shifted to the main drawing room where John stood with the remnants of the party. She caught a breath and moved into the kitchen where the catering staff were washing up the final glasses and clearing everything away into cardboard boxes; soon there would be nothing to show that over a hundred people had been there at all. Elizabeth passed through into the sitting room, the best room, the prettiest room, the only place where she felt really at home.

'Well, that's that . . .'

John's voice made her turn.

'All gone?'

'Yes,' he said. 'Would you like a drink?'

She nodded and sat down.

'I'm so pleased about Oliver and Clare – she looks ten years younger.'

'He deserves it.'

'Yes.'

John placed a glass on the table next to her.

'G and T – is that okay?'

'Fine.'

'Oh, yes . . . I've been meaning to mention this to you . . .'

She looked into his face with trepidation, wondering what he was about to say.

'You remember Laura Drummond, the girl you saw one afternoon who seemed so upset. . . ?'

She blushed and picked up her drink.

'Yes.'

'She's been sent home.'

Elizabeth's eyes widened.

'The poor girl got herself involved with some sort of agent.'

'You mean a spy?'

'I suppose so.' John took a gulp of his drink. 'He seduced her, basically, and then took a few pretty snapshots and a video.'

'Oh, God . . .' And he would be good at seduction, she thought with a flicker of unease as she recalled his square, handsome face, the slick, practised manner of his courtesy, the way his mouth had lingered on her hand.

'Quite.' He shook his head. 'I thought I'd seen him somewhere before, it's a pity it took me so long to remember exactly where.'

'Who is he?'

'He told Laura his name was Ralf Müller and that he was a West German businessman, but in actual fact his mother was Hungarian and his father Russian, at least that is the version I have. He's called Gennady Levchenko. I met him in London in 1980 at the Soviet Embassy and in the following year he achieved the doubtful distinction of being one of the first Russian diplomats to be expelled since the mass clear-out of a hundred and five spies from Britain in 1971.'

'What did he do?'

'I only know the official story – that he tried to lure a British civil servant into an espionage ring, a woman, coincidentally. But I do know for sure that he was or is a KGB officer specializing in technology and scientific affairs.'

'Laura didn't stand much of a chance, did she?'

'No,' John said.

'How was Sir Nigel with her?'

'Kind, of course, but she had to return to London, there was no alternative.'

'And her career?'

'Not ruined, exactly, because she did the right thing by admitting what had happened . . . but a setback nevertheless. Vienna was an excellent posting for her.'

'Poor Laura,' she said quietly. 'And Ralf Müller, or Gennady?'

'Disappeared,' he said, shaking his head. 'I heard from Lawrence that Sir Nigel tried to set him up, but he never showed. Instinct, I suppose.'

'So he's still out there somewhere.'

'I'm afraid so.'

'It's strange . . .' she said slowly, 'I knew this sort of thing went on, but it's hard to believe when it actually happens.'

'I suppose that could be said about a lot of things.' He looked back at her sharply, carefully.

Her heart was beating slowly in her chest, but it seemed terribly loud, the pounding, as he waited for her to speak. She cleared her throat.

'It's over, John.'

He looked at her and said nothing, and as the silence went on and on she thought she might scream with the tension and the disquiet and his eyes boring into her.

'Over?' he said without expression. 'What's over?'

She looked down at her hands as her fingers pressed against one another, pushing them together in slow twisting pain.

'I think you know,' she said quietly.

'No, I don't know.' He wanted her to say it, say it out loud.

'I'm not seeing him any more.'

'Who?' He swallowed.

Her eyes flew open, pleading.

'Who?'

'Karl Nielsen.'

He moved over to the window, not trusting himself to speak, unable to stem the tide of bleak sadness spreading through him.

'John?'

'What do you want me to say?'

Her mind seemed to freeze up with despair, tight and helpless. 'I knew him before . . .'

He caught a breath. 'Before what?'

'Before you.'

'Is that supposed to make it better?'

'I'm not trying to make it better – I can't do that, can I?' She stared at his back as he stood looking out of the window. 'I'm trying to explain.'

'But there's nothing to explain – is there?'

'What do you mean?'

'Well, an affair is an affair, isn't it? What difference does it make whether you knew him before, after, or in between, it comes to the same thing.'

'No, John.'

'Oh?' he said. 'So *your* affair is different from all the other torrid, tawdry, hole-in-the-corner encounters that flesh is heir to . . .?'

'It wasn't like that.'

'*DON'T TELL ME WHAT IT WAS LIKE!*'

His voice made her stomach jump and she bowed her head in submission as the fear and the anguish began to dance inside.

When he spoke again his voice was soft, desolate.

'Don't tell me what is was like, Elizabeth, don't do that to me.' He didn't want to be reminded of her with him, together, making love, saying all the things that lovers say to one another. He couldn't bear it.

'I didn't mean what you think.'

'All right,' he said. 'All right.'

'I'm sorry, John,' she said suddenly, hopelessly. 'So very sorry . . .' The tears were coming, she could feel them behind her eyes and she hated that he should see them, as if she were asking for pity.

He made no answer and the fear began to grow big inside her.

'I met him over a year before you . . .' she said, her words stammering, rushing. 'We had a brief, heady romance and then he left for the States.' She paused as the words began to slow, to stick in her throat. 'I thought I loved him, John,' she said quietly. 'But he didn't keep in touch – there was no other meeting, nothing.'

'Until now.'

'Yes,' she said reluctantly.

'And you felt compelled to renew your "heady romance" – literally?' He didn't want to use the word 'love', not that.

She said nothing, because it was true.

'Did I come into this at all – did you think of me, once?'

'Of course.'

'Of course,' he repeated and turned to look at her. 'And now that your fling is over, I presume that you think everything will return to normal?'

'Stop it, John.'

'You have no right to say that.'

The silence was heavy then, powerful, but her voice snapped it in two.

'Do you want me to go?'

'Do-I-want-you-to-go?' His words were laced with cynicism. 'Now that really is a good question.' He laughed then, but the laugh was broken and devoid of joy and she closed her eyes. He turned back into the room to look at her. 'Do you think it is that simple?' He shook his head. 'I don't know how you define love, and I don't understand what it means to you, Elizabeth, but for me it is different – I can't tell you to go because I still love you and I don't know what to do about it.'

She lifted her eyes to his face, but his gaze beat her down.

'Have you ever really loved me?' He stared at the partly bowed head as memories began to pour into his mind, crushing him. It seemed to him a long time ago when he had seen her at a dinner party for the first time, had looked up to see the lovely wide cheekbones and the mass of honey-coloured hair falling below creamy shoulders. Wanting her. He had pursued her and discovered that she was also intelligent and witty and warm and even funny, but she had placed herself at a distance from him which had been intriguing in the beginning, until it had begun to hurt and then she had almost lost him. But she had come back to him and they had married. She had been happy – he knew she had been happy, they had had a good marriage. Everything had been good. And she had given him a beautiful son. John felt himself stiffen as he thought of Christopher.

'Oh, John . . .' she said softly. 'Yes, yes.'

'I can't believe you,' he said. 'Somehow there has always been a part of you that kept me at arm's length.'

'It was this.'

'Karl-bloody-Nielsen.' He spat the words and his heart knocked furiously in his chest with frightening anger. 'And you were willing to sacrifice what we had – and Christopher – *for him*. Did you ever think what the resumption of your "heady romance" might do to your son?' He swallowed deeply. 'And did you know that that smooth, cheap bastard traded ivory in his spare time!?' Dan Gurney had told him just a little too casually, but confidentially of course, over a drink. John blushed again at the humiliating memory; Dan seemed to have a way of knowing everything.

She closed her eyes and shook her head helplessly.

'I want to hate you, but I can't,' he said and looked away from her.

'I had his baby, John.' It was the only thing she had left and she wondered, suddenly, why she had never told him before, because he would have understood, but she had locked it all away and waited, letting it build and build.

He turned slowly. 'His baby.' He swallowed. 'Nielsen's baby?'

'Yes.'

'When?'

'About a year before I met you.'

She felt sick, suddenly, with uncertainty.

'She died,' she said, answering his unspoken question. 'At five weeks old. She was premature.'

He examined her face carefully and saw how her eyes darkened and the nose which was just a little too round began to redden and he knew that she would cry.

'It was unfinished, you see . . .' Her voice quavered. 'Somehow unfinished.' She tried to clear her throat and her eyes darted to his face. 'Because it was all trapped inside – him, the baby, always, for too long . . . I know that now.' The ghost had fled at last and the grief was creeping, rising.

'You don't love him?' His heart was beating painfully. Aching, because there would be no going back now, no other chance.

She shook her head. 'No.'

'So it's gone.' He said it for them both and then closed his eyes with dizzying relief. 'It's finished.' He watched her for a long moment and then walked slowly across the room to sit down beside her.

'What was her name?'

He pulled her in to his chest and began stroking her hair.

'Tell me her name, Elizabeth,' he asked gently.

'Susan.'

He could feel the wild, anxious beat of her heart as she lay against him and the warmth of her heavy tears as they began sinking into his shirt to stain his skin. It would be all right now. All right. After all, they had the rest of their lives.